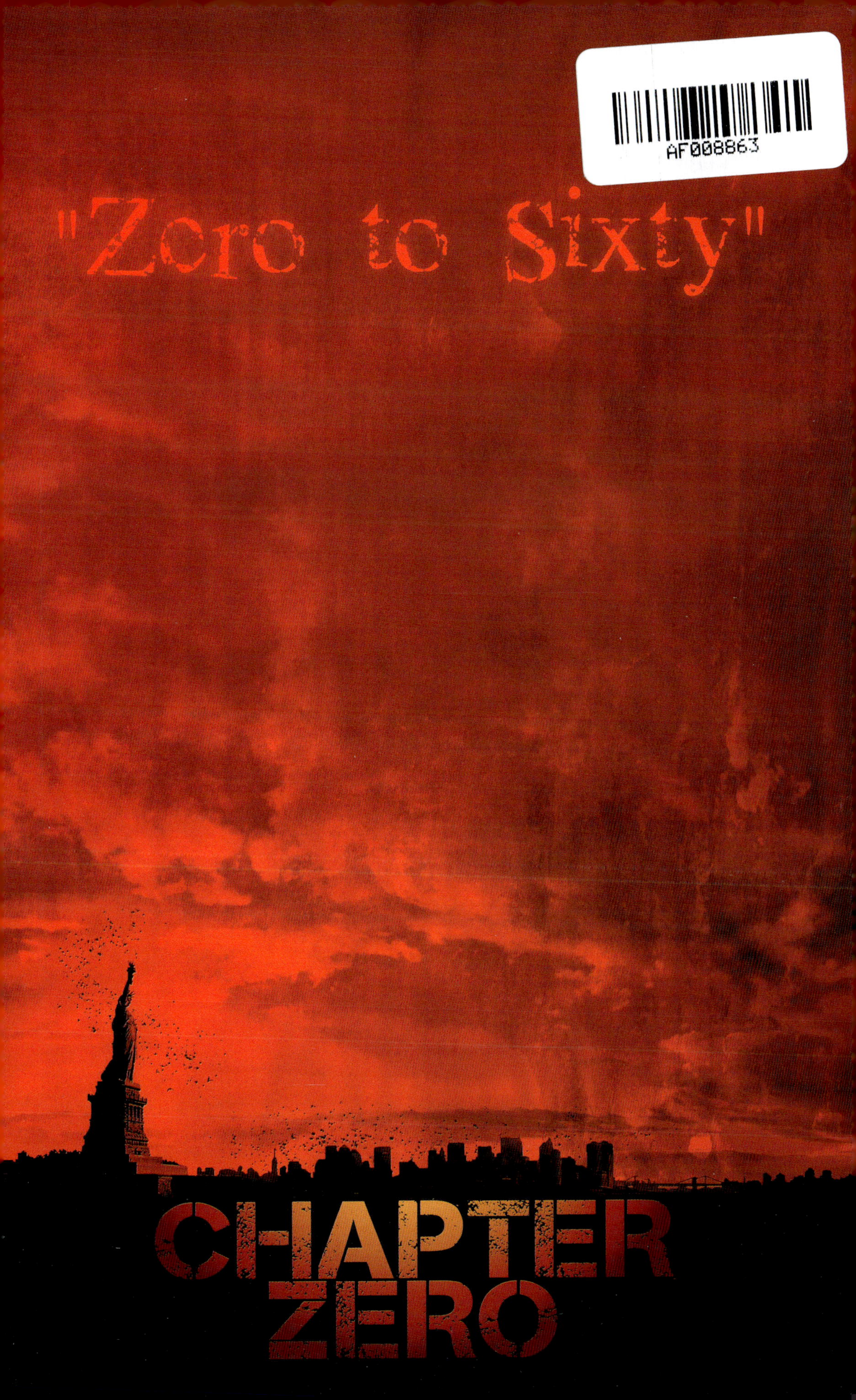
"Zero to Sixty"
CHAPTER
ZERO

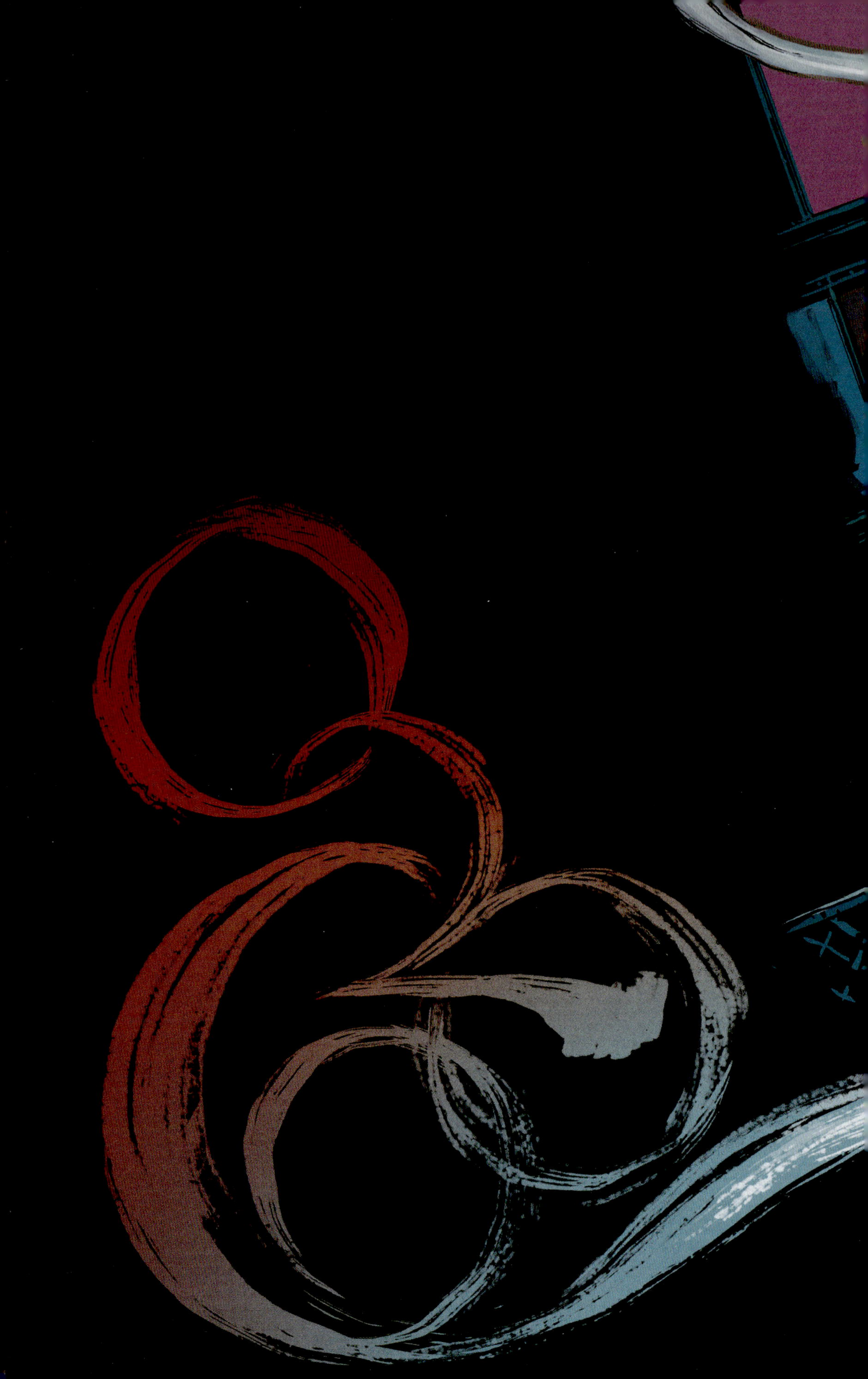

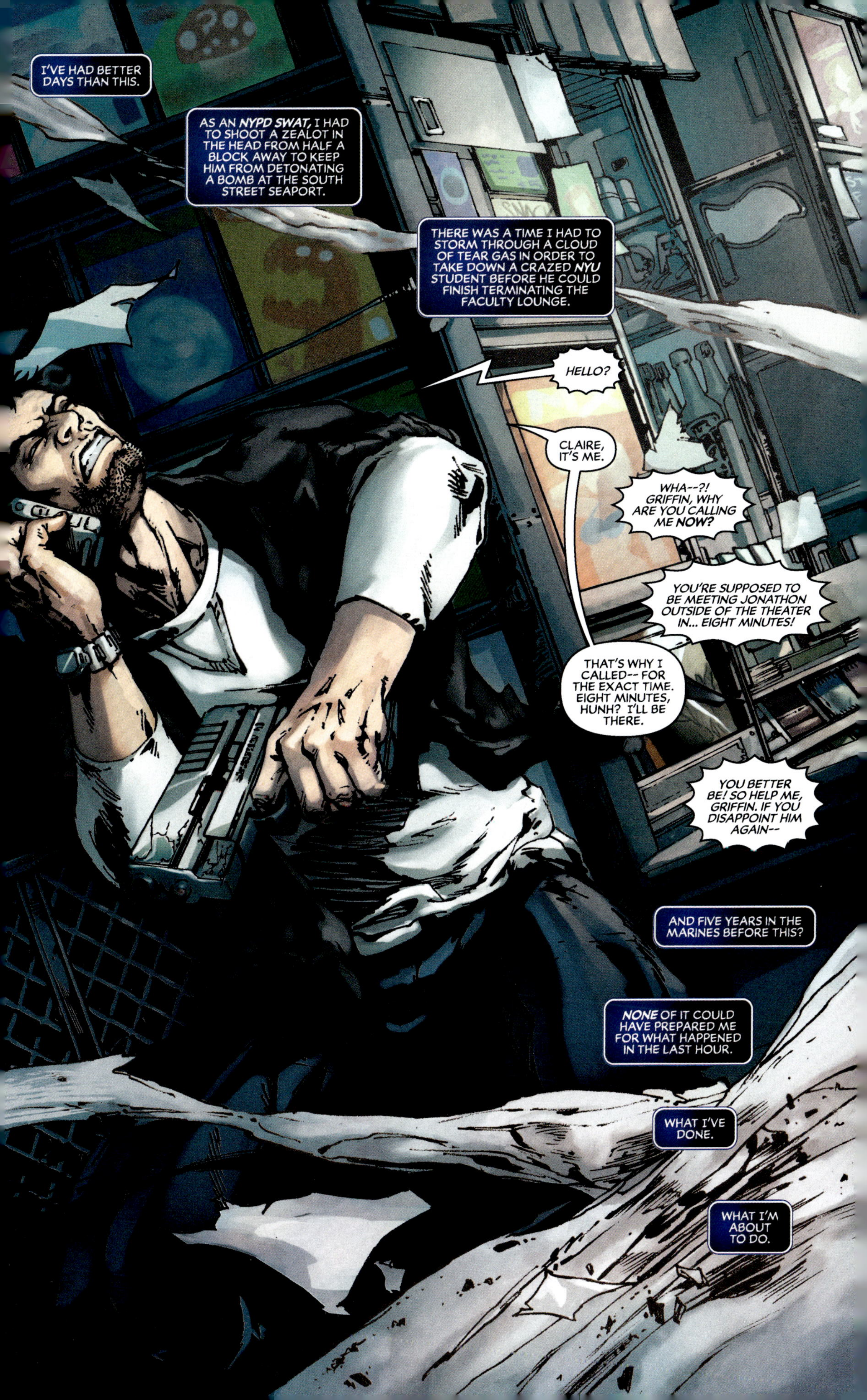
I'VE HAD BETTER DAYS THAN THIS.
AS AN NYPD SWAT, I HAD TO SHOOT A ZEALOT IN THE HEAD FROM HALF A BLOCK AWAY TO KEEP HIM FROM DETONATING A BOMB AT THE SOUTH STREET SEAPORT.
THERE WAS A TIME I HAD TO STORM THROUGH A CLOUD OF TEAR GAS IN ORDER TO TAKE DOWN A CRAZED NYU STUDENT BEFORE HE COULD FINISH TERMINATING THE FACULTY LOUNGE.
HELLO?
CLAIRE, IT'S ME.
WHA--?! GRIFFIN, WHY ARE YOU CALLING ME NOW?
YOU'RE SUPPOSED TO BE MEETING JONATHON OUTSIDE OF THE THEATER IN... EIGHT MINUTES!
THAT'S WHY I CALLED-- FOR THE EXACT TIME. EIGHT MINUTES, HUNH? I'LL BE THERE.
YOU BETTER BE! SO HELP ME, GRIFFIN. IF YOU DISAPPOINT HIM AGAIN--
AND FIVE YEARS IN THE MARINES BEFORE THIS?
NONE OF IT COULD HAVE PREPARED ME FOR WHAT HAPPENED IN THE LAST HOUR.
WHAT I'VE DONE.
WHAT I'M ABOUT TO DO.

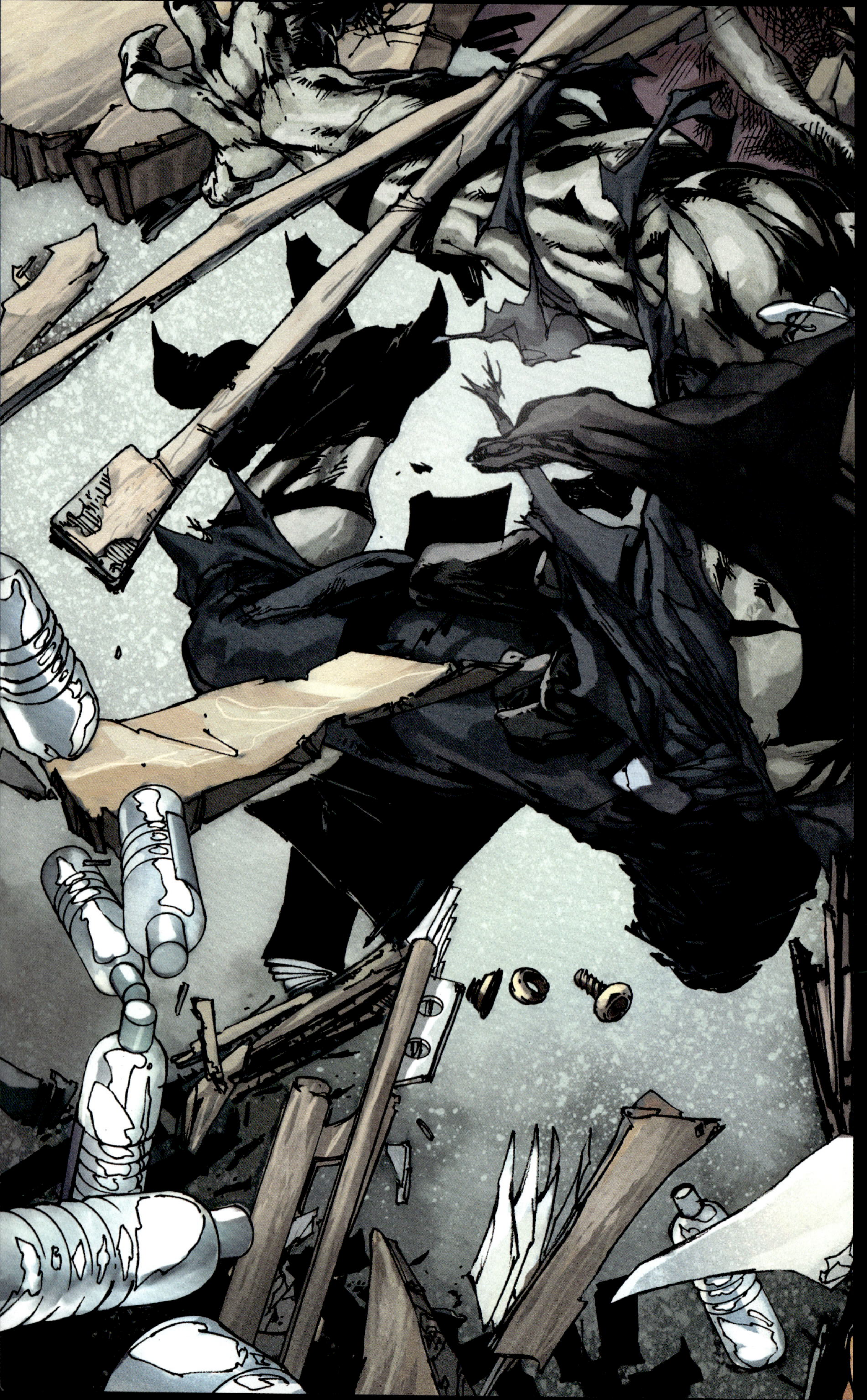

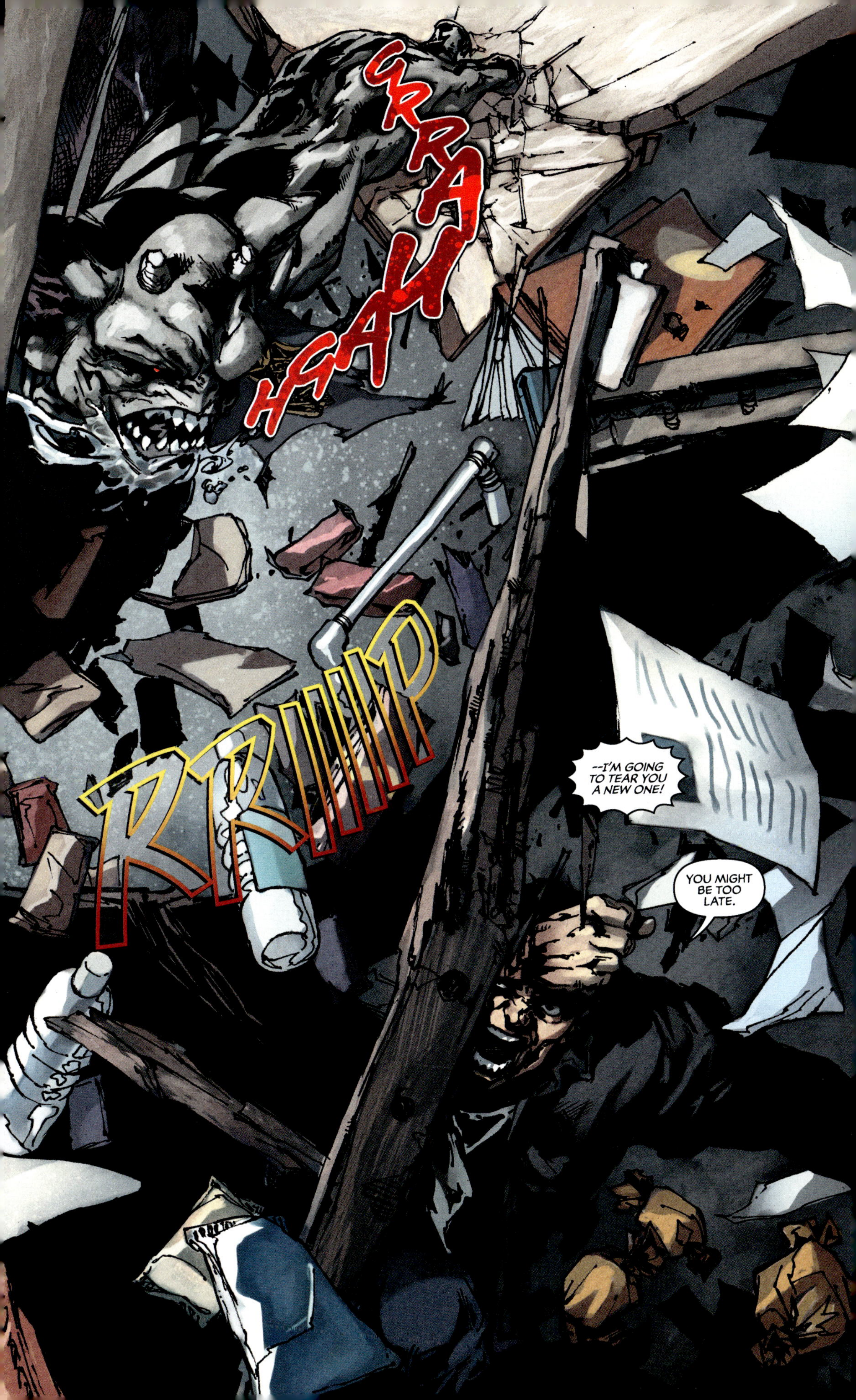
GRRAAUHGAAH
RRIIIIP
--I'M GOING TO TEAR YOU A NEW ONE!
YOU MIGHT BE TOO LATE.

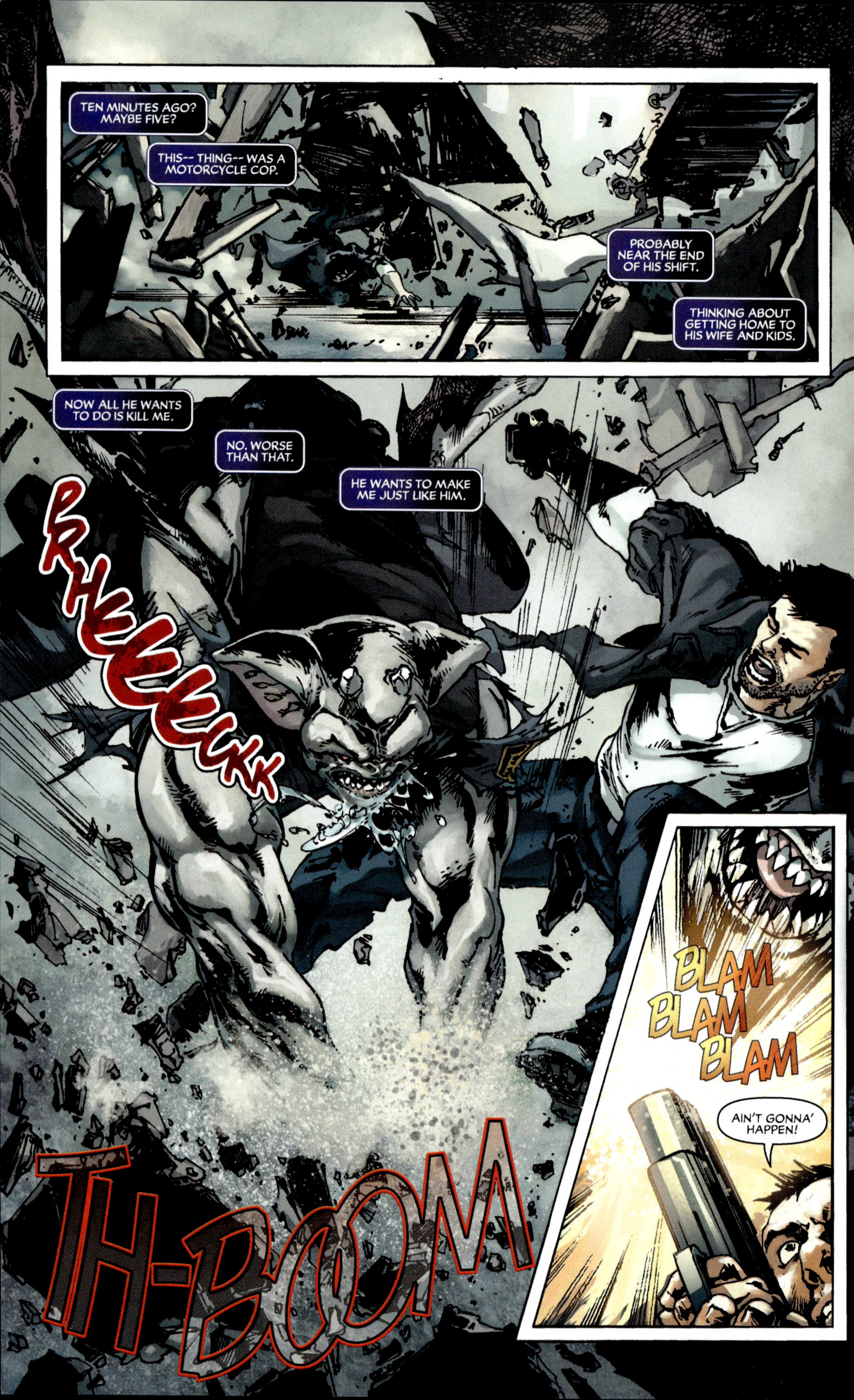

TEN MINUTES AGO? MAYBE FIVE?
THIS-- THING-- WAS A MOTORCYCLE COP.
PROBABLY NEAR THE END OF HIS SHIFT.
THINKING ABOUT GETTING HOME TO HIS WIFE AND KIDS.
NOW ALL HE WANTS TO DO IS KILL ME.
NO. WORSE THAN THAT.
HE WANTS TO MAKE ME JUST LIKE HIM.
TH-BOOM
BLAM
BLAM
BLAM
AIN'T GONNA' HAPPEN!

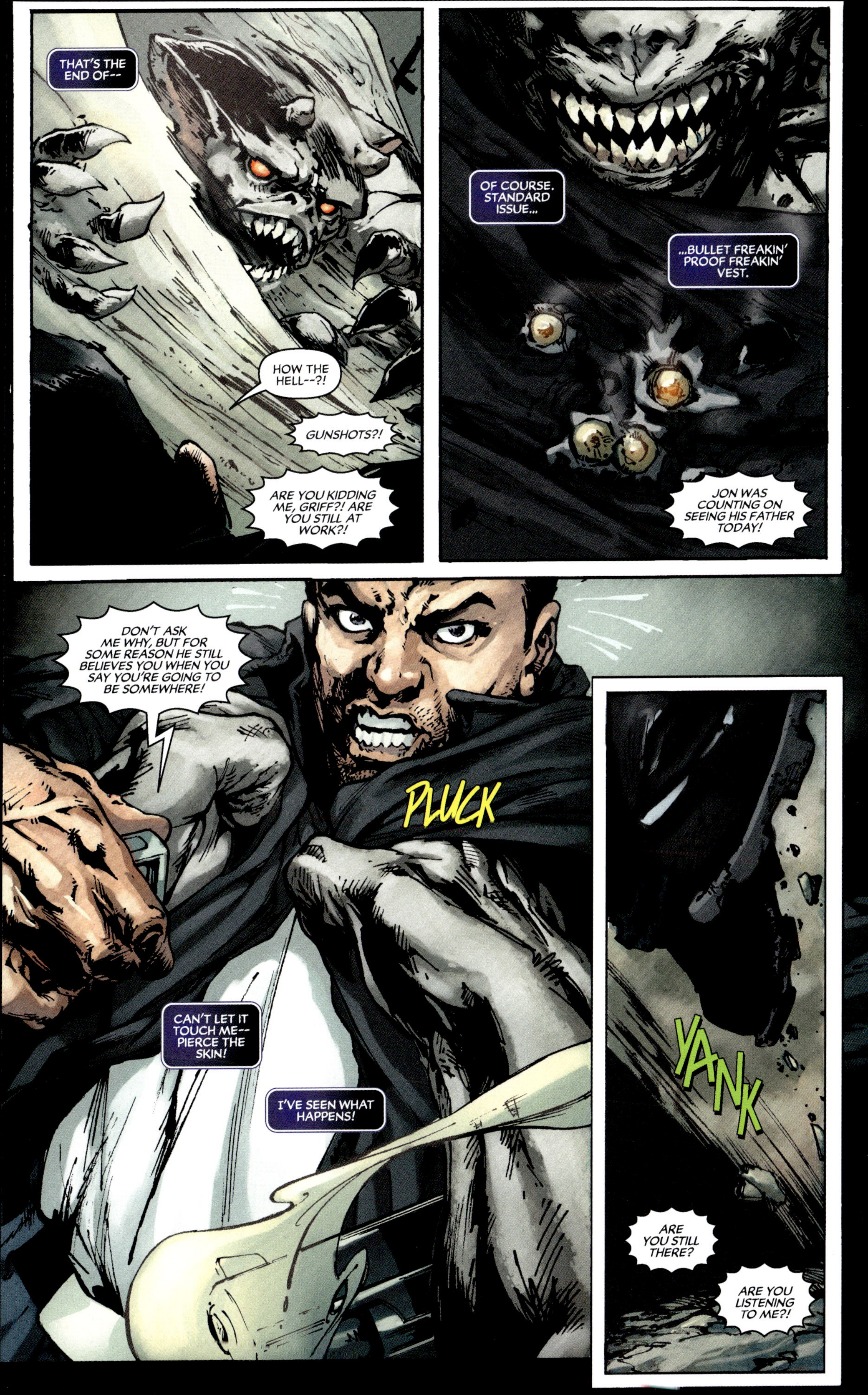
THAT'S THE END OF--
HOW THE HELL--?!
GUNSHOTS?!
ARE YOU KIDDING ME, GRIFF?! ARE YOU STILL AT WORK?!
OF COURSE. STANDARD ISSUE...
...BULLET FREAKIN' PROOF FREAKIN' VEST.
JON WAS COUNTING ON SEEING HIS FATHER TODAY!
DON'T ASK ME WHY, BUT FOR SOME REASON HE STILL BELIEVES YOU WHEN YOU SAY YOU'RE GOING TO BE SOMEWHERE!
PLUCK
CAN'T LET IT TOUCH ME-- PIERCE THE SKIN!
I'VE SEEN WHAT HAPPENS!
YANK
ARE YOU STILL THERE?
ARE YOU LISTENING TO ME?!

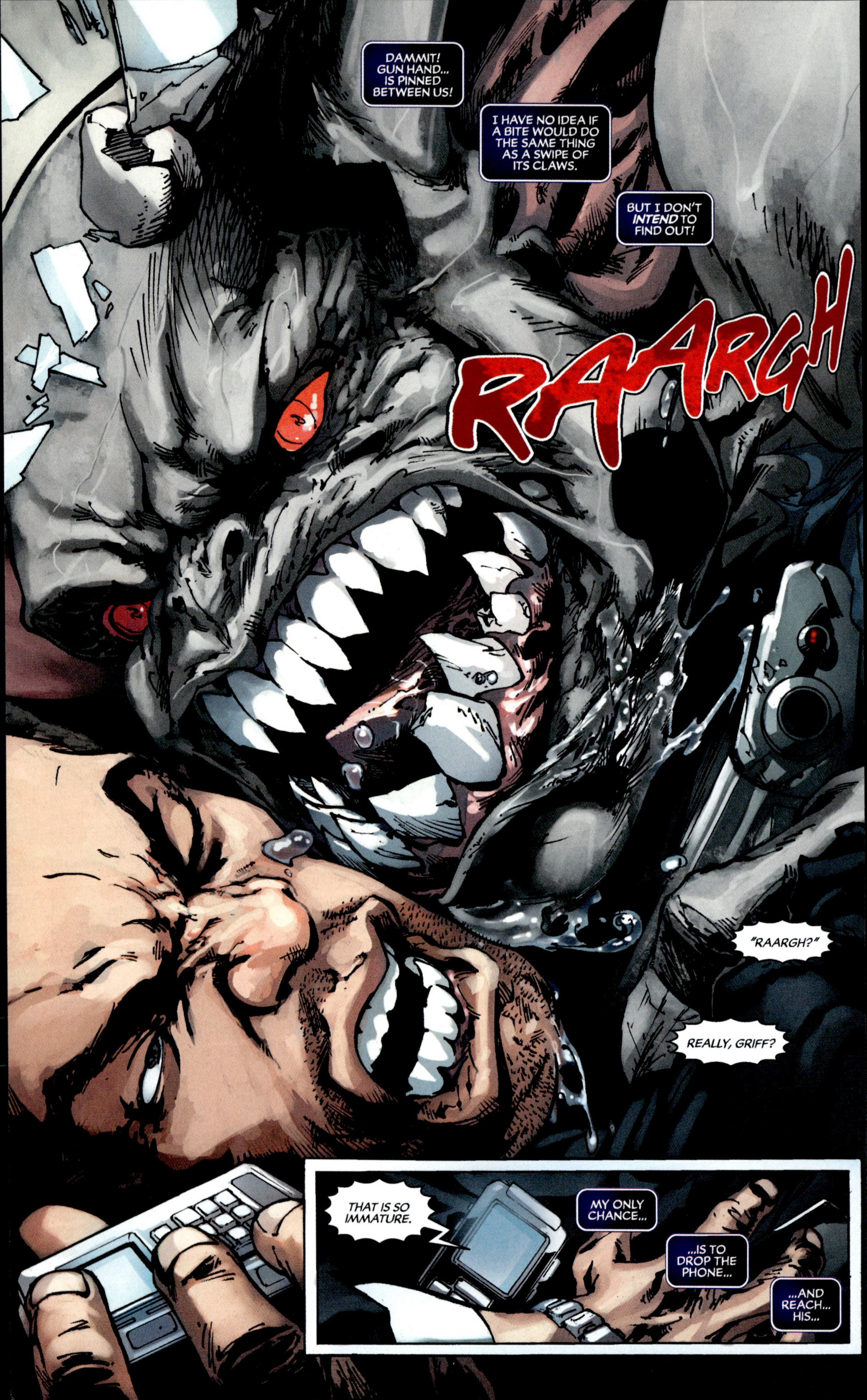
DAMMIT! GUN HAND... IS PINNED BETWEEN US!
I HAVE NO IDEA IF A BITE WOULD DO THE SAME THING AS A SWIPE OF ITS CLAWS.
BUT I DON'T *INTEND* TO FIND OUT!
RAARGH
"RAARGH?"
REALLY, GRIFF?
THAT IS SO IMMATURE.
MY ONLY CHANCE...
...IS TO DROP THE PHONE...
...AND REACH... HIS...

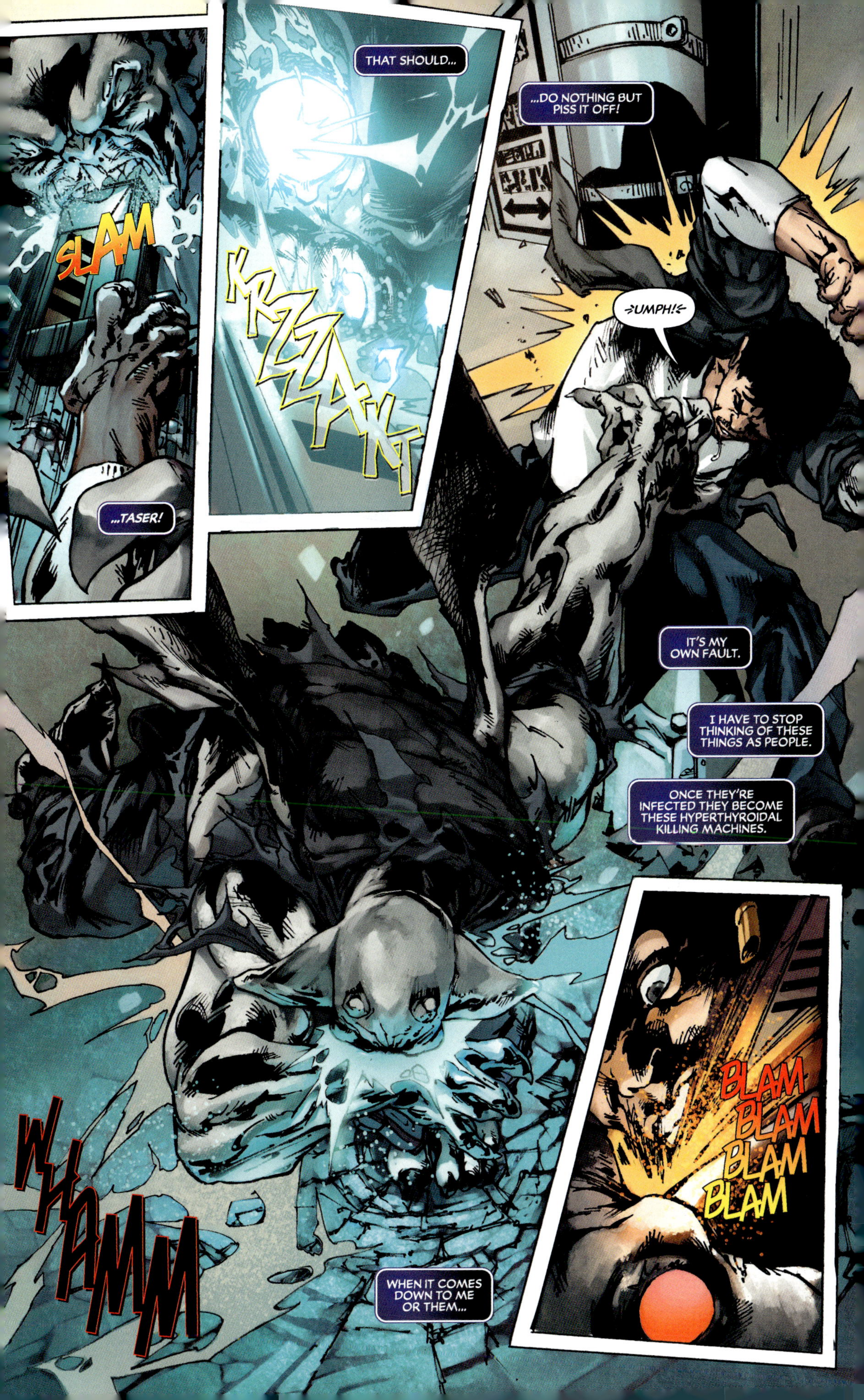
SLAM
...TASER!
THAT SHOULD...
KRZZZAKT
...DO NOTHING BUT PISS IT OFF!
UMPH!
IT'S MY OWN FAULT.
I HAVE TO STOP THINKING OF THESE THINGS AS PEOPLE.
ONCE THEY'RE INFECTED THEY BECOME THESE HYPERTHYROIDAL KILLING MACHINES.
WHAMM
WHEN IT COMES DOWN TO ME OR THEM...
BLAM
BLAM
BLAM
BLAM

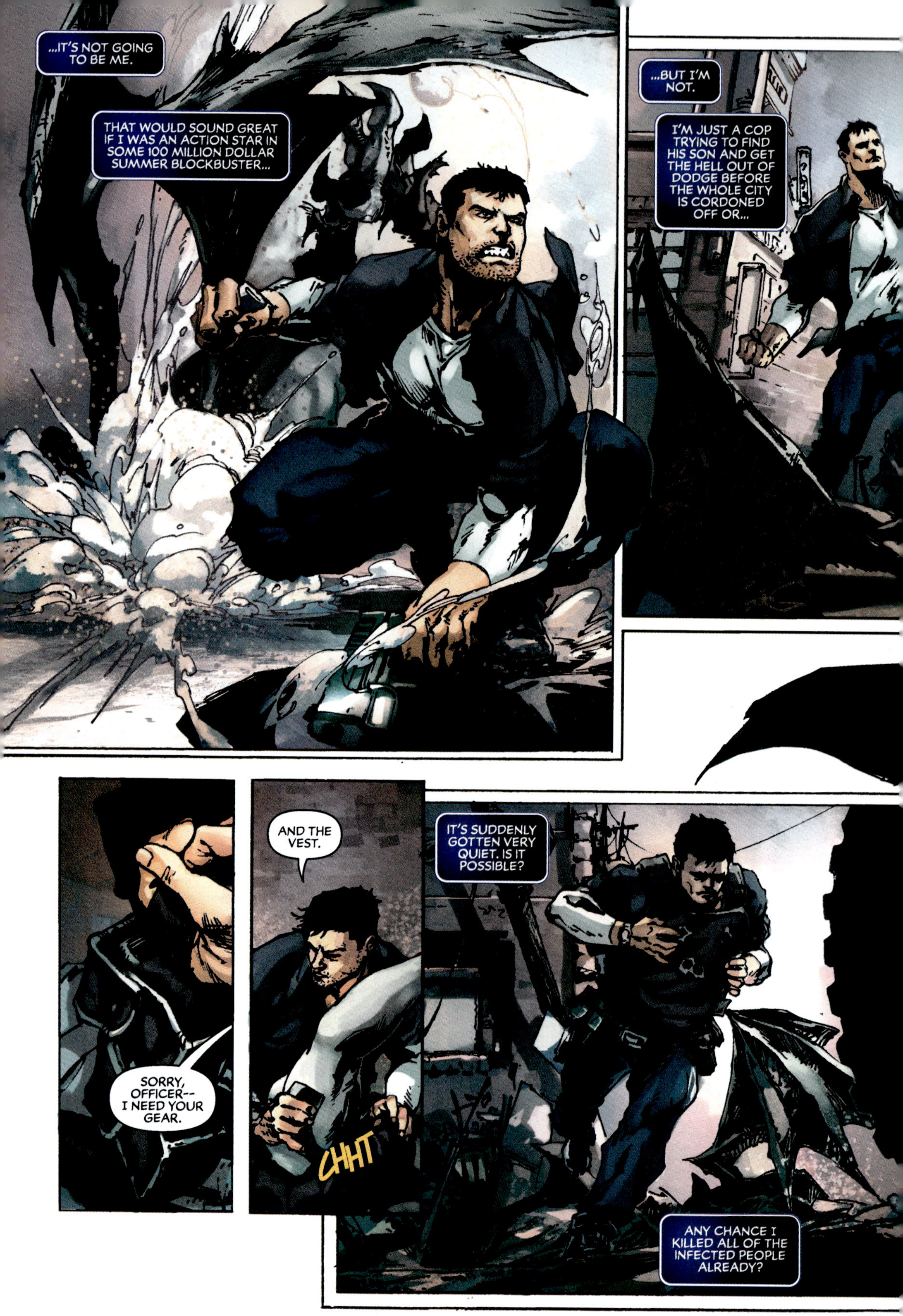
...IT'S NOT GOING TO BE ME.
THAT WOULD SOUND GREAT IF I WAS AN ACTION STAR IN SOME 100 MILLION DOLLAR SUMMER BLOCKBUSTER...
...BUT I'M NOT.
I'M JUST A COP TRYING TO FIND HIS SON AND GET THE HELL OUT OF DODGE BEFORE THE WHOLE CITY IS CORDONED OFF OR...
SORRY, OFFICER-- I NEED YOUR GEAR.
AND THE VEST.
CHHT
IT'S SUDDENLY GOTTEN VERY QUIET. IS IT POSSIBLE?
ANY CHANCE I KILLED ALL OF THE INFECTED PEOPLE ALREADY?

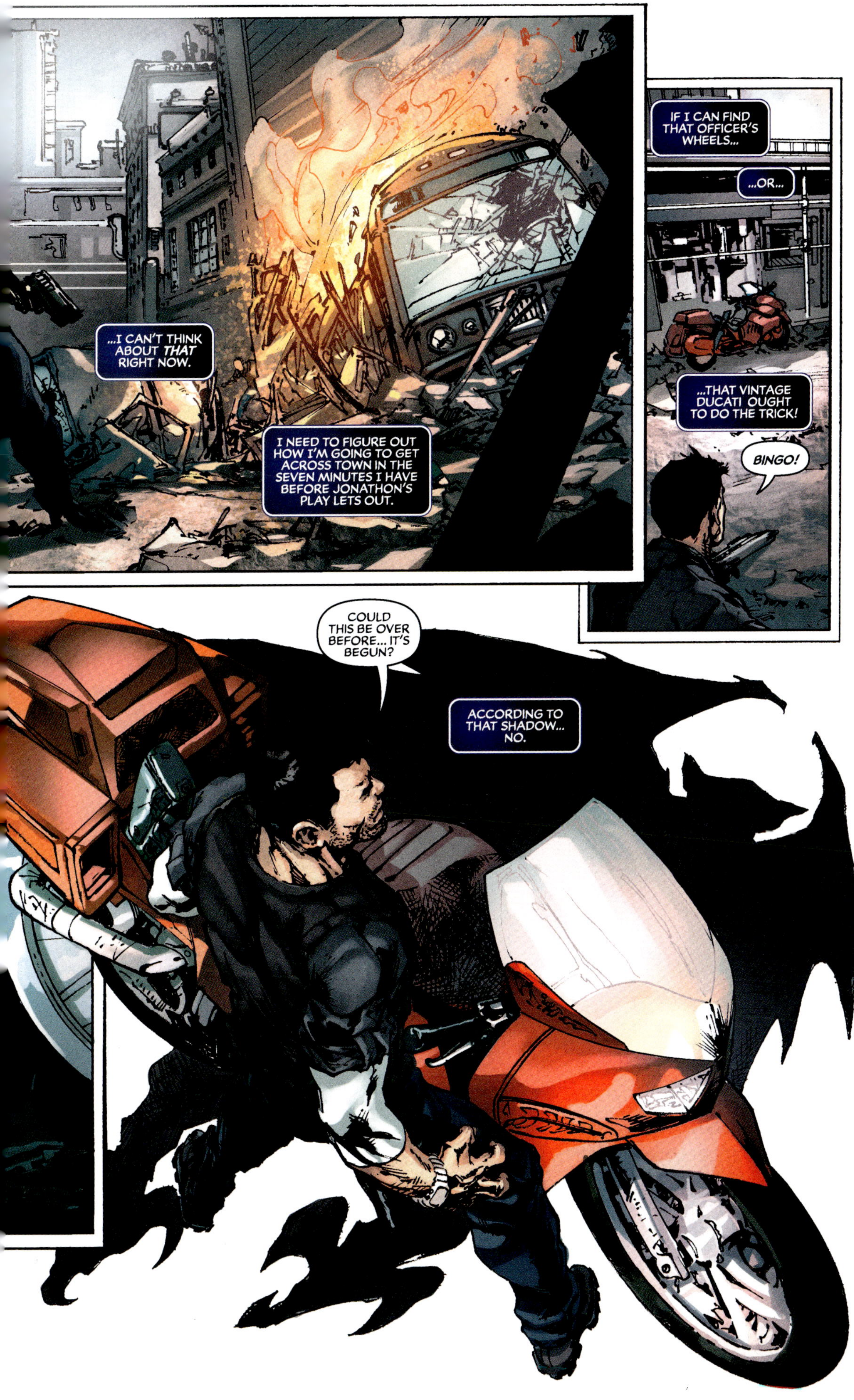
...I CAN'T THINK ABOUT *THAT* RIGHT NOW.
I NEED TO FIGURE OUT HOW I'M GOING TO GET ACROSS TOWN IN THE SEVEN MINUTES I HAVE BEFORE JONATHON'S PLAY LETS OUT.
IF I CAN FIND THAT OFFICER'S WHEELS...
...OR...
...THAT VINTAGE DUCATI OUGHT TO DO THE TRICK!
BINGO!
COULD THIS BE OVER BEFORE... IT'S BEGUN?
ACCORDING TO THAT SHADOW... NO.

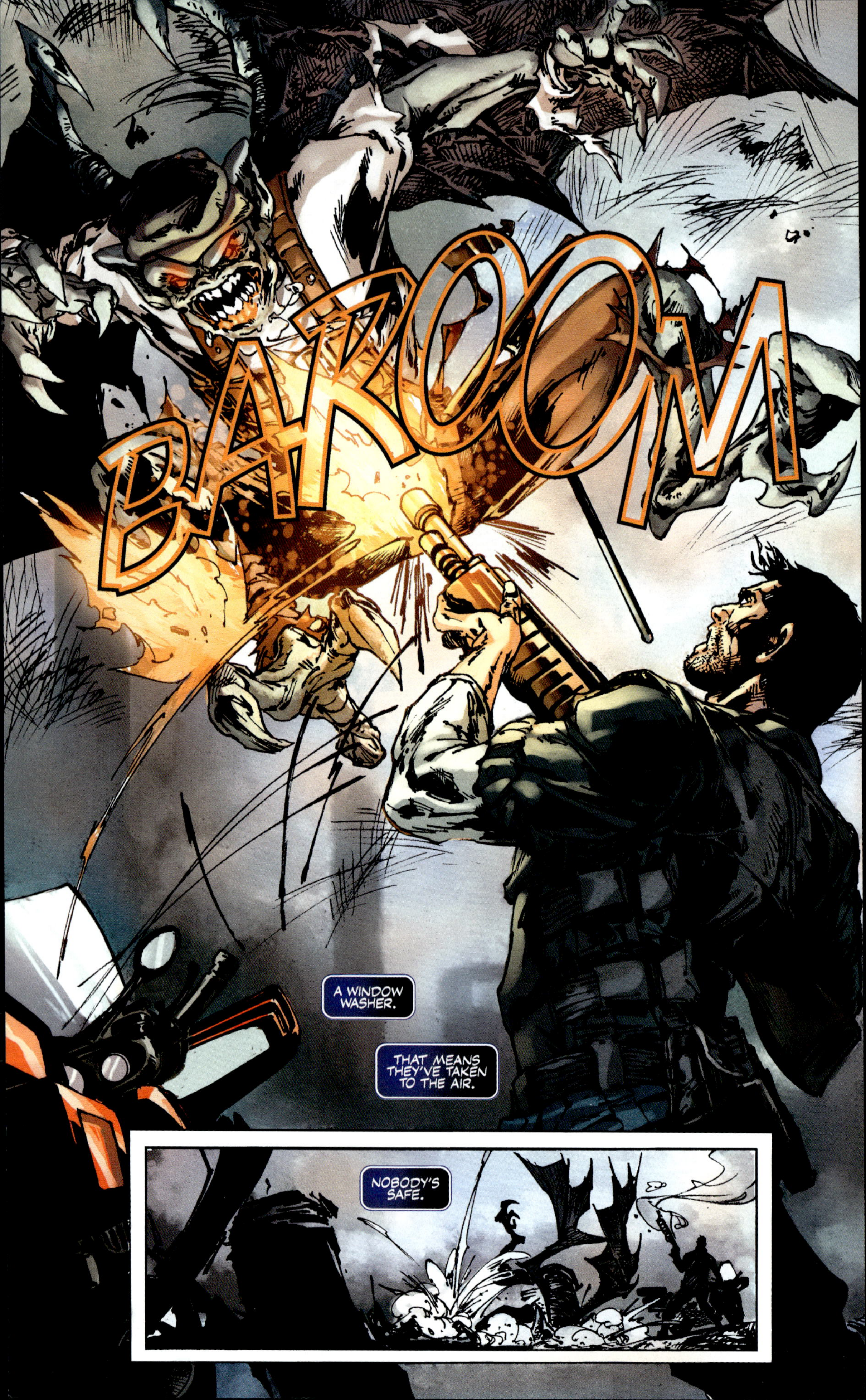
BAROOM
A WINDOW WASHER.
THAT MEANS THEY'VE TAKEN TO THE AIR.
NOBODY'S SAFE.

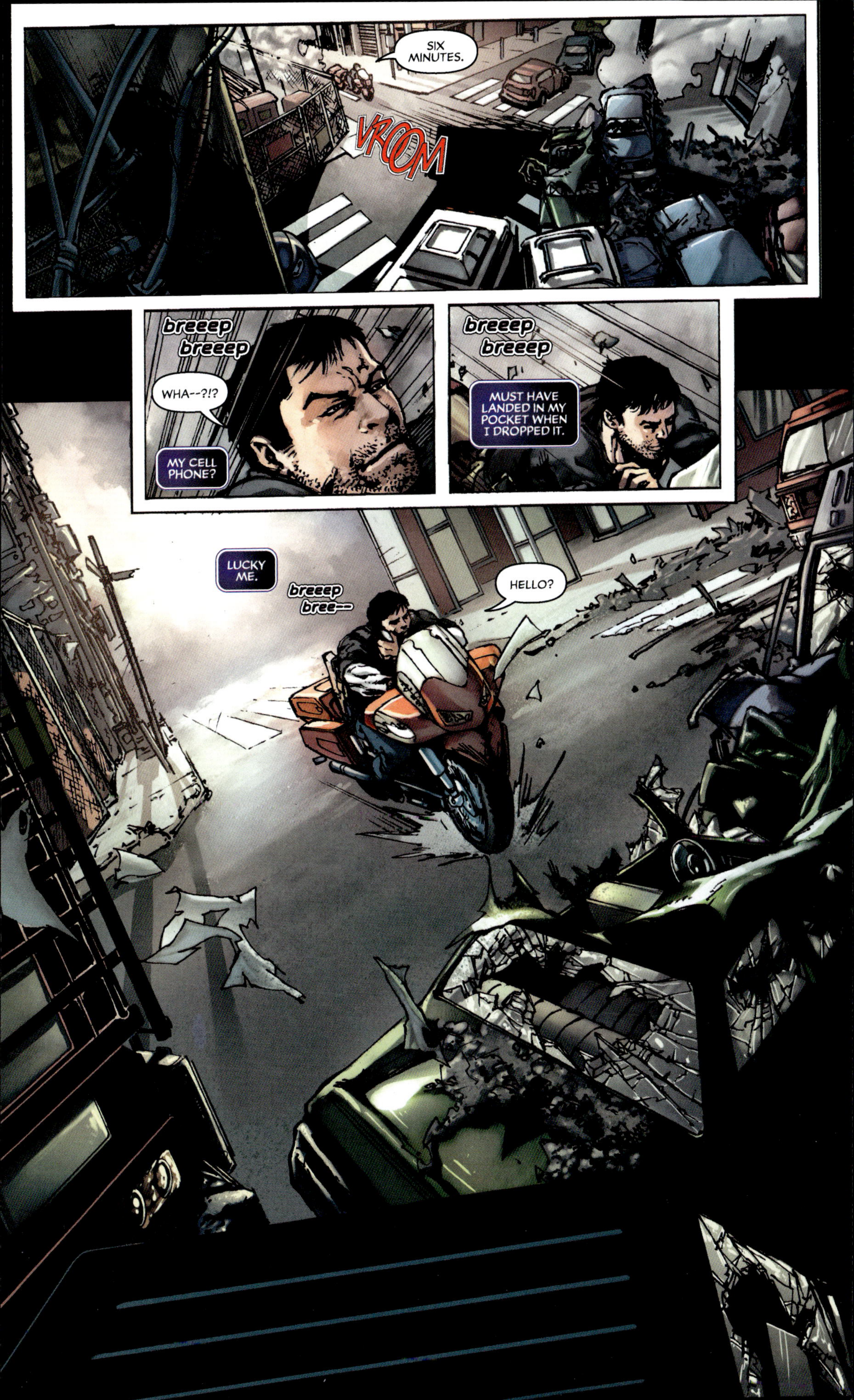

SIX MINUTES.
VROOM
breeep breeep
WHA--?!?
MY CELL PHONE?
breeep breeep
MUST HAVE LANDED IN MY POCKET WHEN I DROPPED IT.
LUCKY ME.
breeep bree--
HELLO?

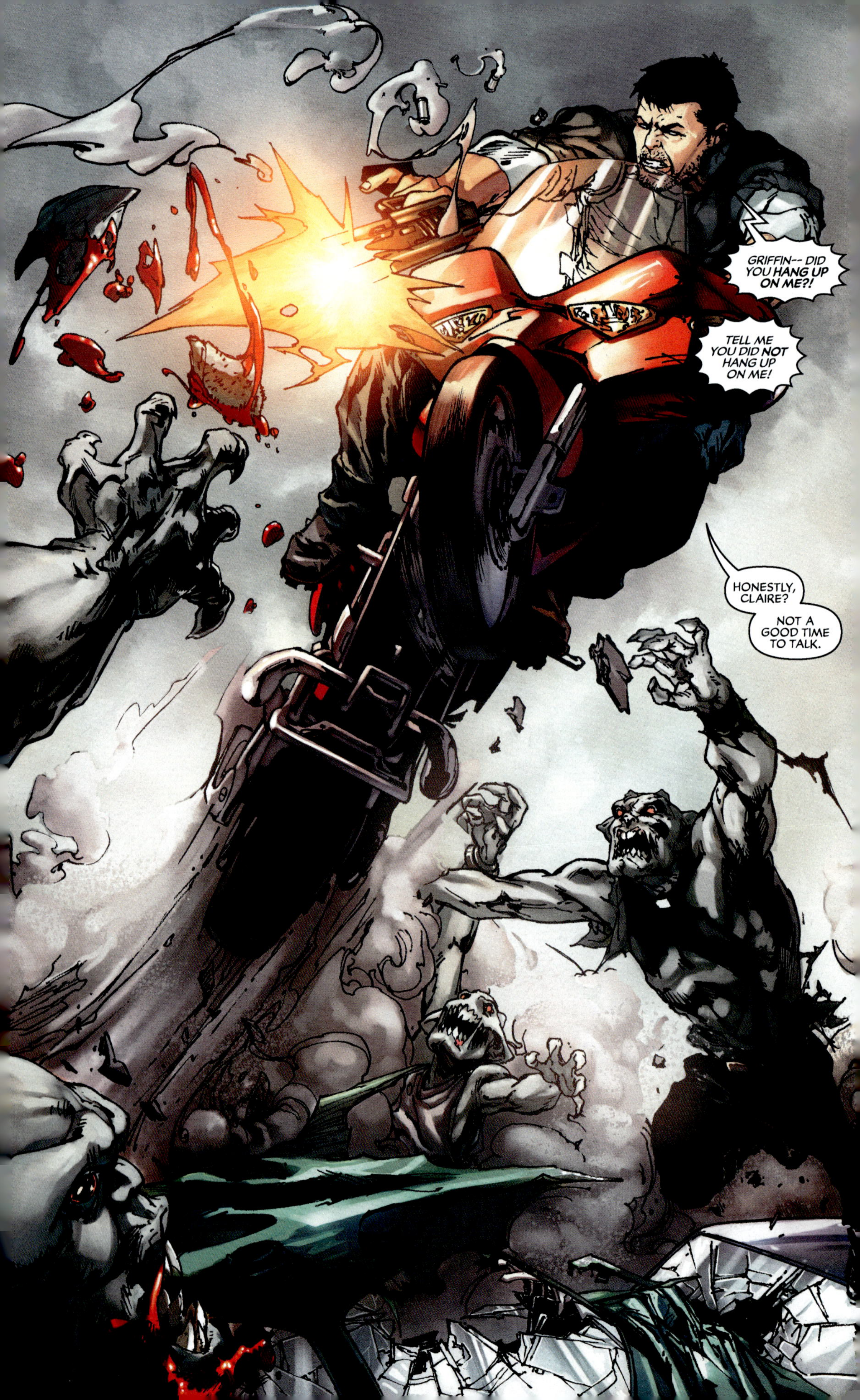
GRIFFIN-- DID YOU HANG UP ON ME?!
TELL ME YOU DID NOT HANG UP ON ME!
HONESTLY, CLAIRE?
NOT A GOOD TIME TO TALK.

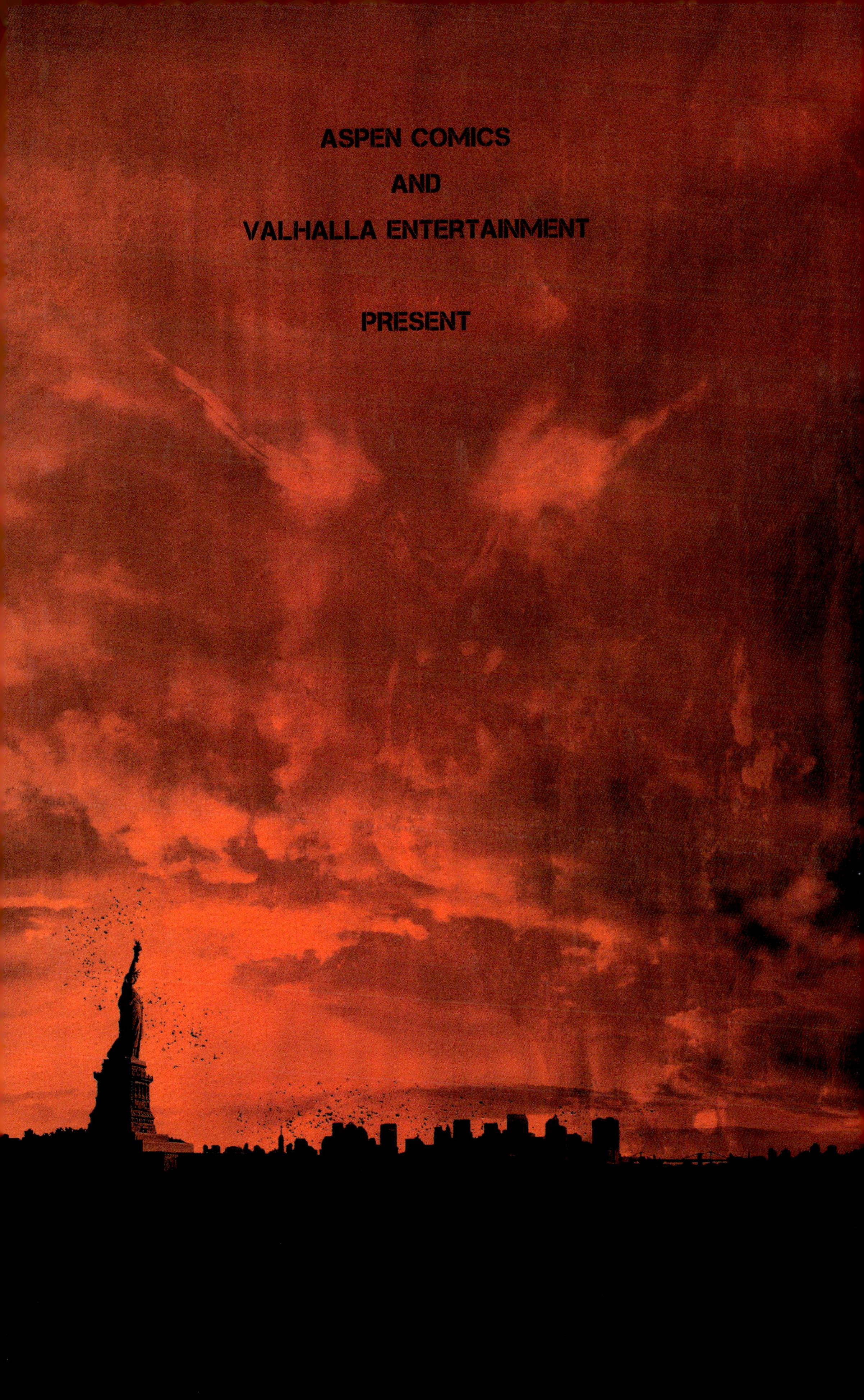
ASPEN COMICS
AND
VALHALLA ENTERTAINMENT
PRESENT

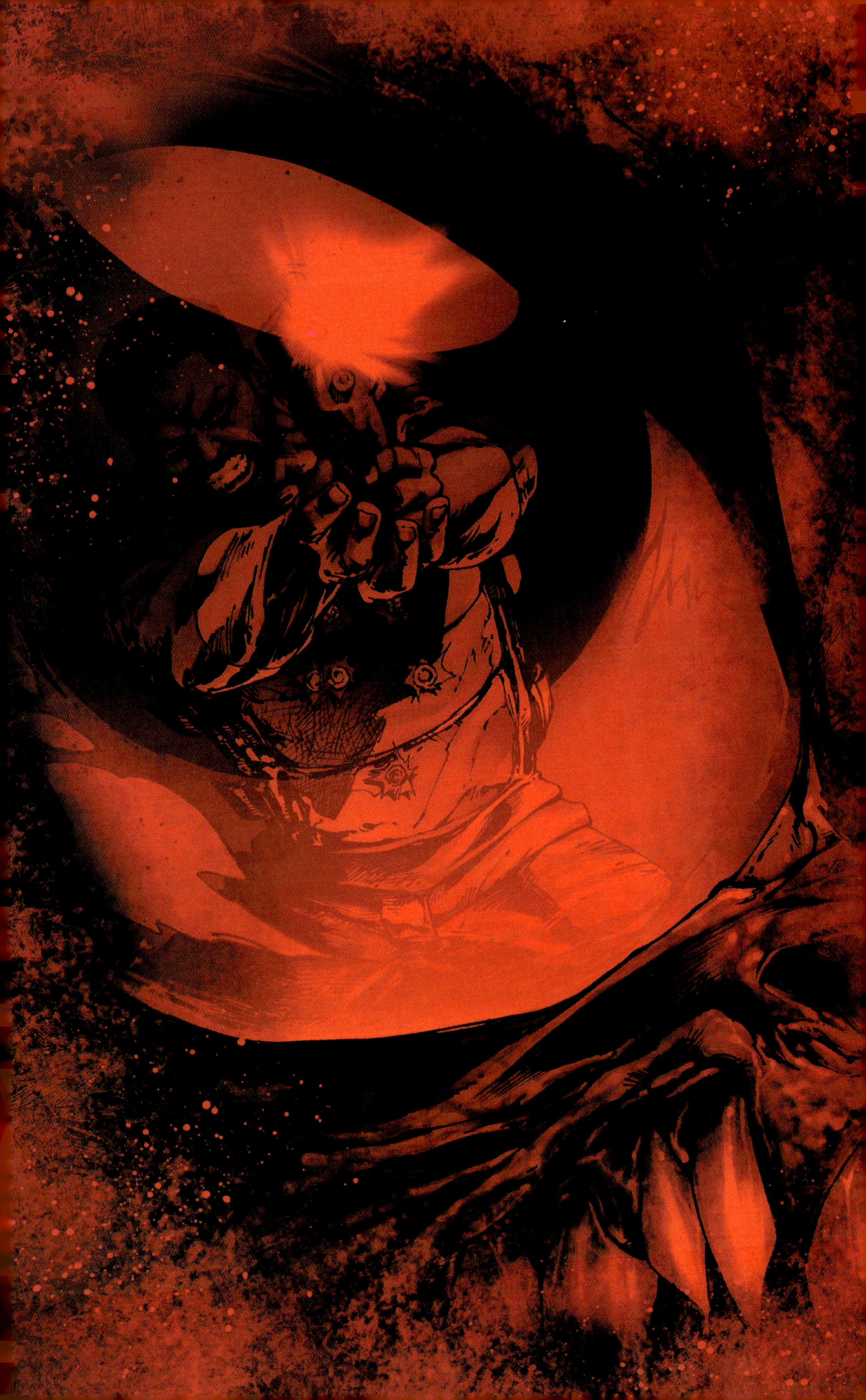

The Scourge

STORY
SCOTT LOBDELL

ILLUSTRATIONS
ERIC BATTLE

COLORS
DAVID CURIEL
AND JORGE FARES

LETTERS
JOSH REED

THE SCOURGE CREATED BY
GALE ANNE HURD

THE SCOURGE CREATED BY GALE ANNE HURD

THE SCOURGE™ VOLUME I
ISBN: 978-1-941511-35-0 FIRST PRINTING, REGULAR EDITION 2017
ISBN: 978-1-941511-43-5 FIRST PRINTING, COMIC BENTO VARIANT EDITION 2017
Collects material originally published as The Scourge vol. 1 Issues 0, 1-6

PUBLISHED BY ASPEN MLT, LLC.
Office of Publication: 5701 W. Slauson Ave. Suite. 120, Culver City, CA 90230.
The Aspen MLT, LLC. logo® is a registered trademark of Aspen MLT, LLC. The Scourge™ and the The Scourge logo, are the trademarks of Valhalla Entertainment, Inc. and Aspen MLT, LLC. The entire contents of this book, all artwork, characters and their likenesses are © 2017 Aspen MLT, LLC. All Rights Reserved. Any similarities between names, characters, persons, and/or institutions in this magazine with persons living or dead or institutions is unintended and is purely coincidental. With the exception of artwork used for review purposes, none of the contents of this book may be reprinted, reproduced or transmitted by any means or in any form without the express written consent of Aspen MLT, LLC.
PRINTED IN U.S.A.

Address correspondence to:
THE SCOURGE c/o Aspen MLT, LLC.
5701 W. Slauson Ave. Suite. 120
Culver City, CA. 90230-6946
or fanmail@aspencomics.com

Visit us on the web at:
aspencomics.com
aspenstore.com
facebook.com/aspencomics
twitter.com/aspencomics

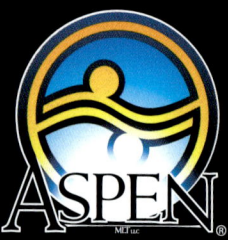
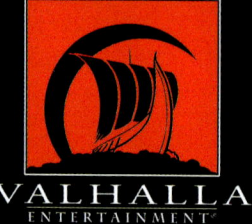

For this Edition:
COLLECTED EDITION EDITORS: GABE CARRASCO, MARK ROSLAN AND FRANK MASTROMAURO
ORIGINAL SERIES EDITORS: FRANK MASTROMAURO AND VINCE HERNANDEZ
COVER AND BOOK DESIGN AND PRODUCTION: MARK ROSLAN
LOGO DESIGN: PETER STEIGERWALD
COVER ILLUSTRATION: ERIC BATTLE AND PETER STEIGERWALD
COMIC BENTO COVER ILLUSTRATION: ERIC BATTLE AND PETER STEIGERWALD

For Aspen Comics:
FOUNDER: MICHAEL TURNER
CO-OWNER: PETER STEIGERWALD
CO-OWNER/PRESIDENT: FRANK MASTROMAURO
VICE PRESIDENT/EDITOR IN CHIEF: VINCE HERNANDEZ
VICE PRESIDENT/DIRECTOR OF DESIGN AND PRODUCTION: MARK ROSLAN
EDITOR: GABE CARRASCO
OFFICE COORDINATOR: MEGAN MADRIGAL
PRODUCTION: JUSTICE
ASPENSTORE.COM: CHRIS RUPP

For Valhalla Entertainment:
CHAIRMAN: GALE ANNE HURD
VICE PRESIDENT: PHILLIP KOBYLANSKI

To find the Comic Shop nearest you...
888-COMIC-BOOK
csls.diamondcomics.com
1-888-266-4226

Also Available from Aspen Comics:
A Tribute to Michael Turner — ISBN: 978-0-9774821-7-7
Aspen Universe: Revelations™ Volume 1 — ISBN: 978-1-941511-25-1
Bubblegun™ Volume 1: Heist Jinks — ISBN: 978-1-941511-15-2
Charismagic™ Volume 1 — ISBN: 978-0-9854473-7-3
Damsels In Excess™ Volume 1 — ISBN: 978-0-941511-32-9
Eternal Soulfire™ Volume I — ISBN: 978-1-941511-26-8
Executive Assistant: Iris™ Volume 1 — ISBN: 978-0-9823628-5-3
Executive Assistant: Iris™ Volume 2 — ISBN: 978-0-9854473-0-4
Executive Assistant: Iris™ Volume 3 — ISBN: 978-1-941511-36-7
Executive Assistant: The Hitlist Agenda™ Volume 1 — ISBN: 978-0-9854473-1-1
Executive Assistant: Assassins™ Volume 1 — ISBN: 978-1-941511-09-1
Fathom™ Volume I: The Definitive Edition — ISBN: 978-0-9774821-5-3
Fathom™ Volume 2: Into The Deep — ISBN: 978-1-6317369-2-6
Fathom™ Volume 3: Worlds at War — ISBN: 978-0-9774821-9-1
Fathom™ Volume 4: The Rig — ISBN: 978-1-941511-07-7
Fathom™ Volume 5: Cold Destiny — ISBN: 978-1-941511-14-5
Fathom Blue™ Volume I — ISBN: 978-1-941511-27-5
Fathom™: Dawn of War — ISBN: 978-1-941511-33-6
Fathom™: Kiani: Volume I: Blade of Fire — ISBN: 978-0-9774821-8-4
Fathom™: Kiani: Volume 2: Blade of Fury — ISBN: 978-1-941511-06-0
Fathom™: Killian's Tide — ISBN: 978-1-941511-00-8
The Four Points™ Volume I: Horsemen — ISBN: 978-1-941511-10-7

Homecoming™ Volume I — ISBN: 978-1-941511-18-3
Jirni™ Volume I: Shadows and Dust — ISBN: 978-0-9854473-8-0
Jirni™ Volume II: New Horizons — ISBN: 978-0-9823628-9-1
Lola XOXO™ Volume I — ISBN: 978-1-941511-03-9
Lola XOXO™: Wasteland Madam Volume I — ISBN: 978-1-941511-04-6
Mindfield™ Volume I — ISBN: 978-1-941511-45-9
Shrugged™ Volume 1: A Little Perspective — ISBN: 978-0-9774821-6-0
Soulfire™ Volume 1: part 1 — ISBN: 978-0-9774821-2-2
Soulfire™ Volume 1: part 2 — ISBN: 978-0-9823628-1-5
Soulfire™ Volume 1: The Definitive Edition — ISBN: 978-0-9823628-6-0
Soulfire™ Volume 2: Dragon Fall — ISBN: 978-0-9854473-2-8
Soulfire™ Volume 3: Seeds of Chaos — ISBN: 978-1-941511-13-8
Soulfire™ Volume 4: Dark Grace — ISBN: 978-1-941511-22-0
Soulfire™ Volume 5: Pandemonium — ISBN: 978-1-941511-30-5
Soulfire™: Chaos Reign — ISBN: 978-0-9774821-4-6
Soulfire™: Dying of the Light — ISBN: 978-0-9774821-1-5
Soulfire™: Shadow Magic — ISBN: 978-0-9823628-7-7

Aspen Novels:
Seven To Die™ — ISBN: 978-1-941511-02-2
The Lost Spark™ — ISBN: 978-0-9854473-3-5

FOREWORD

There's nothing scarier than the faceless monster. Not literally a creature without a face, but a terror whose identity or personality is unknown. And what makes the unknown so frightful is that it forces us to project our own dread and anxieties, thus giving the monster we fear a face that gazes back into our souls like Nietzsche's abyss. No one knows this better than Gale Anne Hurd, the executive producer of one of the biggest TV shows in history, THE WALKING DEAD. Season after season, THE WALKING DEAD proves not only are zombies scary, but just the idea of zombies is even scarier because they are a faceless horde, void of motive and prejudice. All they want is to destroy you, and they won't stop until that happens, much like the creatures of the ALIEN movies. While Ridley Scott explores the larger questions of the ALIEN-verse in the more recent entries, let's not forget the minimalistic terror of the first movie, a movie Gale Anne Hurd produced. Unencumbered and sleek, the first ALIEN was a haunted house movie in space. Haunted by an other-worldly creature before we even knew them as Xenomorphs. At the time, we didn't know its name, how it functioned, or where it came from. All we knew was that it scared the shit out of us, and we took that fear into our nightmares for decades.

THE SCOURGE is a natural extension of Gale's brilliant mind, tapping into the same fears as THE WALKING DEAD and ALIENS. Without giving away too much of the goods here, this is a story about a pandemic of gargoyles. Compared to other monsters, like the well-tread terrain of vampires or werewolves, there hasn't been much exploration of gargoyle mythology. Sure, there are cameos in various iterations of THE HUNCHBACK OF NOTRE DAME, the 1972 Bill Norton-directed movie, and a few other examples, but beyond those, there lacks a real depth of canon for gargoyles.

Which brings us back to the faceless monster. Cormac McCarthy once wrote, "Whatever in creation exists without my knowledge, exists without my consent." Here, McCarthy is articulating the hopeless nature of living in a world where new dangers form and attack us, whether real like a virus that breaks down our immune system or made up like the dead rising from their graves to consume us. THE SCOURGE is a new take on this fear and the entire endeavor is elegantly executed in the pages of this comic by the rest of the creative team, Scott Lobdell, Eric Battle, David Curiel, and Josh Reed. They bring the gargoyle threat to life in one eye-popping panel after the other, giving us a faceless horde so relentless in its goal of destruction that it's almost Biblical, becoming a parable for the end times. If the world ended today and this trade paperback was the last thing you read… At least it would be a perfect ending.

—MIKE LE
Los Angeles, 2017

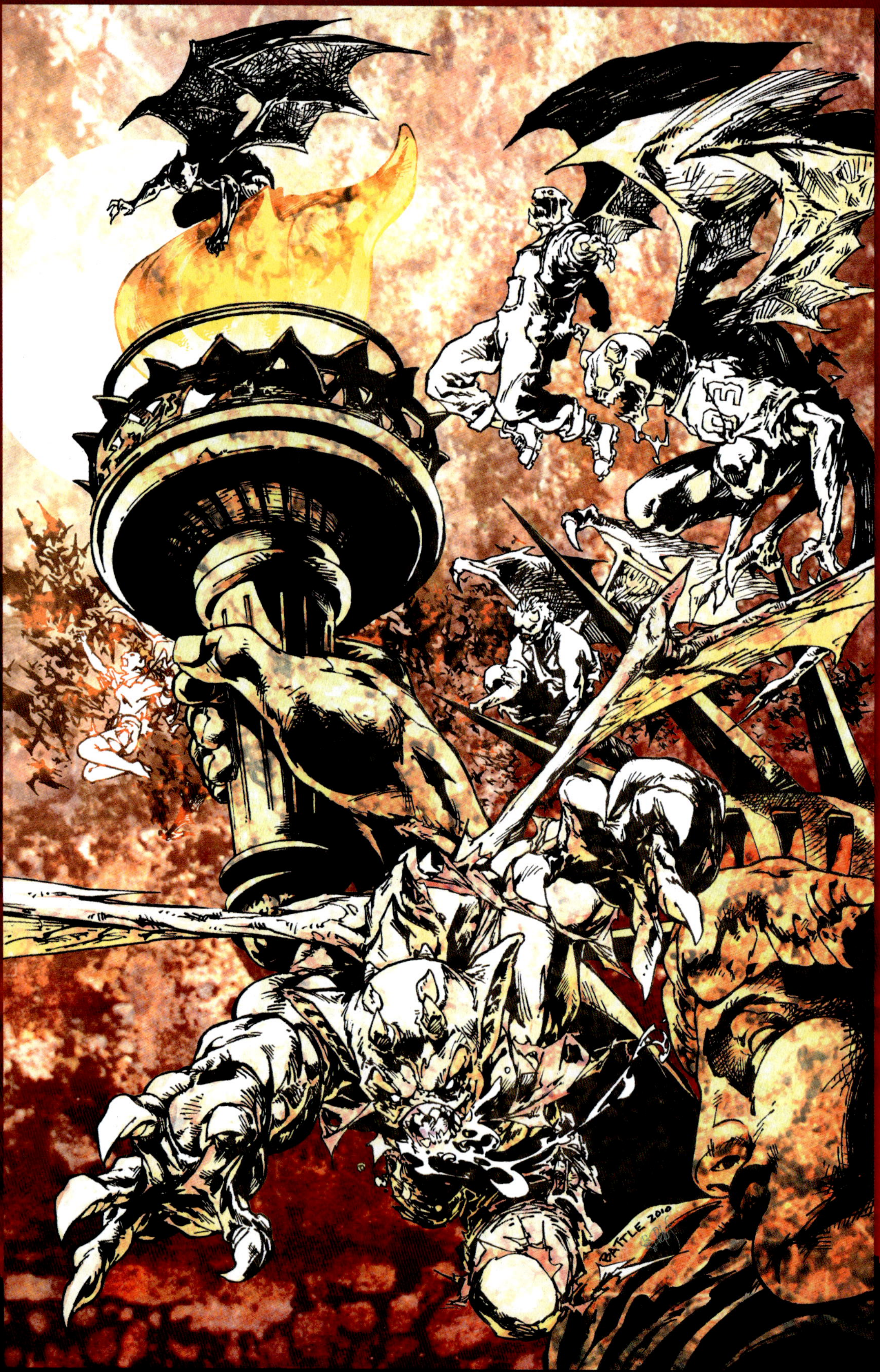

Retailer "Infected" Incentive Edition Cover C to

THE SCOURGE #0

by

Eric **BATTLE** | Peter **STEIGERWALD**

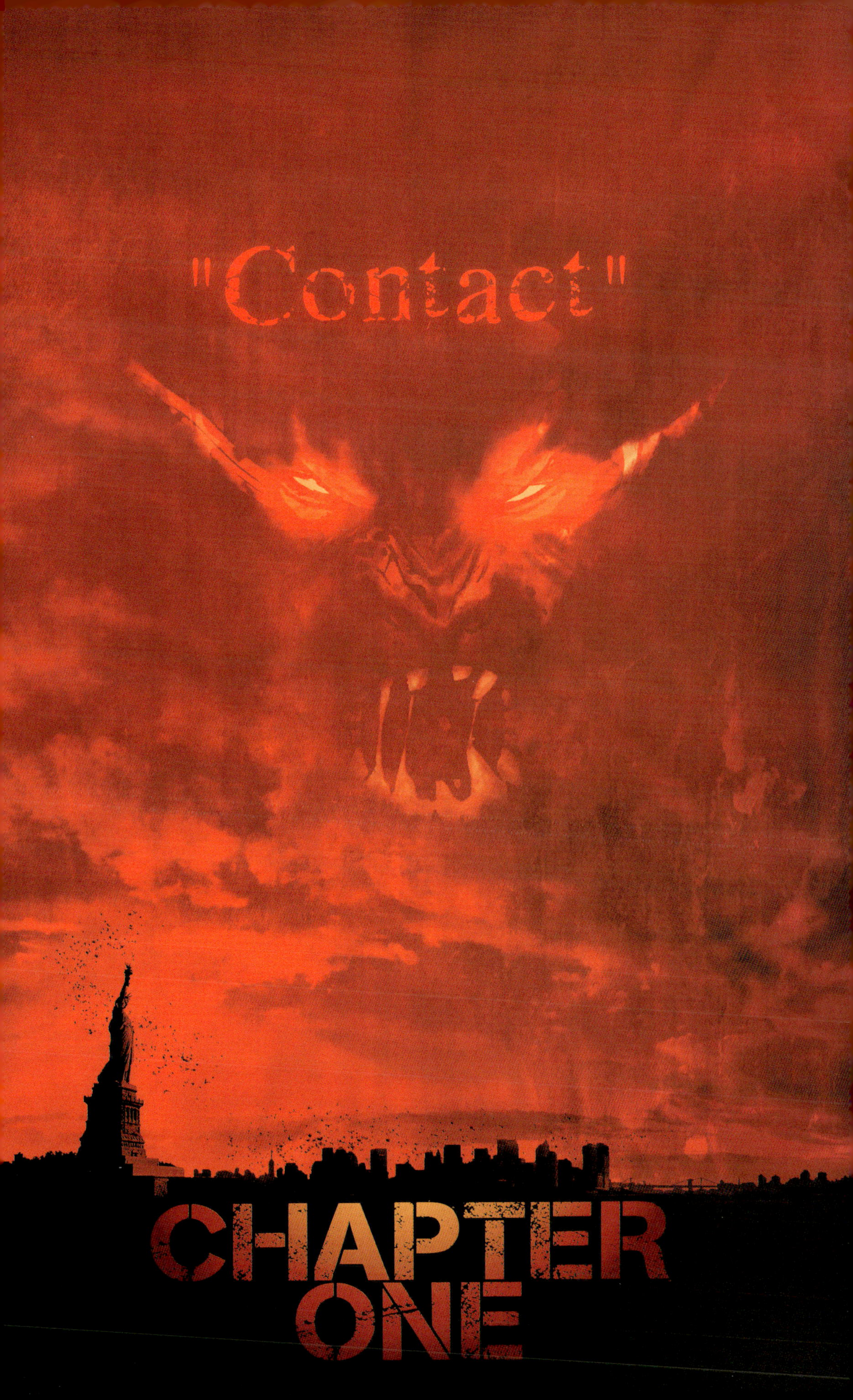
"Contact"
CHAPTER
ONE

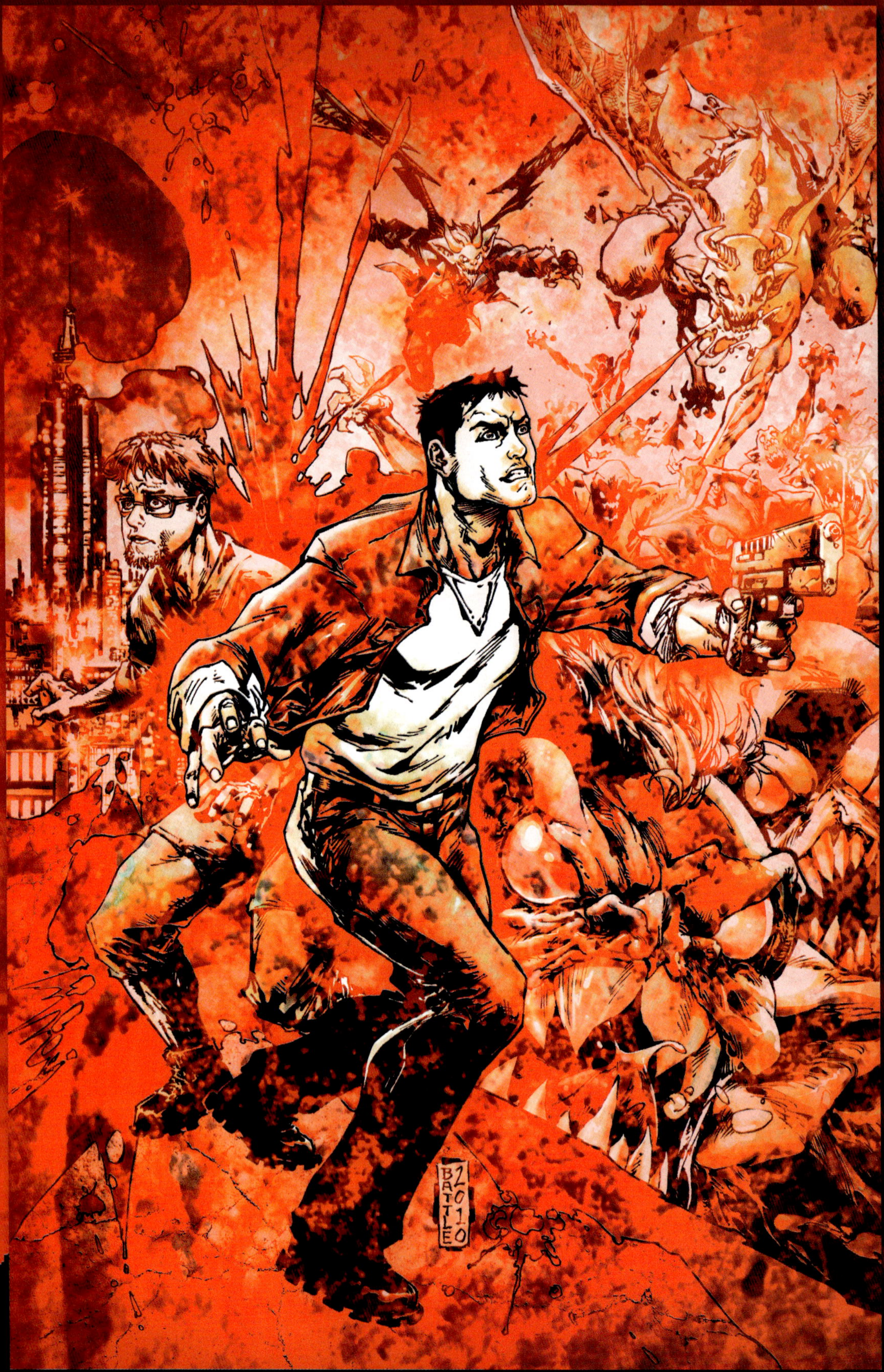
BATTLE 2010

Retailer "Infected" Incentive Edition Cover D to
THE SCOURGE #1

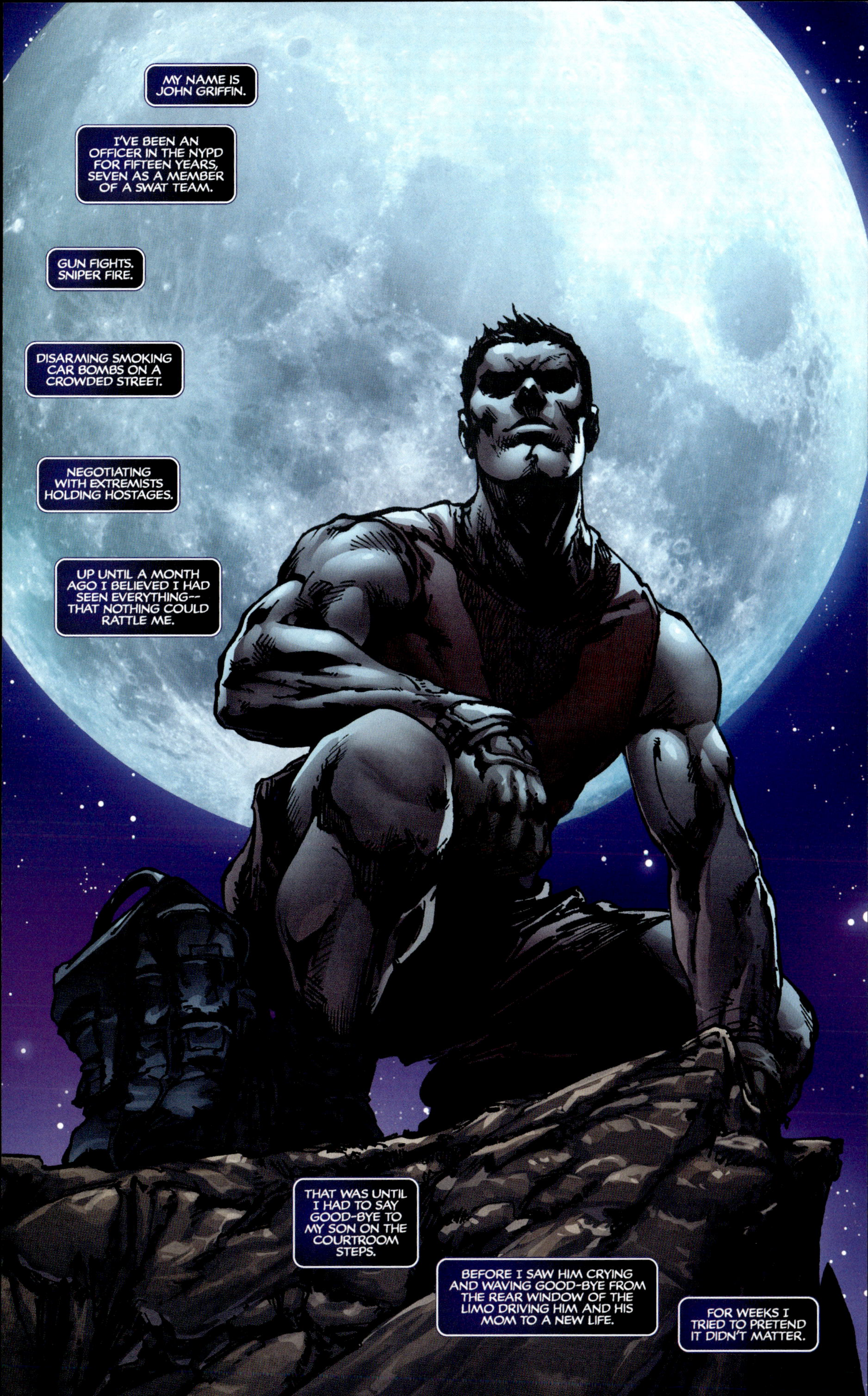
MY NAME IS JOHN GRIFFIN.
I'VE BEEN AN OFFICER IN THE NYPD FOR FIFTEEN YEARS, SEVEN AS A MEMBER OF A SWAT TEAM.
GUN FIGHTS. SNIPER FIRE.
DISARMING SMOKING CAR BOMBS ON A CROWDED STREET.
NEGOTIATING WITH EXTREMISTS HOLDING HOSTAGES.
UP UNTIL A MONTH AGO I BELIEVED I HAD SEEN EVERYTHING-- THAT NOTHING COULD RATTLE ME.
THAT WAS UNTIL I HAD TO SAY GOOD-BYE TO MY SON ON THE COURTROOM STEPS.
BEFORE I SAW HIM CRYING AND WAVING GOOD-BYE FROM THE REAR WINDOW OF THE LIMO DRIVING HIM AND HIS MOM TO A NEW LIFE.
FOR WEEKS I TRIED TO PRETEND IT DIDN'T MATTER.

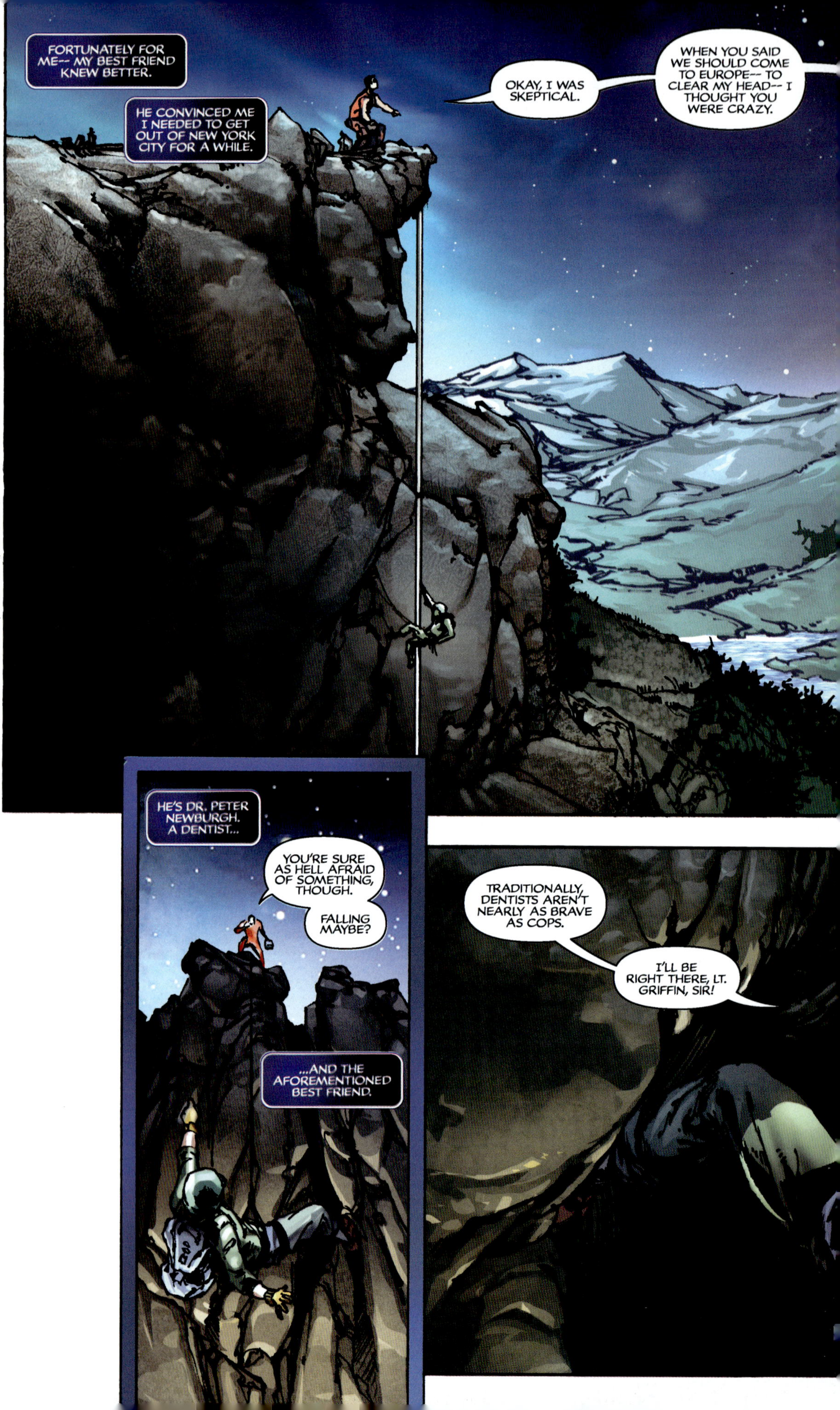
FORTUNATELY FOR ME-- MY BEST FRIEND KNEW BETTER.
HE CONVINCED ME I NEEDED TO GET OUT OF NEW YORK CITY FOR A WHILE.
WHEN YOU SAID WE SHOULD COME TO EUROPE-- TO CLEAR MY HEAD-- I THOUGHT YOU WERE CRAZY.
OKAY, I WAS SKEPTICAL.
HE'S DR. PETER NEWBURGH. A DENTIST...
YOU'RE SURE AS HELL AFRAID OF SOMETHING, THOUGH.
FALLING MAYBE?
...AND THE AFOREMENTIONED BEST FRIEND.
TRADITIONALLY, DENTISTS AREN'T NEARLY AS BRAVE AS COPS.
I'LL BE RIGHT THERE, LT. GRIFFIN, SIR!

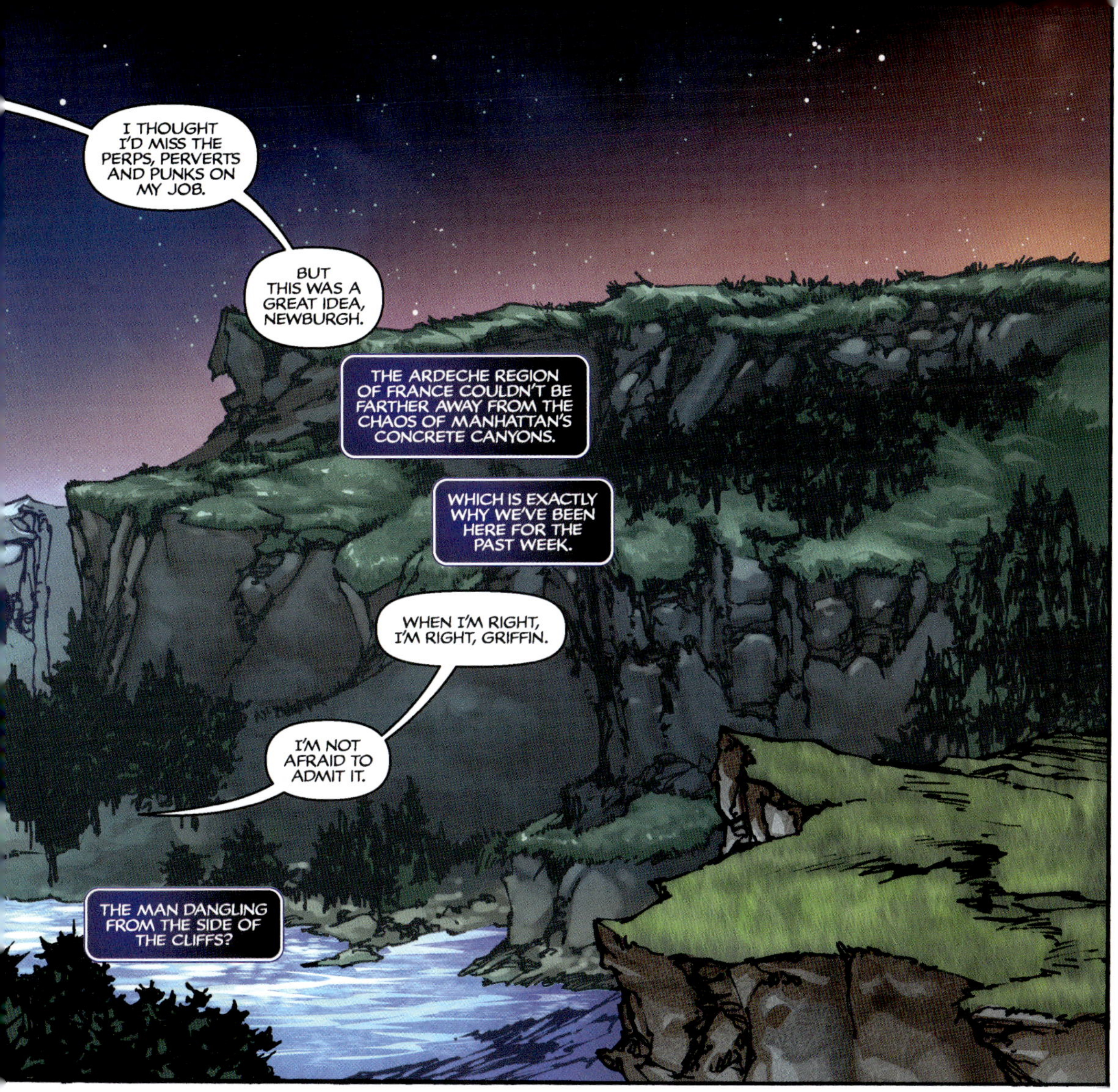
I THOUGHT I'D MISS THE PERPS, PERVERTS AND PUNKS ON MY JOB.
BUT THIS WAS A GREAT IDEA, NEWBURGH.
THE ARDECHE REGION OF FRANCE COULDN'T BE FARTHER AWAY FROM THE CHAOS OF MANHATTAN'S CONCRETE CANYONS.
WHICH IS EXACTLY WHY WE'VE BEEN HERE FOR THE PAST WEEK.
WHEN I'M RIGHT, I'M RIGHT, GRIFFIN.
I'M NOT AFRAID TO ADMIT IT.
THE MAN DANGLING FROM THE SIDE OF THE CLIFFS?

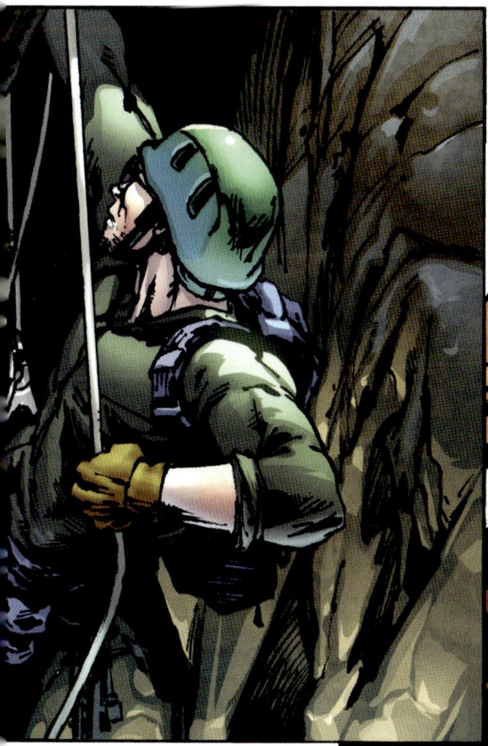

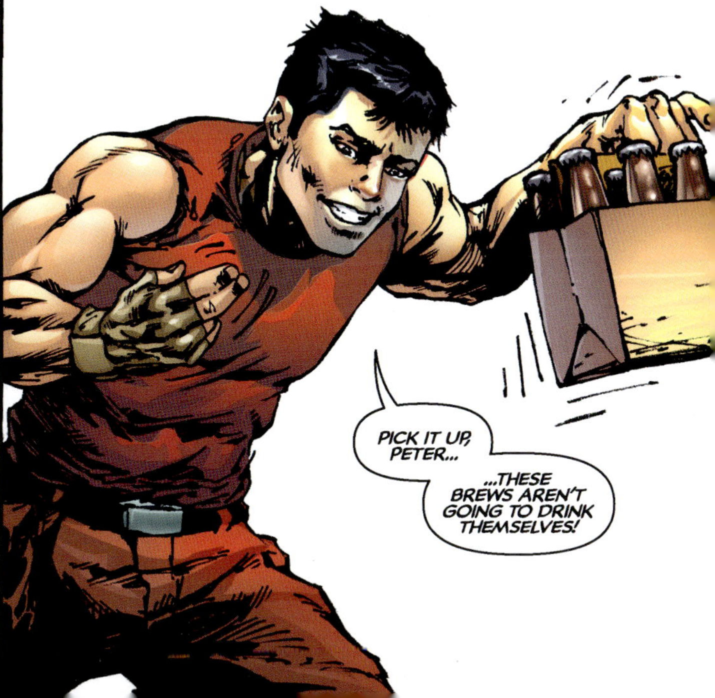
PICK IT UP, PETER...
...THESE BREWS AREN'T GOING TO DRINK THEMSELVES!

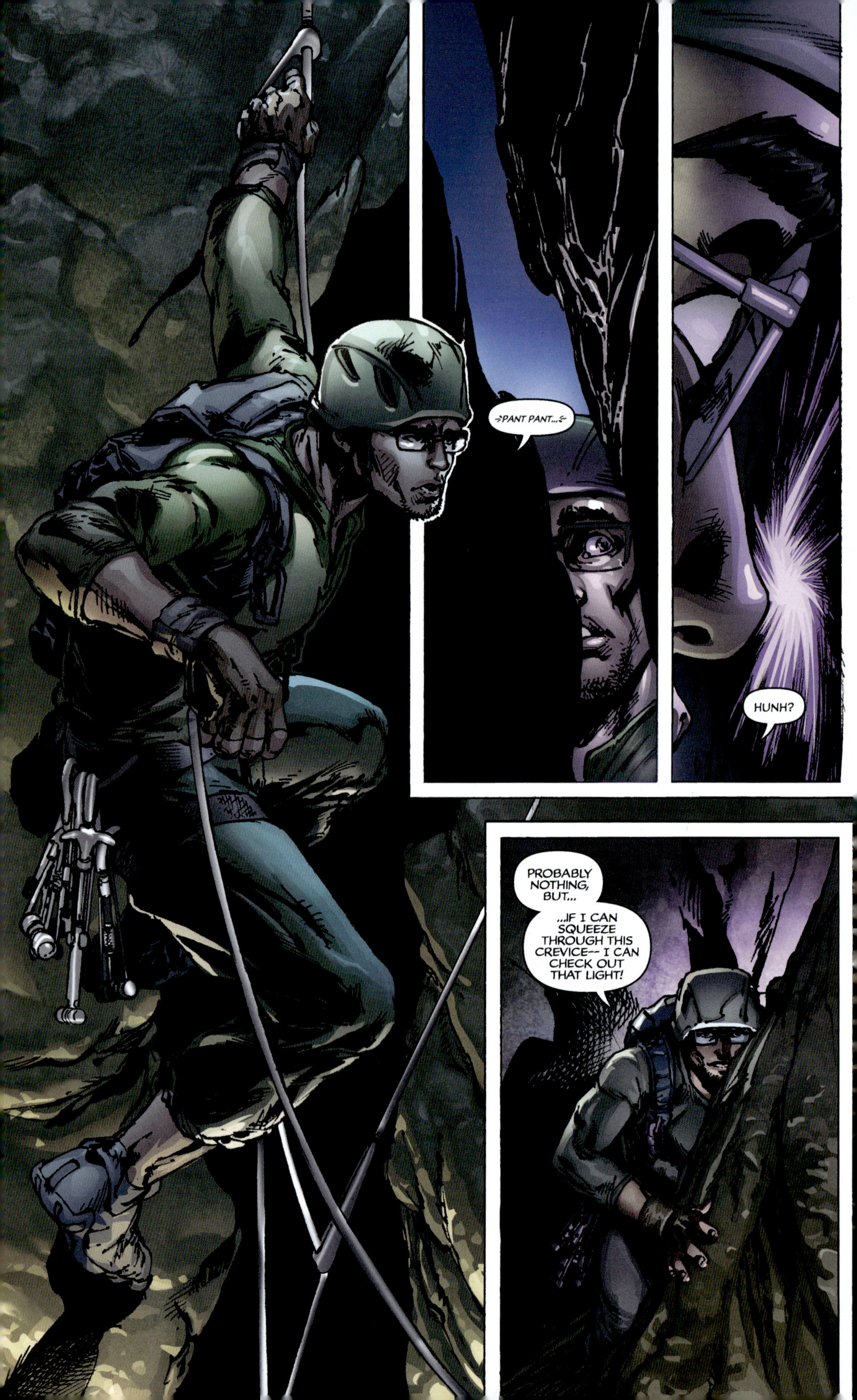
PANT PANT...
HUNH?
PROBABLY NOTHING, BUT...
...IF I CAN SQUEEZE THROUGH THIS CREVICE-- I CAN CHECK OUT THAT LIGHT!

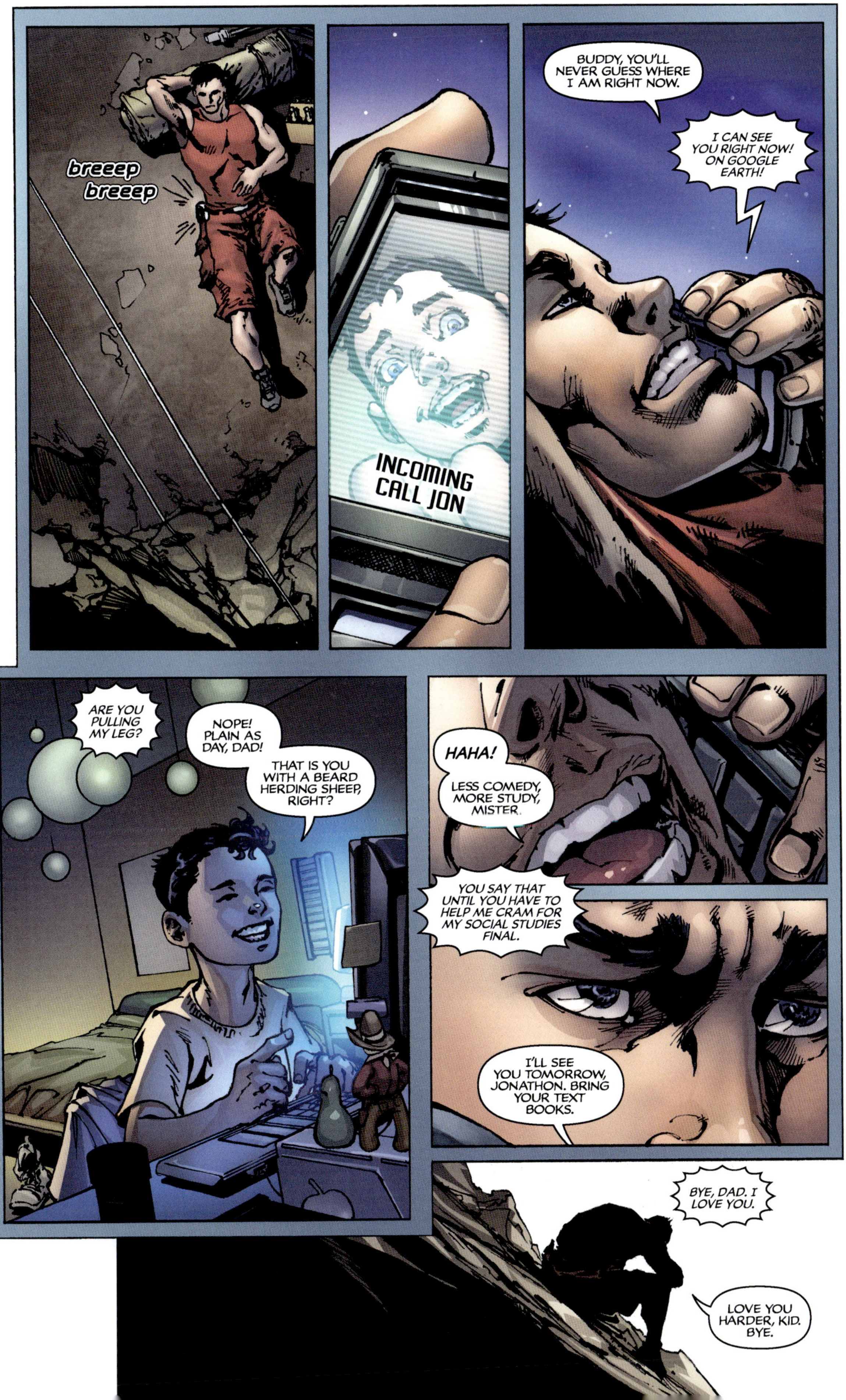
breeep
breeep
INCOMING CALL JON
BUDDY, YOU'LL NEVER GUESS WHERE I AM RIGHT NOW.
I CAN SEE YOU RIGHT NOW! ON GOOGLE EARTH!
ARE YOU PULLING MY LEG?
NOPE! PLAIN AS DAY, DAD!
THAT IS YOU WITH A BEARD HERDING SHEEP, RIGHT?
HAHA!
LESS COMEDY, MORE STUDY, MISTER.
YOU SAY THAT UNTIL YOU HAVE TO HELP ME CRAM FOR MY SOCIAL STUDIES FINAL.
I'LL SEE YOU TOMORROW, JONATHON. BRING YOUR TEXT BOOKS.
BYE, DAD. I LOVE YOU.
LOVE YOU HARDER, KID. BYE.

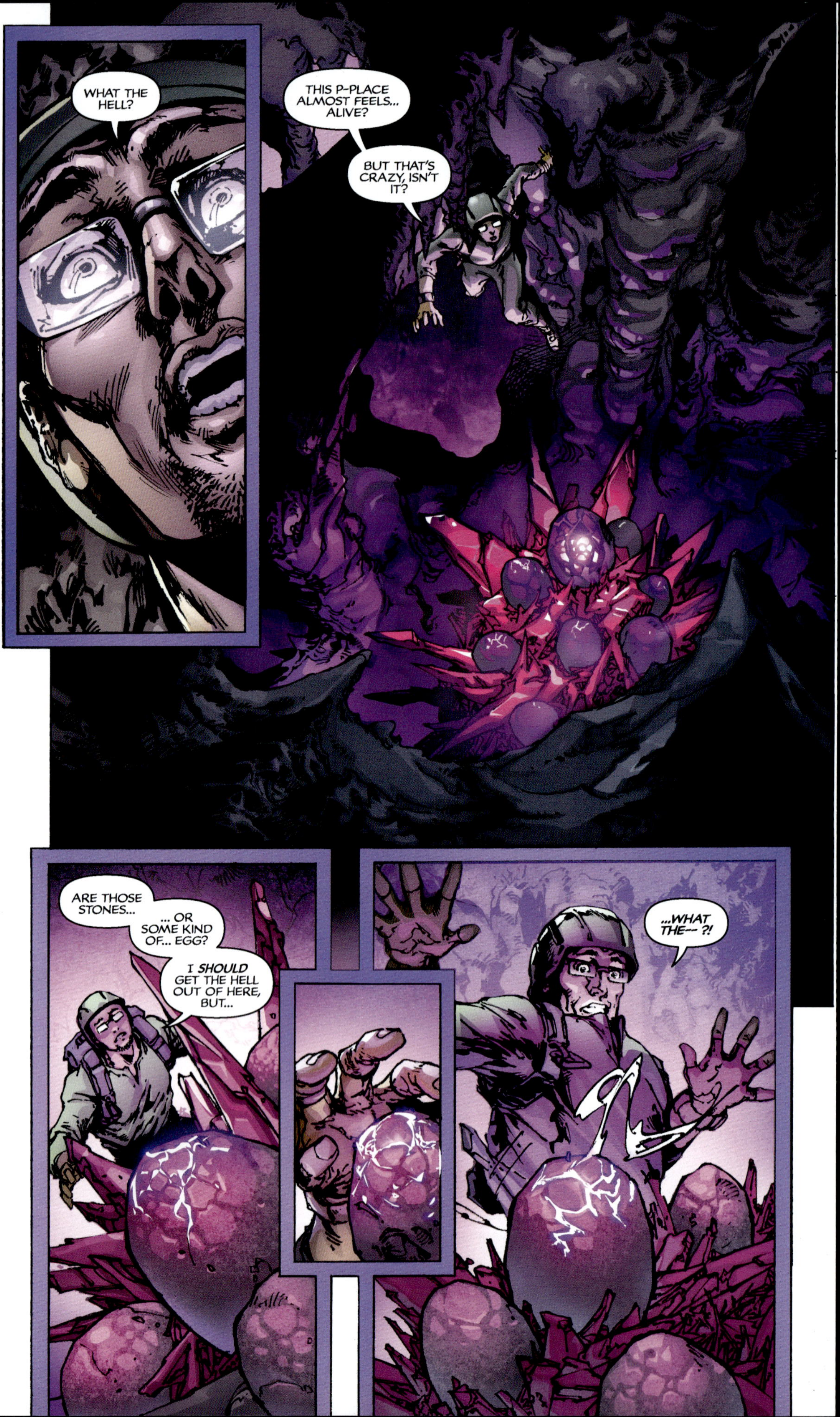
WHAT THE HELL?
THIS P-PLACE ALMOST FEELS... ALIVE?
BUT THAT'S CRAZY, ISN'T IT?
ARE THOSE STONES...
... OR SOME KIND OF... EGG?
I *SHOULD* GET THE HELL OUT OF HERE, BUT...
...WHAT THE-- ?!

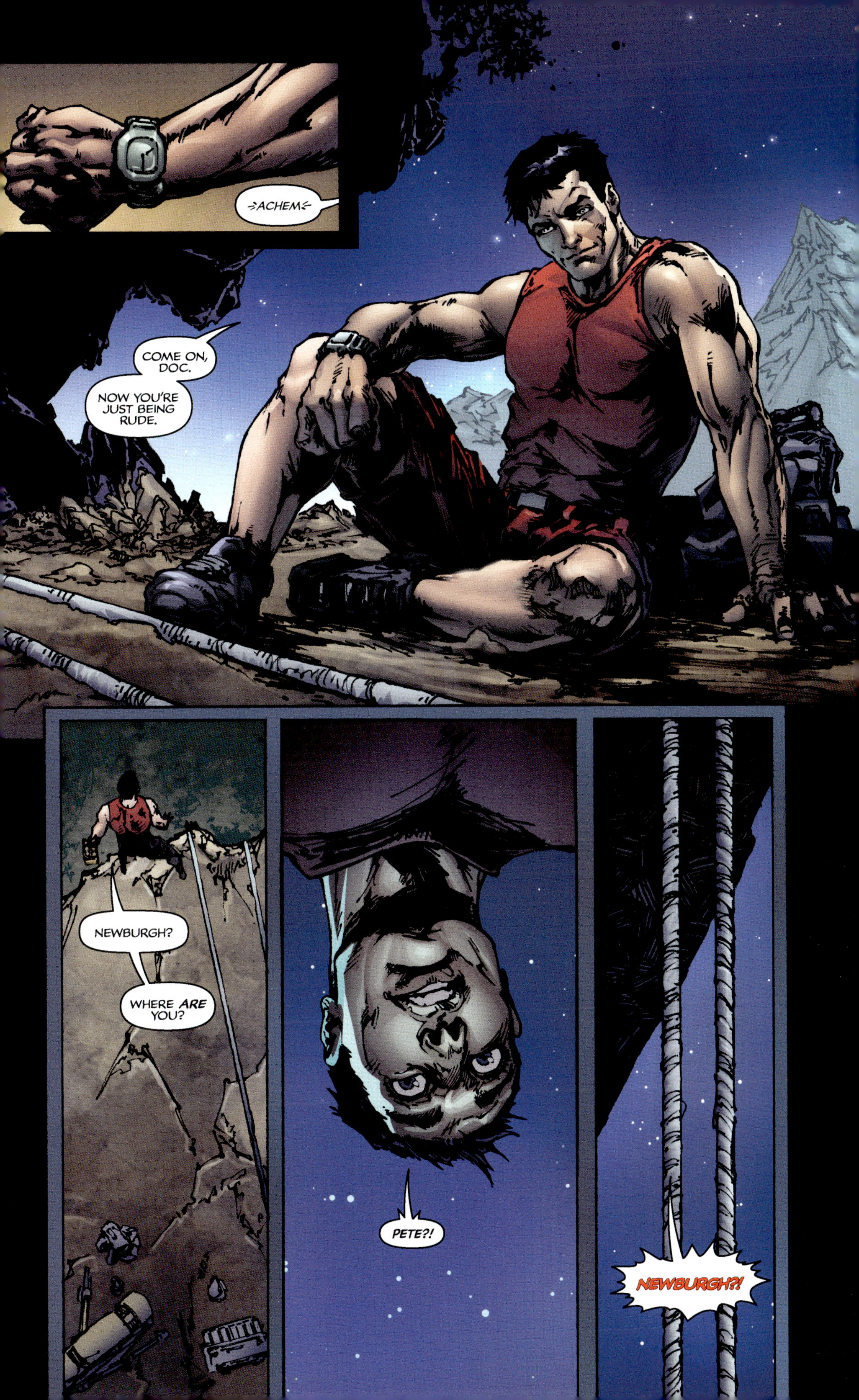

-ACHEM-
COME ON, DOC.
NOW YOU'RE JUST BEING RUDE.
NEWBURGH?
WHERE *ARE* YOU?
PETE?!
NEWBURGH?!

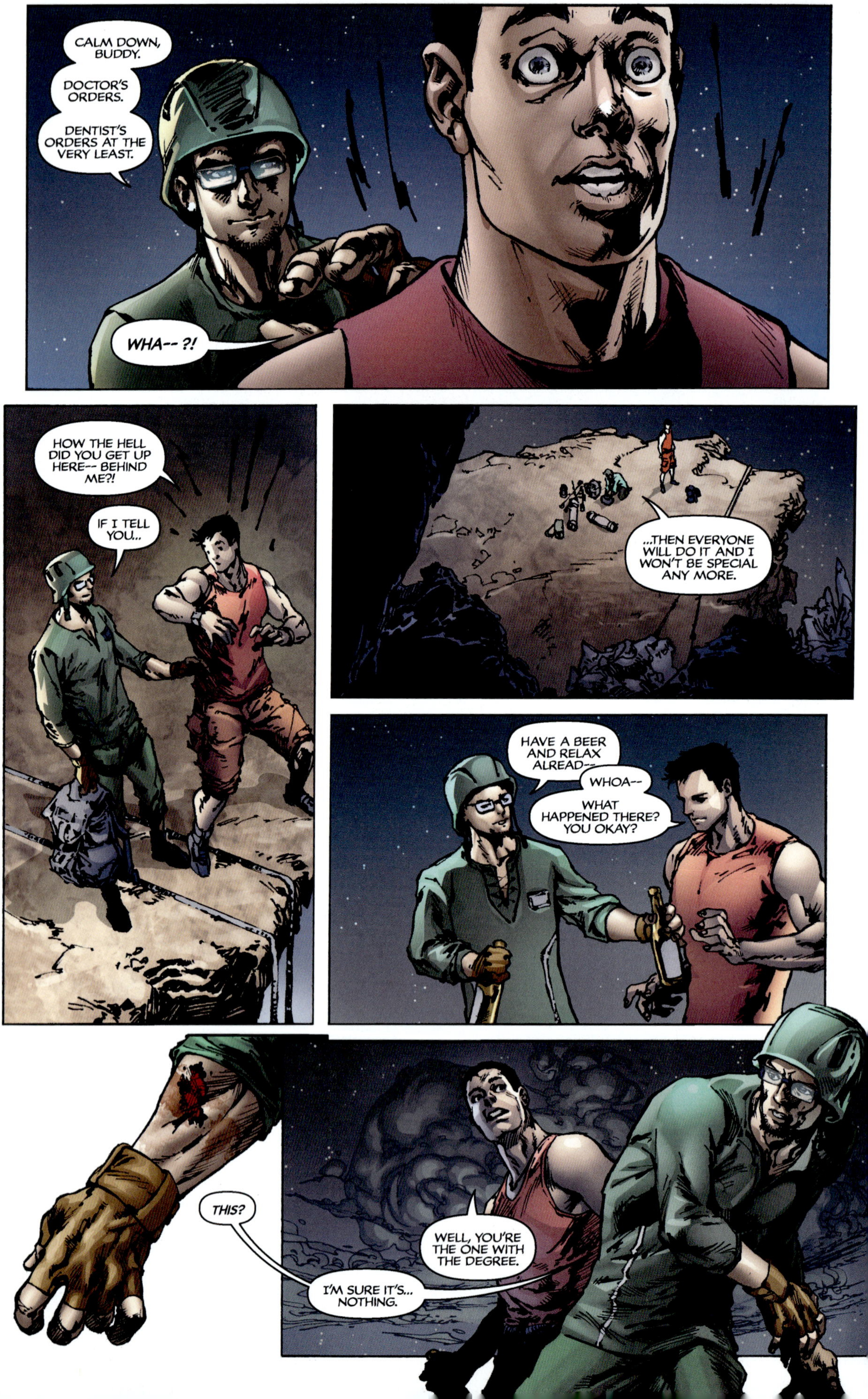
CALM DOWN, BUDDY.
DOCTOR'S ORDERS.
DENTIST'S ORDERS AT THE VERY LEAST.
WHA-- ?!
HOW THE HELL DID YOU GET UP HERE-- BEHIND ME?!
IF I TELL YOU...
...THEN EVERYONE WILL DO IT AND I WON'T BE SPECIAL ANY MORE.
HAVE A BEER AND RELAX ALREAD--
WHOA--
WHAT HAPPENED THERE? YOU OKAY?
THIS?
I'M SURE IT'S... NOTHING.
WELL, YOU'RE THE ONE WITH THE DEGREE.

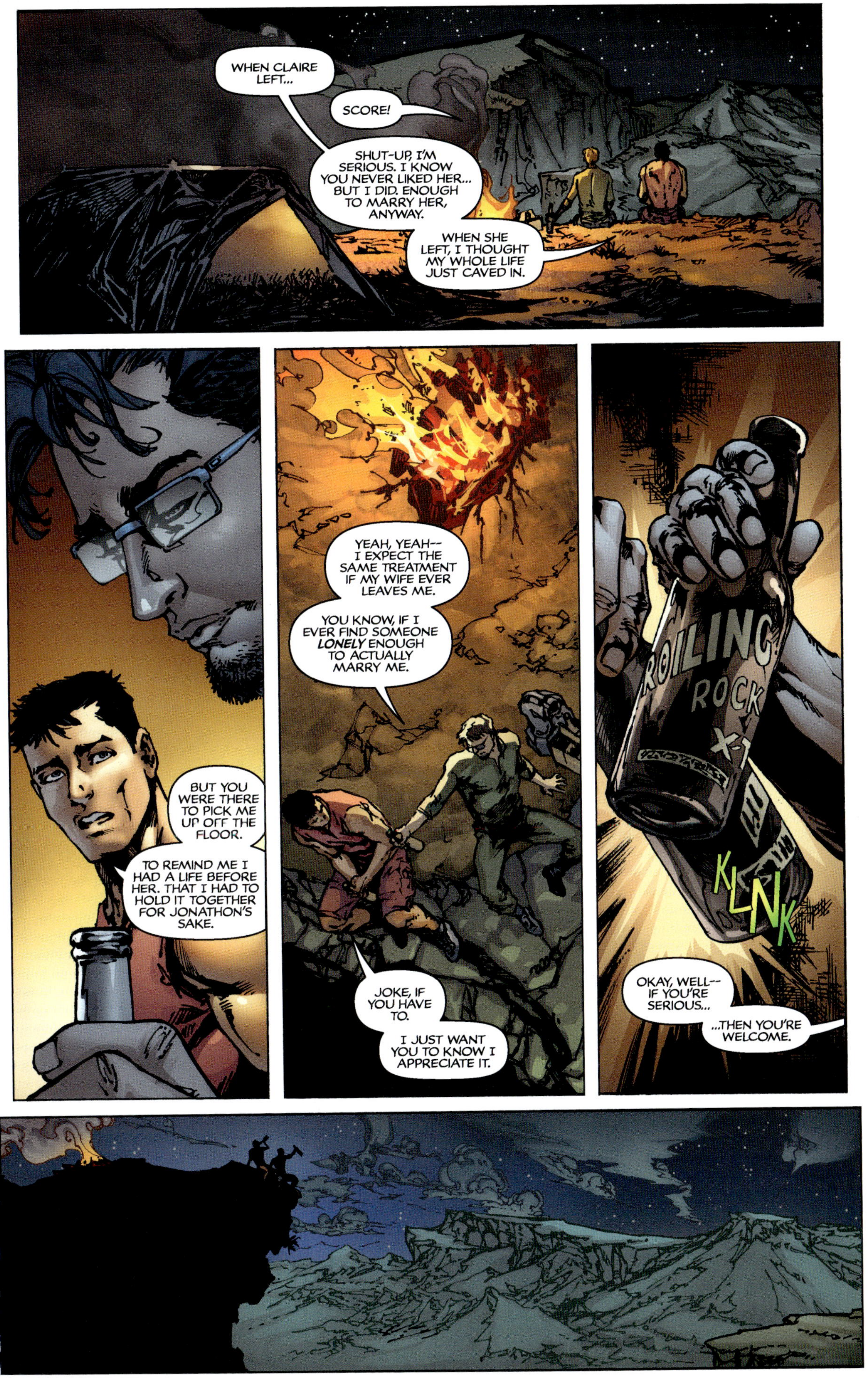
WHEN CLAIRE LEFT...
SCORE!
SHUT-UP, I'M SERIOUS. I KNOW YOU NEVER LIKED HER... BUT I DID. ENOUGH TO MARRY HER, ANYWAY.
WHEN SHE LEFT, I THOUGHT MY WHOLE LIFE JUST CAVED IN.
BUT YOU WERE THERE TO PICK ME UP OFF THE FLOOR.
TO REMIND ME I HAD A LIFE BEFORE HER. THAT I HAD TO HOLD IT TOGETHER FOR JONATHON'S SAKE.
YEAH, YEAH-- I EXPECT THE SAME TREATMENT IF MY WIFE EVER LEAVES ME.
YOU KNOW, IF I EVER FIND SOMEONE **LONELY** ENOUGH TO ACTUALLY MARRY ME.
JOKE, IF YOU HAVE TO.
I JUST WANT YOU TO KNOW I APPRECIATE IT.
ROLLING ROCK
KLNK
OKAY, WELL-- IF YOU'RE SERIOUS...
...THEN YOU'RE WELCOME.

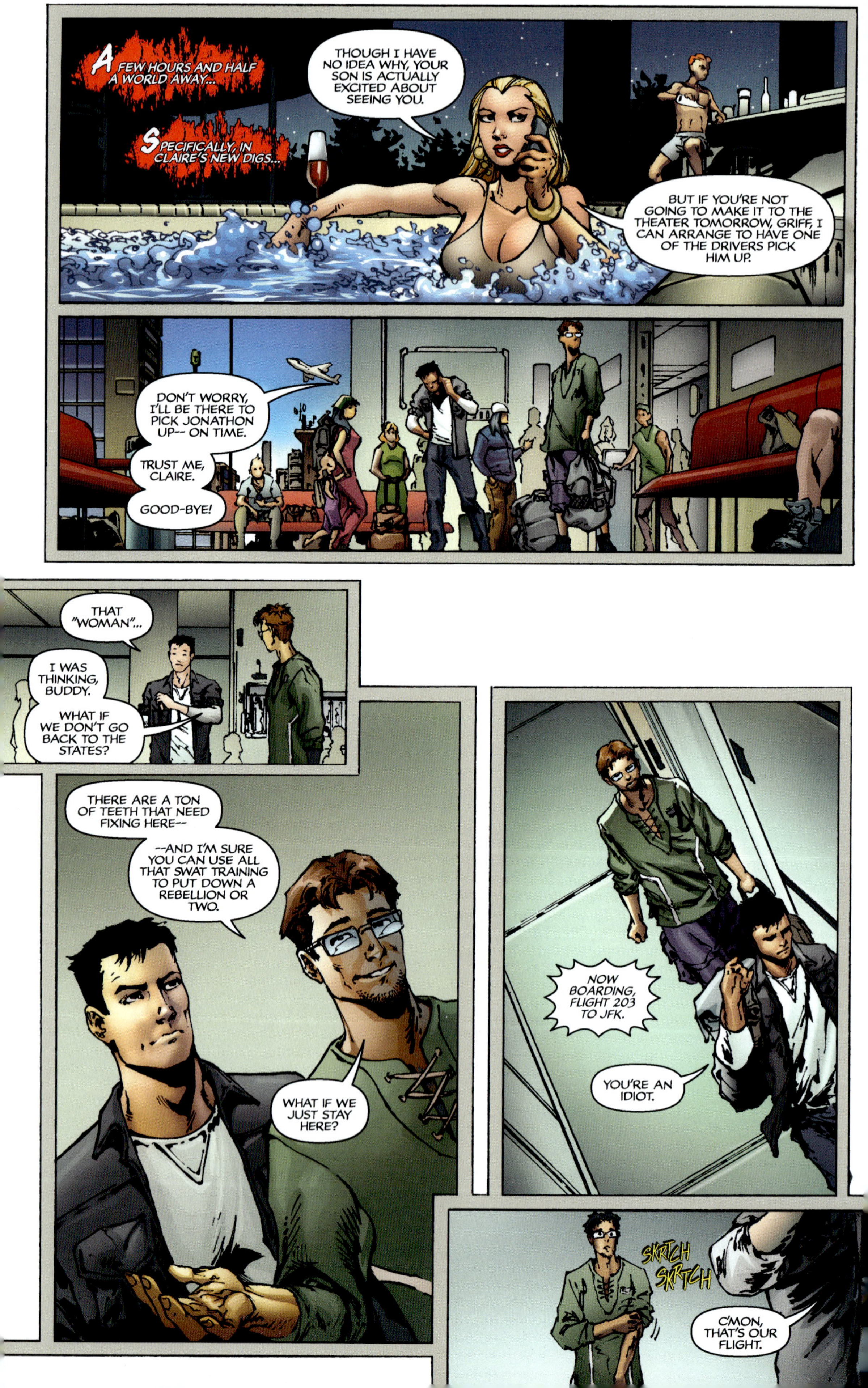
A FEW HOURS AND HALF A WORLD AWAY...
SPECIFICALLY, IN CLAIRE'S NEW DIGS...
THOUGH I HAVE NO IDEA WHY, YOUR SON IS ACTUALLY EXCITED ABOUT SEEING YOU.
BUT IF YOU'RE NOT GOING TO MAKE IT TO THE THEATER TOMORROW, GRIFF, I CAN ARRANGE TO HAVE ONE OF THE DRIVERS PICK HIM UP.
DON'T WORRY, I'LL BE THERE TO PICK JONATHON UP-- ON TIME.
TRUST ME, CLAIRE.
GOOD-BYE!
THAT "WOMAN"...
I WAS THINKING, BUDDY.
WHAT IF WE DON'T GO BACK TO THE STATES?
THERE ARE A TON OF TEETH THAT NEED FIXING HERE--
--AND I'M SURE YOU CAN USE ALL THAT SWAT TRAINING TO PUT DOWN A REBELLION OR TWO.
WHAT IF WE JUST STAY HERE?
NOW BOARDING, FLIGHT 203 TO JFK.
YOU'RE AN IDIOT.
SKRTCH
SKRTCH
C'MON, THAT'S OUR FLIGHT.

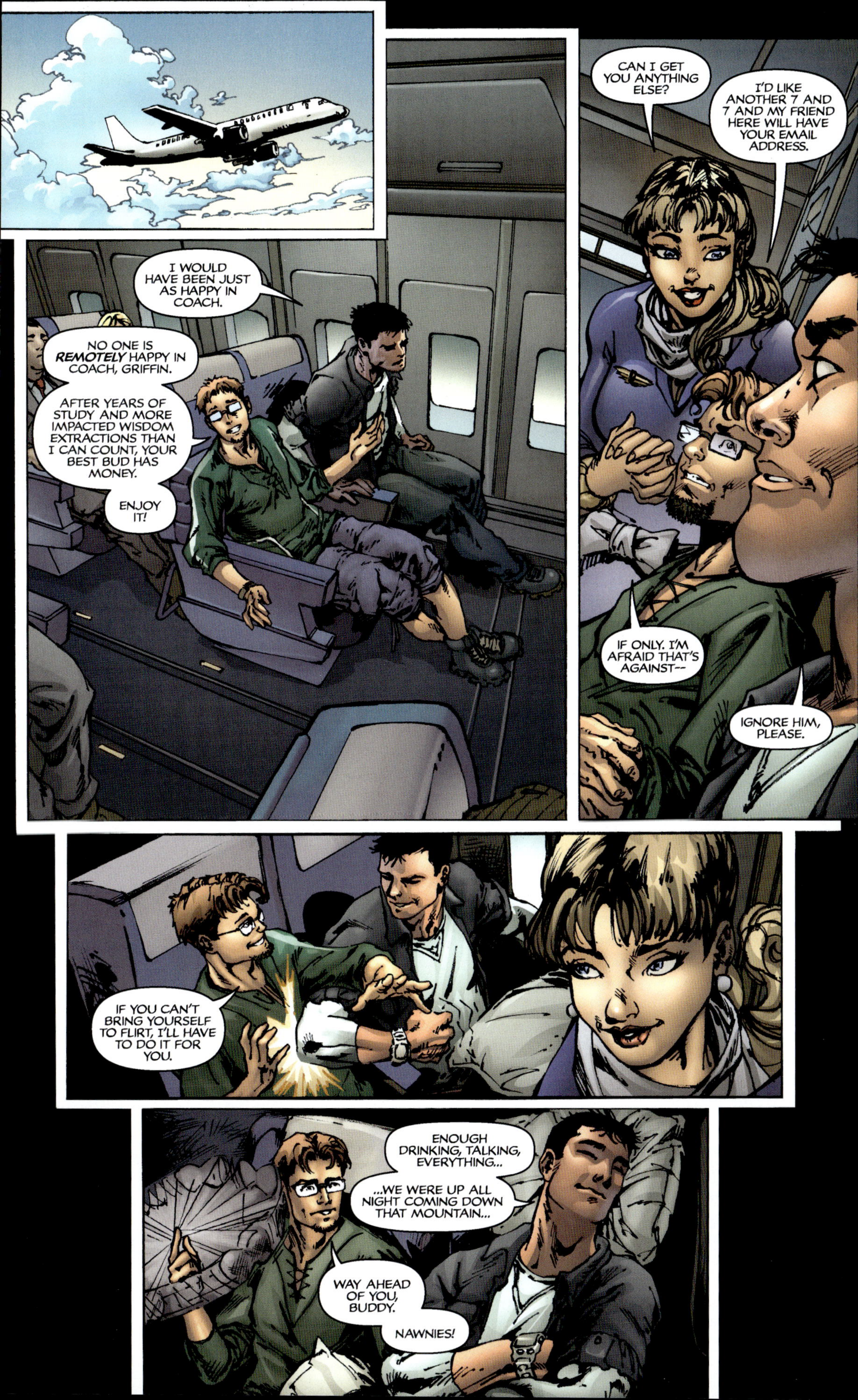
I WOULD HAVE BEEN JUST AS HAPPY IN COACH.
NO ONE IS *REMOTELY* HAPPY IN COACH, GRIFFIN.
AFTER YEARS OF STUDY AND MORE IMPACTED WISDOM EXTRACTIONS THAN I CAN COUNT, YOUR BEST BUD HAS MONEY.
ENJOY IT!
CAN I GET YOU ANYTHING ELSE?
I'D LIKE ANOTHER 7 AND 7 AND MY FRIEND HERE WILL HAVE YOUR EMAIL ADDRESS.
IF ONLY. I'M AFRAID THAT'S AGAINST--
IGNORE HIM, PLEASE.
IF YOU CAN'T BRING YOURSELF TO FLIRT, I'LL HAVE TO DO IT FOR YOU.
ENOUGH DRINKING, TALKING, EVERYTHING...
...WE WERE UP ALL NIGHT COMING DOWN THAT MOUNTAIN...
WAY AHEAD OF YOU, BUDDY.
NAWNIES!

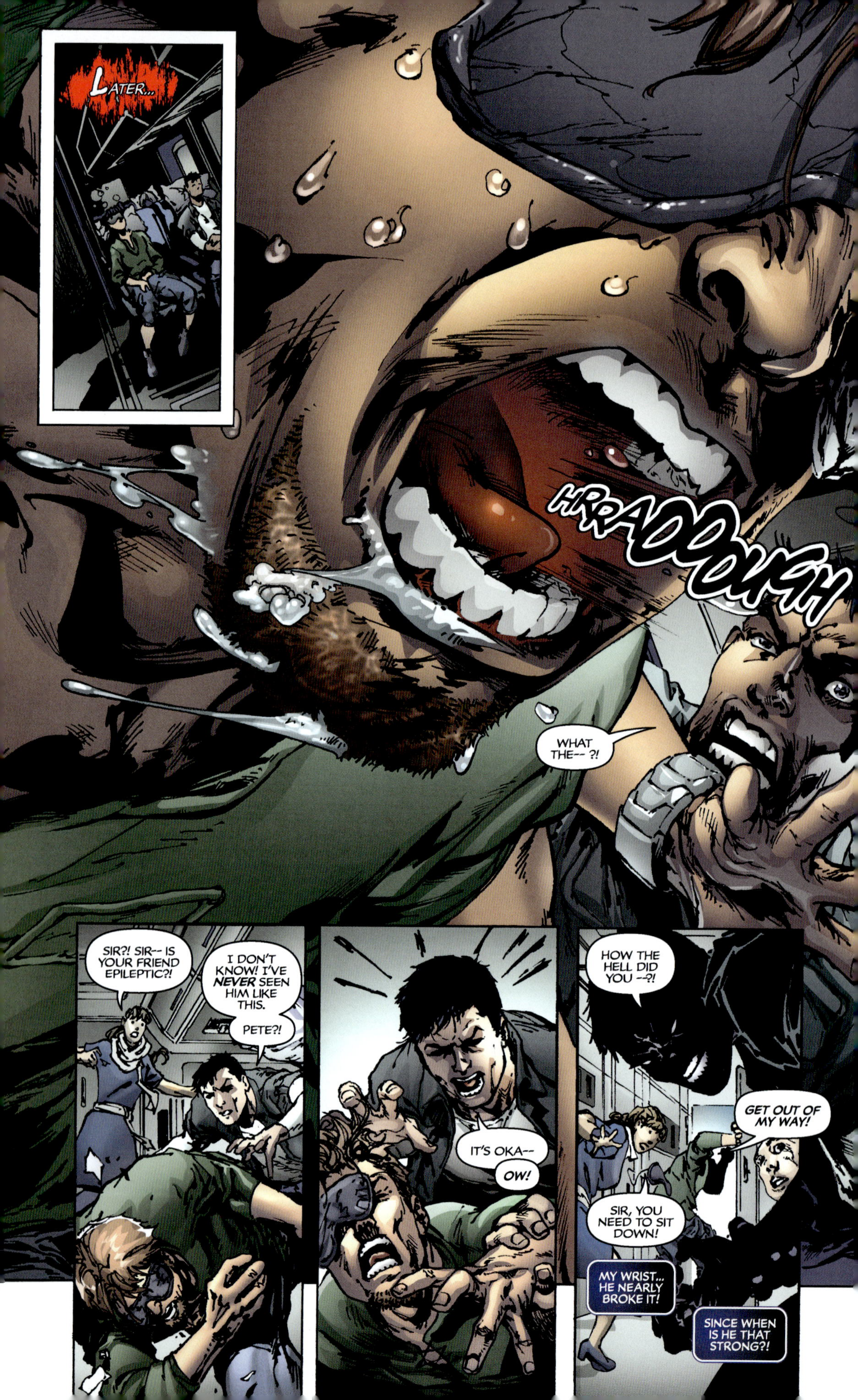
LATER...
HRRADOOUGH
WHAT THE-- ?!
SIR?! SIR-- IS YOUR FRIEND EPILEPTIC?!
I DON'T KNOW! I'VE NEVER SEEN HIM LIKE THIS.
PETE?!
IT'S OKA--
OW!
HOW THE HELL DID YOU --?!
GET OUT OF MY WAY!
SIR, YOU NEED TO SIT DOWN!
MY WRIST... HE NEARLY BROKE IT!
SINCE WHEN IS HE THAT STRONG?!

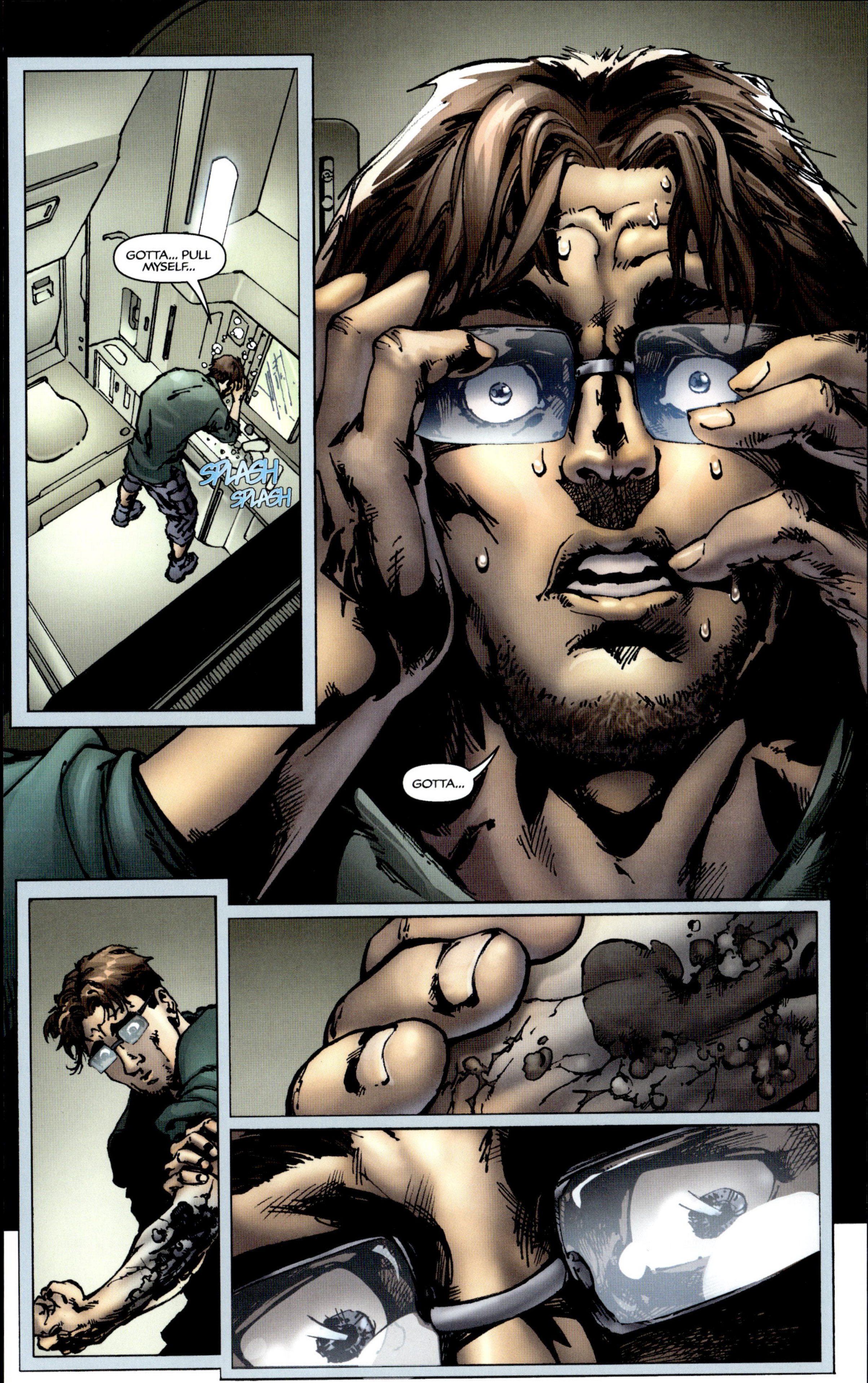
GOTTA... PULL MYSELF...
SPLASH
SPLASH
GOTTA...

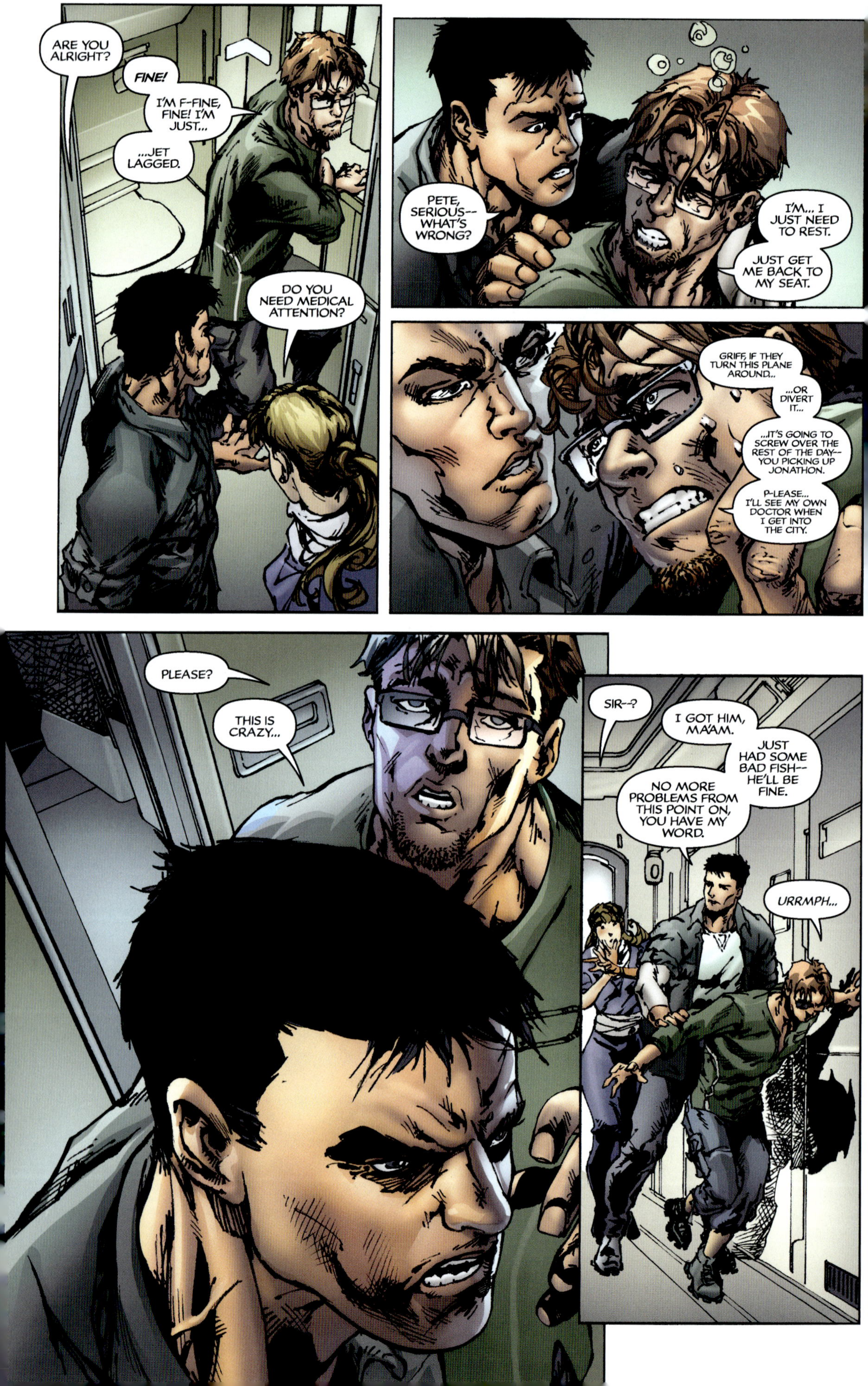
ARE YOU ALRIGHT?
FINE!
I'M F-FINE, FINE! I'M JUST...
...JET LAGGED.
DO YOU NEED MEDICAL ATTENTION?
PETE, SERIOUS-- WHAT'S WRONG?
I'M... I JUST NEED TO REST.
JUST GET ME BACK TO MY SEAT.
GRIFF, IF THEY TURN THIS PLANE AROUND...
...OR DIVERT IT...
...IT'S GOING TO SCREW OVER THE REST OF THE DAY-- YOU PICKING UP JONATHON.
P-LEASE... I'LL SEE MY OWN DOCTOR WHEN I GET INTO THE CITY.
PLEASE?
THIS IS CRAZY...
SIR--?
I GOT HIM, MA'AM.
JUST HAD SOME BAD FISH-- HE'LL BE FINE.
NO MORE PROBLEMS FROM THIS POINT ON, YOU HAVE MY WORD.
URRMPH...

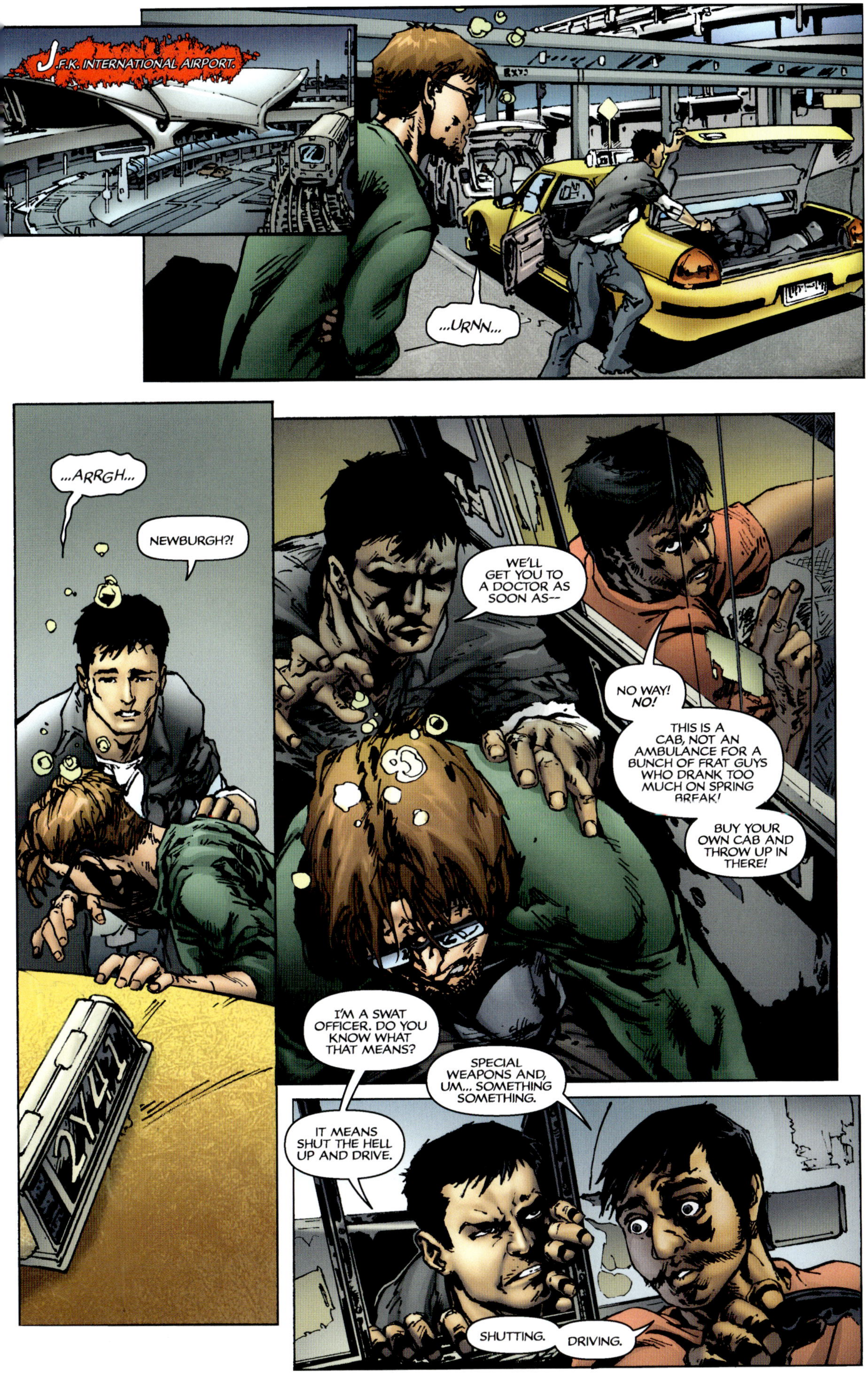
J.F.K. INTERNATIONAL AIRPORT.
...URNN...
...ARRGH...
NEWBURGH?!
WE'LL GET YOU TO A DOCTOR AS SOON AS--
NO WAY! NO!
THIS IS A CAB, NOT AN AMBULANCE FOR A BUNCH OF FRAT GUYS WHO DRANK TOO MUCH ON SPRING BREAK!
BUY YOUR OWN CAB AND THROW UP IN THERE!
I'M A SWAT OFFICER. DO YOU KNOW WHAT THAT MEANS?
SPECIAL WEAPONS AND, UM... SOMETHING SOMETHING.
IT MEANS SHUT THE HELL UP AND DRIVE.
SHUTTING.
DRIVING.

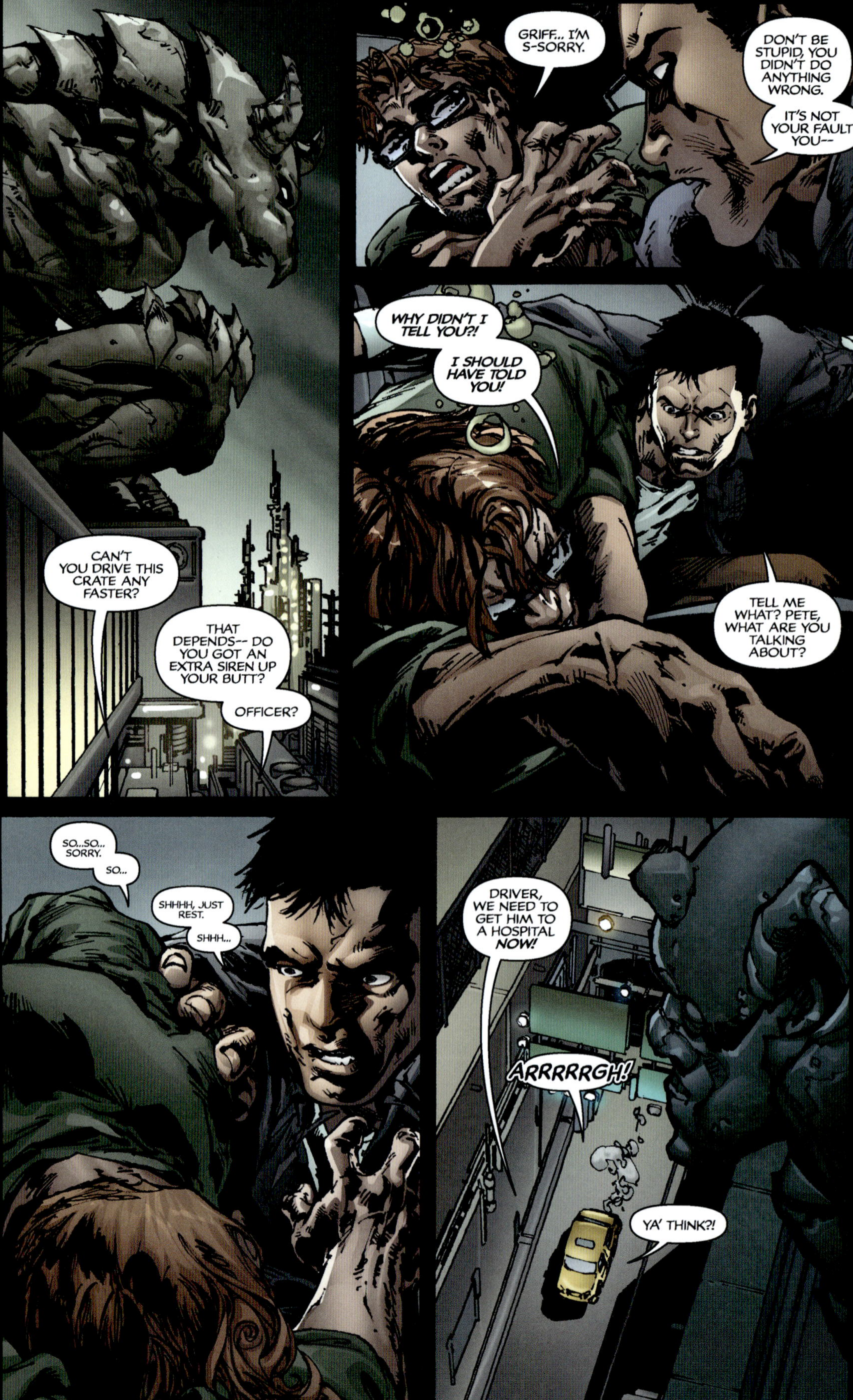
GRIFF... I'M S-SORRY.
DON'T BE STUPID, YOU DIDN'T DO ANYTHING WRONG.
IT'S NOT YOUR FAULT YOU--
CAN'T YOU DRIVE THIS CRATE ANY FASTER?
THAT DEPENDS-- DO YOU GOT AN EXTRA SIREN UP YOUR BUTT?
OFFICER?
WHY DIDN'T I TELL YOU?!
I SHOULD HAVE TOLD YOU!
TELL ME WHAT? PETE, WHAT ARE YOU TALKING ABOUT?
SO...SO... SORRY.
SO...
SHHHH, JUST REST.
SHHH...
DRIVER, WE NEED TO GET HIM TO A HOSPITAL NOW!
ARRRRRGH!
YA' THINK?!

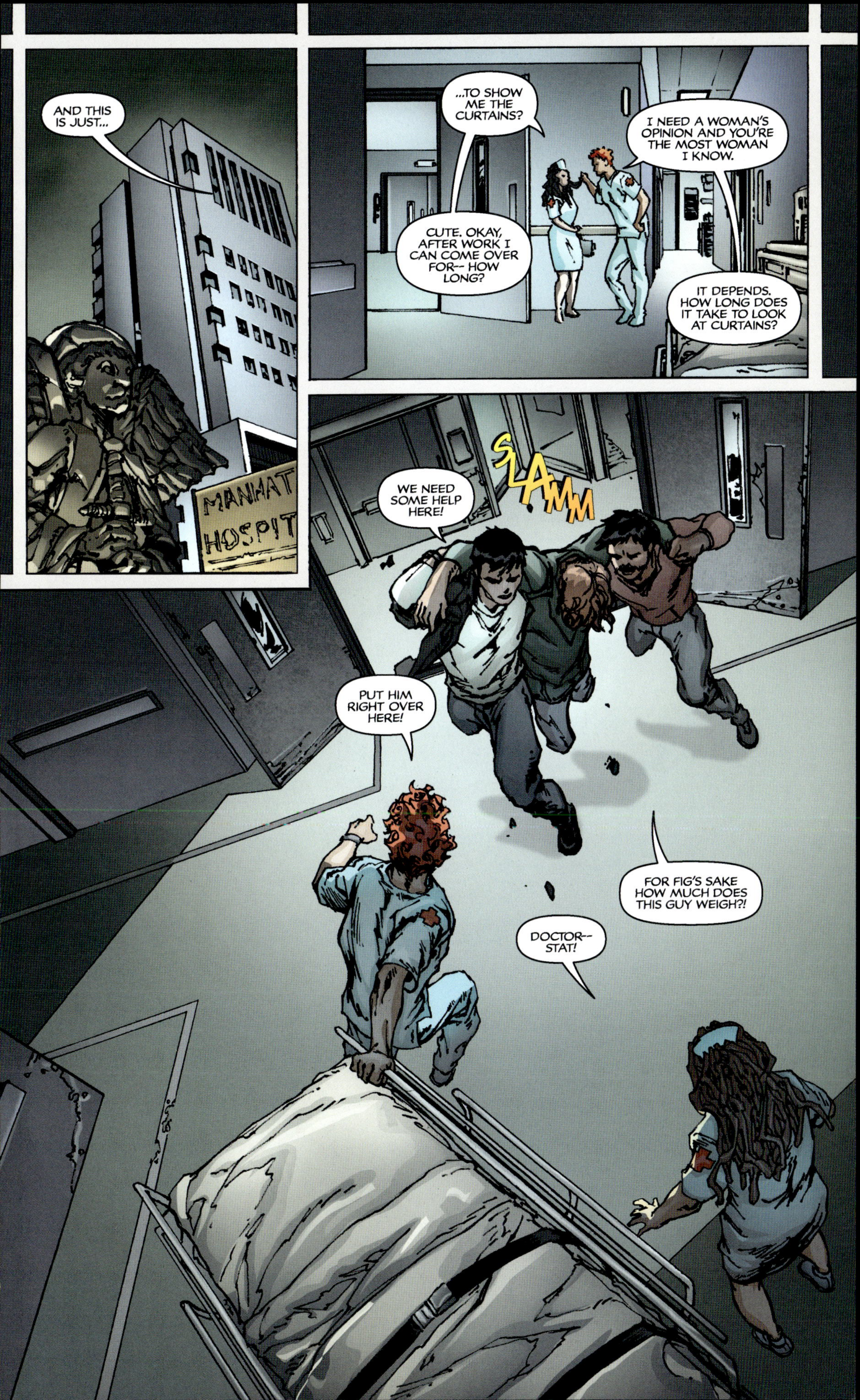
AND THIS IS JUST...
MANHAT
HOSPIT
...TO SHOW ME THE CURTAINS?
I NEED A WOMAN'S OPINION AND YOU'RE THE MOST WOMAN I KNOW.
CUTE. OKAY, AFTER WORK I CAN COME OVER FOR-- HOW LONG?
IT DEPENDS. HOW LONG DOES IT TAKE TO LOOK AT CURTAINS?
SLAMM
WE NEED SOME HELP HERE!
PUT HIM RIGHT OVER HERE!
FOR FIG'S SAKE HOW MUCH DOES THIS GUY WEIGH?!
DOCTOR-- STAT!

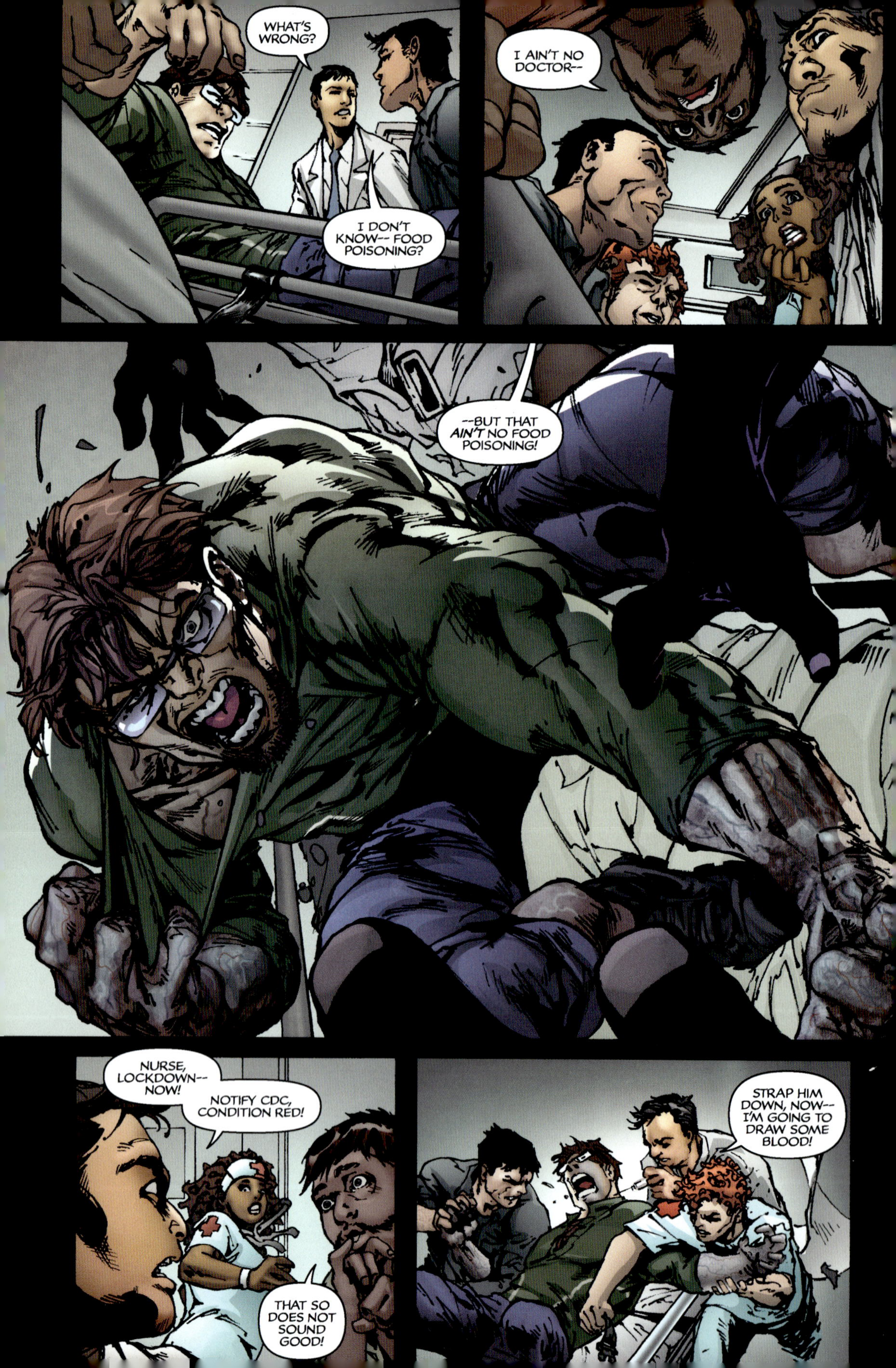
WHAT'S WRONG?
I DON'T KNOW-- FOOD POISONING?
I AIN'T NO DOCTOR--
--BUT THAT AIN'T NO FOOD POISONING!
NURSE, LOCKDOWN--NOW!
NOTIFY CDC, CONDITION RED!
THAT SO DOES NOT SOUND GOOD!
STRAP HIM DOWN, NOW-- I'M GOING TO DRAW SOME BLOOD!

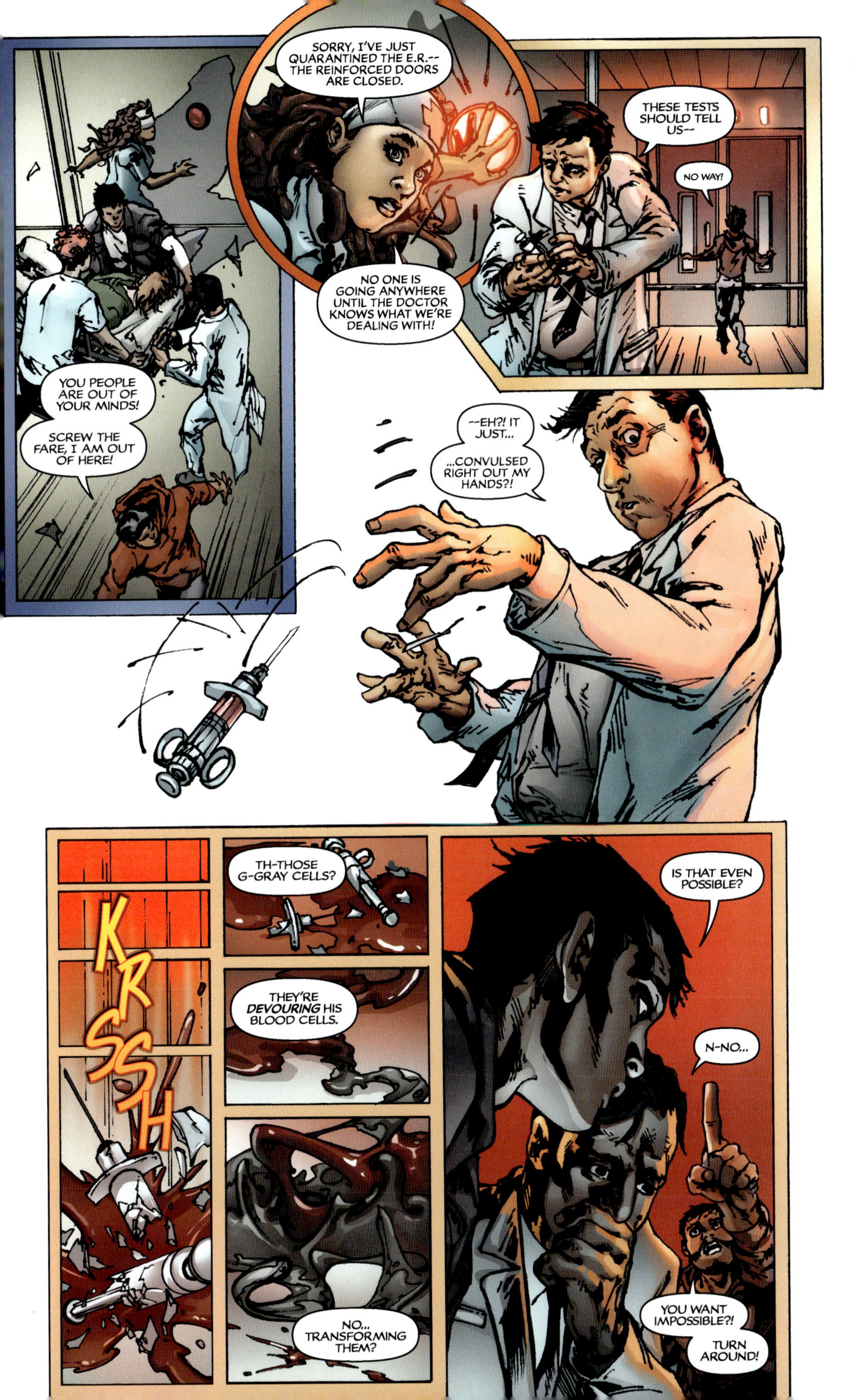
SORRY, I'VE JUST QUARANTINED THE E.R.-- THE REINFORCED DOORS ARE CLOSED.
NO ONE IS GOING ANYWHERE UNTIL THE DOCTOR KNOWS WHAT WE'RE DEALING WITH!
YOU PEOPLE ARE OUT OF YOUR MINDS!
SCREW THE FARE, I AM OUT OF HERE!
THESE TESTS SHOULD TELL US--
NO WAY!
--EH?! IT JUST...
...CONVULSED RIGHT OUT MY HANDS?!
KRSSH
TH-THOSE G-GRAY CELLS?
THEY'RE *DEVOURING* HIS BLOOD CELLS.
NO... TRANSFORMING THEM?
IS THAT EVEN POSSIBLE?
N-NO...
YOU WANT IMPOSSIBLE?!
TURN AROUND!

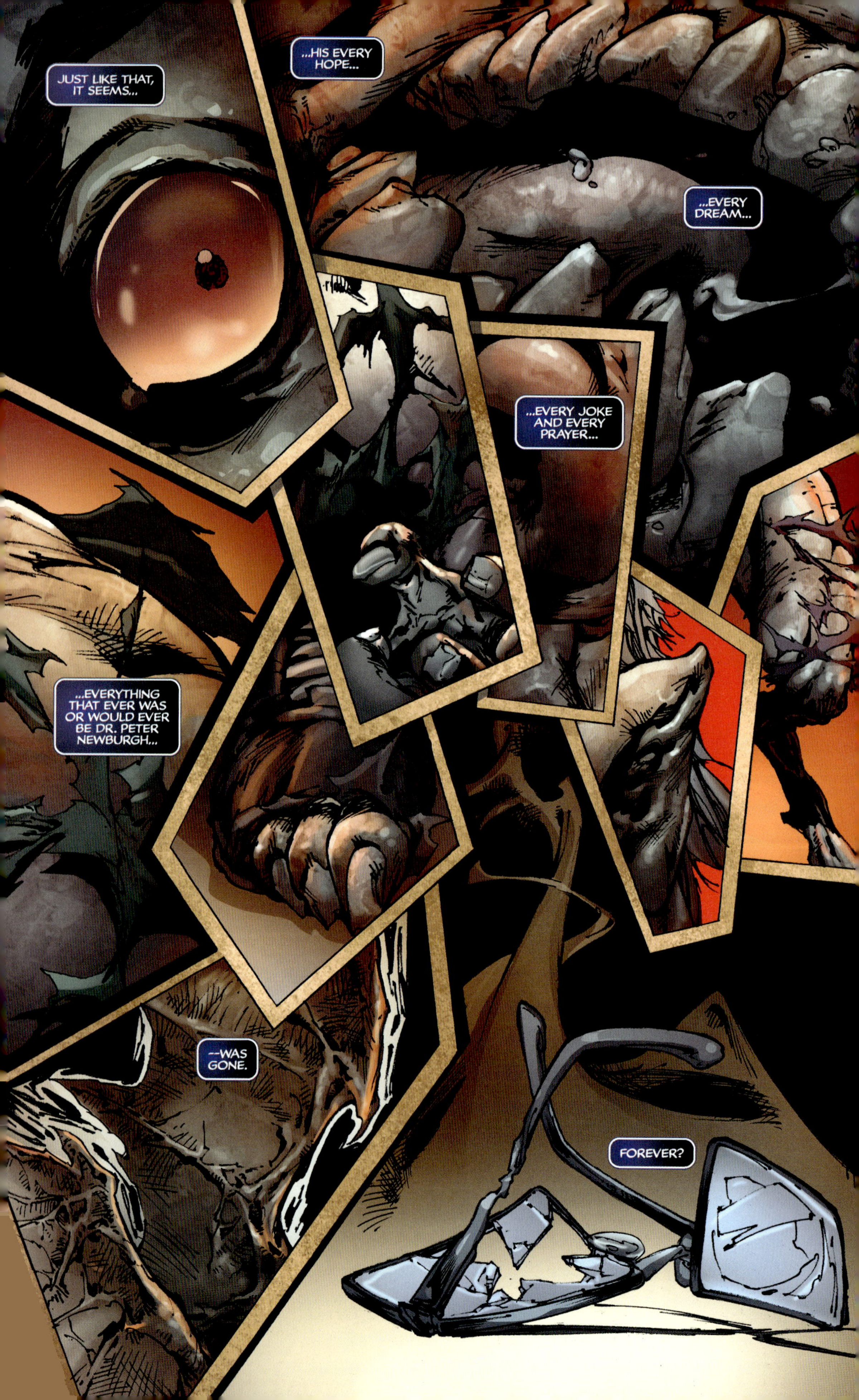
JUST LIKE THAT, IT SEEMS...
...HIS EVERY HOPE...
...EVERY DREAM...
...EVERY JOKE AND EVERY PRAYER...
...EVERYTHING THAT EVER WAS OR WOULD EVER BE DR. PETER NEWBURGH...
--WAS GONE.
FOREVER?

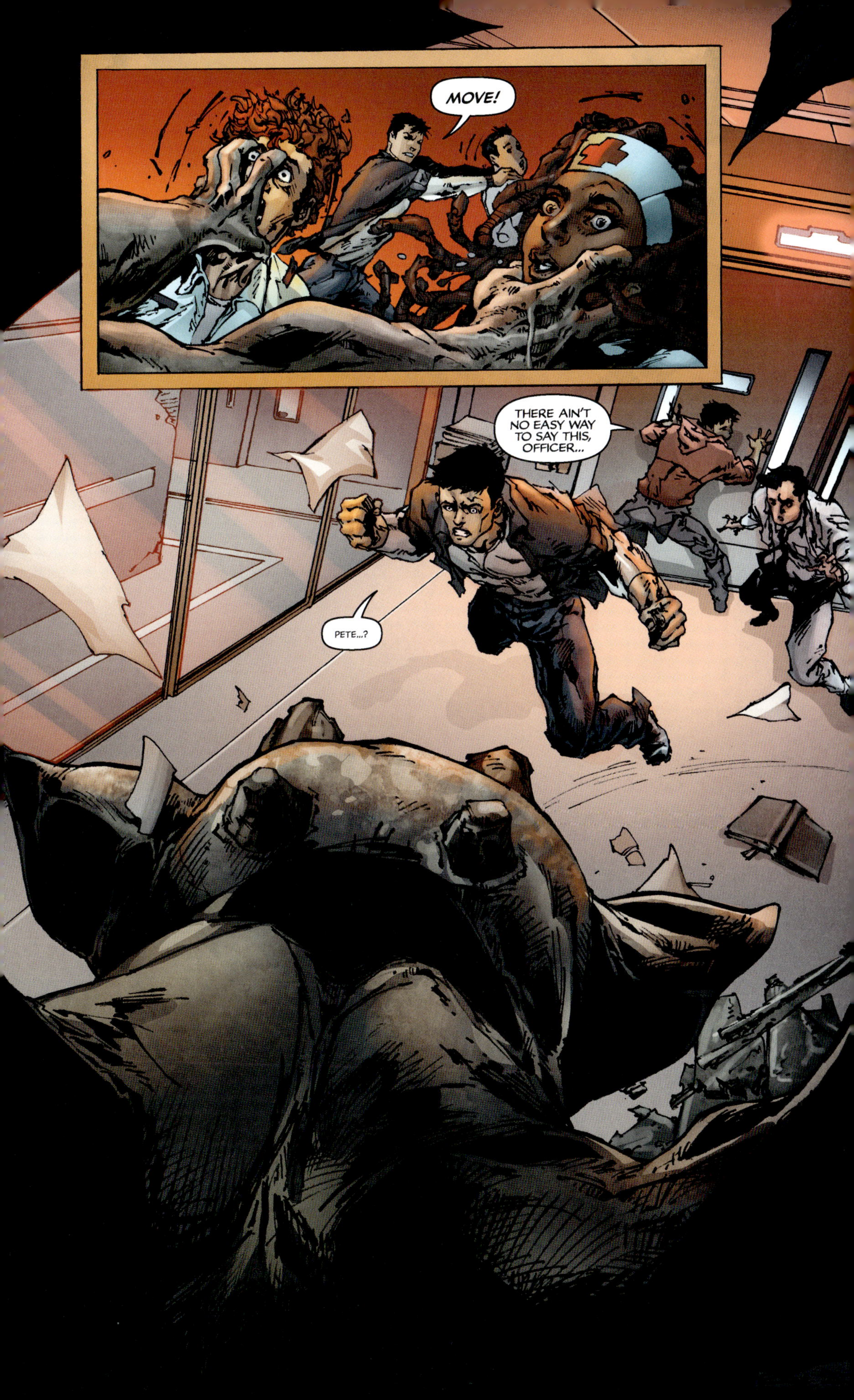
MOVE!
THERE AIN'T NO EASY WAY TO SAY THIS, OFFICER...
PETE...?

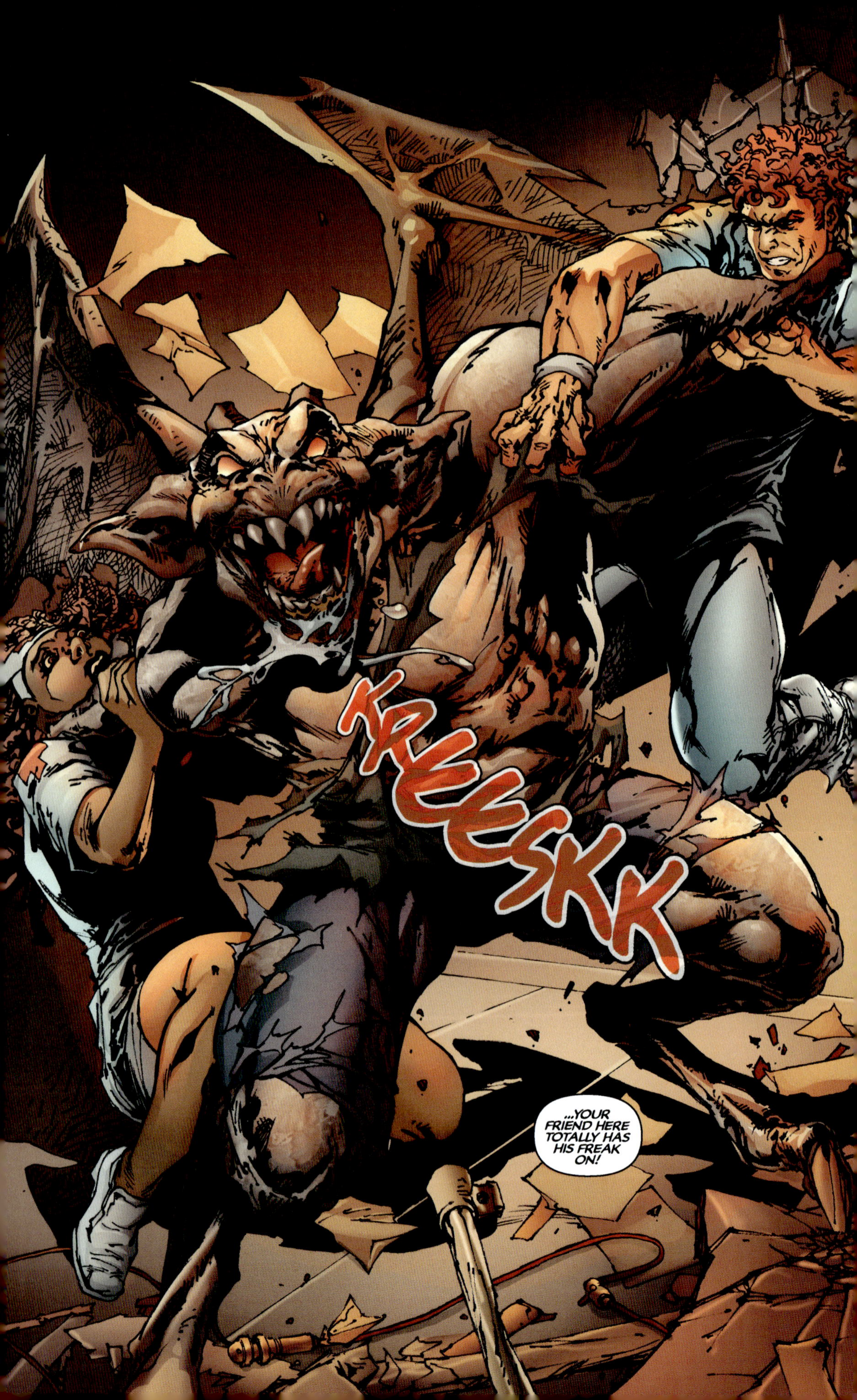
KRUESKK
...YOUR FRIEND HERE TOTALLY HAS HIS FREAK ON!

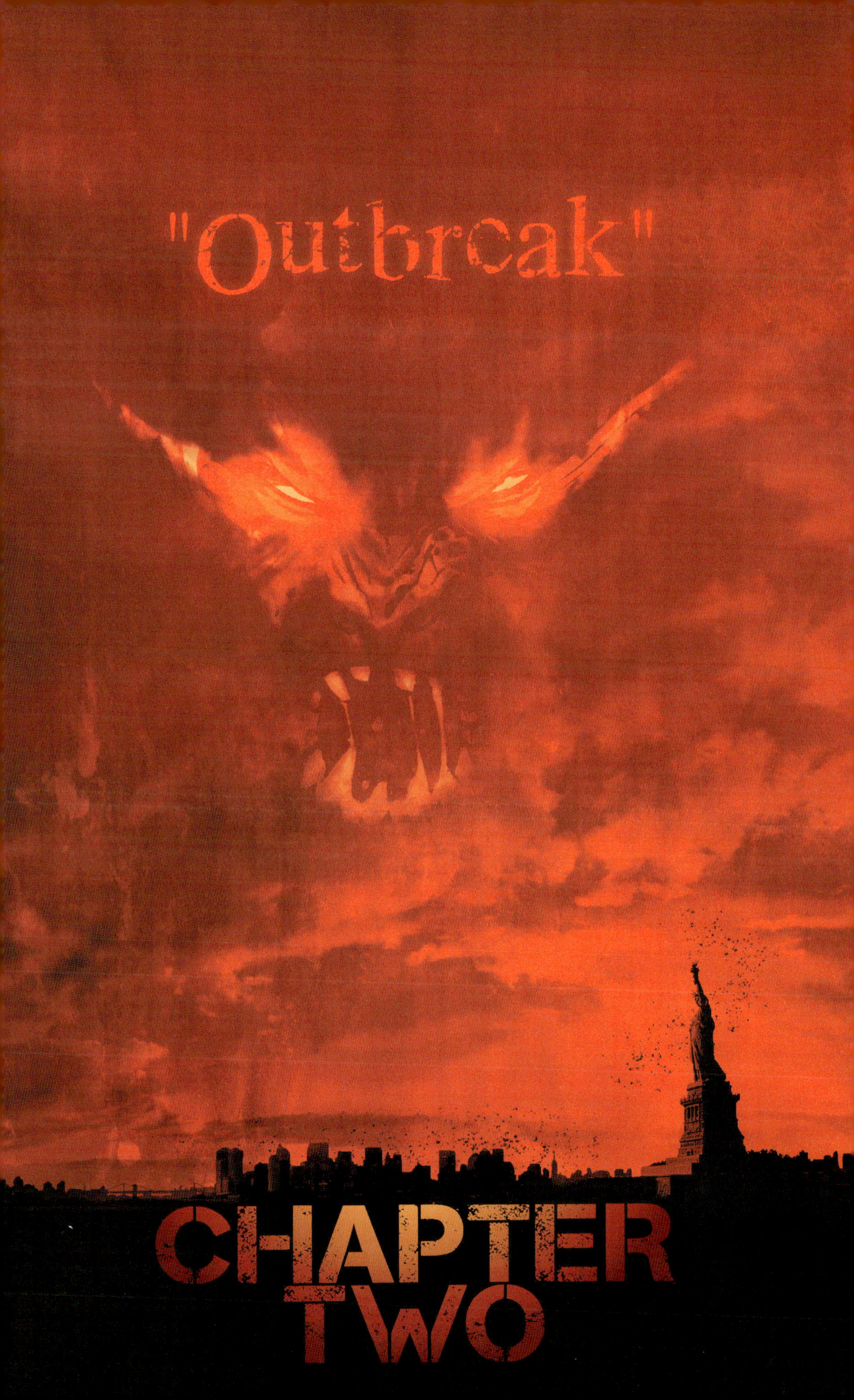
"Outbreak"
CHAPTER
TWO

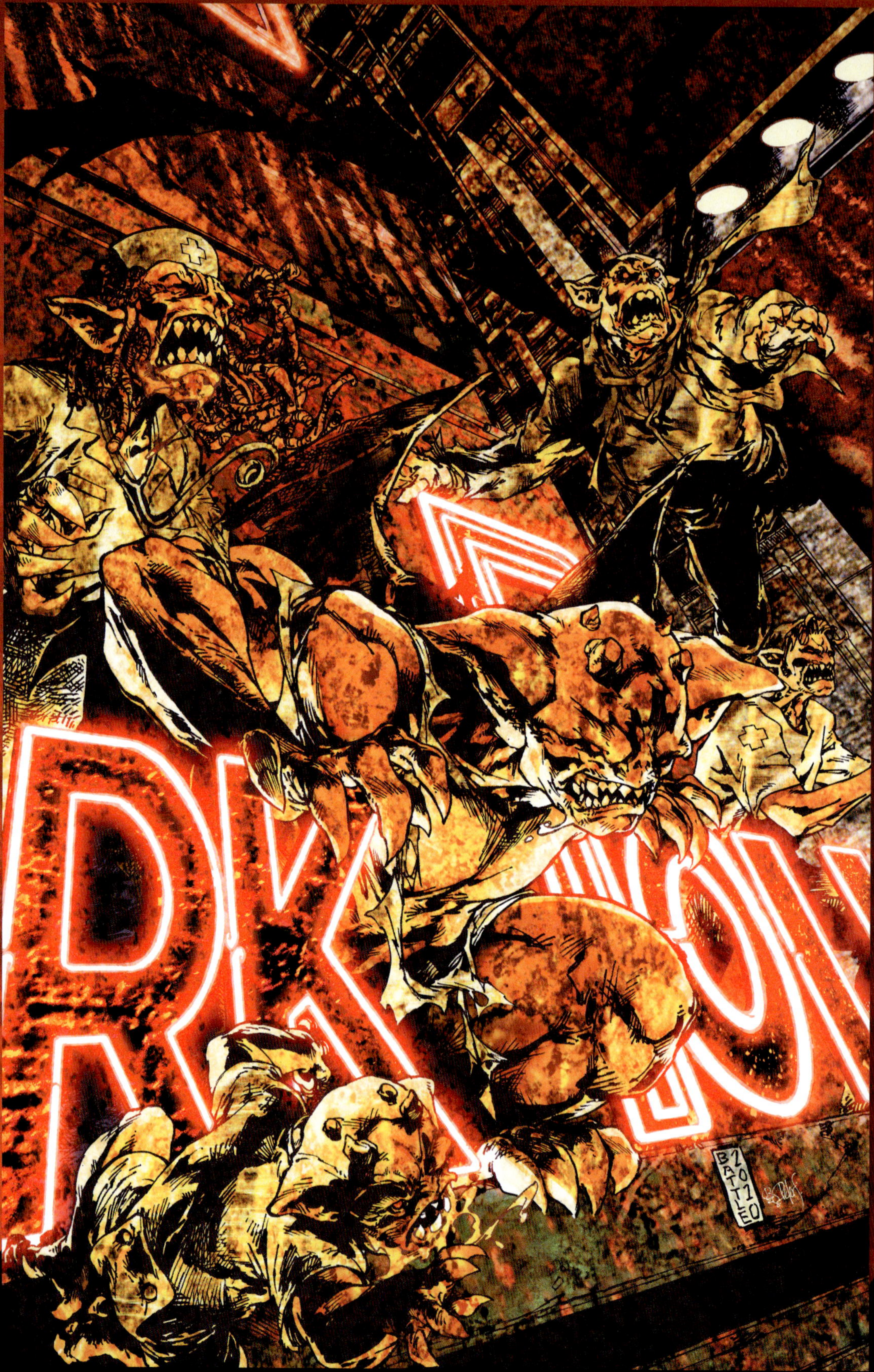

Retailer "Infected" Incentive Edition Cover C to
THE SCOURGE #2
by
Eric **BATTLE** | Peter **STEIGERWALD**

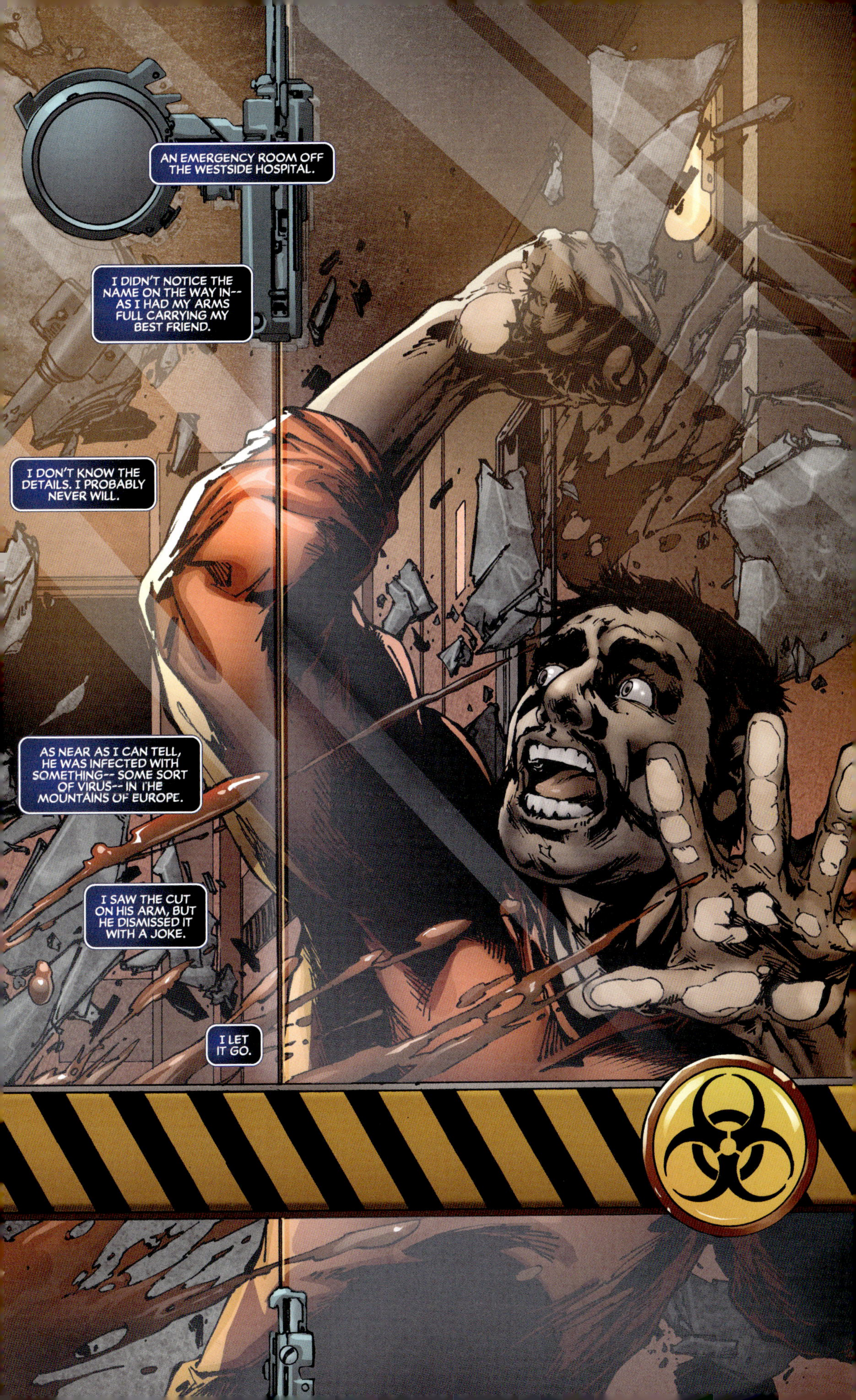
AN EMERGENCY ROOM OFF THE WESTSIDE HOSPITAL.
I DIDN'T NOTICE THE NAME ON THE WAY IN-- AS I HAD MY ARMS FULL CARRYING MY BEST FRIEND.
I DON'T KNOW THE DETAILS. I PROBABLY NEVER WILL.
AS NEAR AS I CAN TELL, HE WAS INFECTED WITH SOMETHING-- SOME SORT OF VIRUS-- IN THE MOUNTAINS OF EUROPE.
I SAW THE CUT ON HIS ARM, BUT HE DISMISSED IT WITH A JOKE.
I LET IT GO.

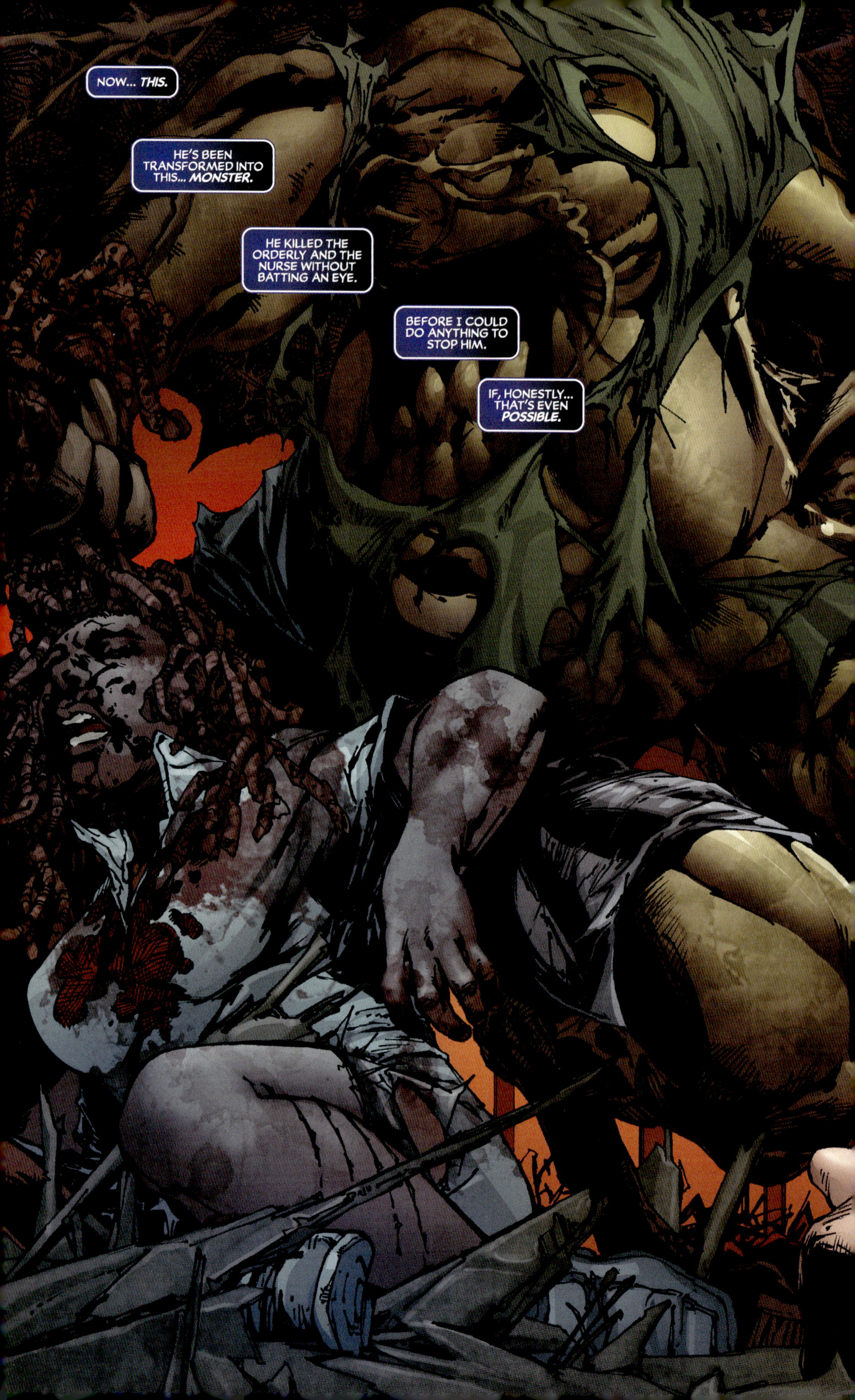
NOW... THIS.
HE'S BEEN TRANSFORMED INTO THIS... MONSTER.
HE KILLED THE ORDERLY AND THE NURSE WITHOUT BATTING AN EYE.
BEFORE I COULD DO ANYTHING TO STOP HIM.
IF, HONESTLY... THAT'S EVEN POSSIBLE.

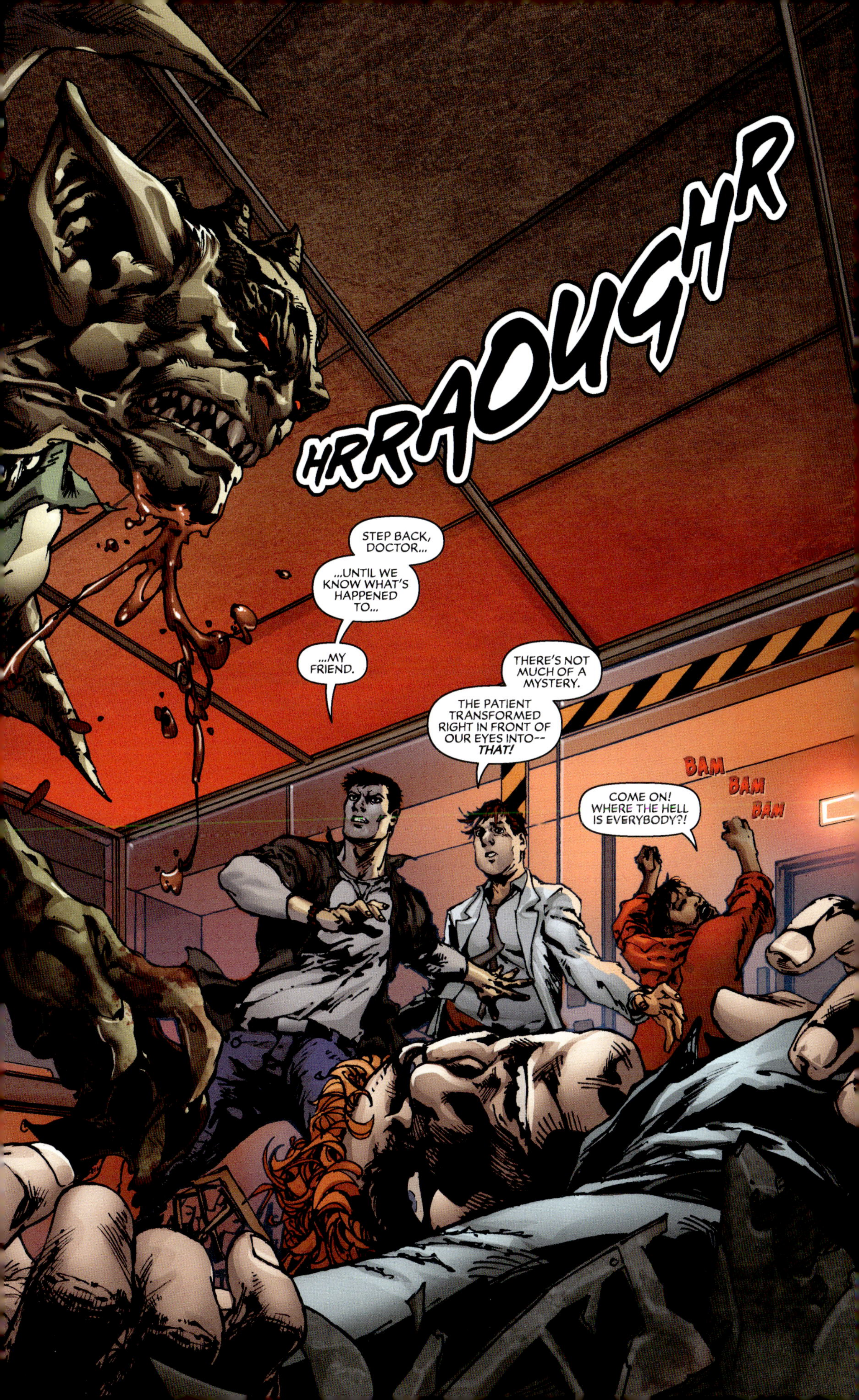
HRRAOUGHR
STEP BACK, DOCTOR...
...UNTIL WE KNOW WHAT'S HAPPENED TO...
...MY FRIEND.
THERE'S NOT MUCH OF A MYSTERY.
THE PATIENT TRANSFORMED RIGHT IN FRONT OF OUR EYES INTO-- THAT!
BAM BAM BAM
COME ON! WHERE THE HELL IS EVERYBODY?!

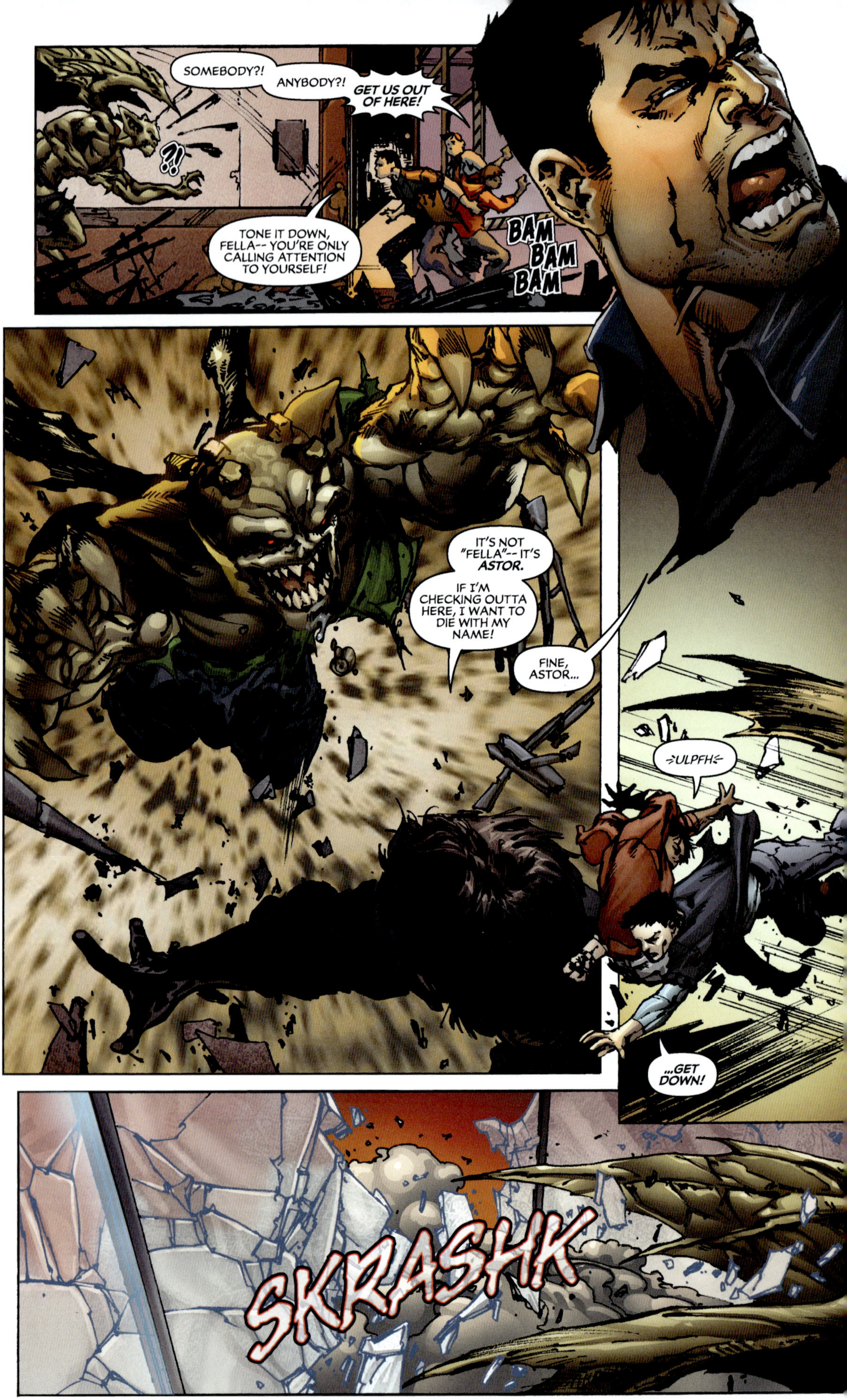
SOMEBODY?!
ANYBODY?!
GET US OUT OF HERE!
?!
TONE IT DOWN, FELLA-- YOU'RE ONLY CALLING ATTENTION TO YOURSELF!
BAM BAM BAM
IT'S NOT "FELLA"-- IT'S ASTOR.
IF I'M CHECKING OUTTA HERE, I WANT TO DIE WITH MY NAME!
FINE, ASTOR...
ULPFH
...GET DOWN!
SKRASHK

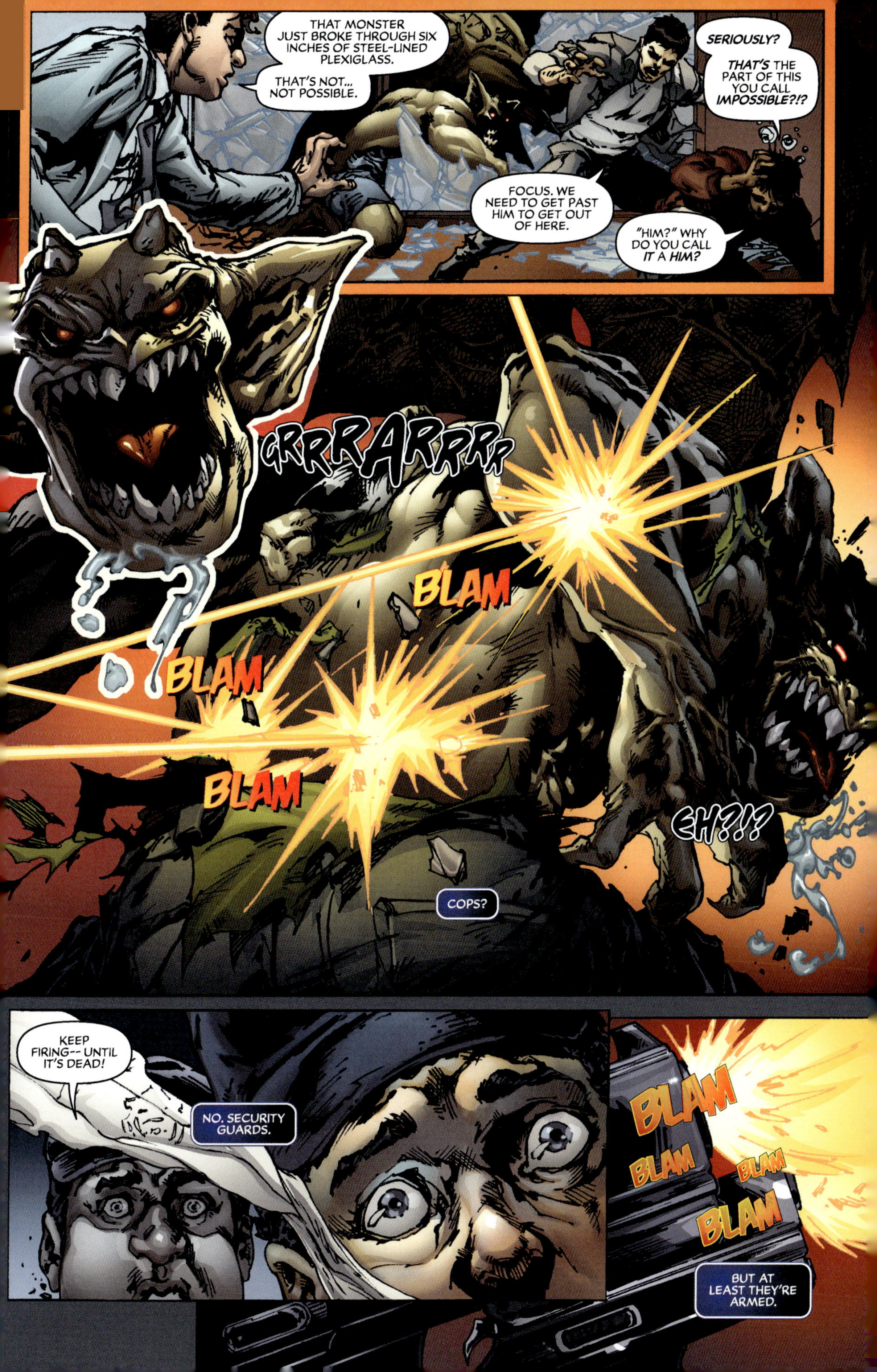
THAT MONSTER JUST BROKE THROUGH SIX INCHES OF STEEL-LINED PLEXIGLASS.
THAT'S NOT... NOT POSSIBLE.
SERIOUSLY?
THAT'S THE PART OF THIS YOU CALL IMPOSSIBLE?!?
FOCUS. WE NEED TO GET PAST HIM TO GET OUT OF HERE.
"HIM?" WHY DO YOU CALL IT A HIM?
GRRRARRRR
BLAM
BLAM
BLAM
EH?!?
COPS?
KEEP FIRING-- UNTIL IT'S DEAD!
NO. SECURITY GUARDS.
BLAM
BLAM
BLAM
BLAM
BUT AT LEAST THEY'RE ARMED.

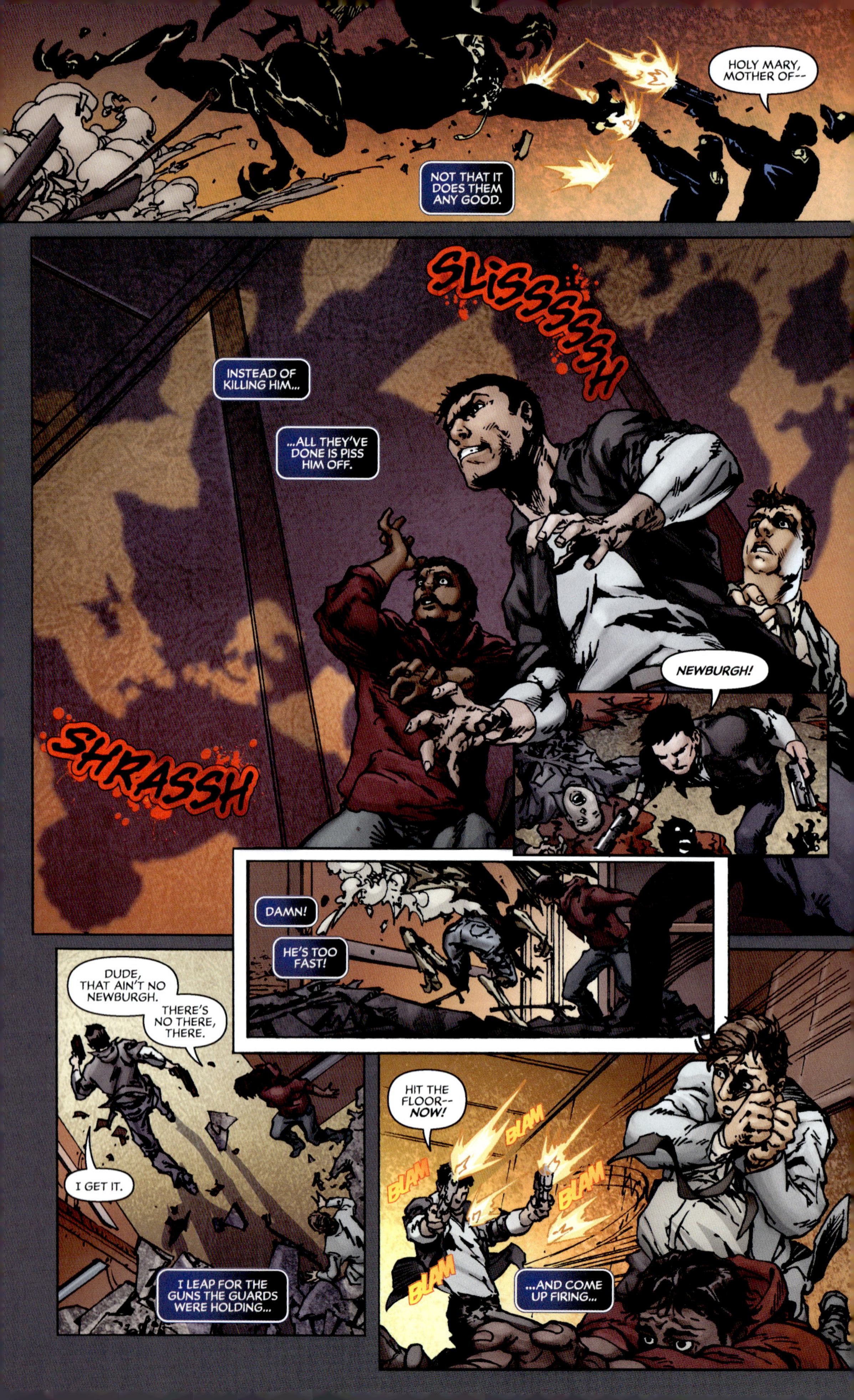
HOLY MARY, MOTHER OF--
NOT THAT IT DOES THEM ANY GOOD.
SLISSSSSH
INSTEAD OF KILLING HIM...
...ALL THEY'VE DONE IS PISS HIM OFF.
NEWBURGH!
SHRASSH
DAMN!
HE'S TOO FAST!
DUDE, THAT AIN'T NO NEWBURGH.
THERE'S NO THERE, THERE.
I GET IT.
I LEAP FOR THE GUNS THE GUARDS WERE HOLDING...
HIT THE FLOOR-- NOW!
BLAM
BLAM
BLAM
BLAM
...AND COME UP FIRING...

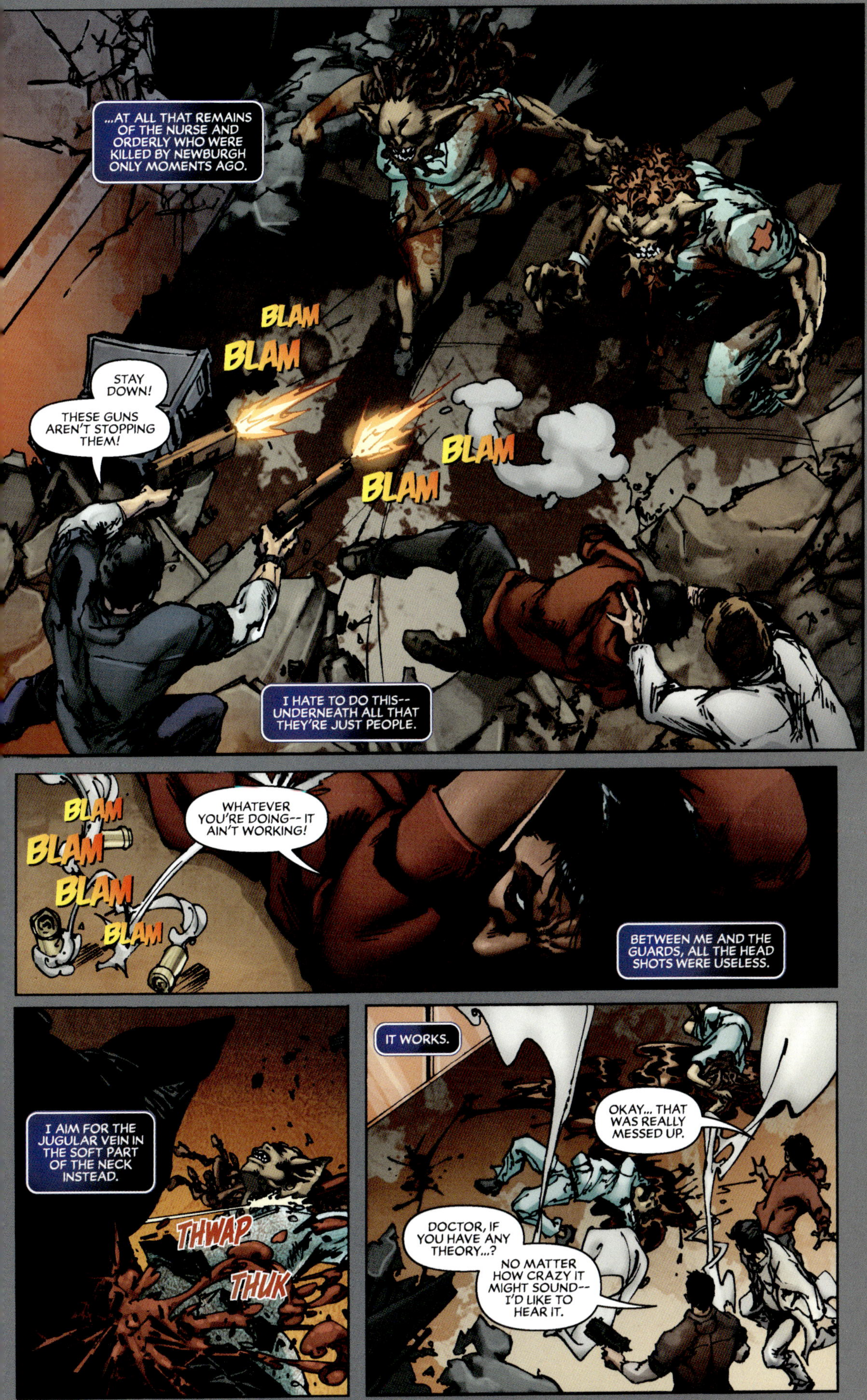

...AT ALL THAT REMAINS OF THE NURSE AND ORDERLY WHO WERE KILLED BY NEWBURGH ONLY MOMENTS AGO.
BLAM
BLAM
STAY DOWN!
THESE GUNS AREN'T STOPPING THEM!
BLAM
BLAM
I HATE TO DO THIS-- UNDERNEATH ALL THAT THEY'RE JUST PEOPLE.
BLAM
BLAM
BLAM
BLAM
WHATEVER YOU'RE DOING-- IT AIN'T WORKING!
BETWEEN ME AND THE GUARDS, ALL THE HEAD SHOTS WERE USELESS.
I AIM FOR THE JUGULAR VEIN IN THE SOFT PART OF THE NECK INSTEAD.
THWAP
THUK
IT WORKS.
OKAY... THAT WAS REALLY MESSED UP.
DOCTOR, IF YOU HAVE ANY THEORY...?
NO MATTER HOW CRAZY IT MIGHT SOUND-- I'D LIKE TO HEAR IT.

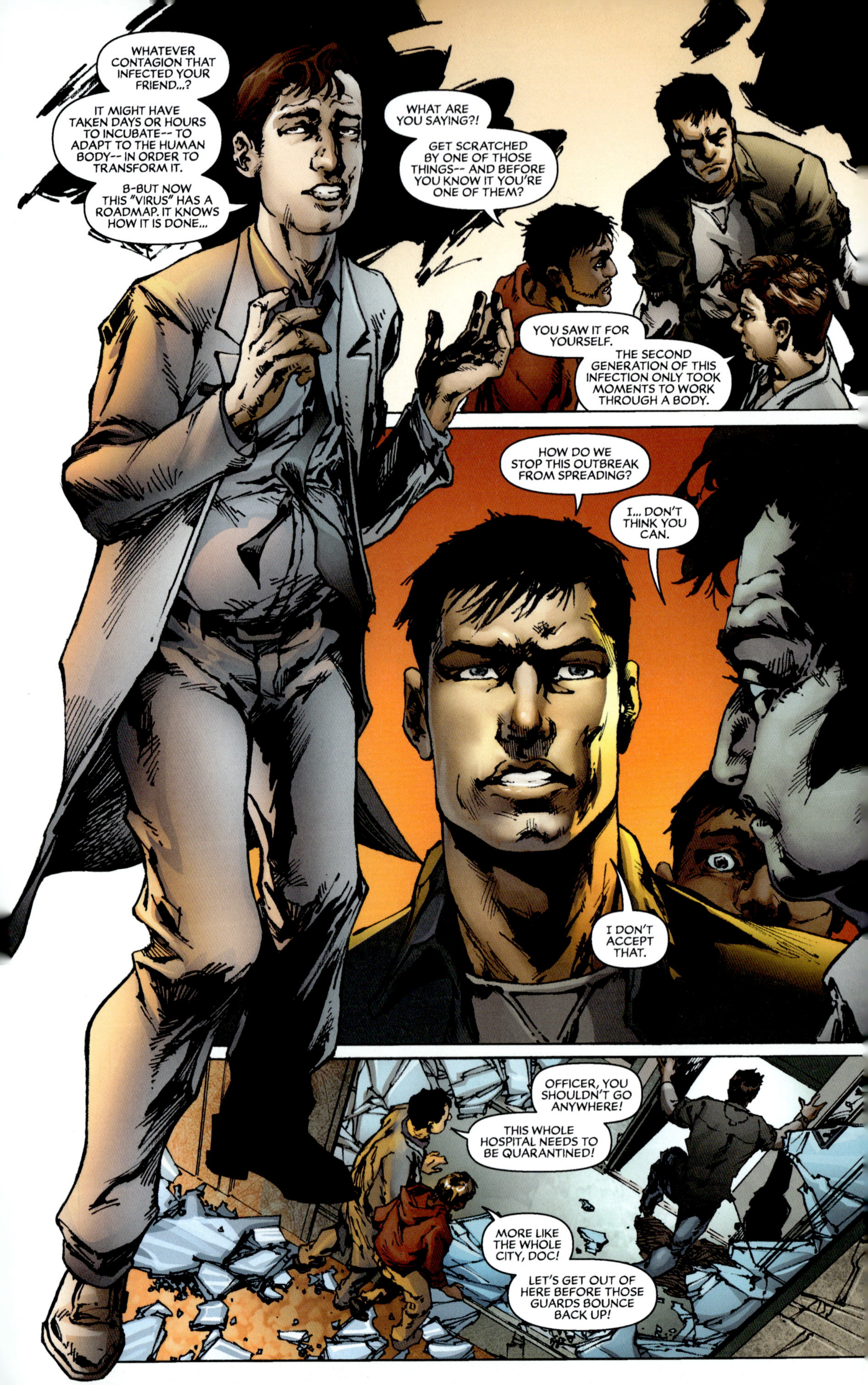
WHATEVER CONTAGION THAT INFECTED YOUR FRIEND...?
IT MIGHT HAVE TAKEN DAYS OR HOURS TO INCUBATE-- TO ADAPT TO THE HUMAN BODY-- IN ORDER TO TRANSFORM IT.
B-BUT NOW THIS "VIRUS" HAS A ROADMAP. IT KNOWS HOW IT IS DONE...
WHAT ARE YOU SAYING?!
GET SCRATCHED BY ONE OF THOSE THINGS-- AND BEFORE YOU KNOW IT YOU'RE ONE OF THEM?
YOU SAW IT FOR YOURSELF.
THE SECOND GENERATION OF THIS INFECTION ONLY TOOK MOMENTS TO WORK THROUGH A BODY.
HOW DO WE STOP THIS OUTBREAK FROM SPREADING?
I... DON'T THINK YOU CAN.
I DON'T ACCEPT THAT.
OFFICER, YOU SHOULDN'T GO ANYWHERE!
THIS WHOLE HOSPITAL NEEDS TO BE QUARANTINED!
MORE LIKE THE WHOLE CITY, DOC!
LET'S GET OUT OF HERE BEFORE THOSE GUARDS BOUNCE BACK UP!

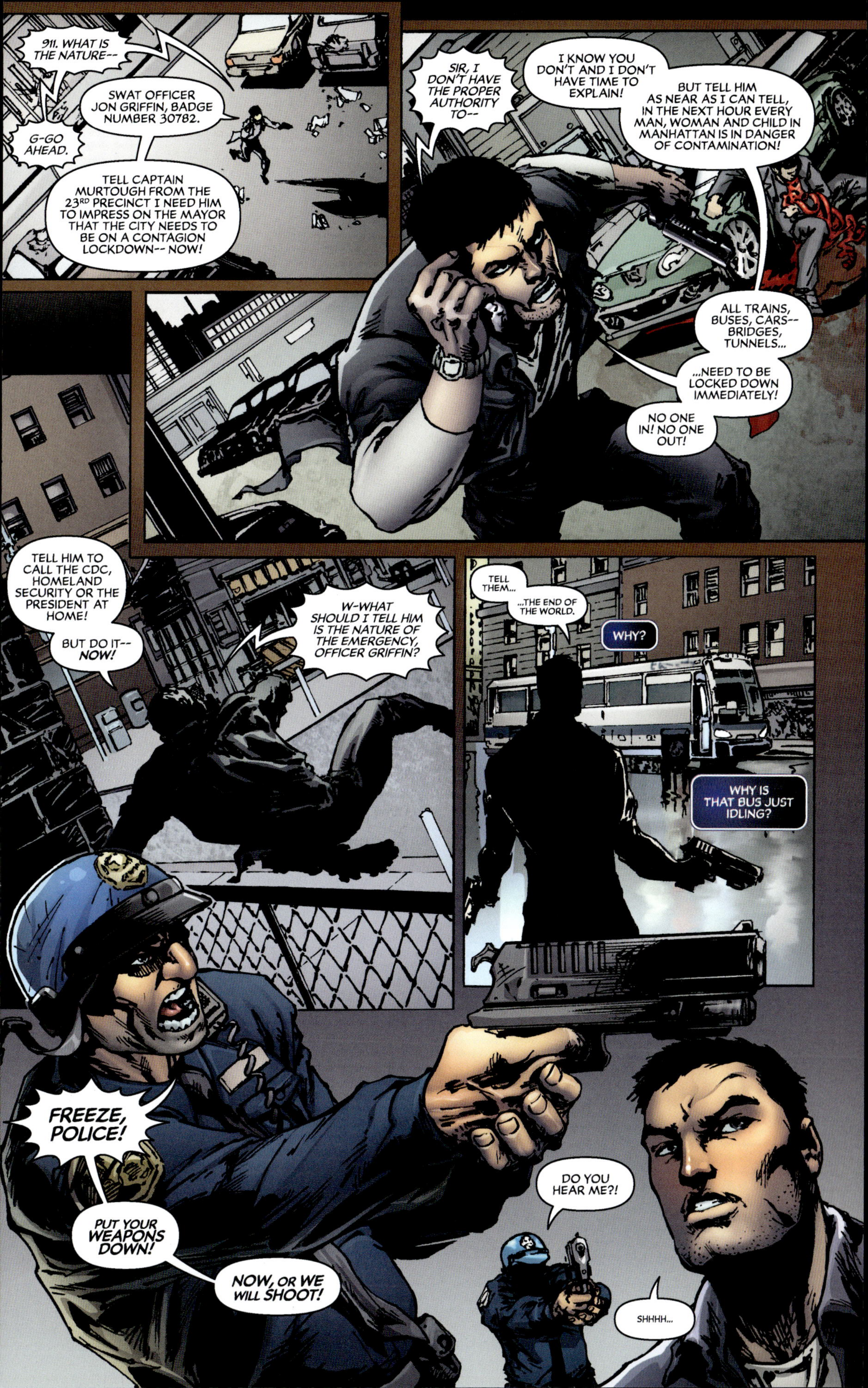
911. WHAT IS THE NATURE--
SWAT OFFICER JON GRIFFIN, BADGE NUMBER 30782.
G-GO AHEAD.
TELL CAPTAIN MURTOUGH FROM THE 23RD PRECINCT I NEED HIM TO IMPRESS ON THE MAYOR THAT THE CITY NEEDS TO BE ON A CONTAGION LOCKDOWN-- NOW!
SIR, I DON'T HAVE THE PROPER AUTHORITY TO--
I KNOW YOU DON'T AND I DON'T HAVE TIME TO EXPLAIN!
BUT TELL HIM AS NEAR AS I CAN TELL, IN THE NEXT HOUR EVERY MAN, WOMAN AND CHILD IN MANHATTAN IS IN DANGER OF CONTAMINATION!
ALL TRAINS, BUSES, CARS-- BRIDGES, TUNNELS...
...NEED TO BE LOCKED DOWN IMMEDIATELY!
NO ONE IN! NO ONE OUT!
TELL HIM TO CALL THE CDC, HOMELAND SECURITY OR THE PRESIDENT AT HOME!
BUT DO IT-- NOW!
W-WHAT SHOULD I TELL HIM IS THE NATURE OF THE EMERGENCY, OFFICER GRIFFIN?
TELL THEM...
...THE END OF THE WORLD.
WHY?
WHY IS THAT BUS JUST IDLING?
FREEZE, POLICE!
PUT YOUR WEAPONS DOWN!
NOW, OR WE WILL SHOOT!
DO YOU HEAR ME?!
SHHHH...

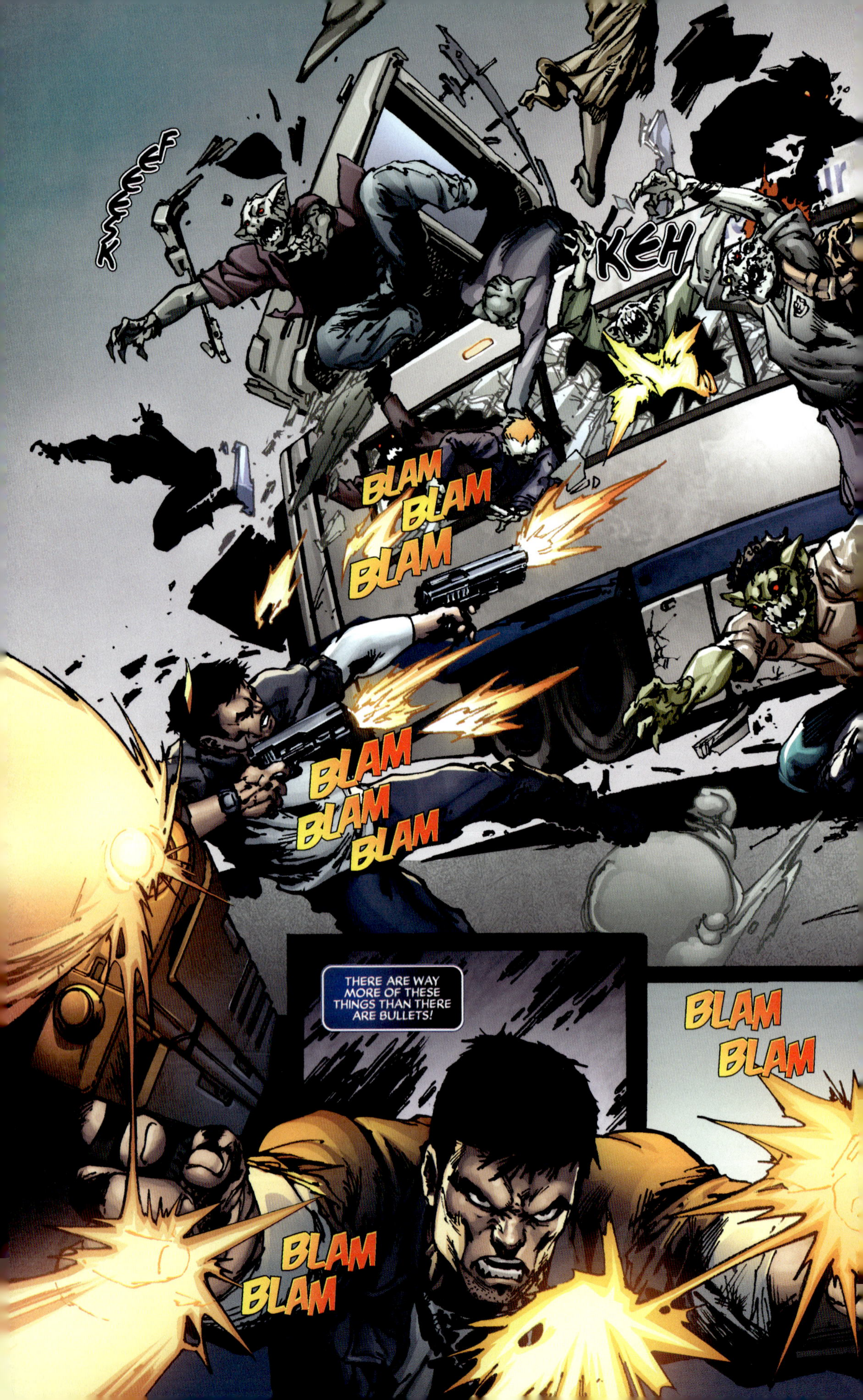
FFWWK
KEH
BLAM
BLAM
BLAM
BLAM
BLAM
BLAM
THERE ARE WAY MORE OF THESE THINGS THAN THERE ARE BULLETS!
BLAM
BLAM
BLAM
BLAM

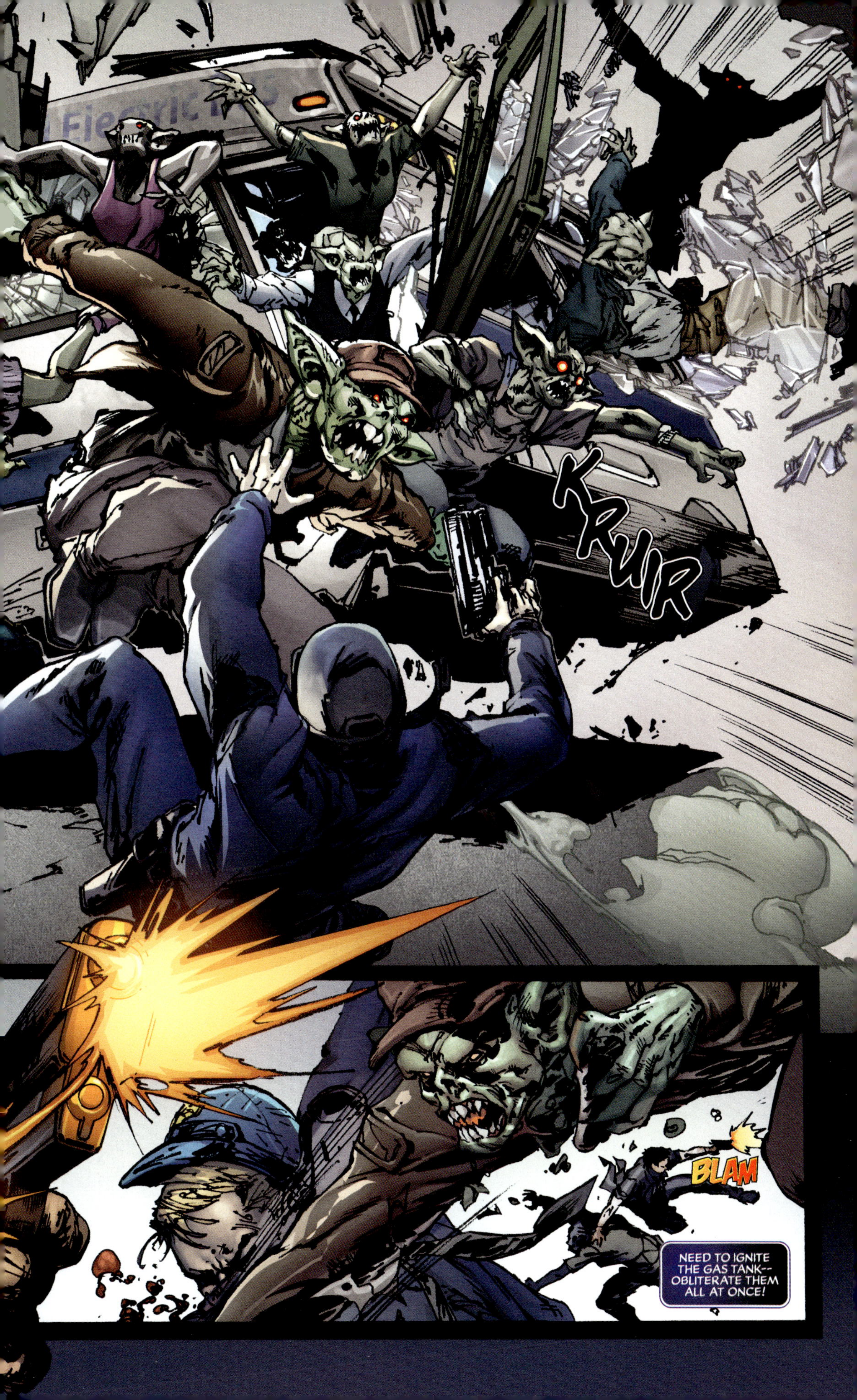
KRUIR
BLAM
NEED TO IGNITE THE GAS TANK-- OBLITERATE THEM ALL AT ONCE!

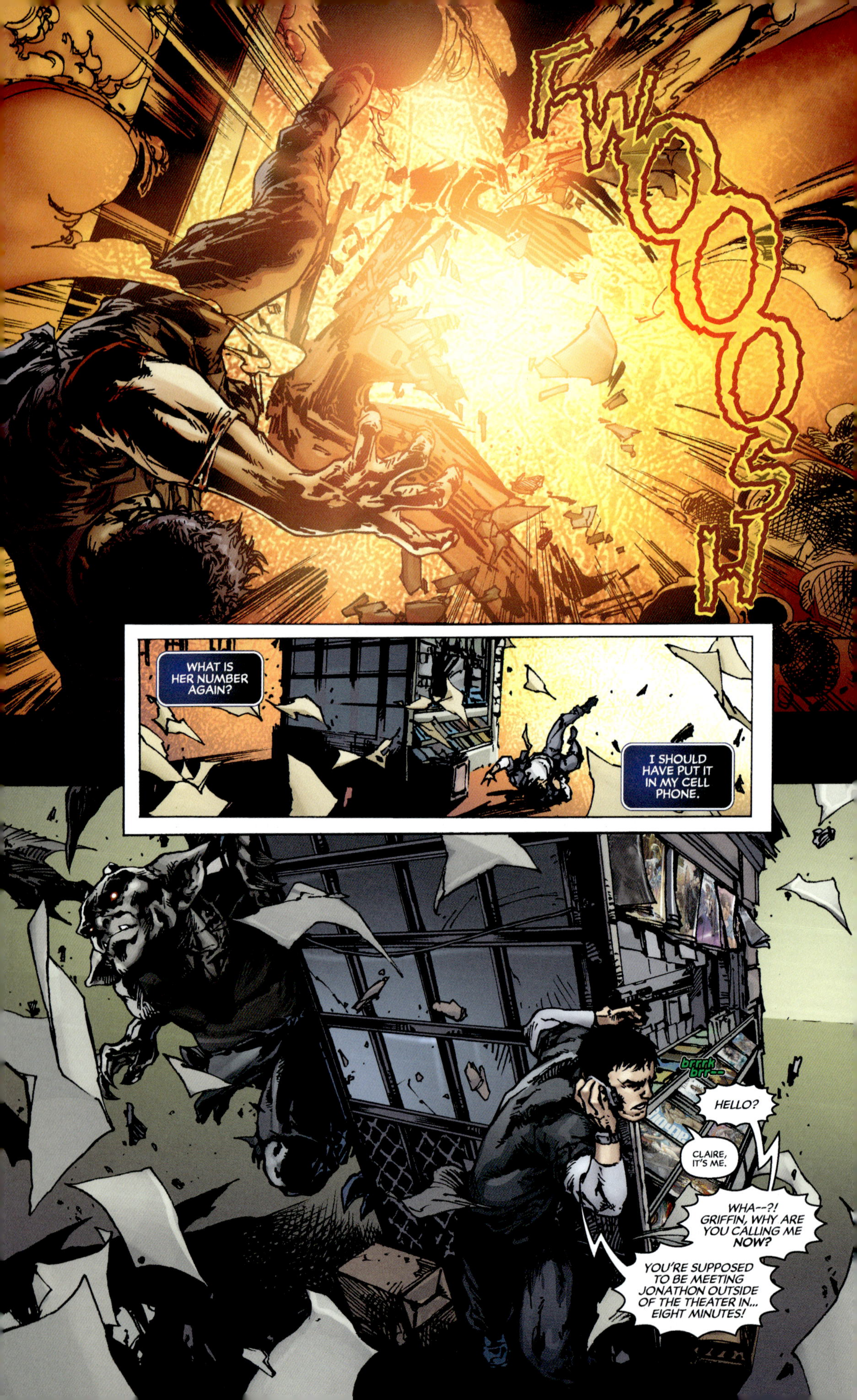
FWOOOOSH
WHAT IS HER NUMBER AGAIN?
I SHOULD HAVE PUT IT IN MY CELL PHONE.
brrrk brr--
HELLO?
CLAIRE, IT'S ME.
WHA--?! GRIFFIN, WHY ARE YOU CALLING ME NOW?
YOU'RE SUPPOSED TO BE MEETING JONATHON OUTSIDE OF THE THEATER IN... EIGHT MINUTES!

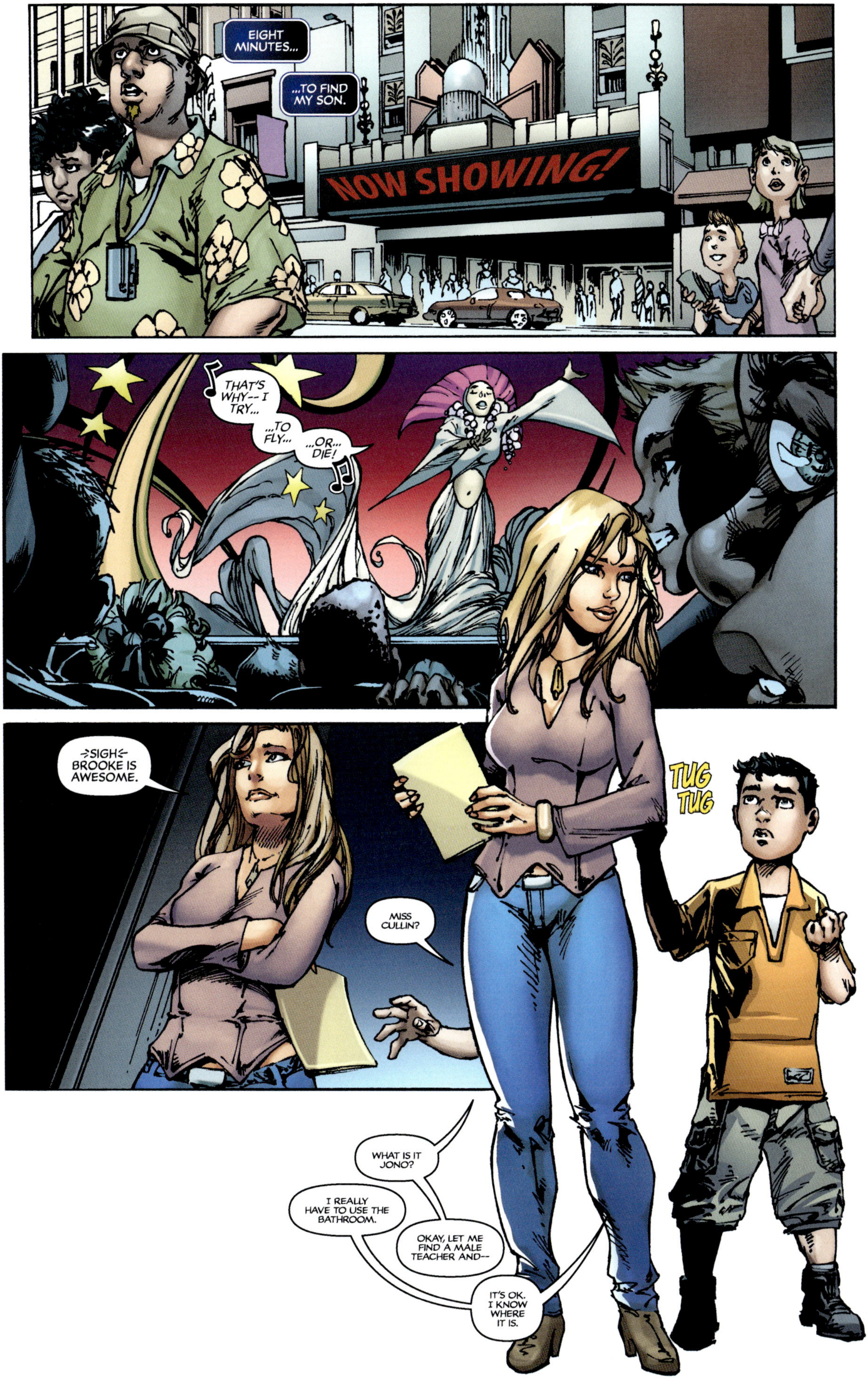
EIGHT MINUTES...
...TO FIND MY SON.
NOW SHOWING!
THAT'S WHY-- I TRY...
...TO FLY...
...OR... DIE!
-SIGH- BROOKE IS AWESOME.
TUG TUG
MISS CULLIN?
WHAT IS IT JONO?
I REALLY HAVE TO USE THE BATHROOM.
OKAY, LET ME FIND A MALE TEACHER AND--
IT'S OK. I KNOW WHERE IT IS.

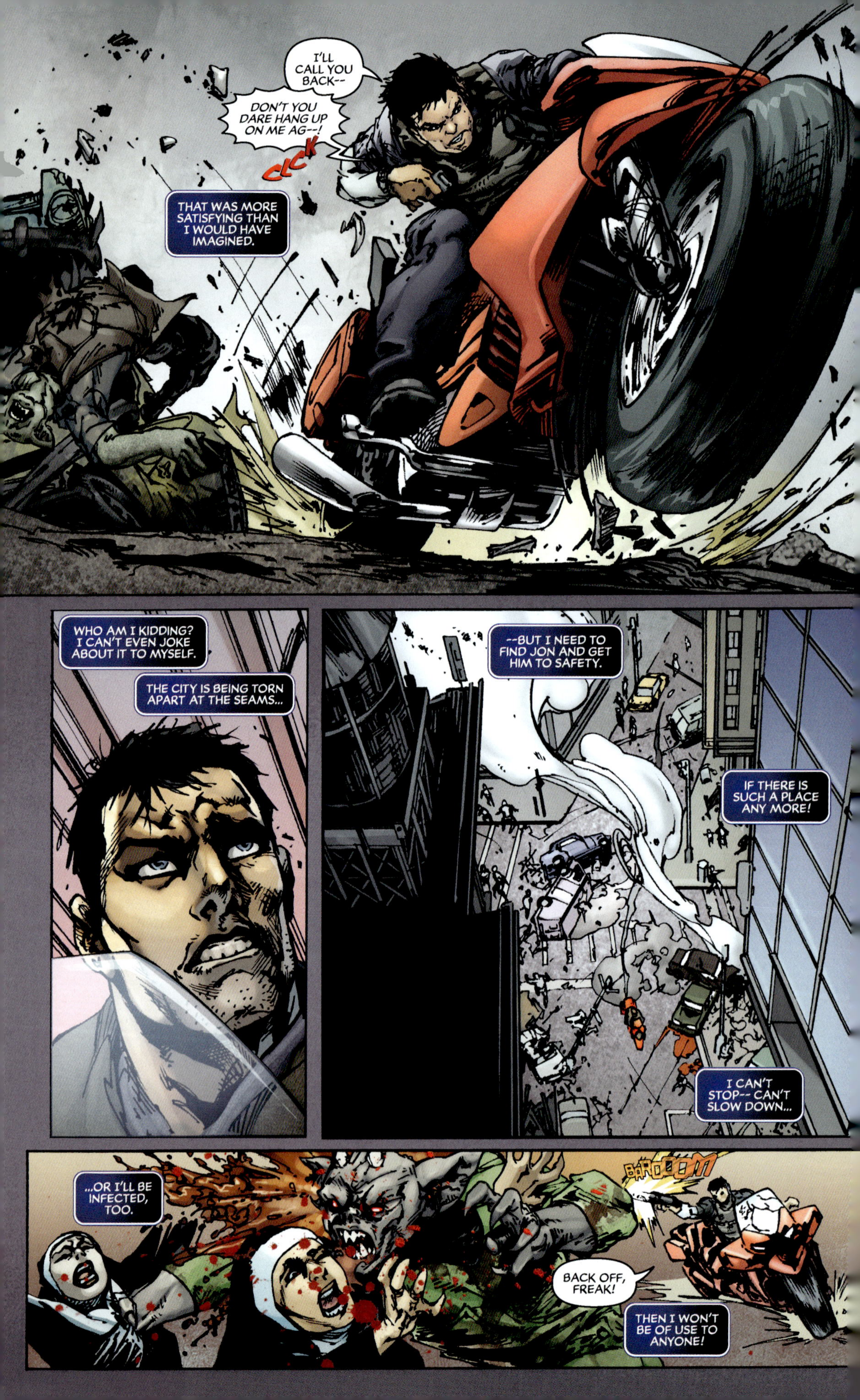
I'LL CALL YOU BACK--
DON'T YOU DARE HANG UP ON ME AG--!
CLICK
THAT WAS MORE SATISFYING THAN I WOULD HAVE IMAGINED.
WHO AM I KIDDING? I CAN'T EVEN JOKE ABOUT IT TO MYSELF.
THE CITY IS BEING TORN APART AT THE SEAMS...
--BUT I NEED TO FIND JON AND GET HIM TO SAFETY.
IF THERE IS SUCH A PLACE ANY MORE!
I CAN'T STOP-- CAN'T SLOW DOWN...
...OR I'LL BE INFECTED, TOO.
BAROOOM
BACK OFF, FREAK!
THEN I WON'T BE OF USE TO ANYONE!

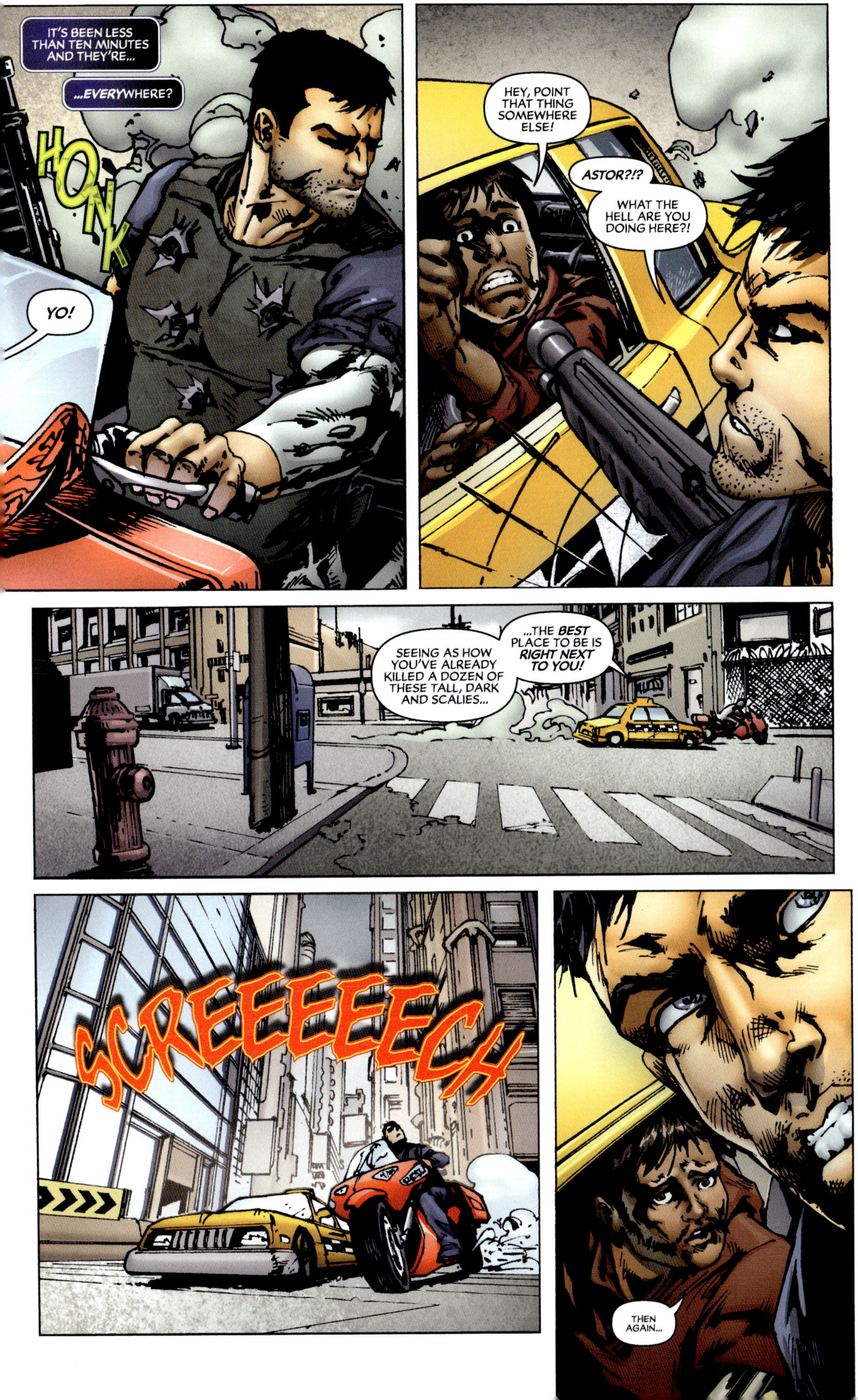
IT'S BEEN LESS THAN TEN MINUTES AND THEY'RE...
...EVERYWHERE?
HONK
YO!
HEY, POINT THAT THING SOMEWHERE ELSE!
ASTOR?!?
WHAT THE HELL ARE YOU DOING HERE?!
SEEING AS HOW YOU'VE ALREADY KILLED A DOZEN OF THESE TALL, DARK AND SCALIES...
...THE BEST PLACE TO BE IS RIGHT NEXT TO YOU!
SCREEEEEECH
THEN AGAIN...

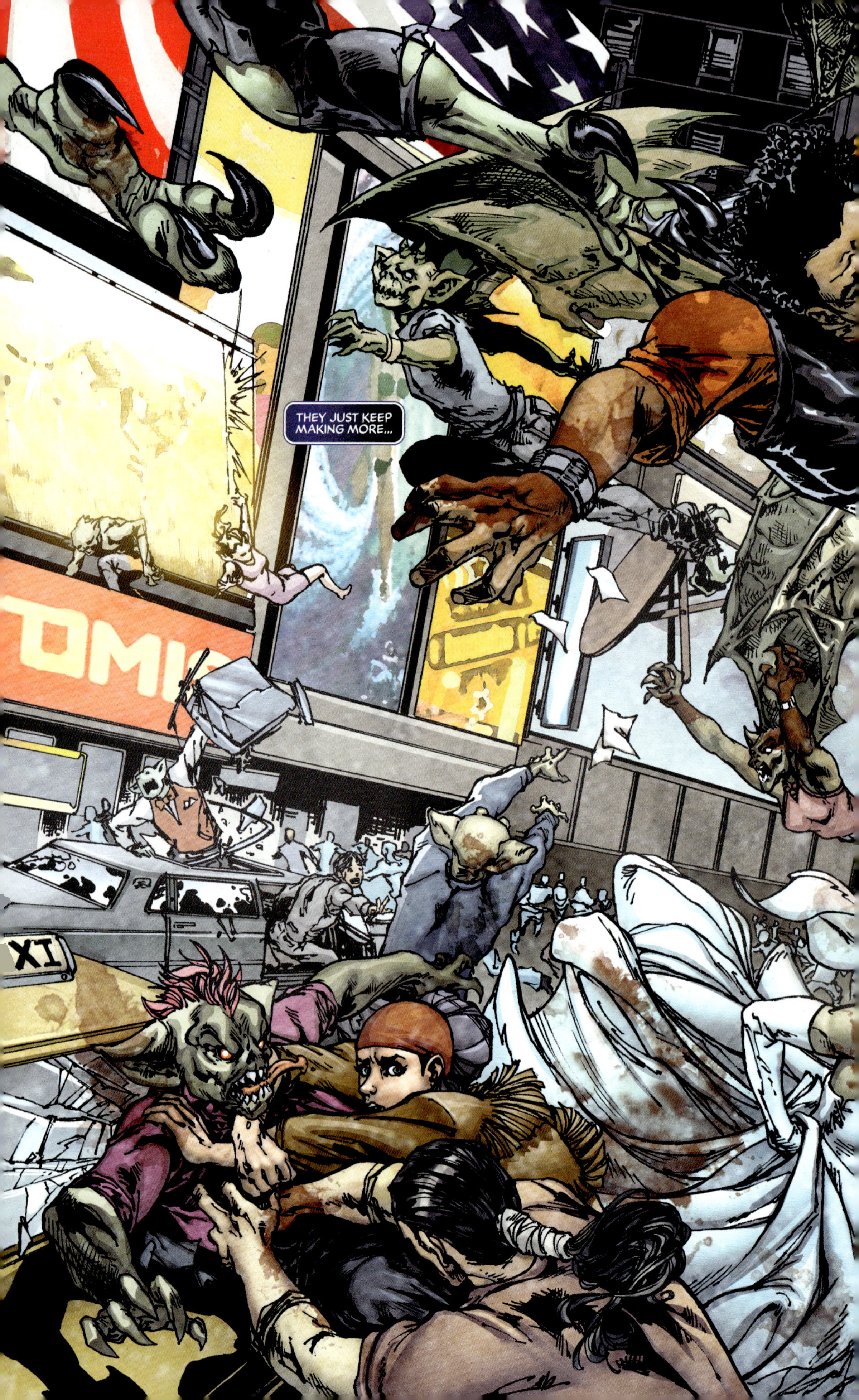
THEY JUST KEEP MAKING MORE...

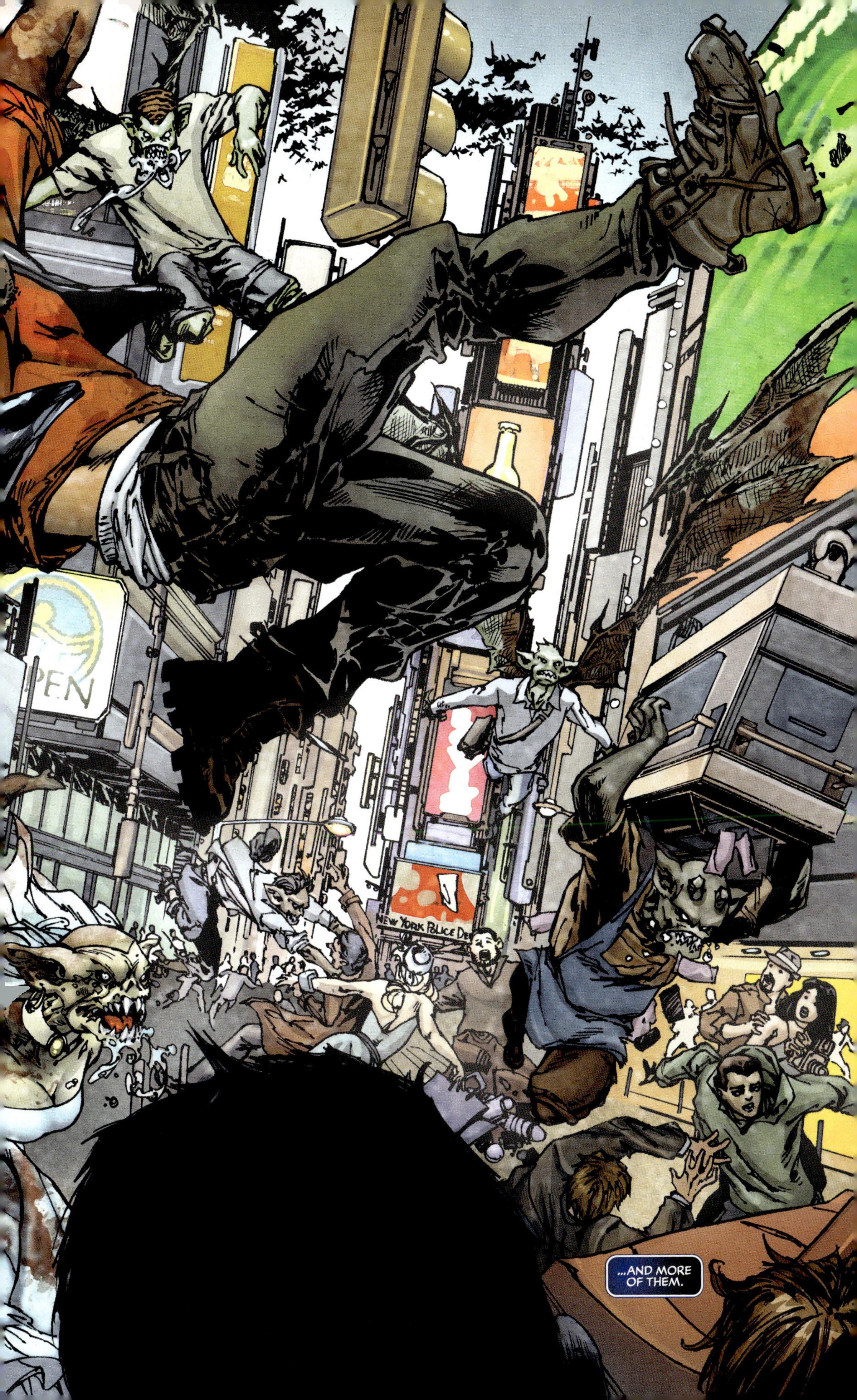
...AND MORE
OF THEM.
OPEN
NEW YORK POLICE DE

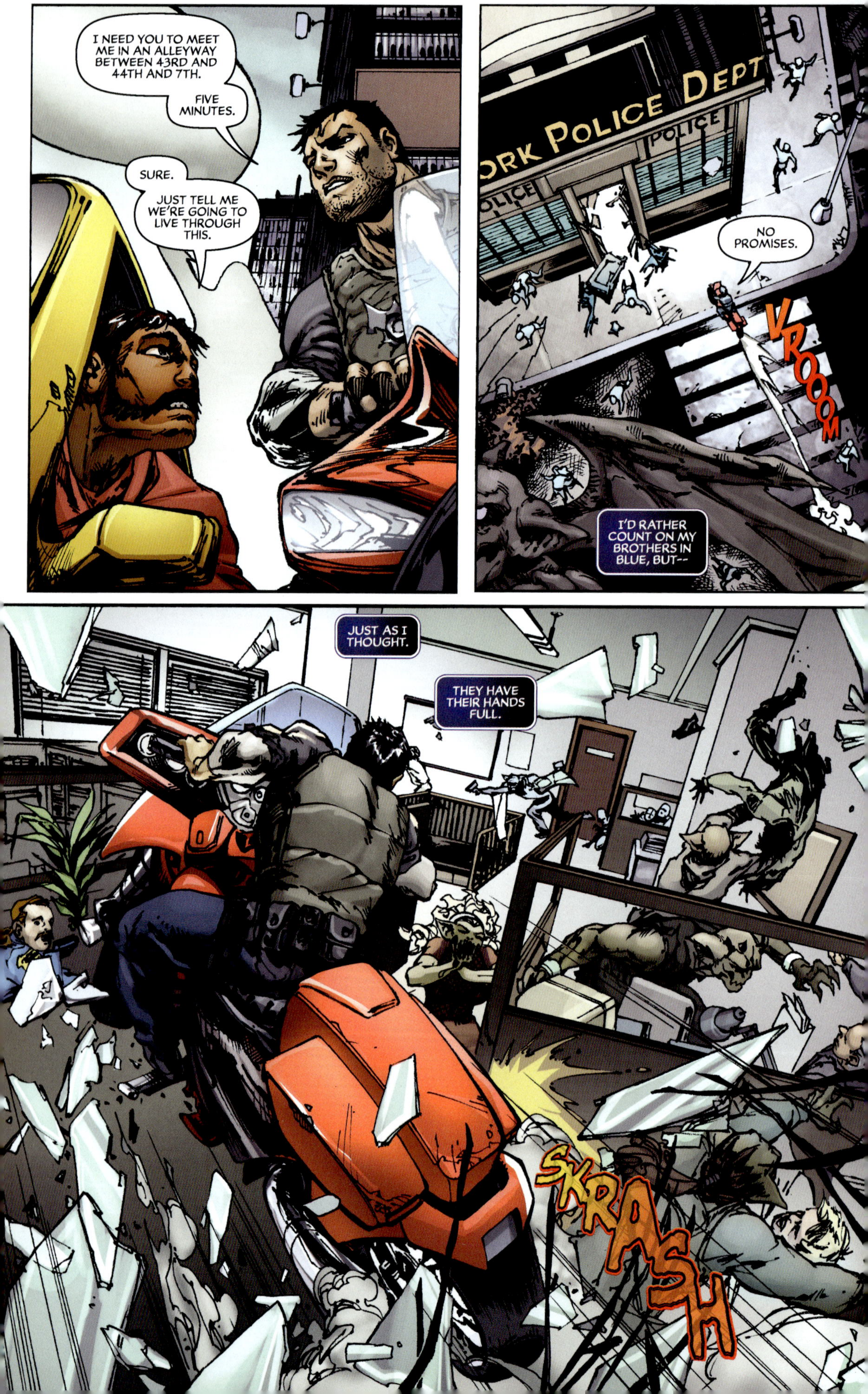

I NEED YOU TO MEET ME IN AN ALLEYWAY BETWEEN 43RD AND 44TH AND 7TH.
FIVE MINUTES.
SURE.
JUST TELL ME WE'RE GOING TO LIVE THROUGH THIS.
ORK POLICE DEPT
POLICE
OLICE
NO PROMISES.
VROOOOM
I'D RATHER COUNT ON MY BROTHERS IN BLUE, BUT--
JUST AS I THOUGHT.
THEY HAVE THEIR HANDS FULL.
SKRASH

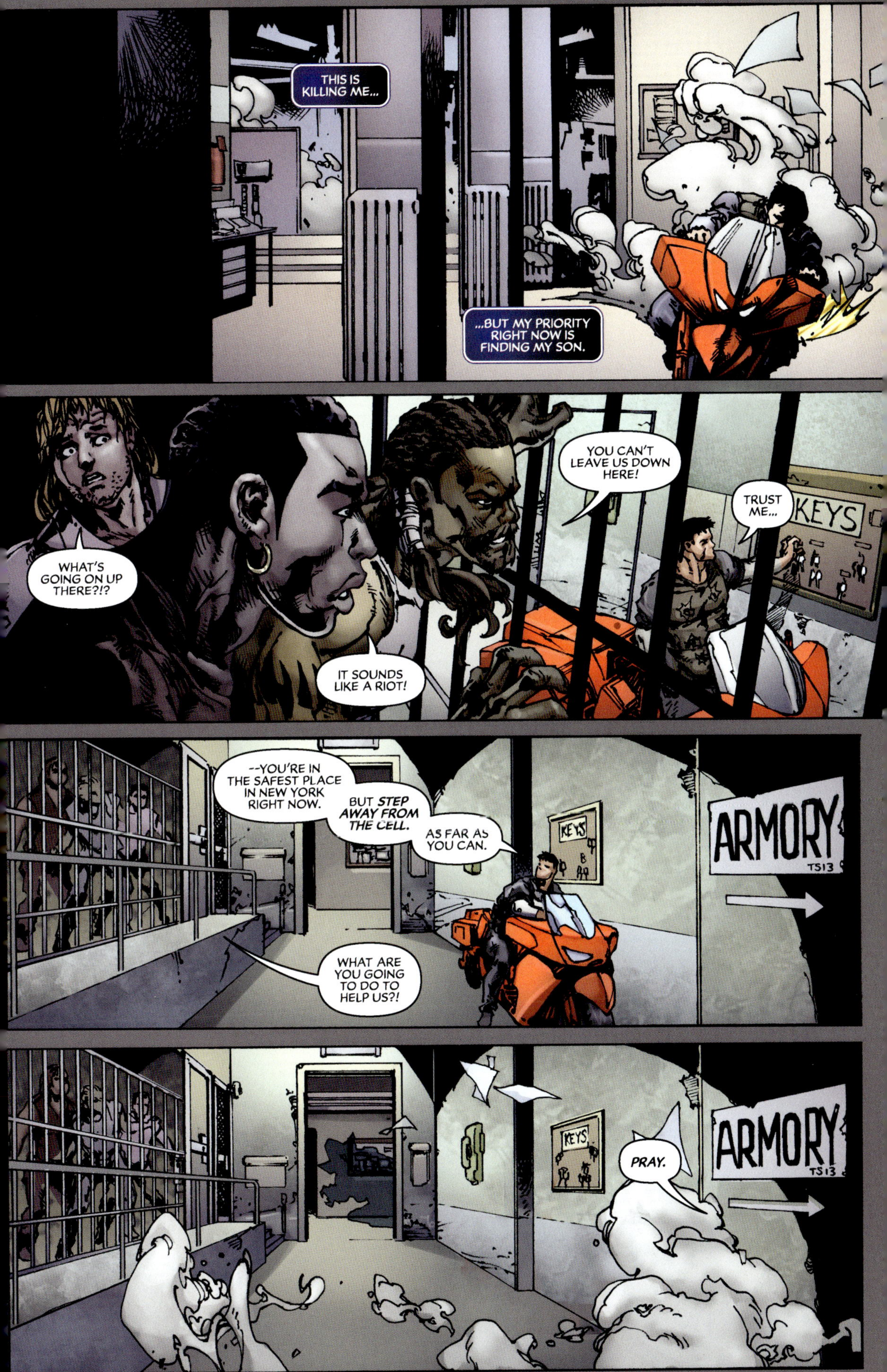
THIS IS KILLING ME...
...BUT MY PRIORITY RIGHT NOW IS FINDING MY SON.
WHAT'S GOING ON UP THERE?!?
IT SOUNDS LIKE A RIOT!
YOU CAN'T LEAVE US DOWN HERE!
TRUST ME...
KEYS
--YOU'RE IN THE SAFEST PLACE IN NEW YORK RIGHT NOW.
BUT STEP AWAY FROM THE CELL.
AS FAR AS YOU CAN.
KEYS
ARMORY
TS13
WHAT ARE YOU GOING TO DO TO HELP US?!
KEYS
PRAY.
ARMORY
TS13

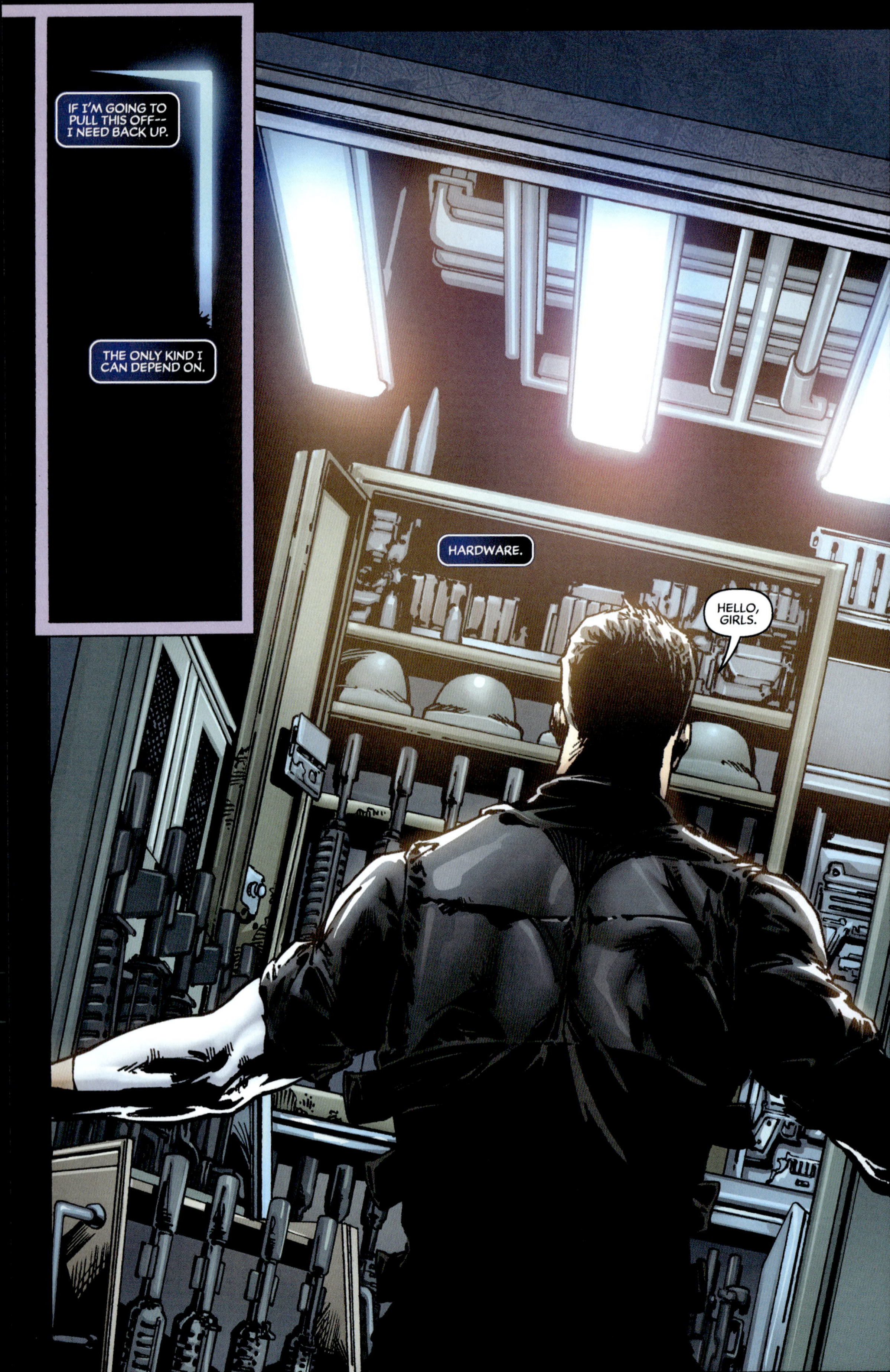
IF I'M GOING TO PULL THIS OFF-- I NEED BACK UP.
THE ONLY KIND I CAN DEPEND ON.
HARDWARE.
HELLO, GIRLS.

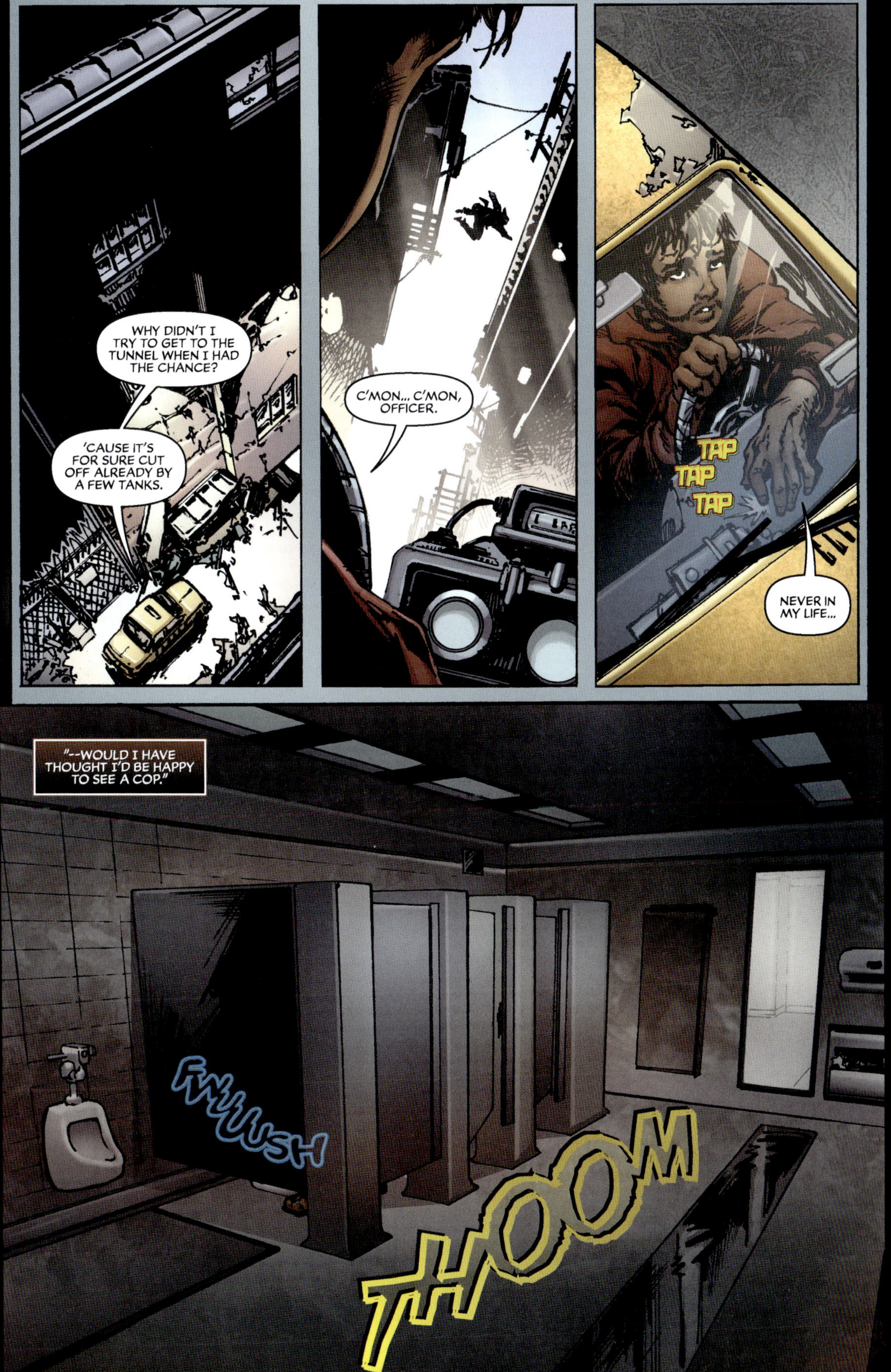
WHY DIDN'T I TRY TO GET TO THE TUNNEL WHEN I HAD THE CHANCE?
'CAUSE IT'S FOR SURE CUT OFF ALREADY BY A FEW TANKS.
C'MON... C'MON, OFFICER.
TAP
TAP
TAP
NEVER IN MY LIFE...
"--WOULD I HAVE THOUGHT I'D BE HAPPY TO SEE A COP."
FWUUSH
THOOM

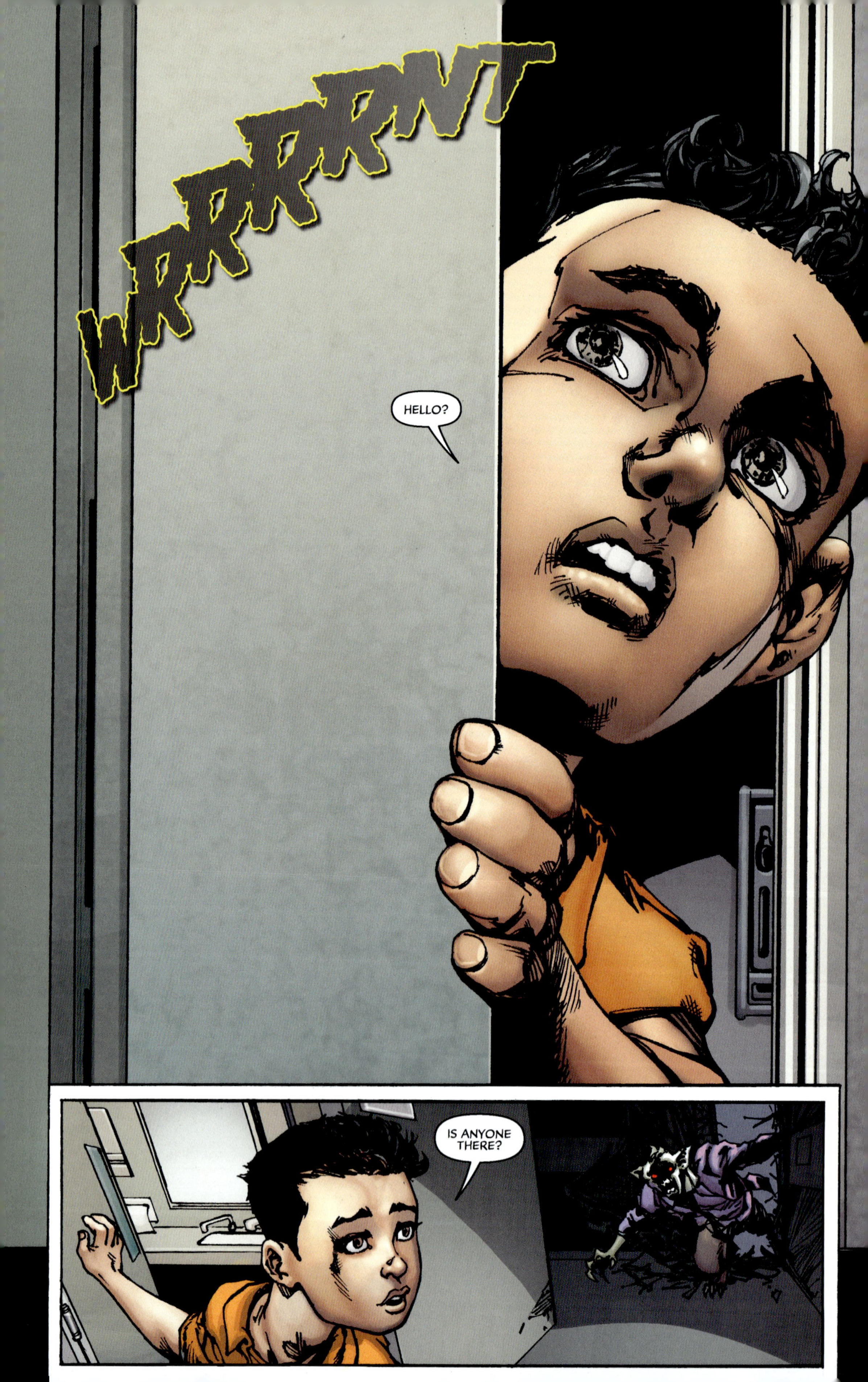
WRRRRRNT
HELLO?
IS ANYONE THERE?

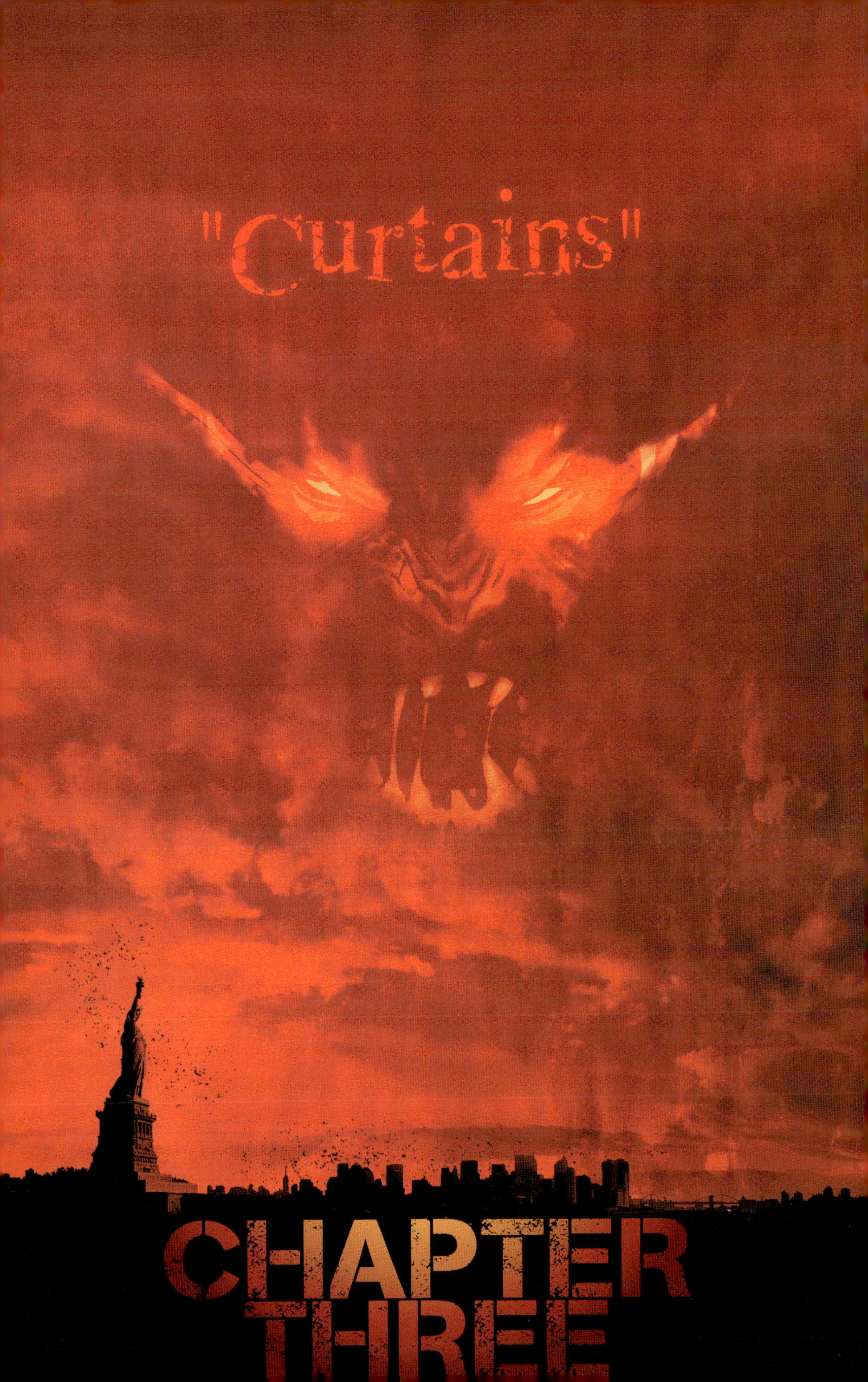
"Curtains"
CHAPTER
THREE

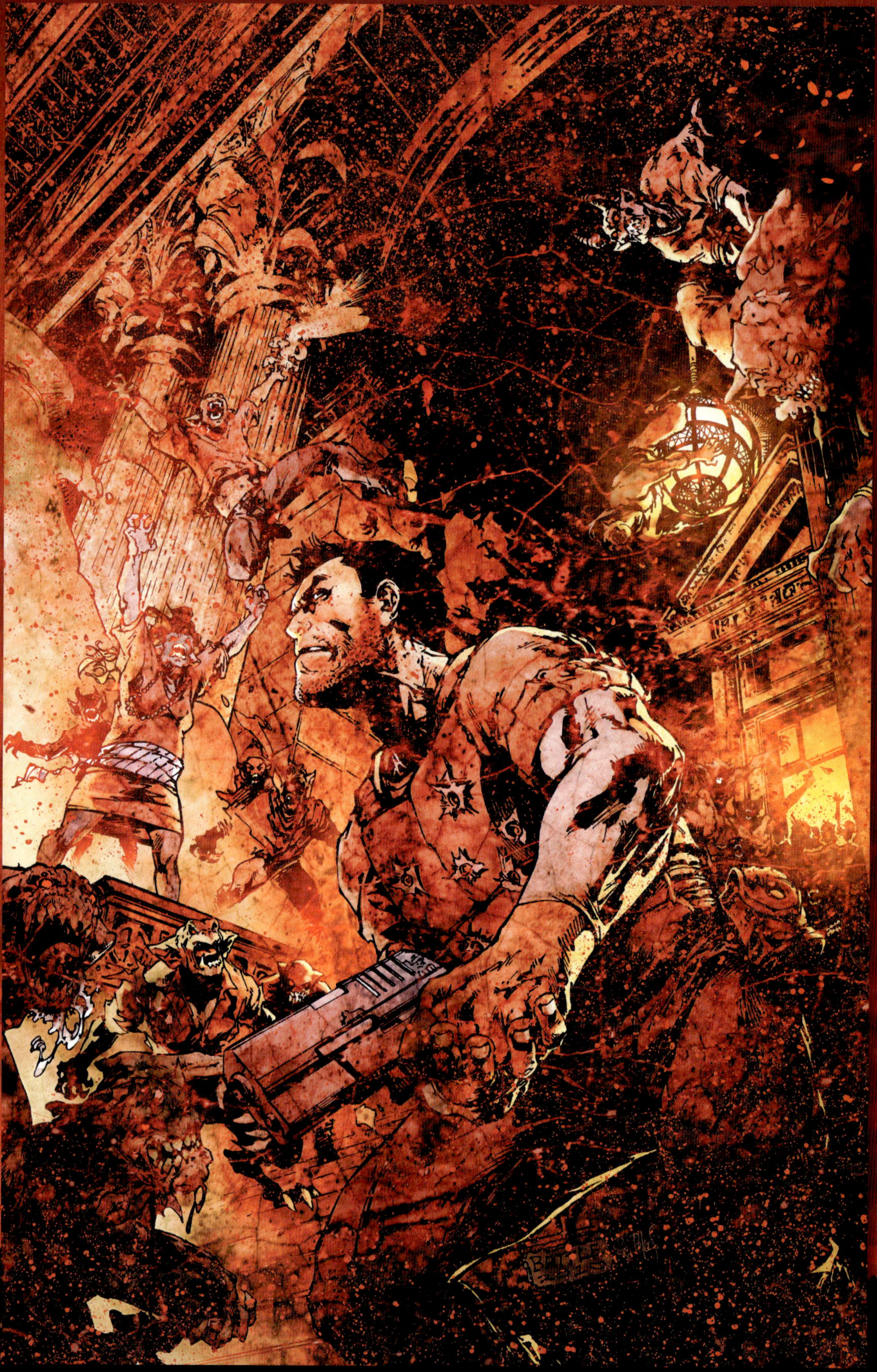

Retailer "Infected" Incentive Edition Cover C to

THE SCOURGE #3

by

Eric BATTLE | Peter STEIGERWALD

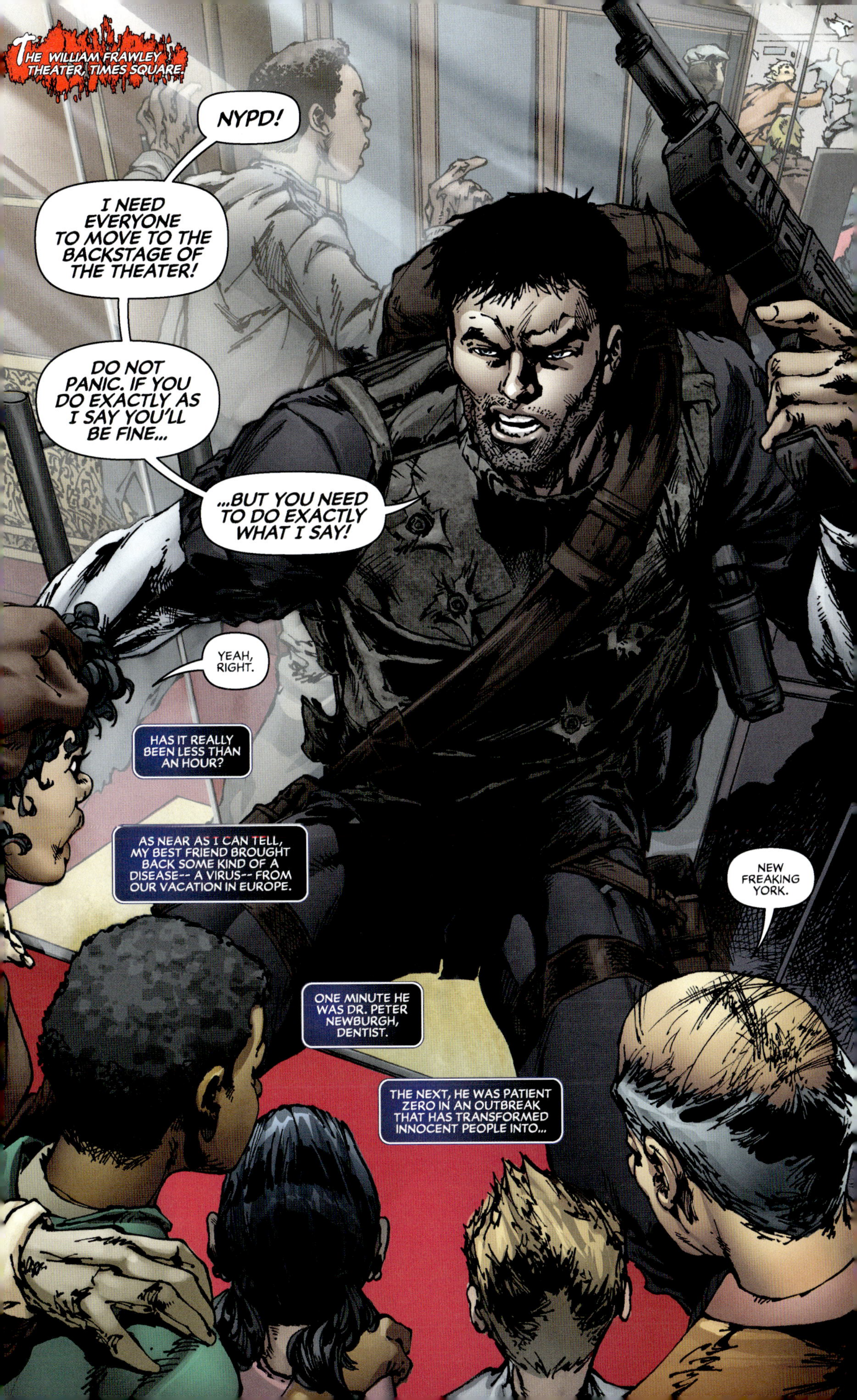
THE WILLIAM FRAWLEY THEATER, TIMES SQUARE.
NYPD!
I NEED EVERYONE TO MOVE TO THE BACKSTAGE OF THE THEATER!
DO NOT PANIC. IF YOU DO EXACTLY AS I SAY YOU'LL BE FINE...
...BUT YOU NEED TO DO EXACTLY WHAT I SAY!
YEAH, RIGHT.
HAS IT REALLY BEEN LESS THAN AN HOUR?
AS NEAR AS I CAN TELL, MY BEST FRIEND BROUGHT BACK SOME KIND OF A DISEASE-- A VIRUS-- FROM OUR VACATION IN EUROPE.
NEW FREAKING YORK.
ONE MINUTE HE WAS DR. PETER NEWBURGH, DENTIST.
THE NEXT, HE WAS PATIENT ZERO IN AN OUTBREAK THAT HAS TRANSFORMED INNOCENT PEOPLE INTO...

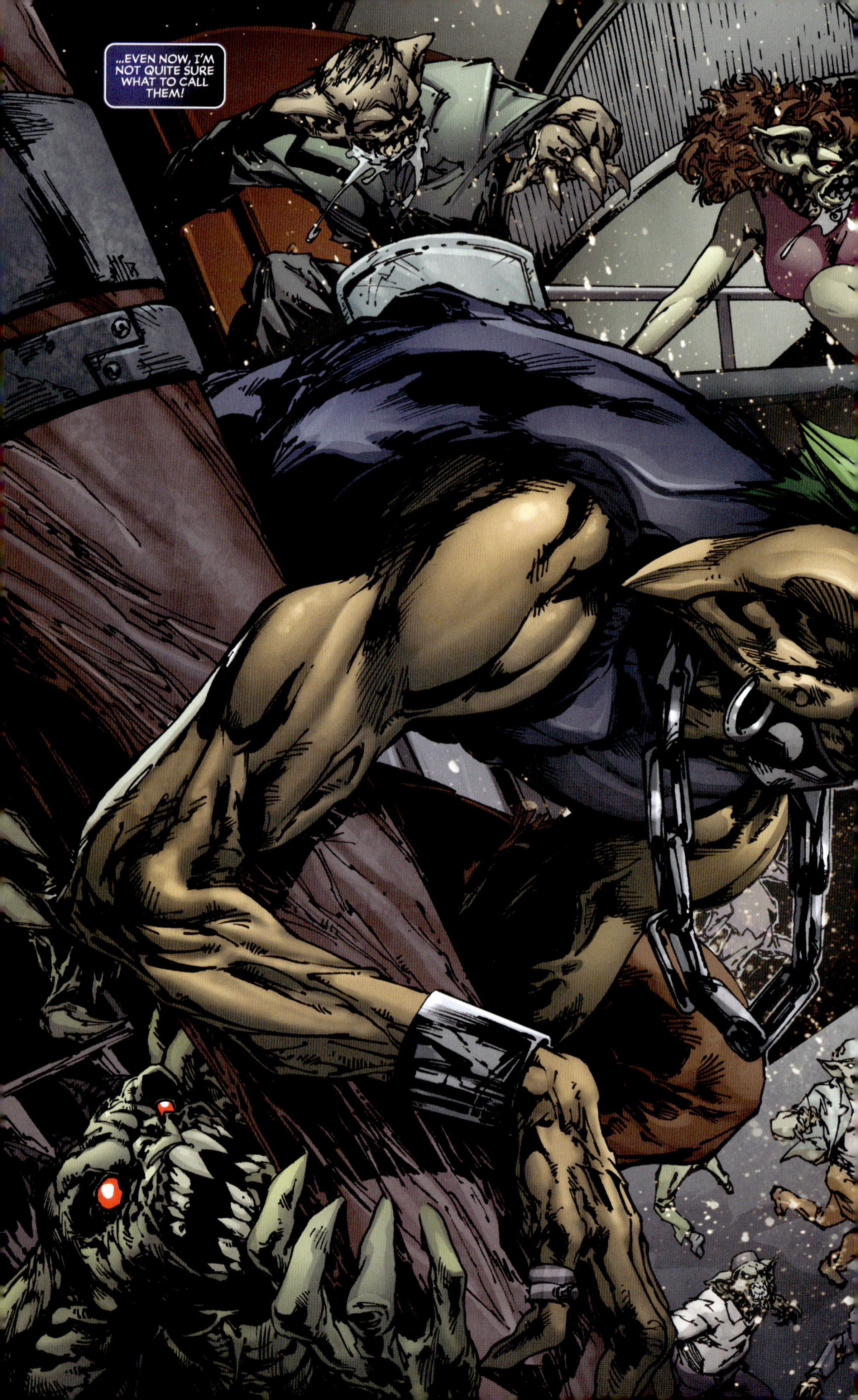
...EVEN NOW, I'M NOT QUITE SURE WHAT TO CALL THEM!

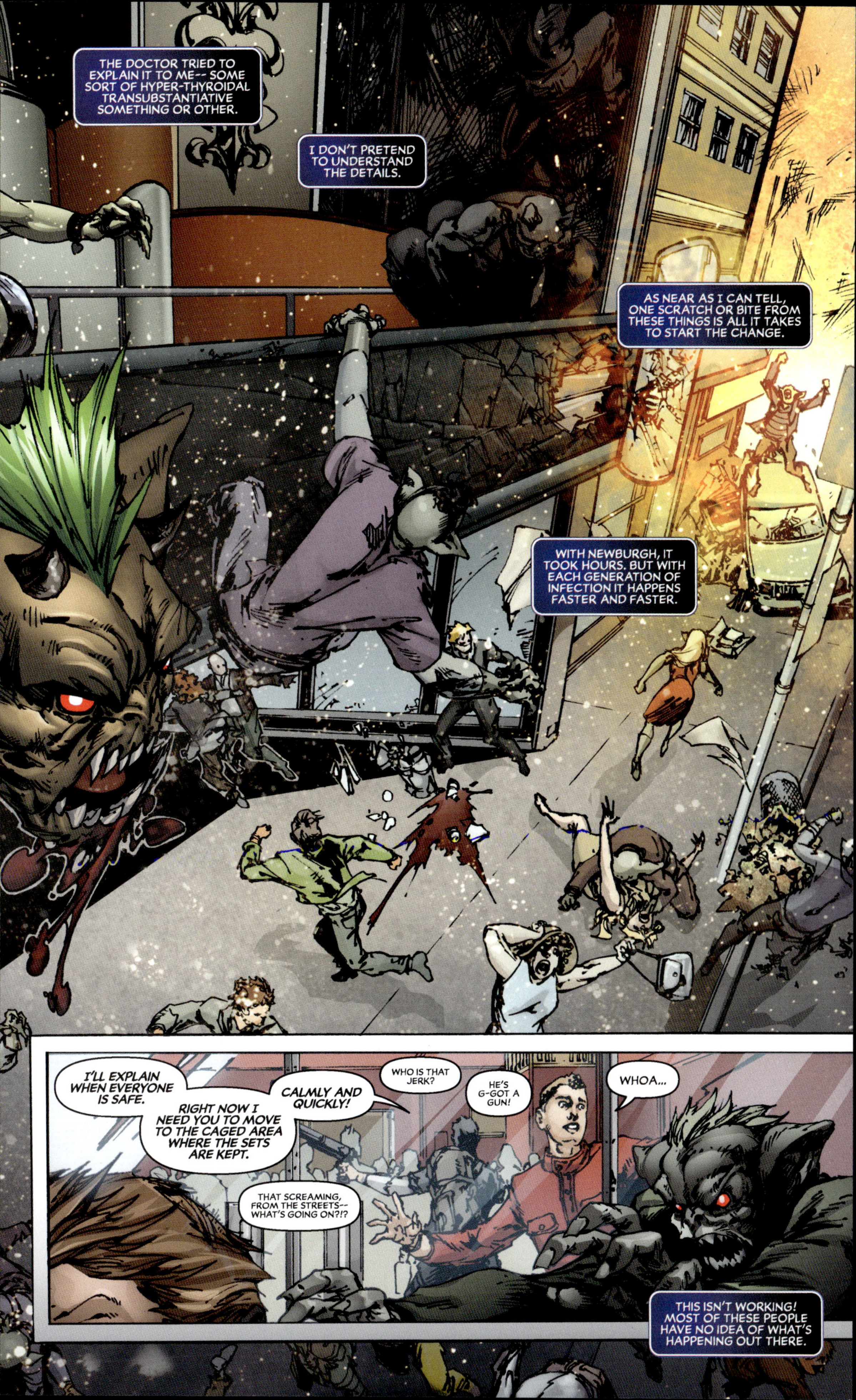
THE DOCTOR TRIED TO EXPLAIN IT TO ME-- SOME SORT OF HYPER-THYROIDAL TRANSUBSTANTIATIVE SOMETHING OR OTHER.
I DON'T PRETEND TO UNDERSTAND THE DETAILS.
AS NEAR AS I CAN TELL, ONE SCRATCH OR BITE FROM THESE THINGS IS ALL IT TAKES TO START THE CHANGE.
WITH NEWBURGH, IT TOOK HOURS. BUT WITH EACH GENERATION OF INFECTION IT HAPPENS FASTER AND FASTER.
I'LL EXPLAIN WHEN EVERYONE IS SAFE.
RIGHT NOW I NEED YOU TO MOVE TO THE CAGED AREA WHERE THE SETS ARE KEPT.
CALMLY AND QUICKLY!
WHO IS THAT JERK?
HE'S G-GOT A GUN!
WHOA...
THAT SCREAMING, FROM THE STREETS-- WHAT'S GOING ON?!?
THIS ISN'T WORKING! MOST OF THESE PEOPLE HAVE NO IDEA OF WHAT'S HAPPENING OUT THERE.

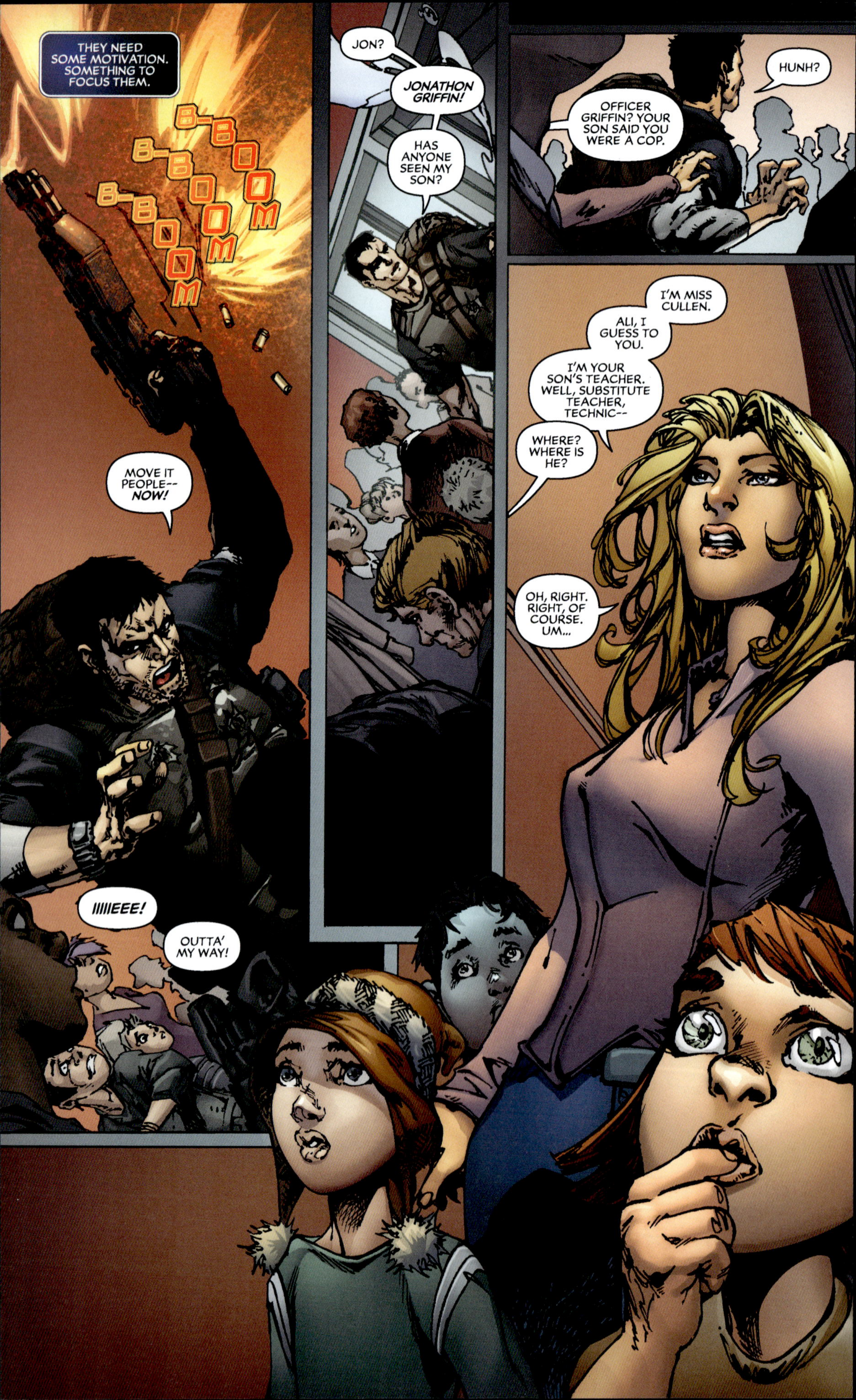

THEY NEED SOME MOTIVATION. SOMETHING TO FOCUS THEM.
B-BOOM
B-BOOM
B-BOOM
MOVE IT PEOPLE-- NOW!
IIIIIEEE!
OUTTA' MY WAY!
JON?
JONATHON GRIFFIN!
HAS ANYONE SEEN MY SON?
HUNH?
OFFICER GRIFFIN? YOUR SON SAID YOU WERE A COP.
I'M MISS CULLEN.
ALI, I GUESS TO YOU.
I'M YOUR SON'S TEACHER. WELL, SUBSTITUTE TEACHER, TECHNIC--
WHERE? WHERE IS HE?
OH, RIGHT. RIGHT, OF COURSE. UM...

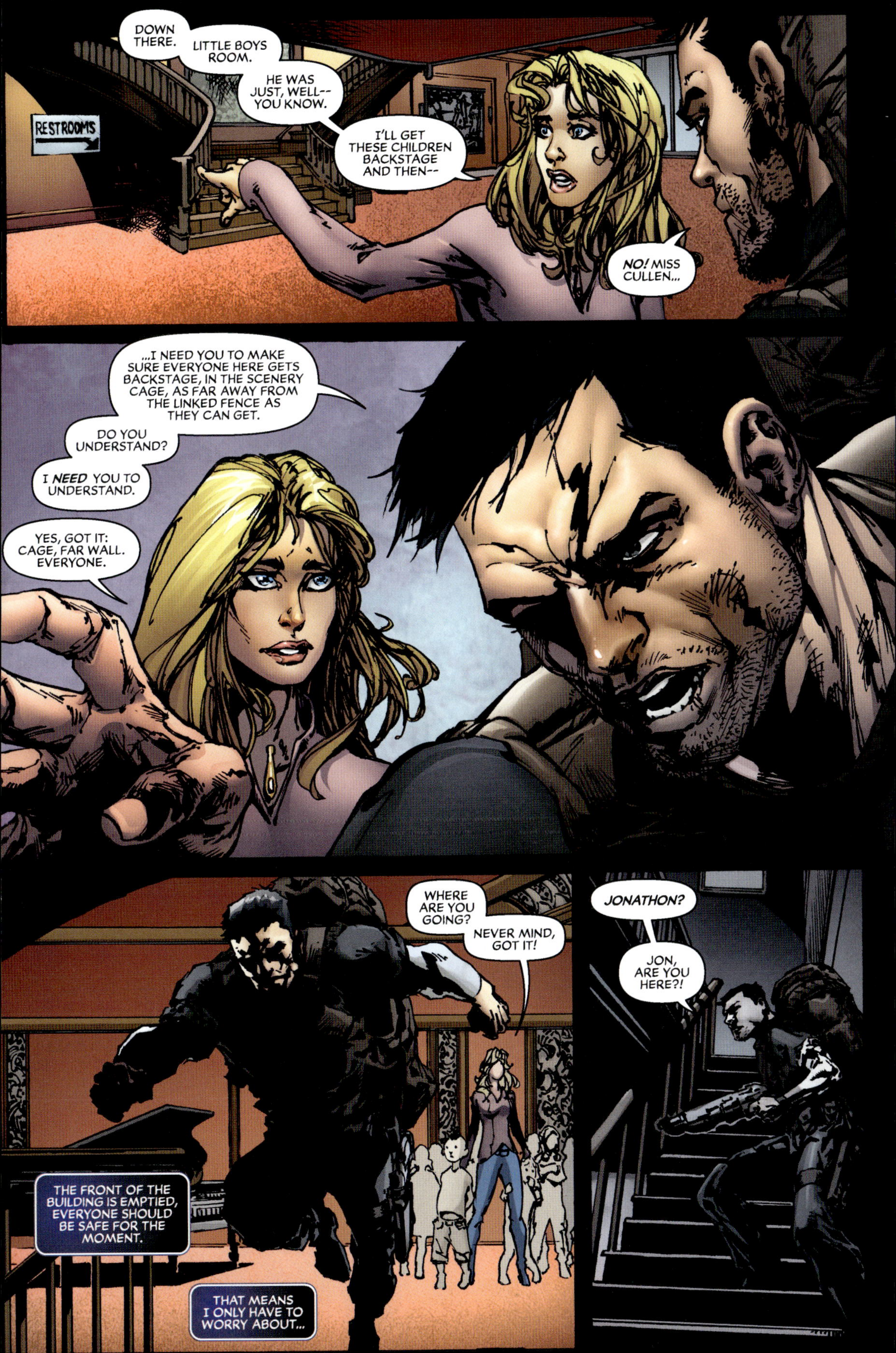
DOWN THERE.
LITTLE BOYS ROOM.
HE WAS JUST, WELL-- YOU KNOW.
I'LL GET THESE CHILDREN BACKSTAGE AND THEN--
RESTROOMS
NO! MISS CULLEN...
...I NEED YOU TO MAKE SURE EVERYONE HERE GETS BACKSTAGE, IN THE SCENERY CAGE, AS FAR AWAY FROM THE LINKED FENCE AS THEY CAN GET.
DO YOU UNDERSTAND?
I NEED YOU TO UNDERSTAND.
YES, GOT IT: CAGE, FAR WALL. EVERYONE.
WHERE ARE YOU GOING?
NEVER MIND, GOT IT!
THE FRONT OF THE BUILDING IS EMPTIED, EVERYONE SHOULD BE SAFE FOR THE MOMENT.
THAT MEANS I ONLY HAVE TO WORRY ABOUT...
JONATHON?
JON, ARE YOU HERE?!

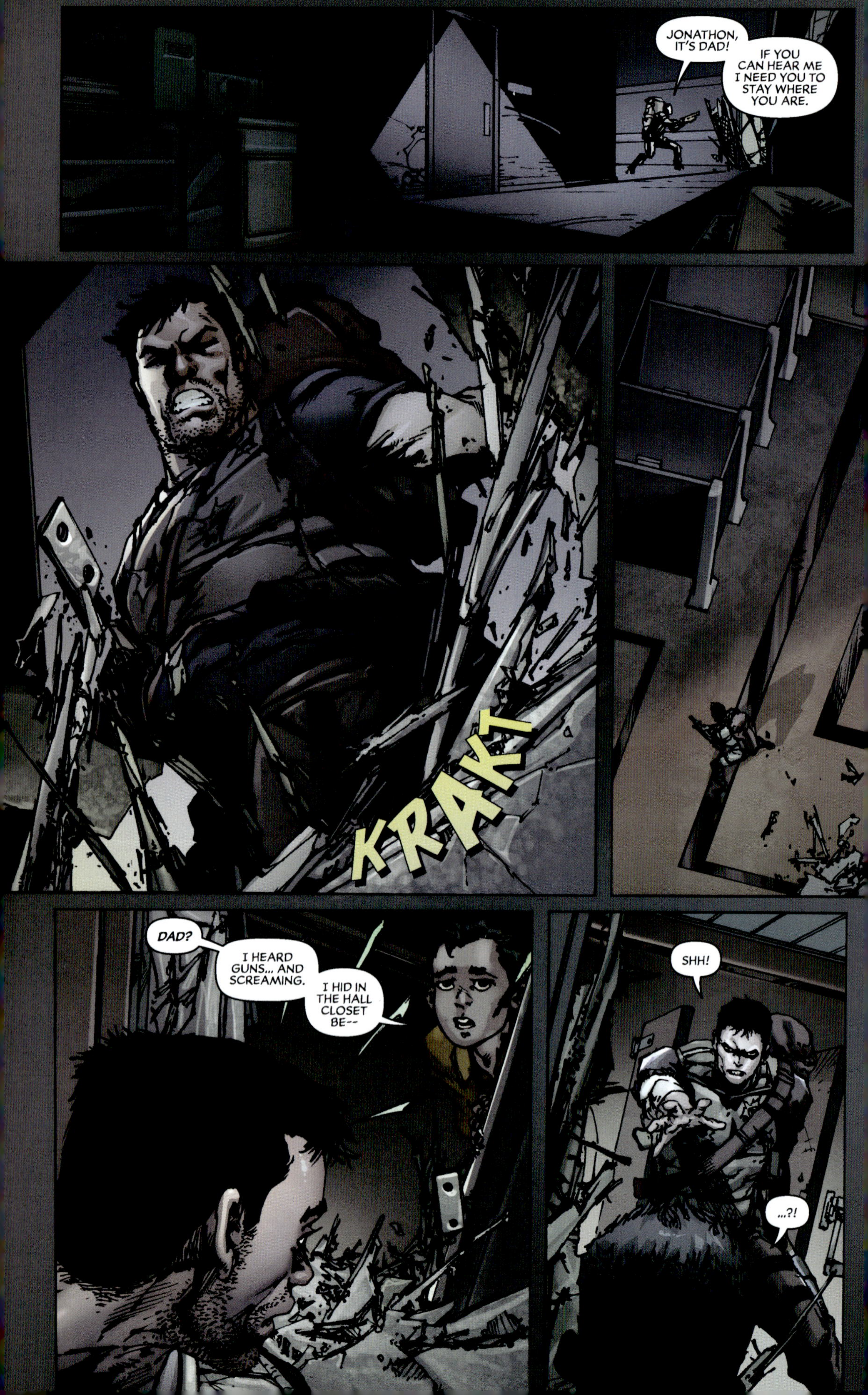
JONATHON, IT'S DAD!
IF YOU CAN HEAR ME I NEED YOU TO STAY WHERE YOU ARE.
KRAKT
DAD?
I HEARD GUNS... AND SCREAMING.
I HID IN THE HALL CLOSET BE--
SHH!
...?!

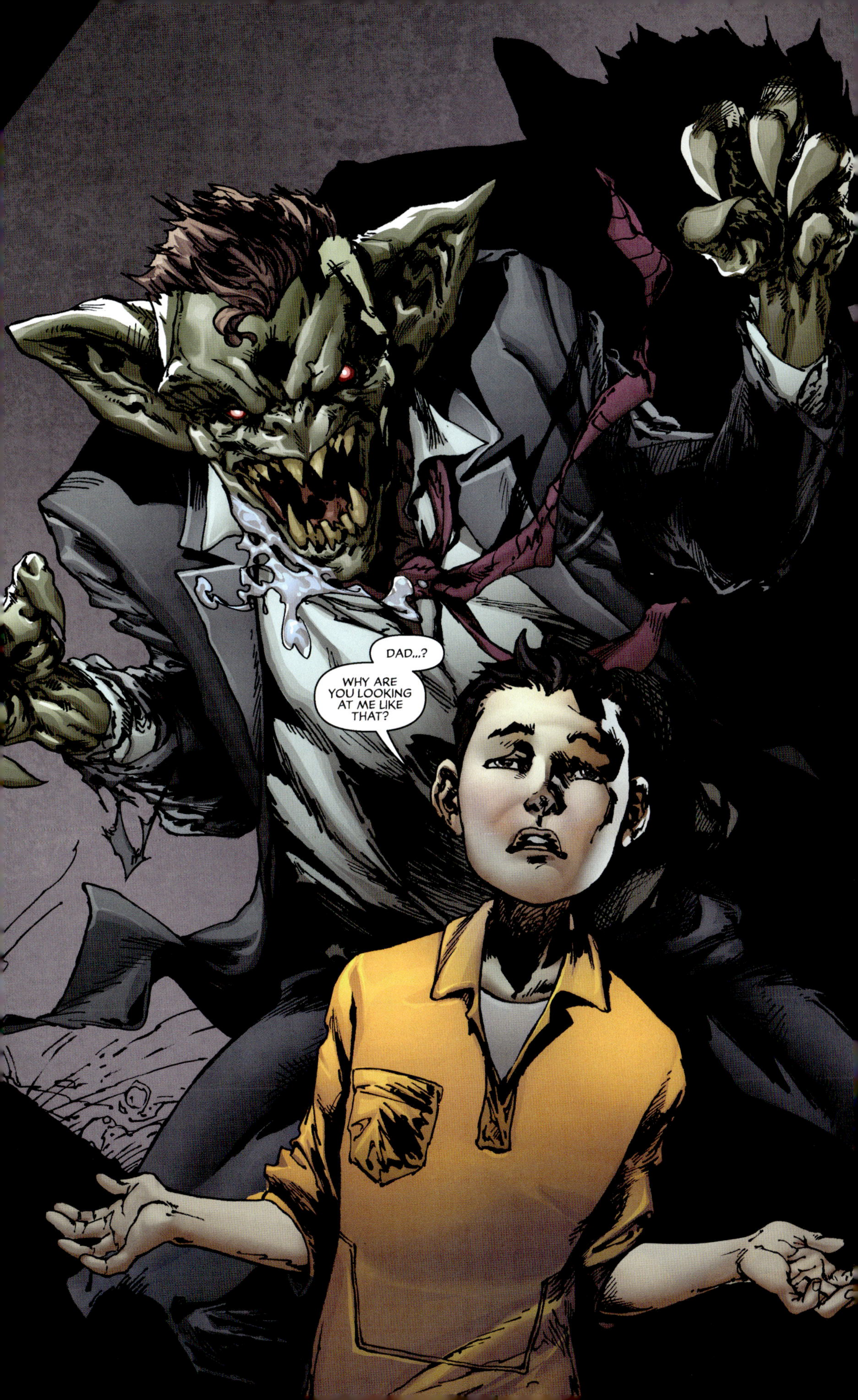
DAD...?
WHY ARE YOU LOOKING AT ME LIKE THAT?

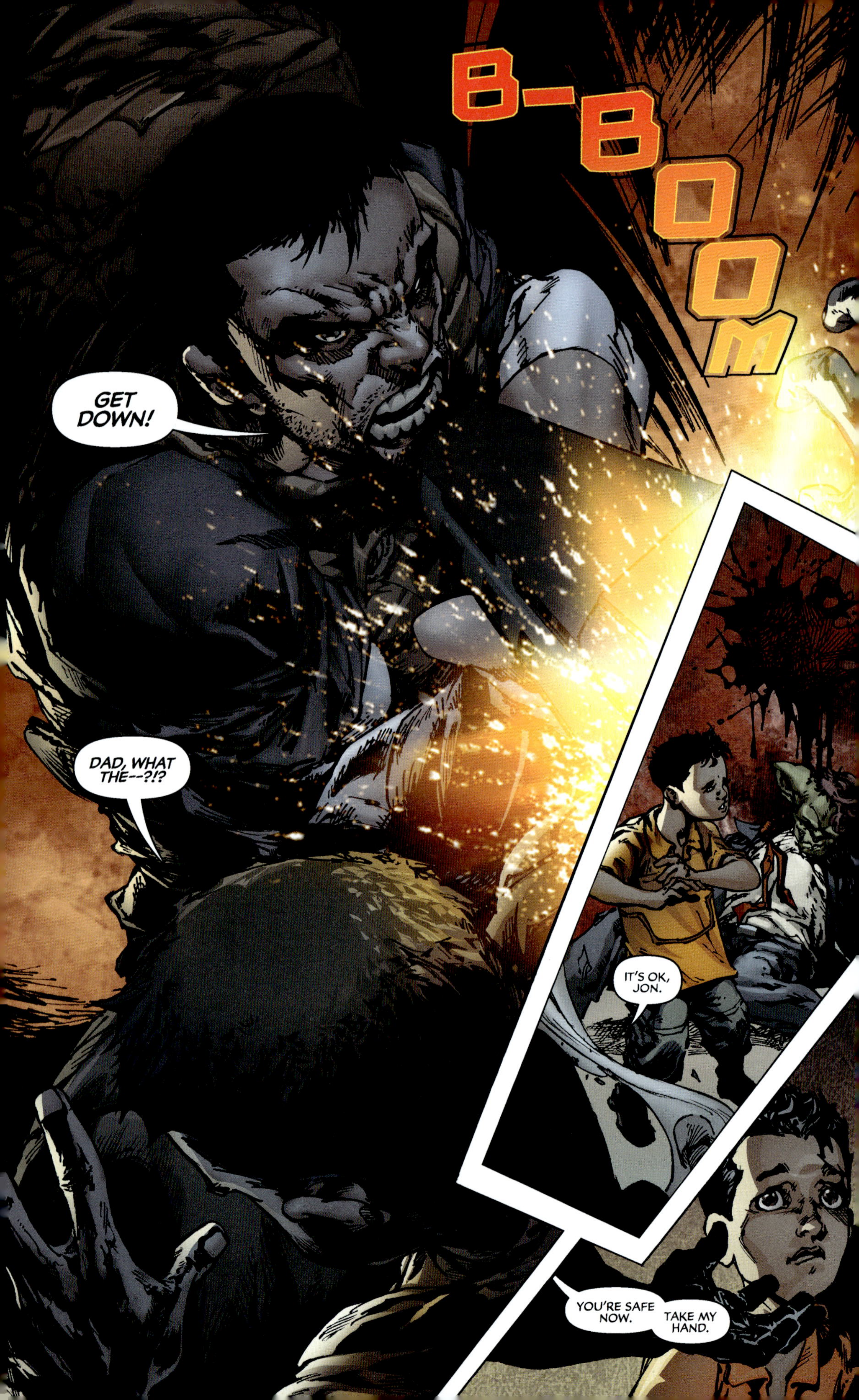
B-BOOM
GET DOWN!
DAD, WHAT THE--?!?
IT'S OK, JON.
YOU'RE SAFE NOW.
TAKE MY HAND.

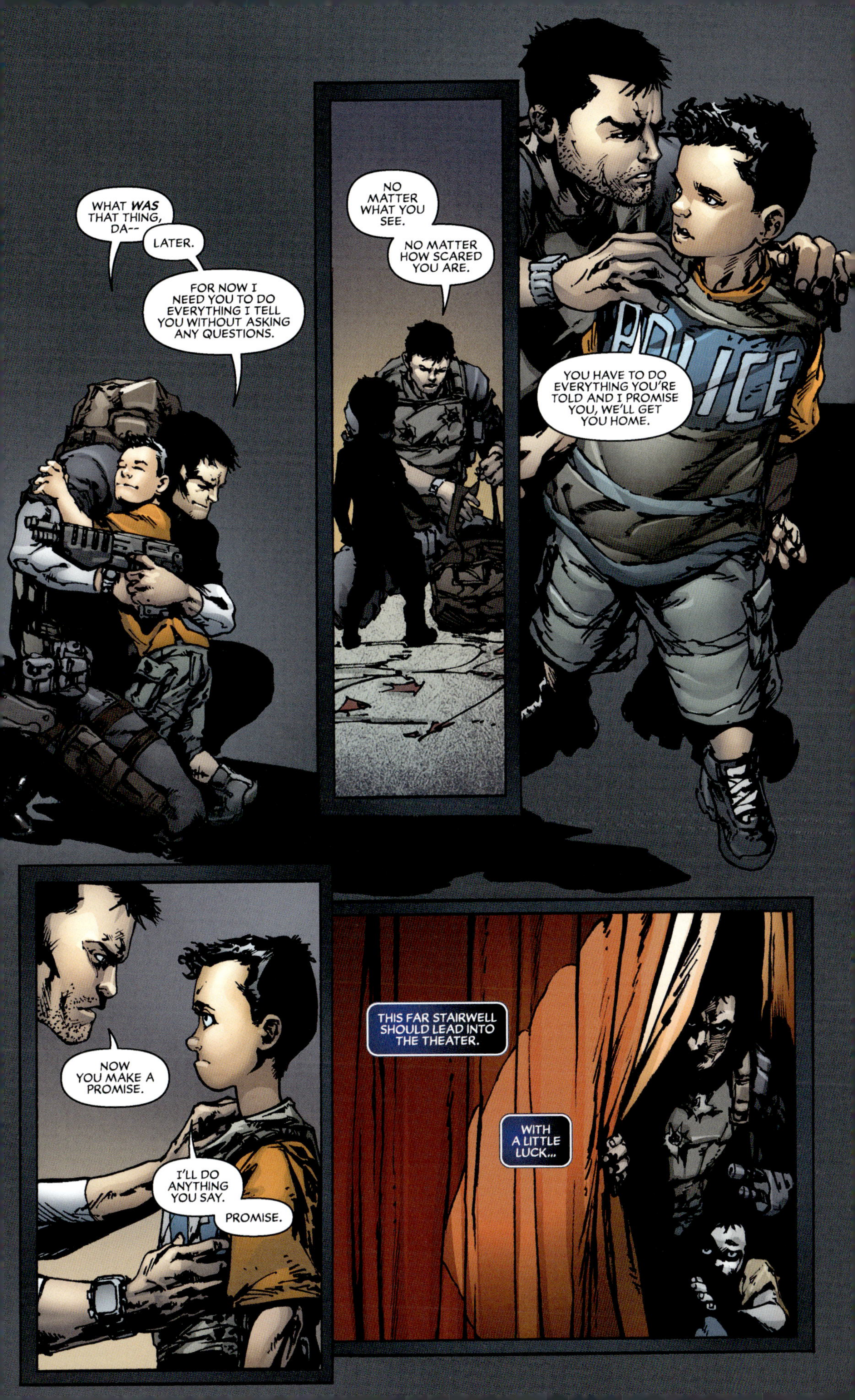

WHAT *WAS* THAT THING, DA--
LATER.
FOR NOW I NEED YOU TO DO EVERYTHING I TELL YOU WITHOUT ASKING ANY QUESTIONS.
NO MATTER WHAT YOU SEE.
NO MATTER HOW SCARED YOU ARE.
POLICE
YOU HAVE TO DO EVERYTHING YOU'RE TOLD AND I PROMISE YOU, WE'LL GET YOU HOME.
NOW YOU MAKE A PROMISE.
I'LL DO ANYTHING YOU SAY.
PROMISE.
THIS FAR STAIRWELL SHOULD LEAD INTO THE THEATER.
WITH A LITTLE LUCK...

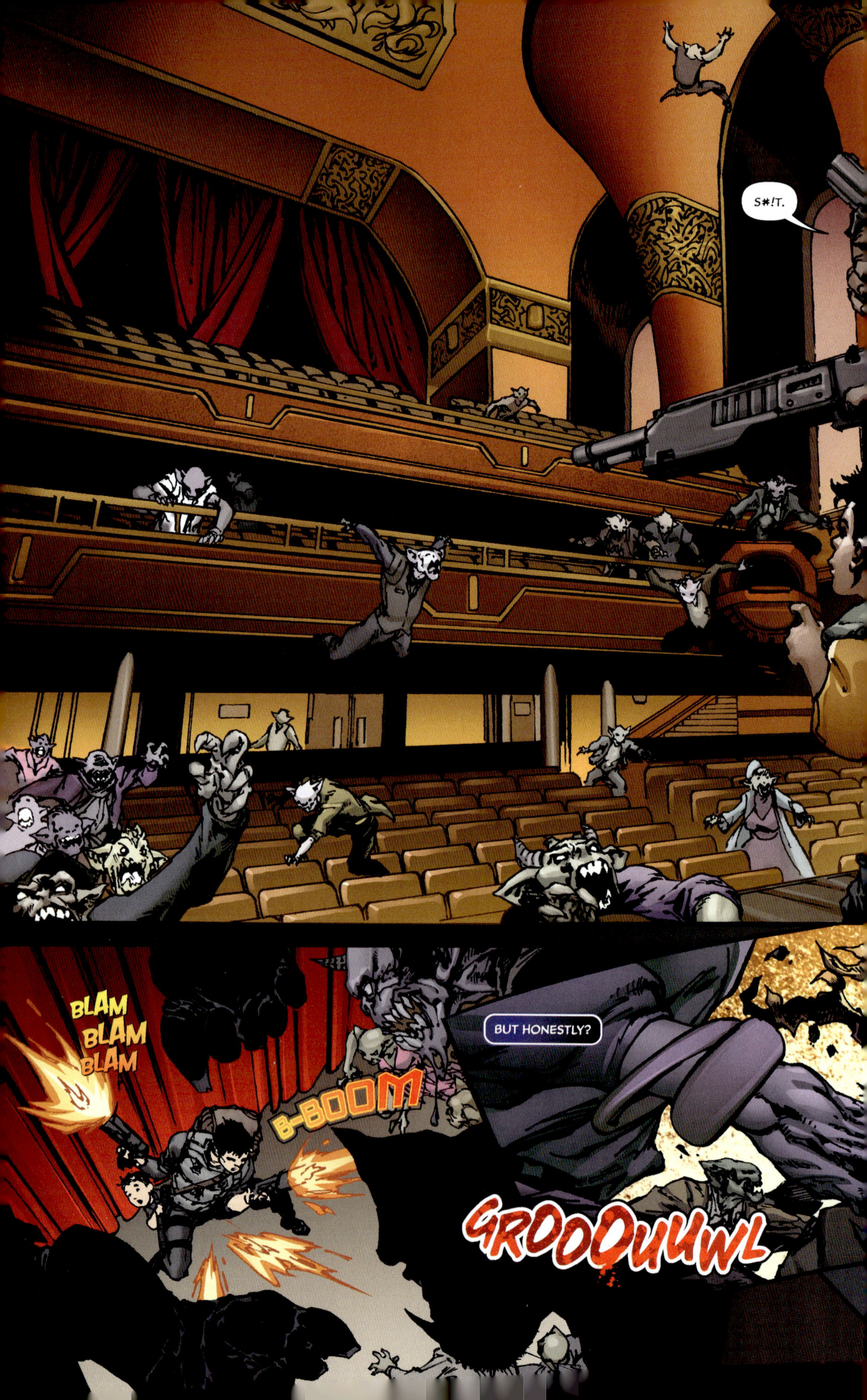
S#!T.
BLAM
BLAM
BLAM
B-BOOM
BUT HONESTLY?
GROOOUUUWL

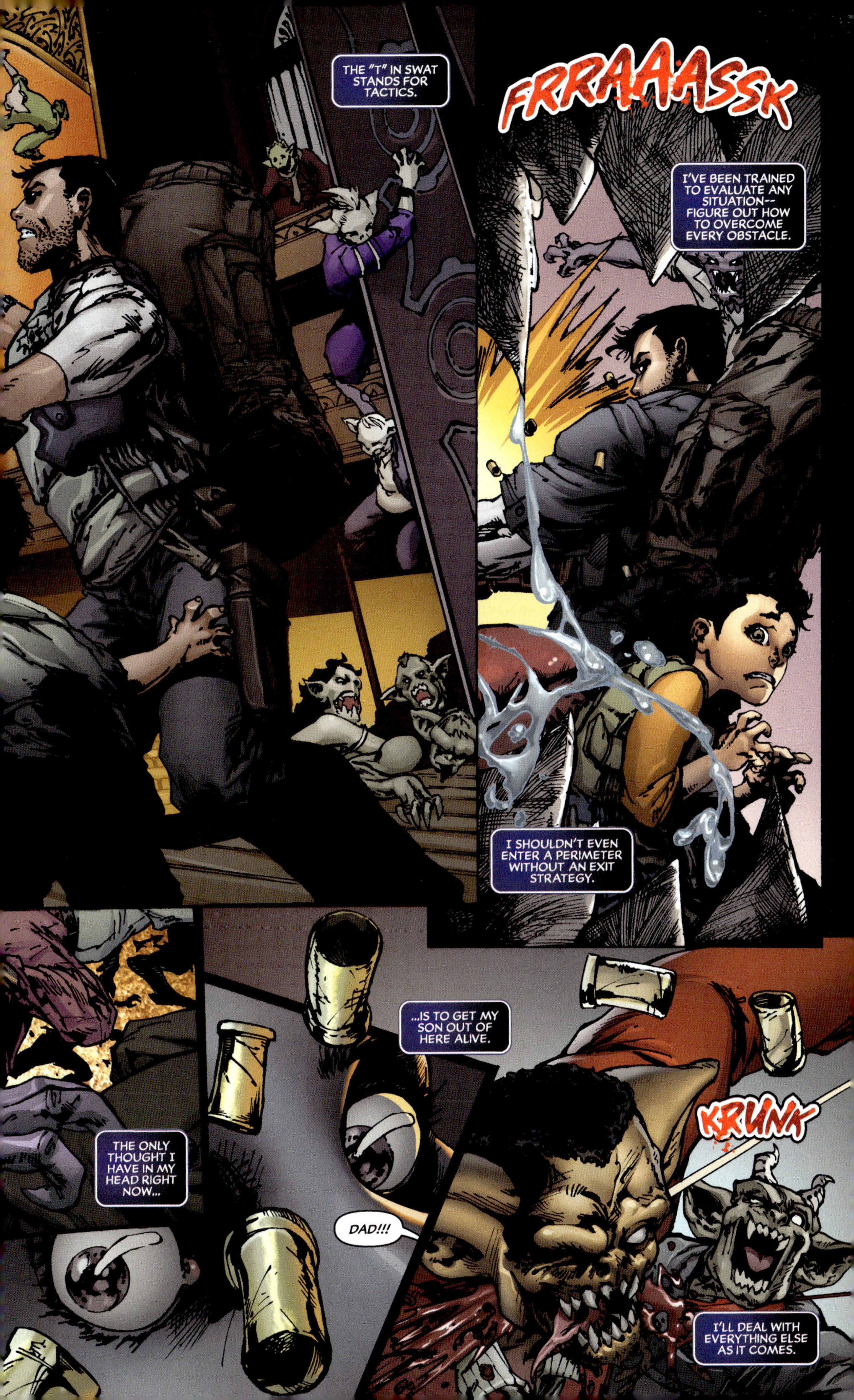
THE "T" IN SWAT STANDS FOR TACTICS.
FRRAAASSK
I'VE BEEN TRAINED TO EVALUATE ANY SITUATION-- FIGURE OUT HOW TO OVERCOME EVERY OBSTACLE.
I SHOULDN'T EVEN ENTER A PERIMETER WITHOUT AN EXIT STRATEGY.
THE ONLY THOUGHT I HAVE IN MY HEAD RIGHT NOW...
...IS TO GET MY SON OUT OF HERE ALIVE.
DAD!!!
KRUNK
I'LL DEAL WITH EVERYTHING ELSE AS IT COMES.

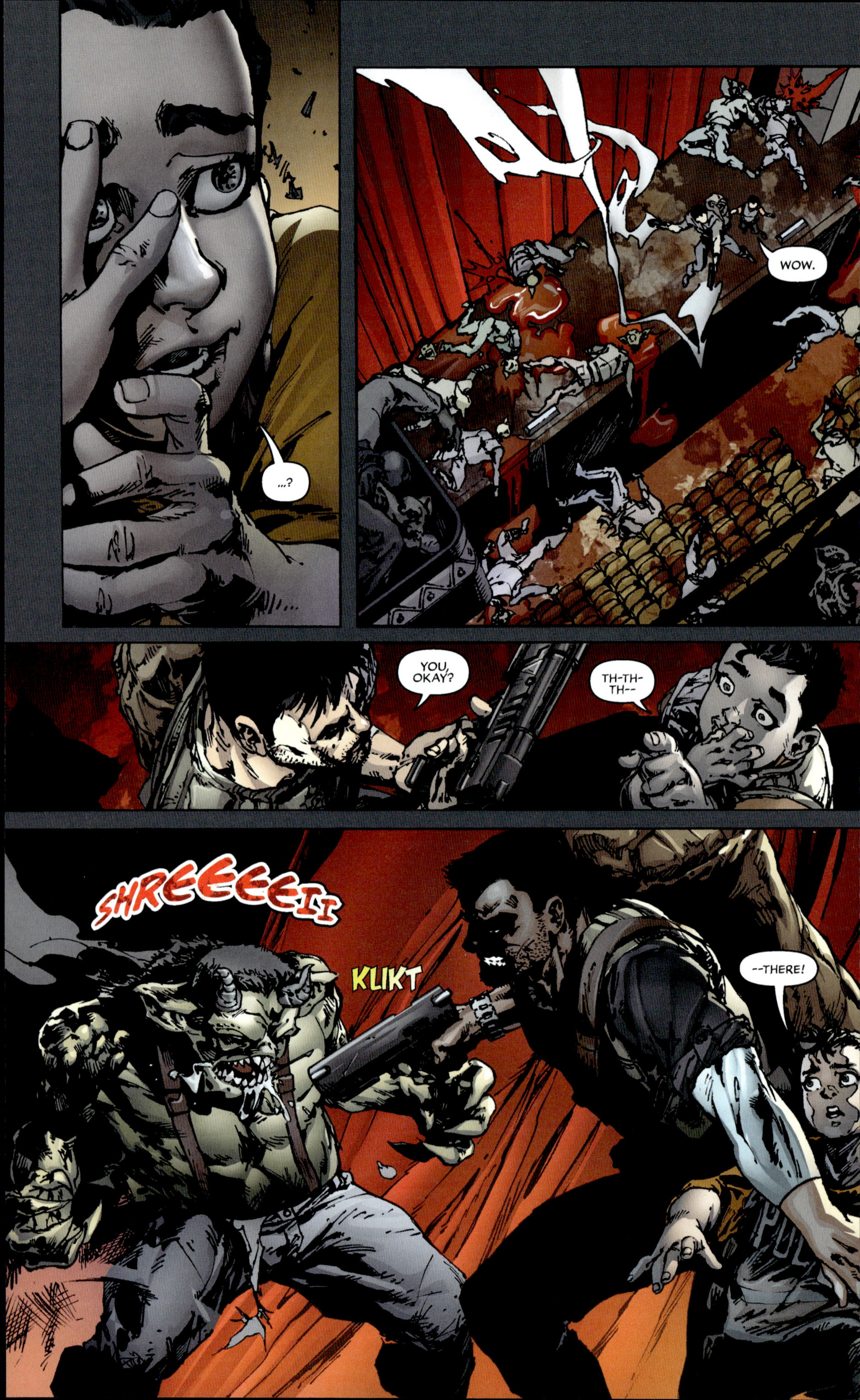
...?
WOW.
YOU, OKAY?
TH-TH-TH--
SHREEEEEII
KLIKT
--THERE!

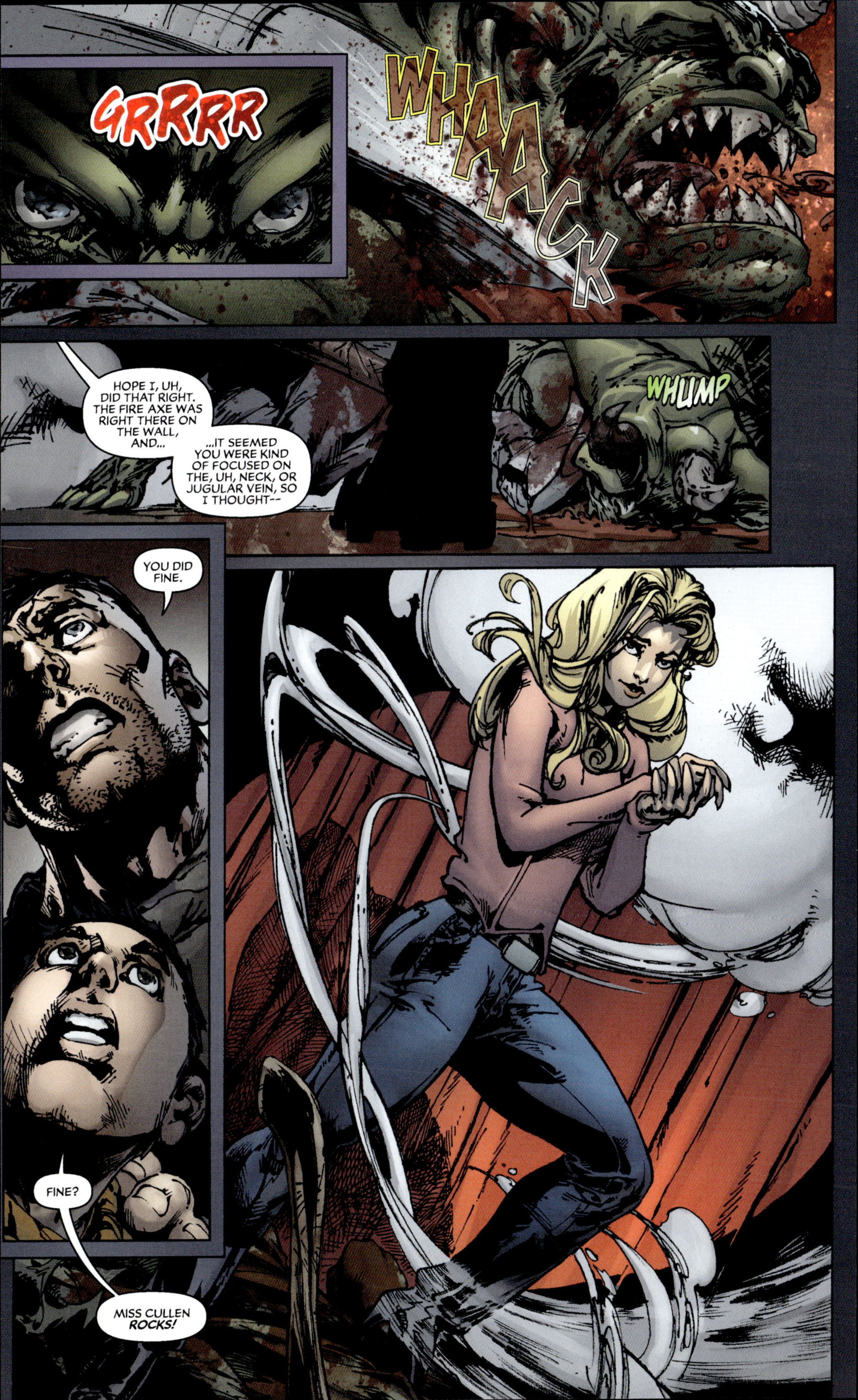
GRRRR
WHAAACK
HOPE I, UH, DID THAT RIGHT. THE FIRE AXE WAS RIGHT THERE ON THE WALL, AND...
...IT SEEMED YOU WERE KIND OF FOCUSED ON THE, UH, NECK, OR JUGULAR VEIN, SO I THOUGHT--
WHUMP
YOU DID FINE.
FINE?
MISS CULLEN *ROCKS!*

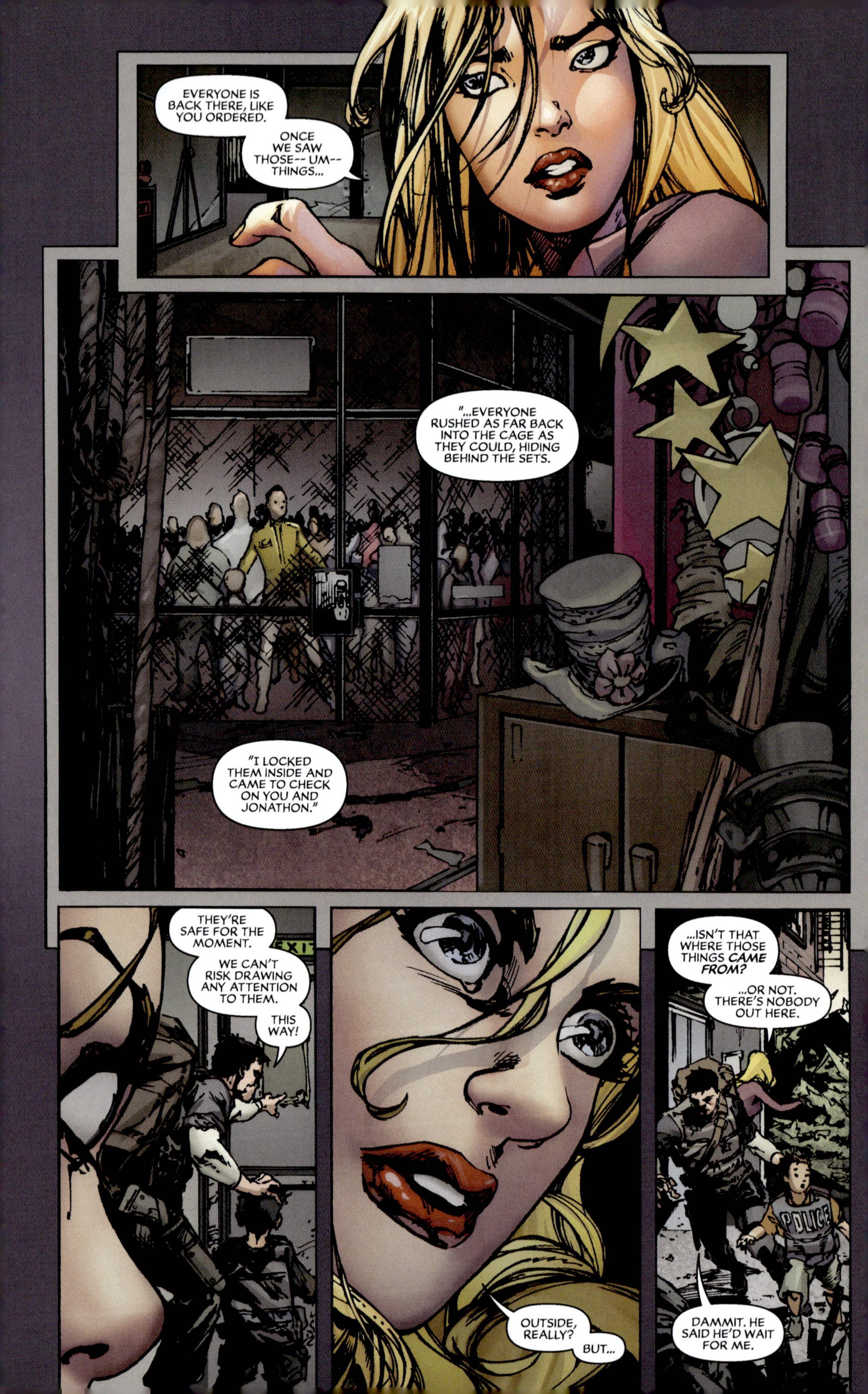
EVERYONE IS BACK THERE, LIKE YOU ORDERED.
ONCE WE SAW THOSE-- UM-- THINGS...
"...EVERYONE RUSHED AS FAR BACK INTO THE CAGE AS THEY COULD, HIDING BEHIND THE SETS.
"I LOCKED THEM INSIDE AND CAME TO CHECK ON YOU AND JONATHON."
THEY'RE SAFE FOR THE MOMENT.
WE CAN'T RISK DRAWING ANY ATTENTION TO THEM.
THIS WAY!
EXIT
OUTSIDE, REALLY? BUT...
...ISN'T THAT WHERE THOSE THINGS *CAME FROM?*
...OR NOT. THERE'S NOBODY OUT HERE.
POLICE
DAMMIT. HE SAID HE'D WAIT FOR ME.

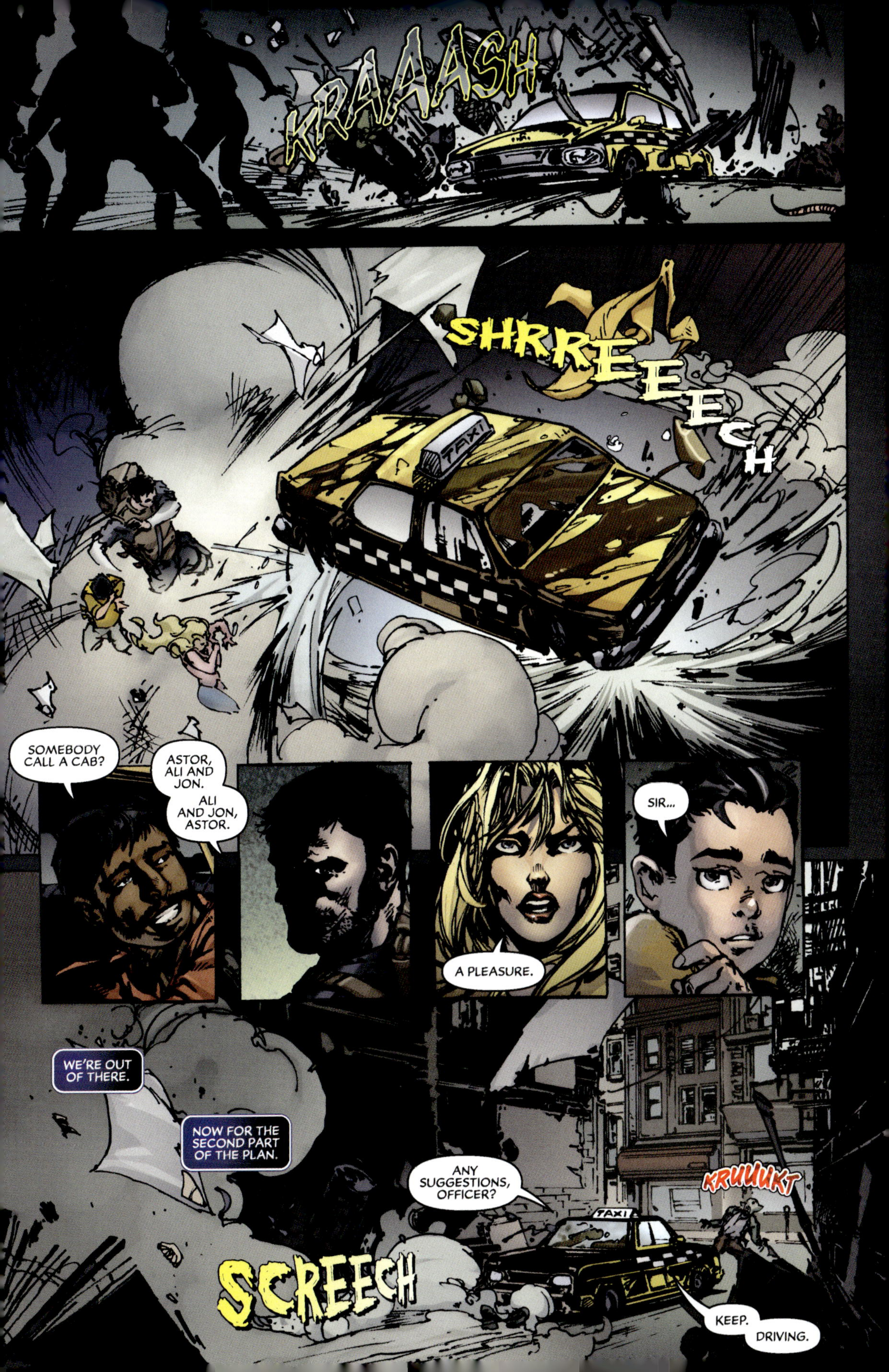
KRAAASH
SHRREEEECH
SOMEBODY CALL A CAB?
ASTOR, ALI AND JON.
ALI AND JON, ASTOR.
A PLEASURE.
SIR...
WE'RE OUT OF THERE.
NOW FOR THE SECOND PART OF THE PLAN.
ANY SUGGESTIONS, OFFICER?
KRUUUKT
SCREECH
KEEP.
DRIVING.

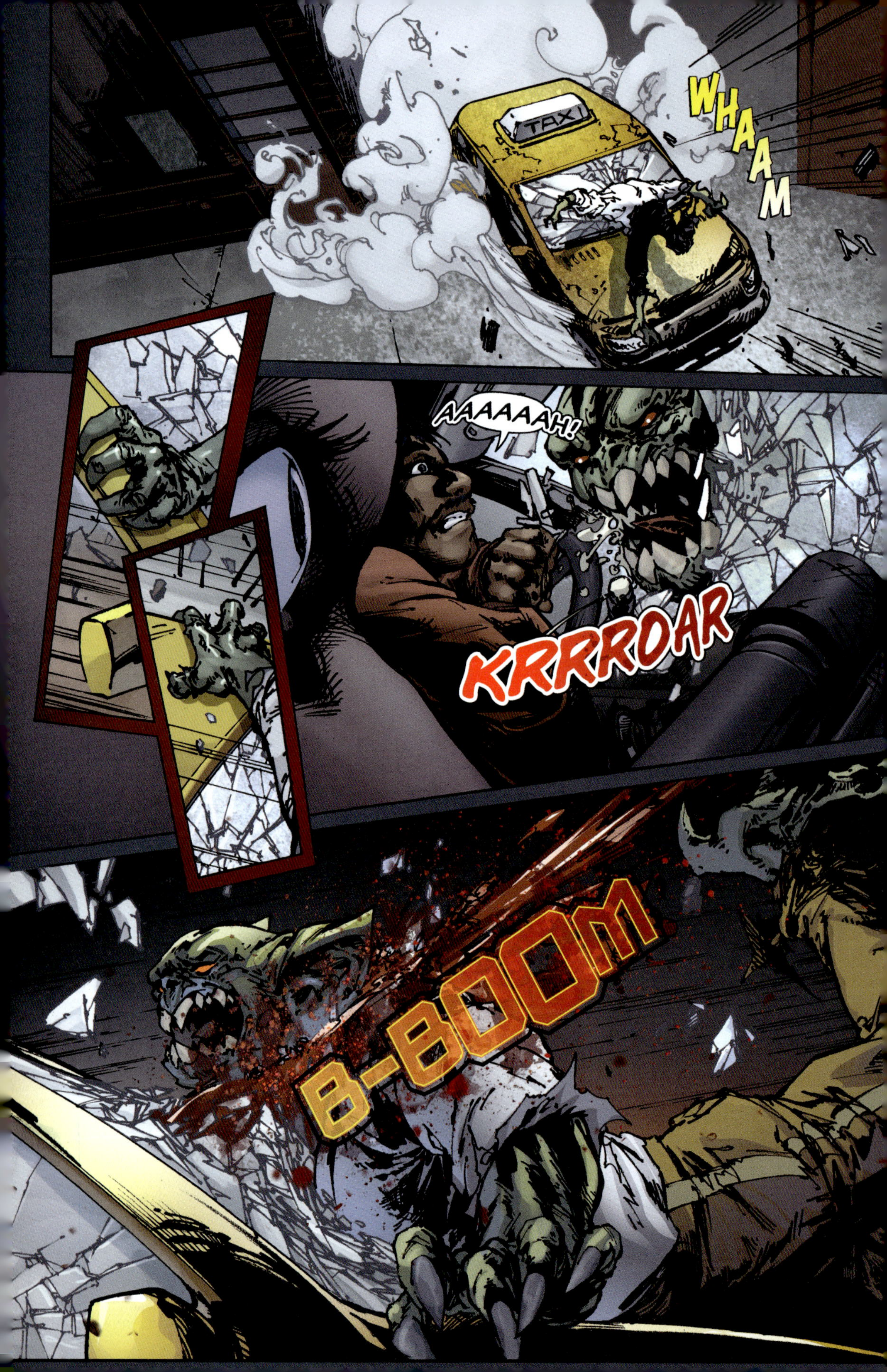

WHAAAM
TAX
AAAAAAH!
KRRROAR
B-BOOM

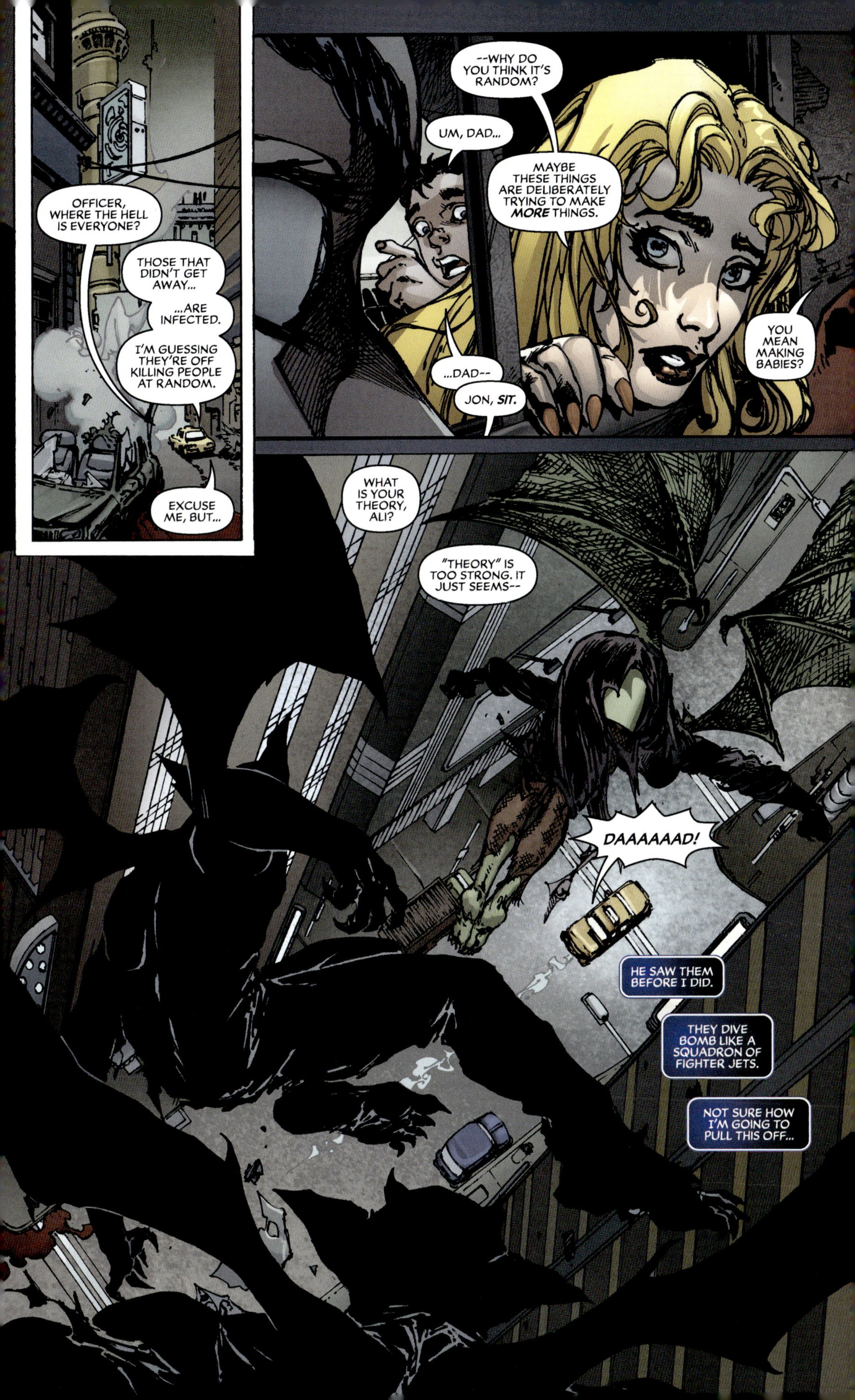
OFFICER, WHERE THE HELL IS EVERYONE?
THOSE THAT DIDN'T GET AWAY...
...ARE INFECTED.
I'M GUESSING THEY'RE OFF KILLING PEOPLE AT RANDOM.
EXCUSE ME, BUT...
--WHY DO YOU THINK IT'S RANDOM?
UM, DAD...
MAYBE THESE THINGS ARE DELIBERATELY TRYING TO MAKE *MORE* THINGS.
YOU MEAN MAKING BABIES?
...DAD--
JON, *SIT.*
WHAT IS YOUR THEORY, ALI?
"THEORY" IS TOO STRONG. IT JUST SEEMS--
DAAAAAAD!
HE SAW THEM BEFORE I DID.
THEY DIVE BOMB LIKE A SQUADRON OF FIGHTER JETS.
NOT SURE HOW I'M GOING TO PULL THIS OFF...

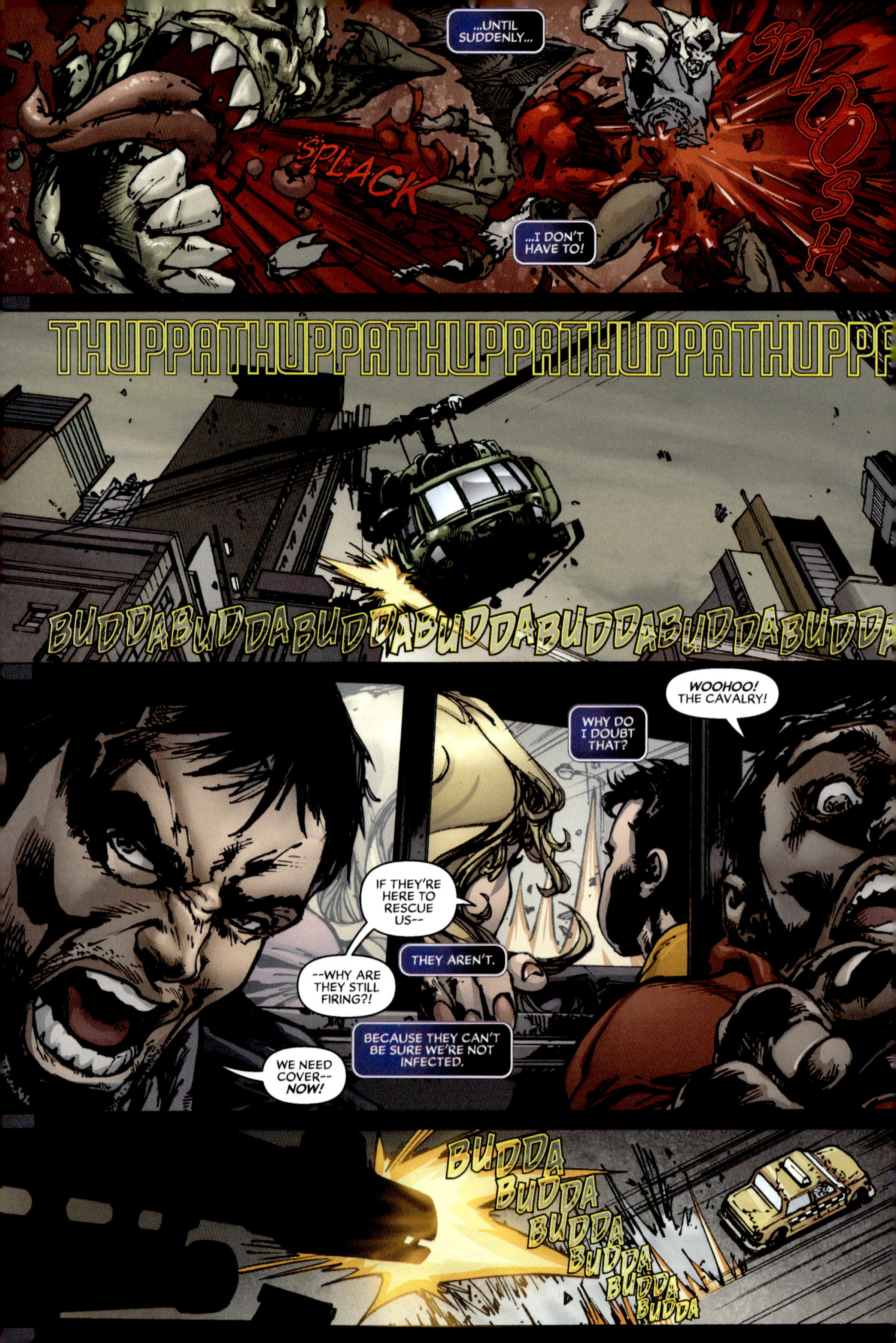

...UNTIL SUDDENLY...
SPLACK
SPLOOSH
...I DON'T HAVE TO!
THUPPATHUPPATHUPPATHUPPATHUPPA
BUDDABUDDABUDDABUDDABUDDABUDDABUDDA
WOOHOO! THE CAVALRY!
WHY DO I DOUBT THAT?
IF THEY'RE HERE TO RESCUE US--
THEY AREN'T.
--WHY ARE THEY STILL FIRING?!
BECAUSE THEY CAN'T BE SURE WE'RE NOT INFECTED.
WE NEED COVER--NOW!
BUDDA BUDDA BUDDA BUDDA BUDDA BUDDA

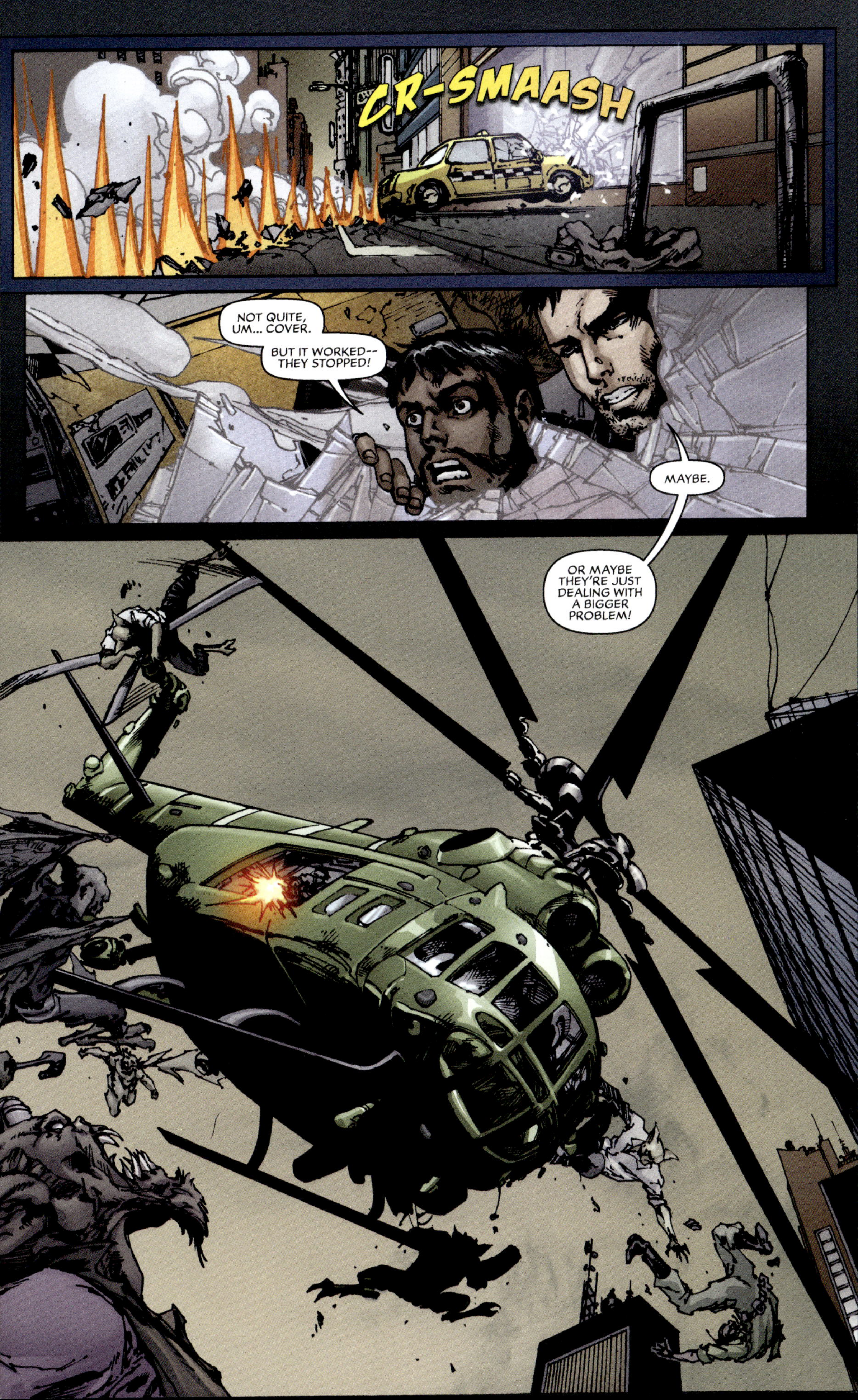
CR-SMAASH
NOT QUITE, UM... COVER.
BUT IT WORKED-- THEY STOPPED!
MAYBE.
OR MAYBE THEY'RE JUST DEALING WITH A BIGGER PROBLEM!

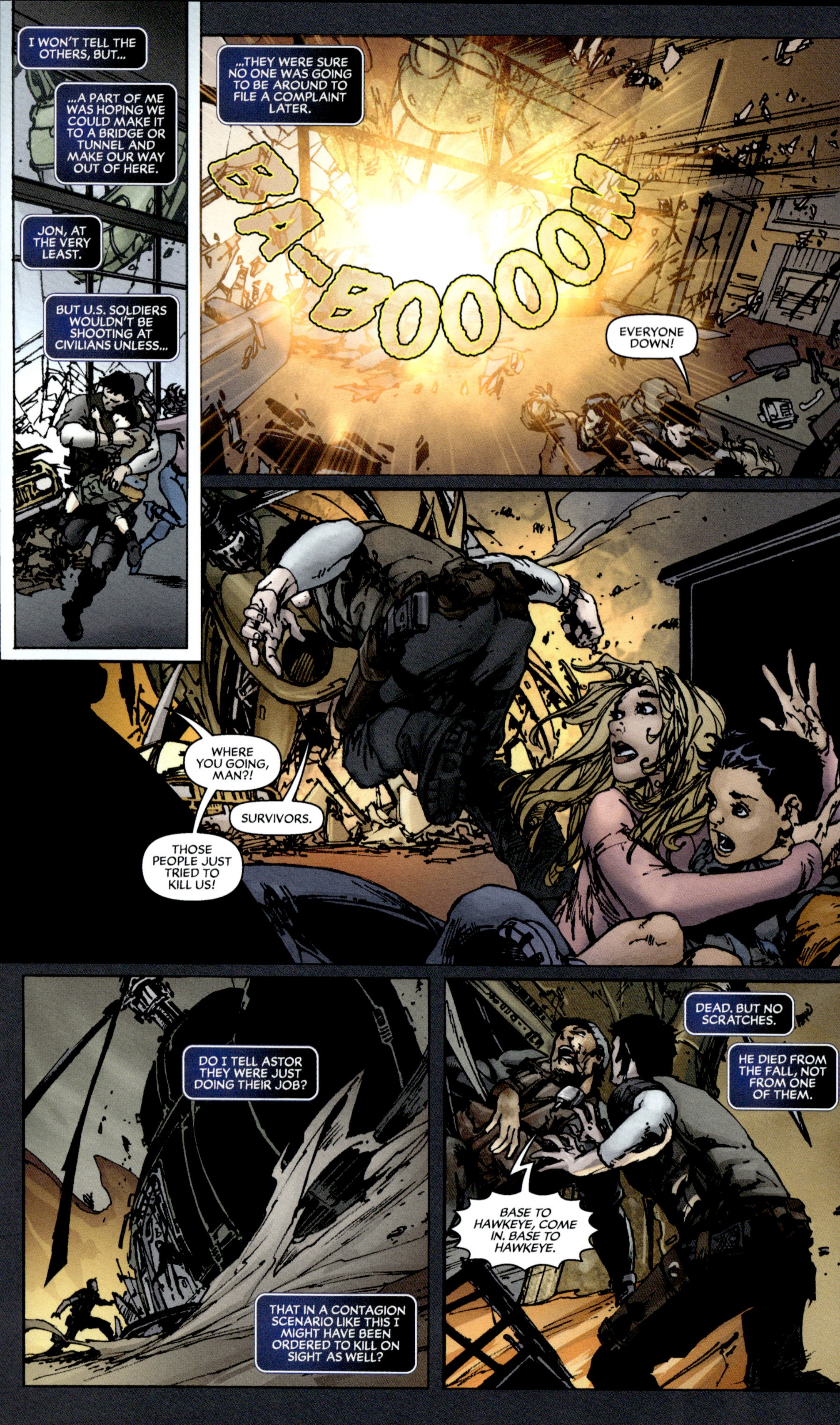

I WON'T TELL THE OTHERS, BUT...
...A PART OF ME WAS HOPING WE COULD MAKE IT TO A BRIDGE OR TUNNEL AND MAKE OUR WAY OUT OF HERE.
JON, AT THE VERY LEAST.
BUT U.S. SOLDIERS WOULDN'T BE SHOOTING AT CIVILIANS UNLESS...
...THEY WERE SURE NO ONE WAS GOING TO BE AROUND TO FILE A COMPLAINT LATER.
BA-BOOOOM!
EVERYONE DOWN!
WHERE YOU GOING, MAN?!
SURVIVORS.
THOSE PEOPLE JUST TRIED TO KILL US!
DO I TELL ASTOR THEY WERE JUST DOING THEIR JOB?
THAT IN A CONTAGION SCENARIO LIKE THIS I MIGHT HAVE BEEN ORDERED TO KILL ON SIGHT AS WELL?
DEAD. BUT NO SCRATCHES.
HE DIED FROM THE FALL, NOT FROM ONE OF THEM.
BASE TO HAWKEYE, COME IN. BASE TO HAWKEYE.

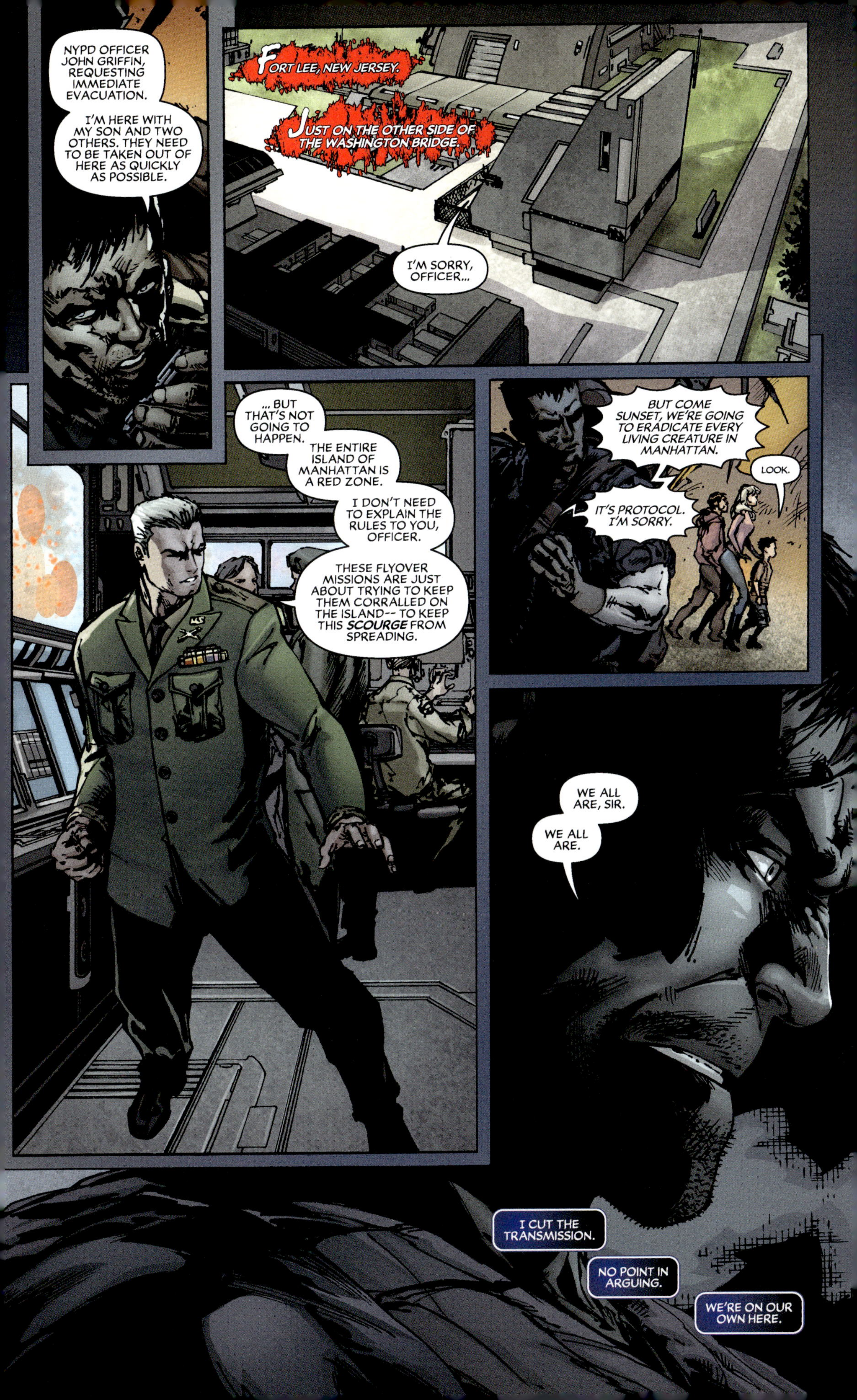
NYPD OFFICER JOHN GRIFFIN, REQUESTING IMMEDIATE EVACUATION.
I'M HERE WITH MY SON AND TWO OTHERS. THEY NEED TO BE TAKEN OUT OF HERE AS QUICKLY AS POSSIBLE.
FORT LEE, NEW JERSEY.
JUST ON THE OTHER SIDE OF THE WASHINGTON BRIDGE.
I'M SORRY, OFFICER...
... BUT THAT'S NOT GOING TO HAPPEN.
THE ENTIRE ISLAND OF MANHATTAN IS A RED ZONE.
I DON'T NEED TO EXPLAIN THE RULES TO YOU, OFFICER.
THESE FLYOVER MISSIONS ARE JUST ABOUT TRYING TO KEEP THEM CORRALLED ON THE ISLAND-- TO KEEP THIS SCOURGE FROM SPREADING.
BUT COME SUNSET, WE'RE GOING TO ERADICATE EVERY LIVING CREATURE IN MANHATTAN.
IT'S PROTOCOL. I'M SORRY.
LOOK.
WE ALL ARE, SIR.
WE ALL ARE.
I CUT THE TRANSMISSION.
NO POINT IN ARGUING.
WE'RE ON OUR OWN HERE.

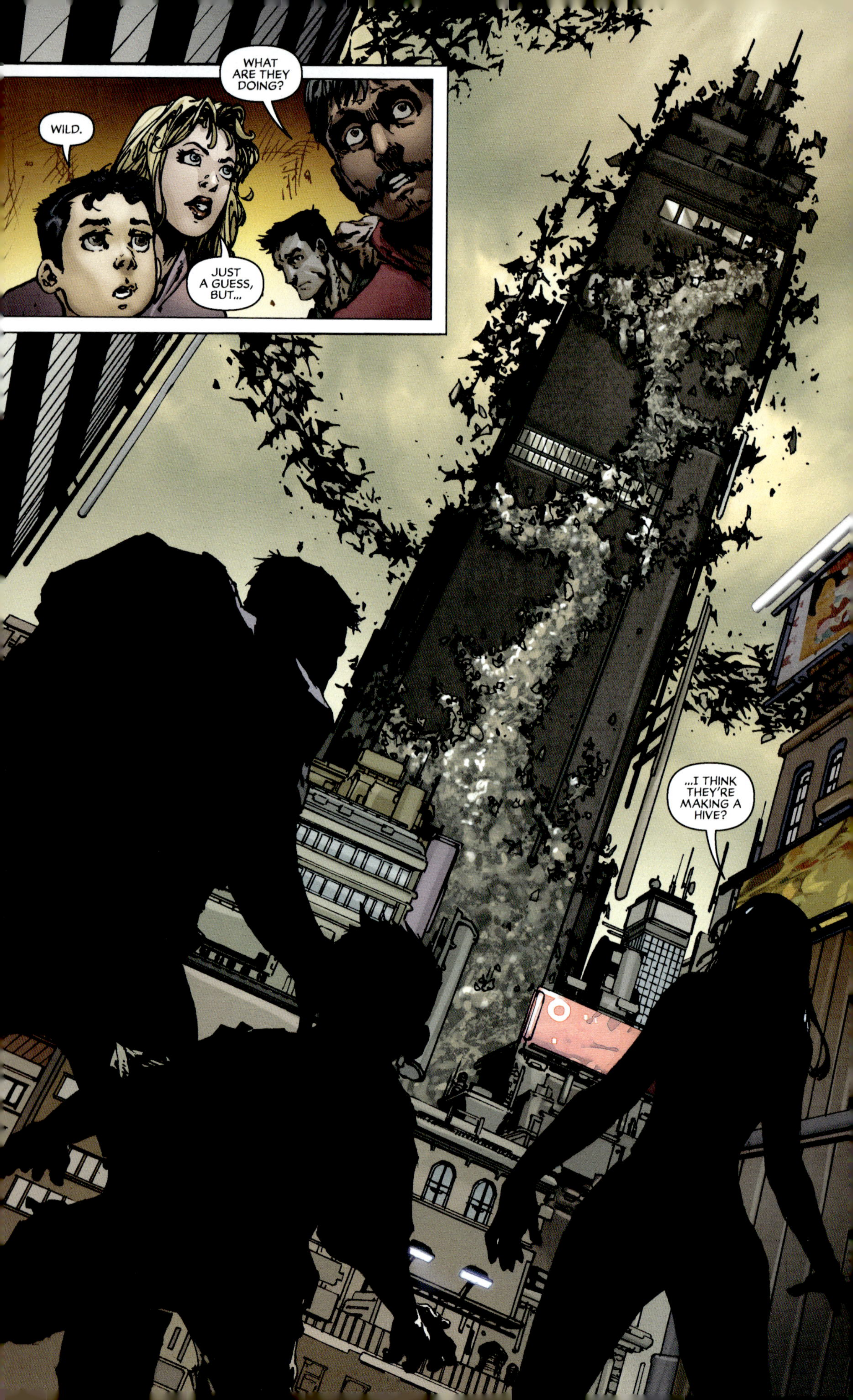
WILD.
WHAT ARE THEY DOING?
JUST A GUESS, BUT...
...I THINK THEY'RE MAKING A HIVE?

CHAPTER FOUR

"Tunnel of Hell"

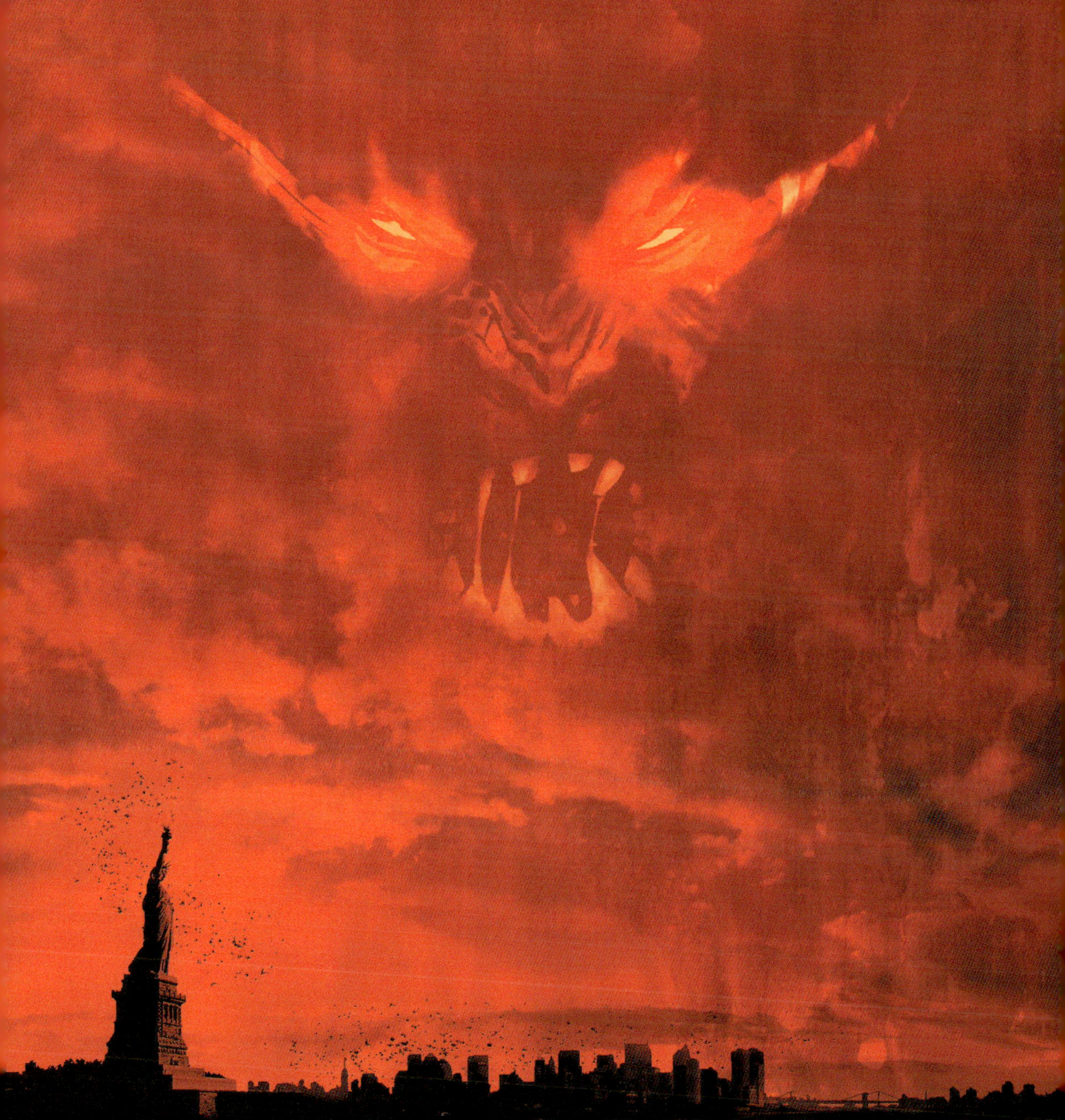

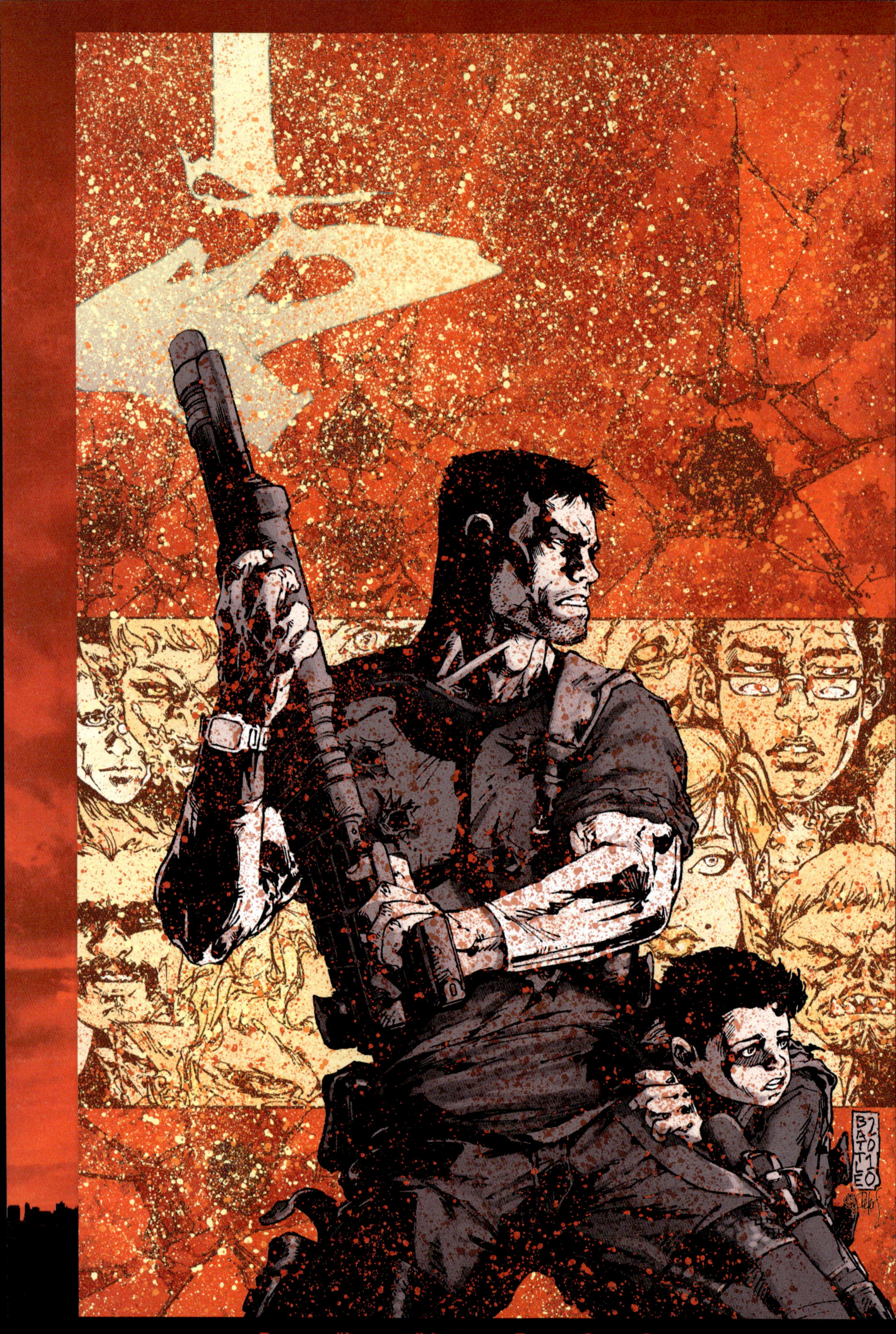

Retailer "Infected" Incentive Edition Cover C to

THE SCOURGE #4

by

Eric **BATTLE** | Peter **STEIGERWALD**

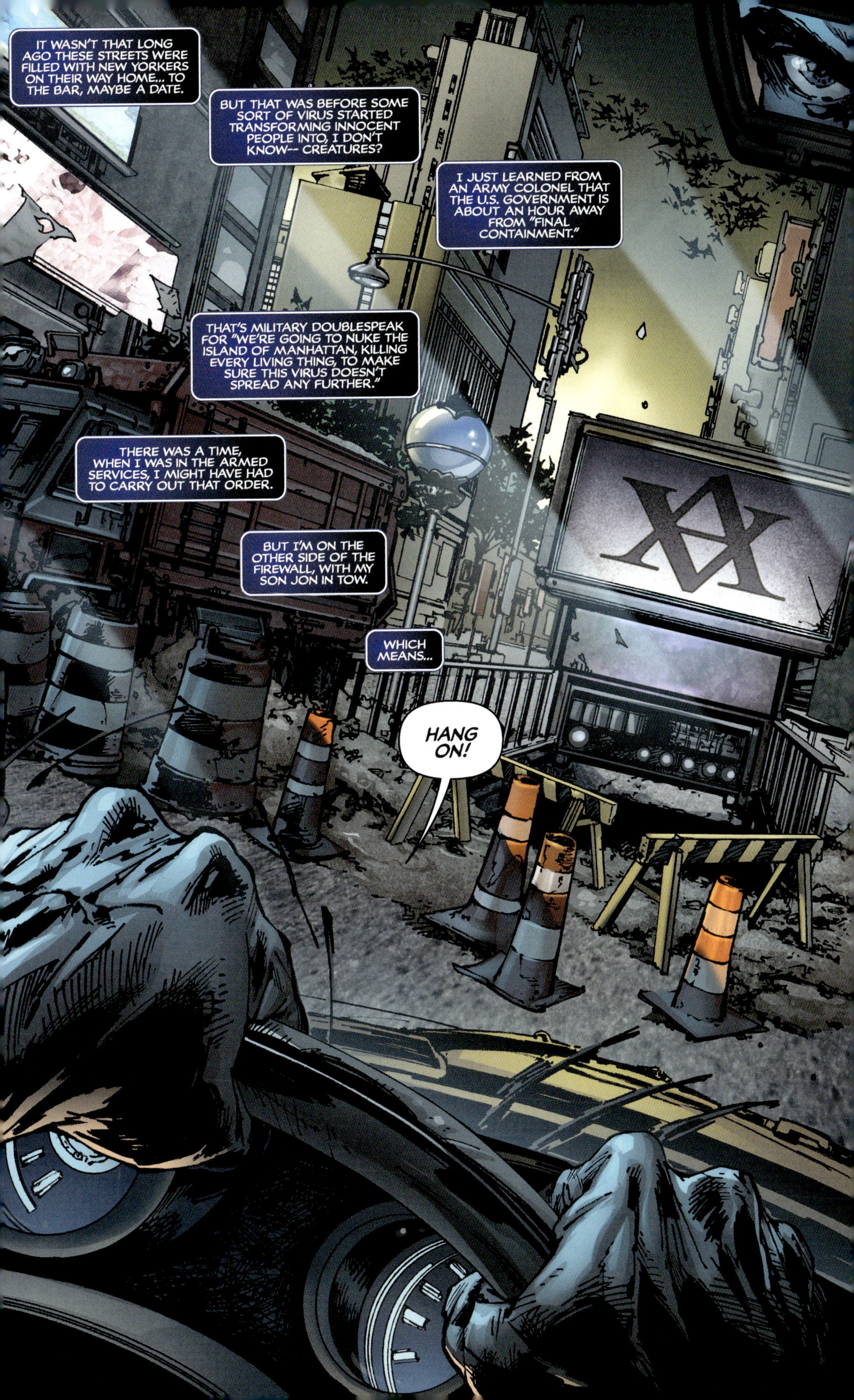
IT WASN'T THAT LONG AGO THESE STREETS WERE FILLED WITH NEW YORKERS ON THEIR WAY HOME... TO THE BAR, MAYBE A DATE.
BUT THAT WAS BEFORE SOME SORT OF VIRUS STARTED TRANSFORMING INNOCENT PEOPLE INTO, I DON'T KNOW-- CREATURES?
I JUST LEARNED FROM AN ARMY COLONEL THAT THE U.S. GOVERNMENT IS ABOUT AN HOUR AWAY FROM "FINAL CONTAINMENT."
THAT'S MILITARY DOUBLESPEAK FOR "WE'RE GOING TO NUKE THE ISLAND OF MANHATTAN, KILLING EVERY LIVING THING, TO MAKE SURE THIS VIRUS DOESN'T SPREAD ANY FURTHER."
THERE WAS A TIME, WHEN I WAS IN THE ARMED SERVICES, I MIGHT HAVE HAD TO CARRY OUT THAT ORDER.
BUT I'M ON THE OTHER SIDE OF THE FIREWALL, WITH MY SON JON IN TOW.
WHICH MEANS...
HANG ON!

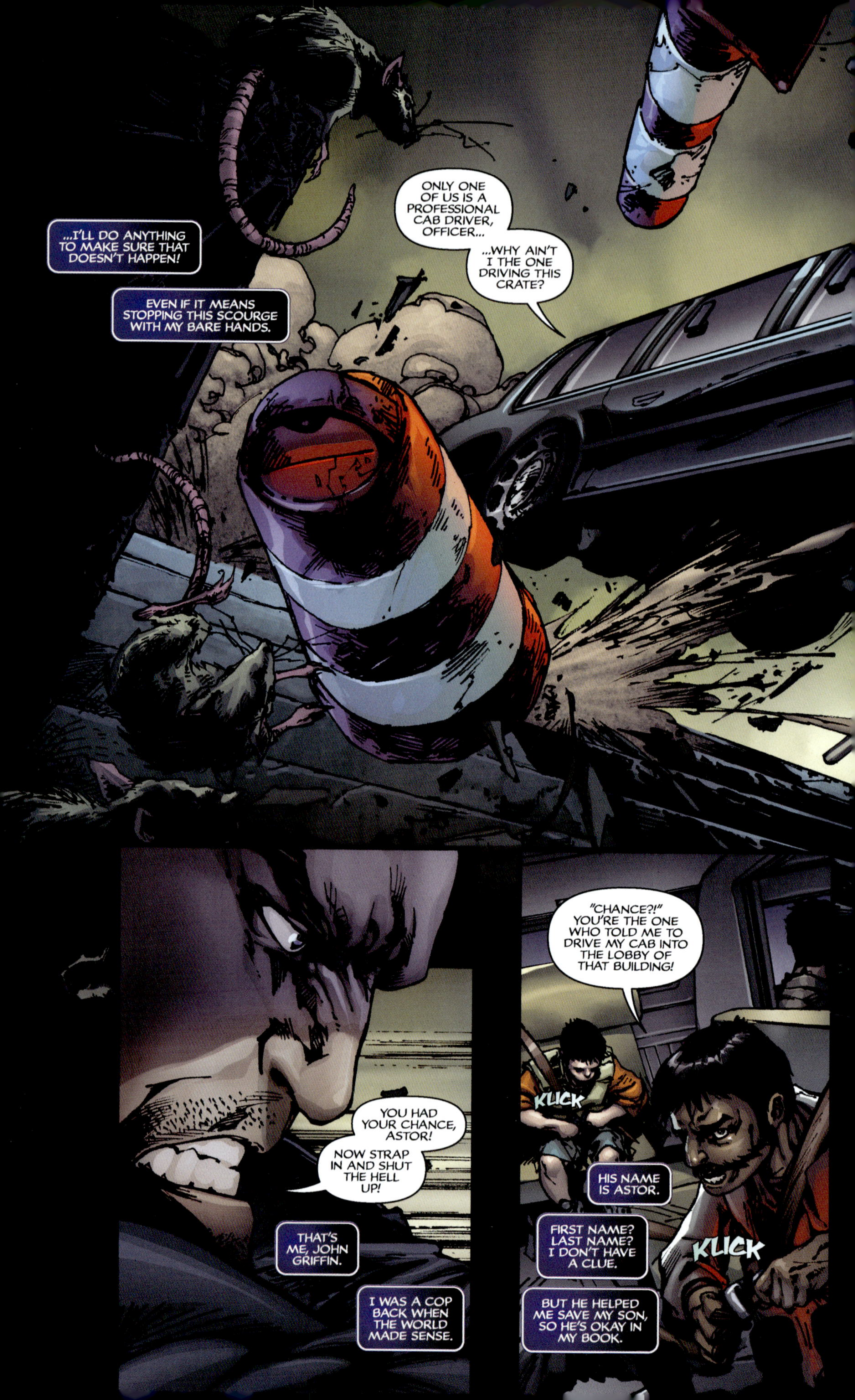

...I'LL DO ANYTHING TO MAKE SURE THAT DOESN'T HAPPEN!
EVEN IF IT MEANS STOPPING THIS SCOURGE WITH MY BARE HANDS.
ONLY ONE OF US IS A PROFESSIONAL CAB DRIVER, OFFICER...
...WHY AIN'T I THE ONE DRIVING THIS CRATE?
YOU HAD YOUR CHANCE, ASTOR!
NOW STRAP IN AND SHUT THE HELL UP!
THAT'S ME, JOHN GRIFFIN.
I WAS A COP BACK WHEN THE WORLD MADE SENSE.
"CHANCE?!" YOU'RE THE ONE WHO TOLD ME TO DRIVE MY CAB INTO THE LOBBY OF THAT BUILDING!
KLICK
HIS NAME IS ASTOR.
FIRST NAME? LAST NAME? I DON'T HAVE A CLUE.
KLICK
BUT HE HELPED ME SAVE MY SON, SO HE'S OKAY IN MY BOOK.

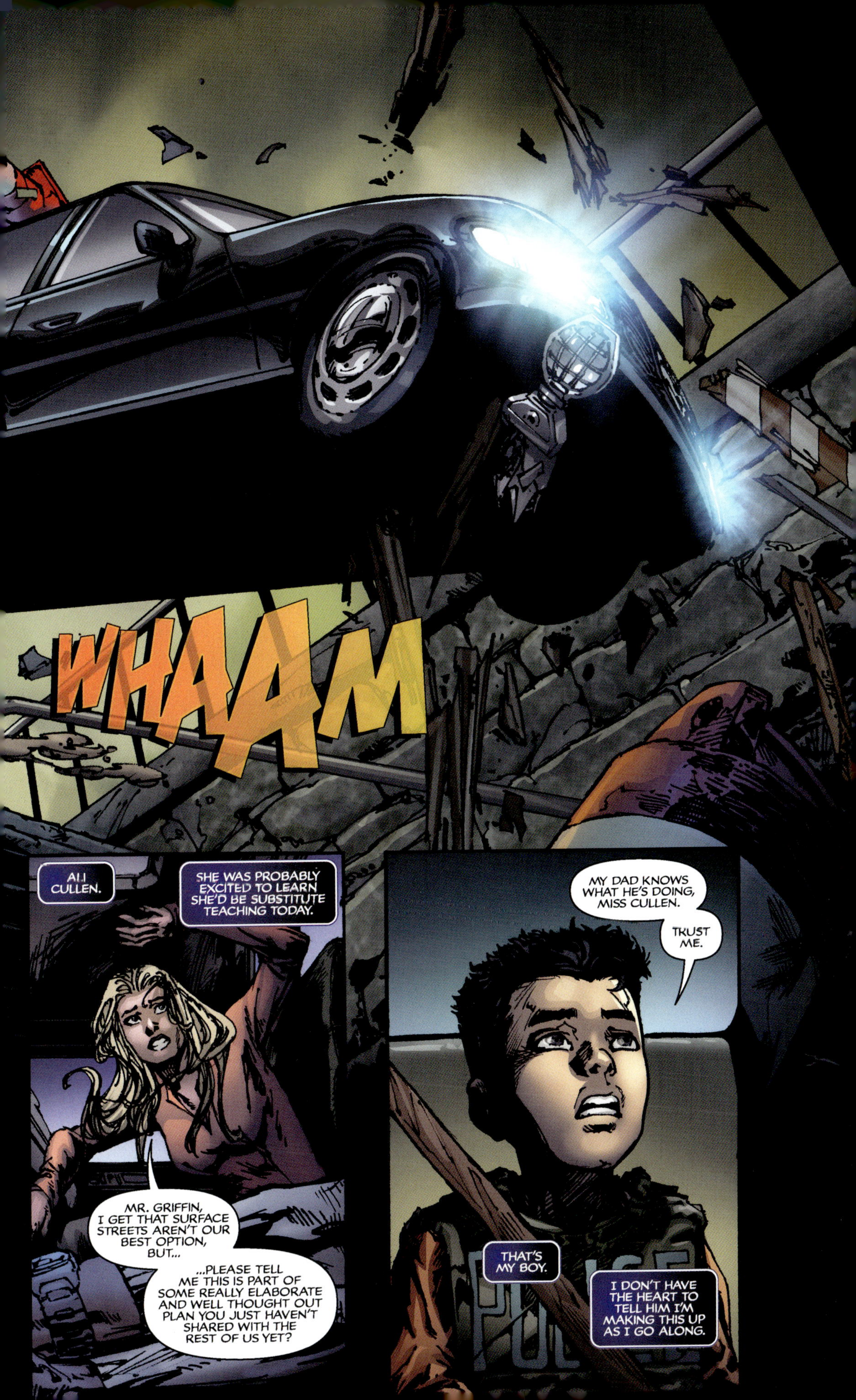
WHAAAM
ALI CULLEN.
SHE WAS PROBABLY EXCITED TO LEARN SHE'D BE SUBSTITUTE TEACHING TODAY.
MR. GRIFFIN, I GET THAT SURFACE STREETS AREN'T OUR BEST OPTION, BUT...
...PLEASE TELL ME THIS IS PART OF SOME REALLY ELABORATE AND WELL THOUGHT OUT PLAN YOU JUST HAVEN'T SHARED WITH THE REST OF US YET?
MY DAD KNOWS WHAT HE'S DOING, MISS CULLEN.
TRUST ME.
THAT'S MY BOY.
I DON'T HAVE THE HEART TO TELL HIM I'M MAKING THIS UP AS I GO ALONG.

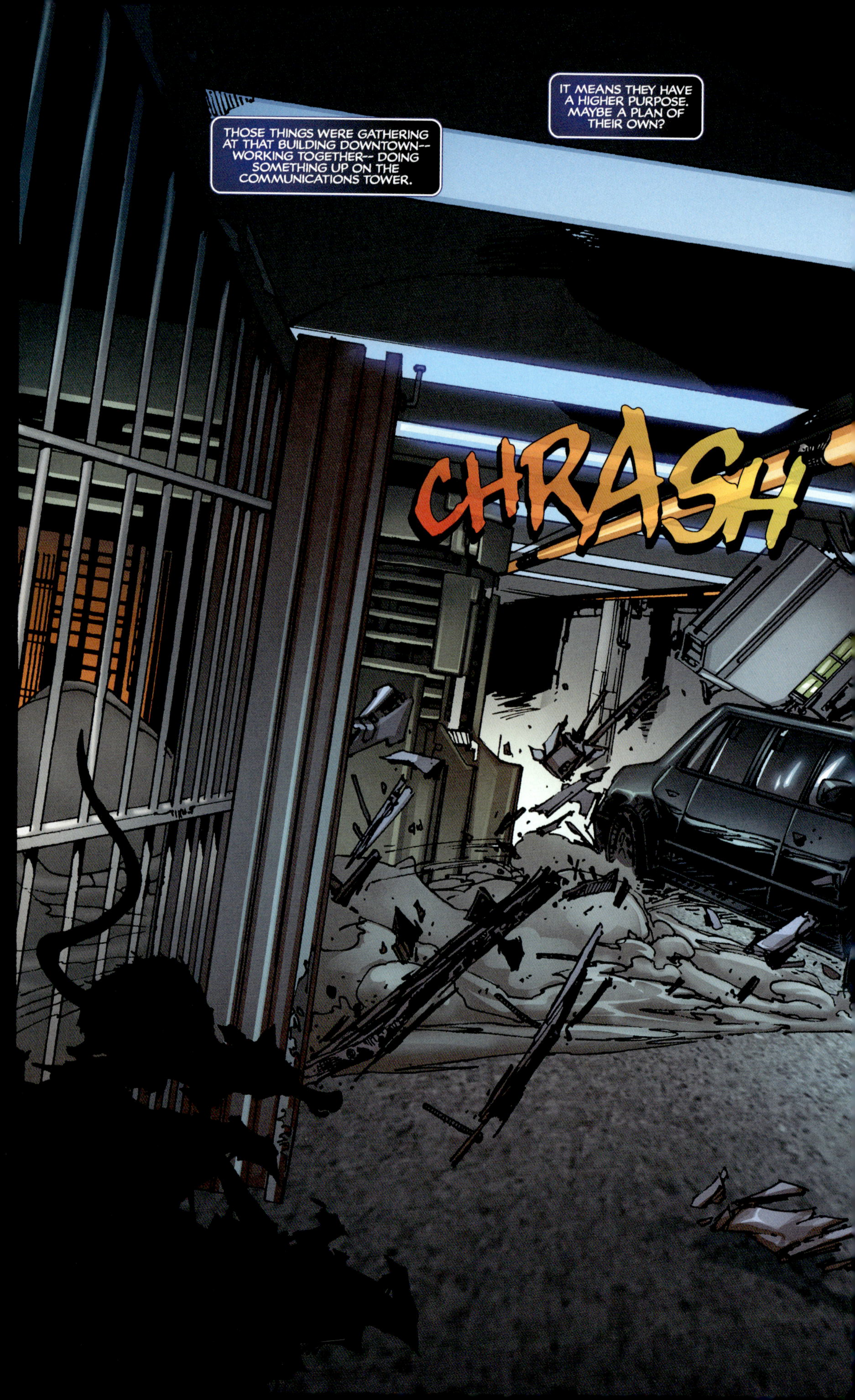
THOSE THINGS WERE GATHERING AT THAT BUILDING DOWNTOWN-- WORKING TOGETHER-- DOING SOMETHING UP ON THE COMMUNICATIONS TOWER.
IT MEANS THEY HAVE A HIGHER PURPOSE. MAYBE A PLAN OF THEIR OWN?
CHRASH

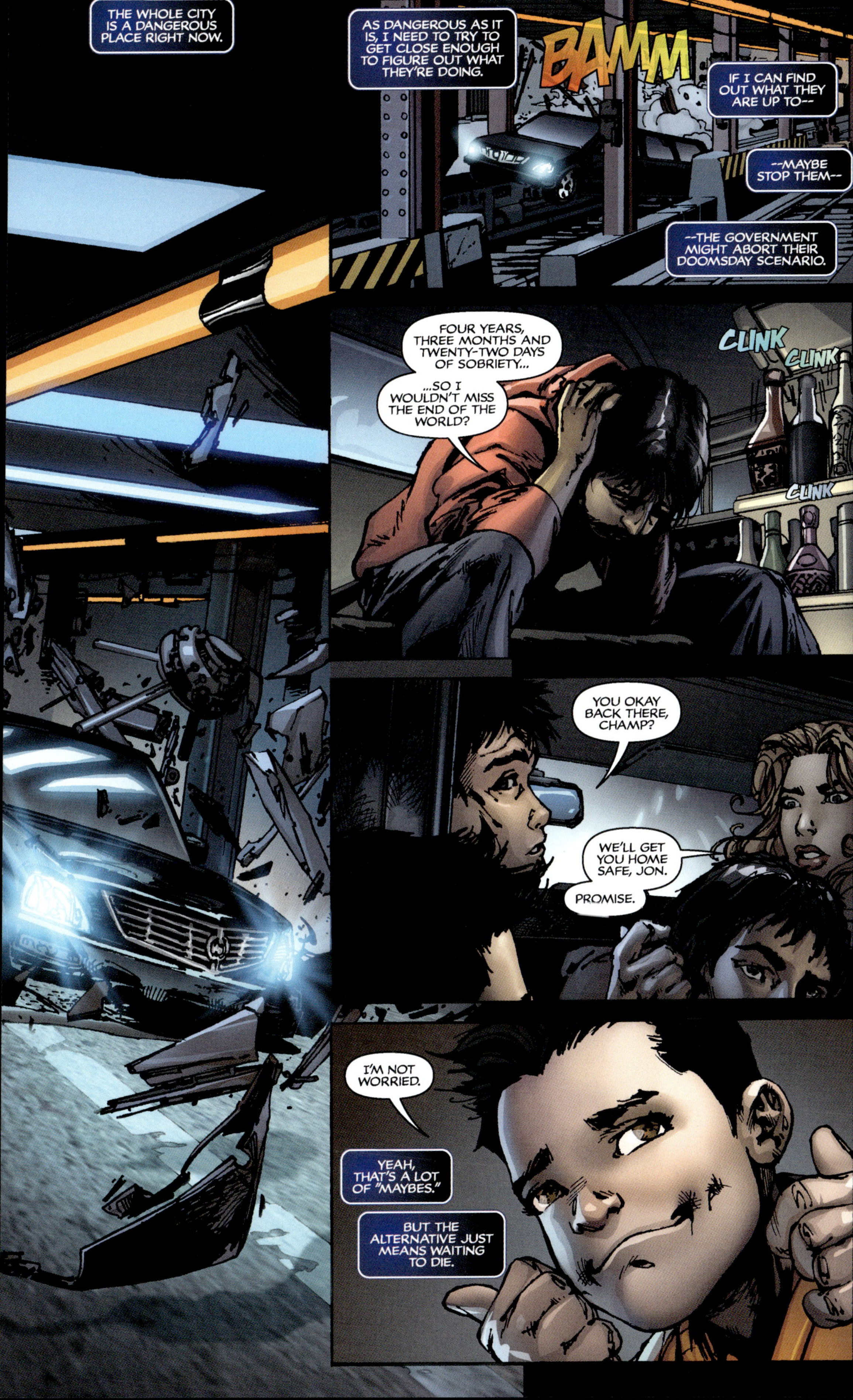
THE WHOLE CITY IS A DANGEROUS PLACE RIGHT NOW.
AS DANGEROUS AS IT IS, I NEED TO TRY TO GET CLOSE ENOUGH TO FIGURE OUT WHAT THEY'RE DOING.
BAMM
IF I CAN FIND OUT WHAT THEY ARE UP TO--
--MAYBE STOP THEM--
--THE GOVERNMENT MIGHT ABORT THEIR DOOMSDAY SCENARIO.
FOUR YEARS, THREE MONTHS AND TWENTY-TWO DAYS OF SOBRIETY...
...SO I WOULDN'T MISS THE END OF THE WORLD?
CLINK
CLINK
CLINK
YOU OKAY BACK THERE, CHAMP?
WE'LL GET YOU HOME SAFE, JON.
PROMISE.
I'M NOT WORRIED.
YEAH, THAT'S A LOT OF "MAYBES."
BUT THE ALTERNATIVE JUST MEANS WAITING TO DIE.

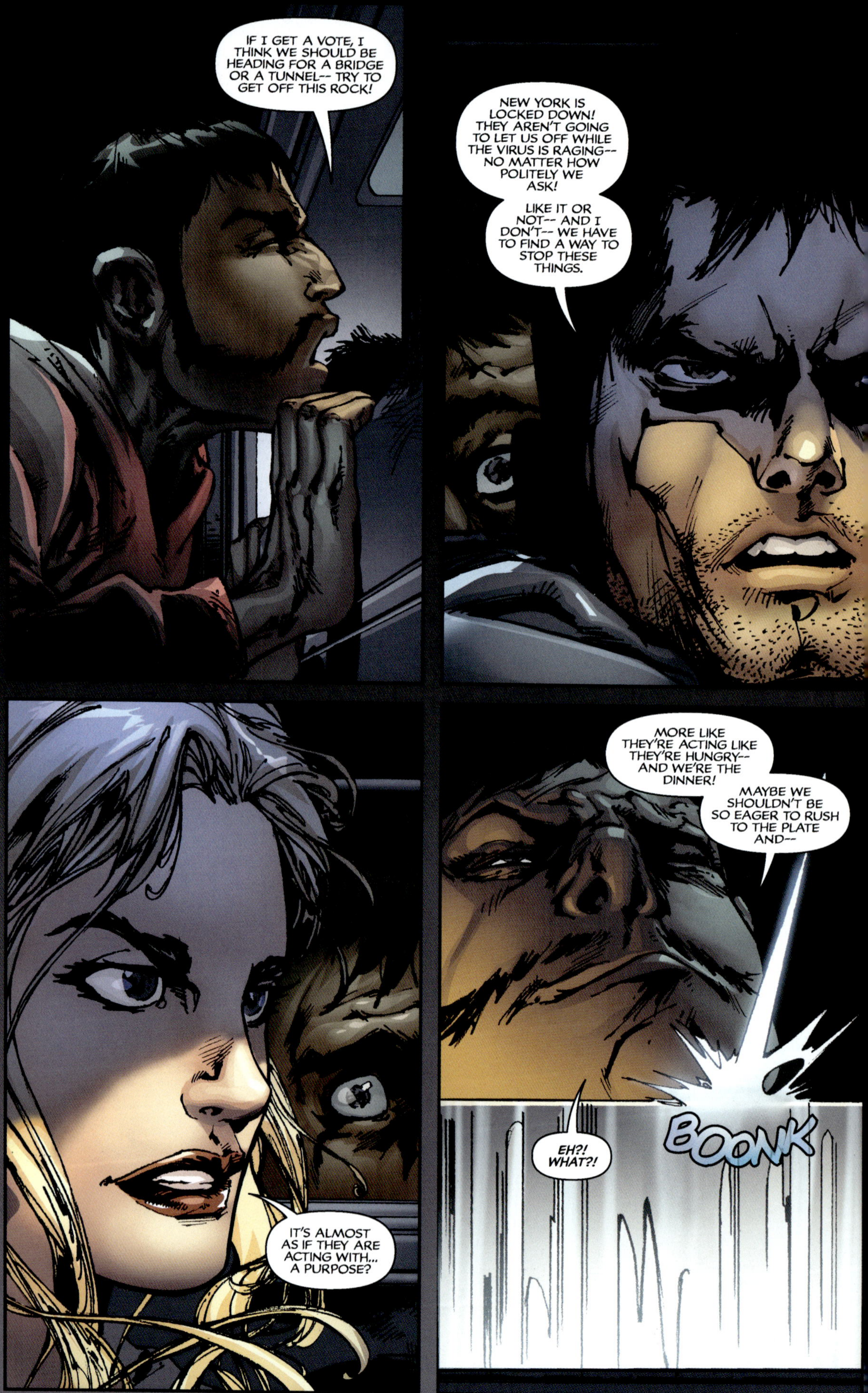
IF I GET A VOTE, I THINK WE SHOULD BE HEADING FOR A BRIDGE OR A TUNNEL-- TRY TO GET OFF THIS ROCK!
NEW YORK IS LOCKED DOWN! THEY AREN'T GOING TO LET US OFF WHILE THE VIRUS IS RAGING-- NO MATTER HOW POLITELY WE ASK!
LIKE IT OR NOT-- AND I DON'T-- WE HAVE TO FIND A WAY TO STOP THESE THINGS.
IT'S ALMOST AS IF THEY ARE ACTING WITH... A PURPOSE?
MORE LIKE THEY'RE ACTING LIKE THEY'RE HUNGRY-- AND WE'RE THE DINNER!
MAYBE WE SHOULDN'T BE SO EAGER TO RUSH TO THE PLATE AND--
BOONK
EH?! WHAT?!

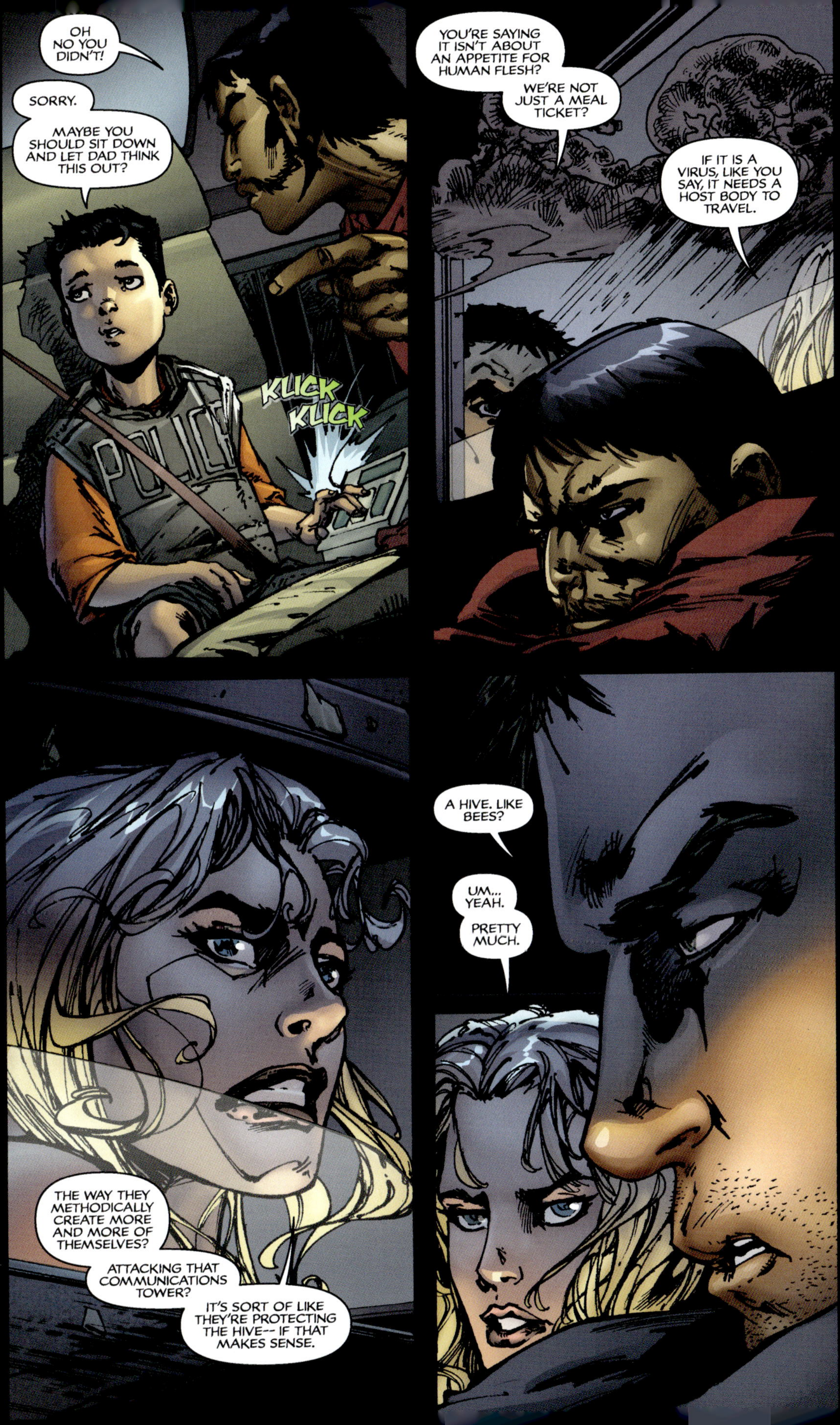
OH NO YOU DIDN'T!
SORRY.
MAYBE YOU SHOULD SIT DOWN AND LET DAD THINK THIS OUT?
POLICE
KLICK KLICK
YOU'RE SAYING IT ISN'T ABOUT AN APPETITE FOR HUMAN FLESH?
WE'RE NOT JUST A MEAL TICKET?
IF IT IS A VIRUS, LIKE YOU SAY, IT NEEDS A HOST BODY TO TRAVEL.
THE WAY THEY METHODICALLY CREATE MORE AND MORE OF THEMSELVES?
ATTACKING THAT COMMUNICATIONS TOWER?
IT'S SORT OF LIKE THEY'RE PROTECTING THE HIVE-- IF THAT MAKES SENSE.
A HIVE. LIKE BEES?
UM... YEAH.
PRETTY MUCH.

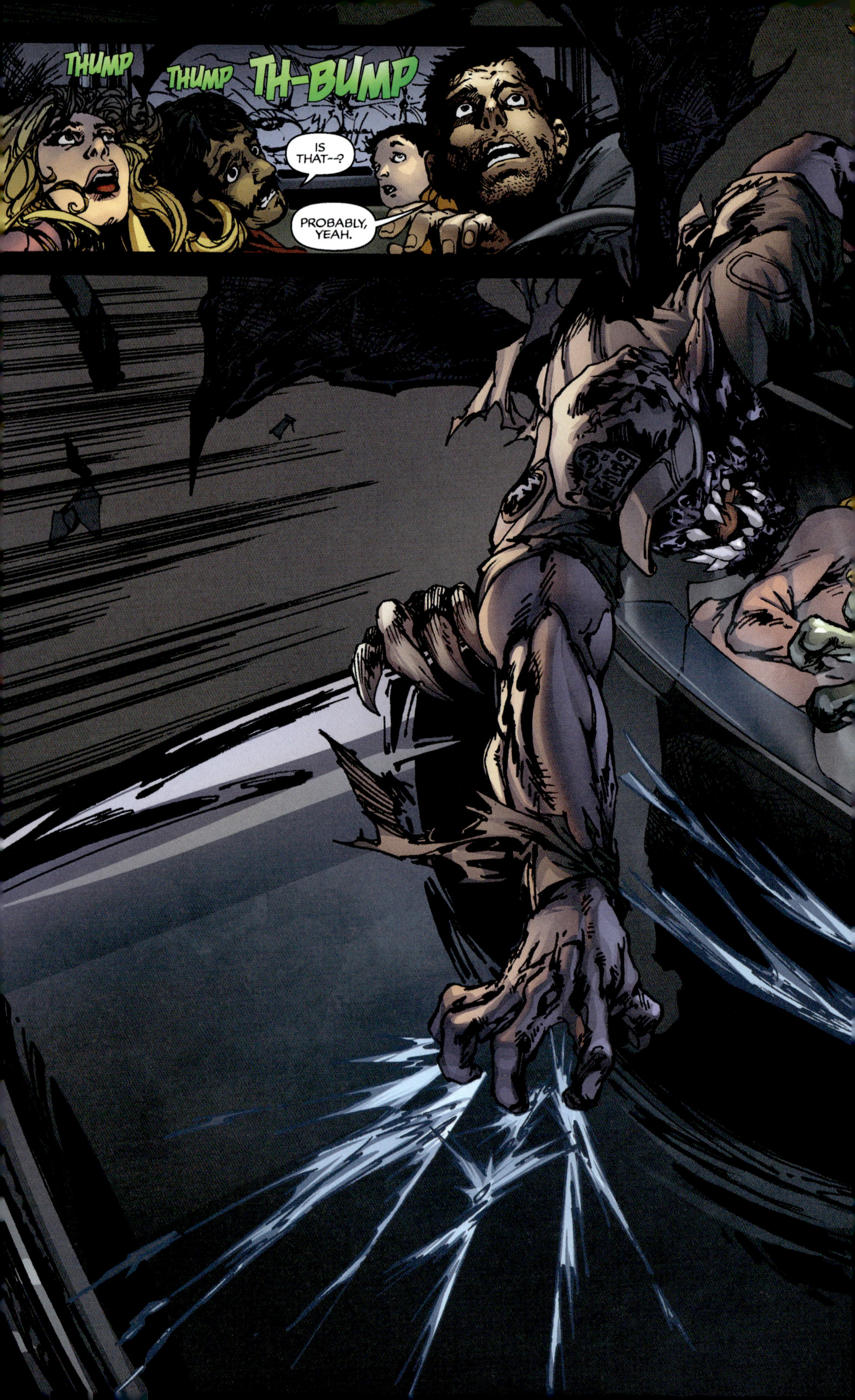
THUMP
THUMP
TH-BUMP
IS THAT--?
PROBABLY, YEAH.

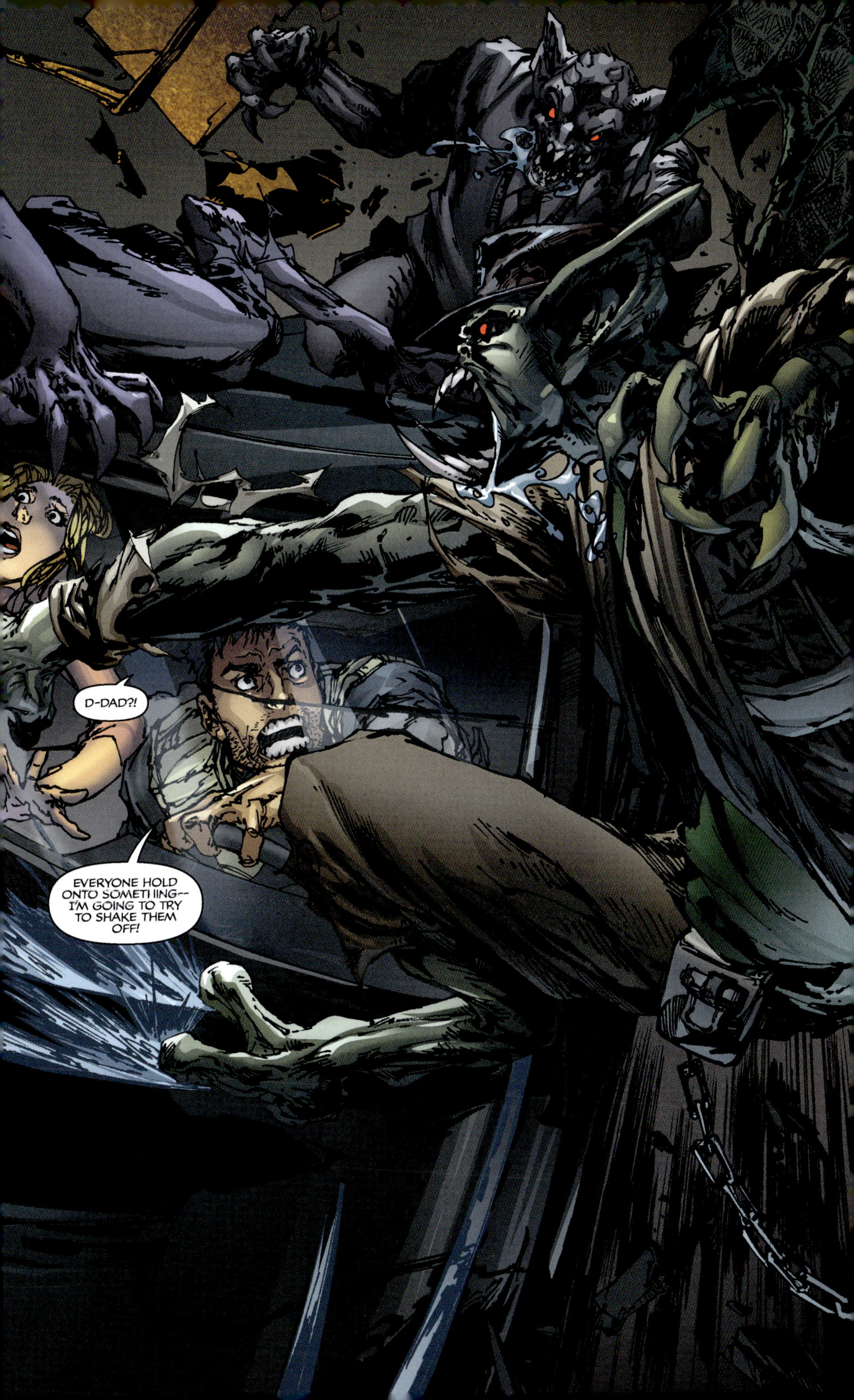
D-DAD?!
EVERYONE HOLD ONTO SOMETHING-- I'M GOING TO TRY TO SHAKE THEM OFF!

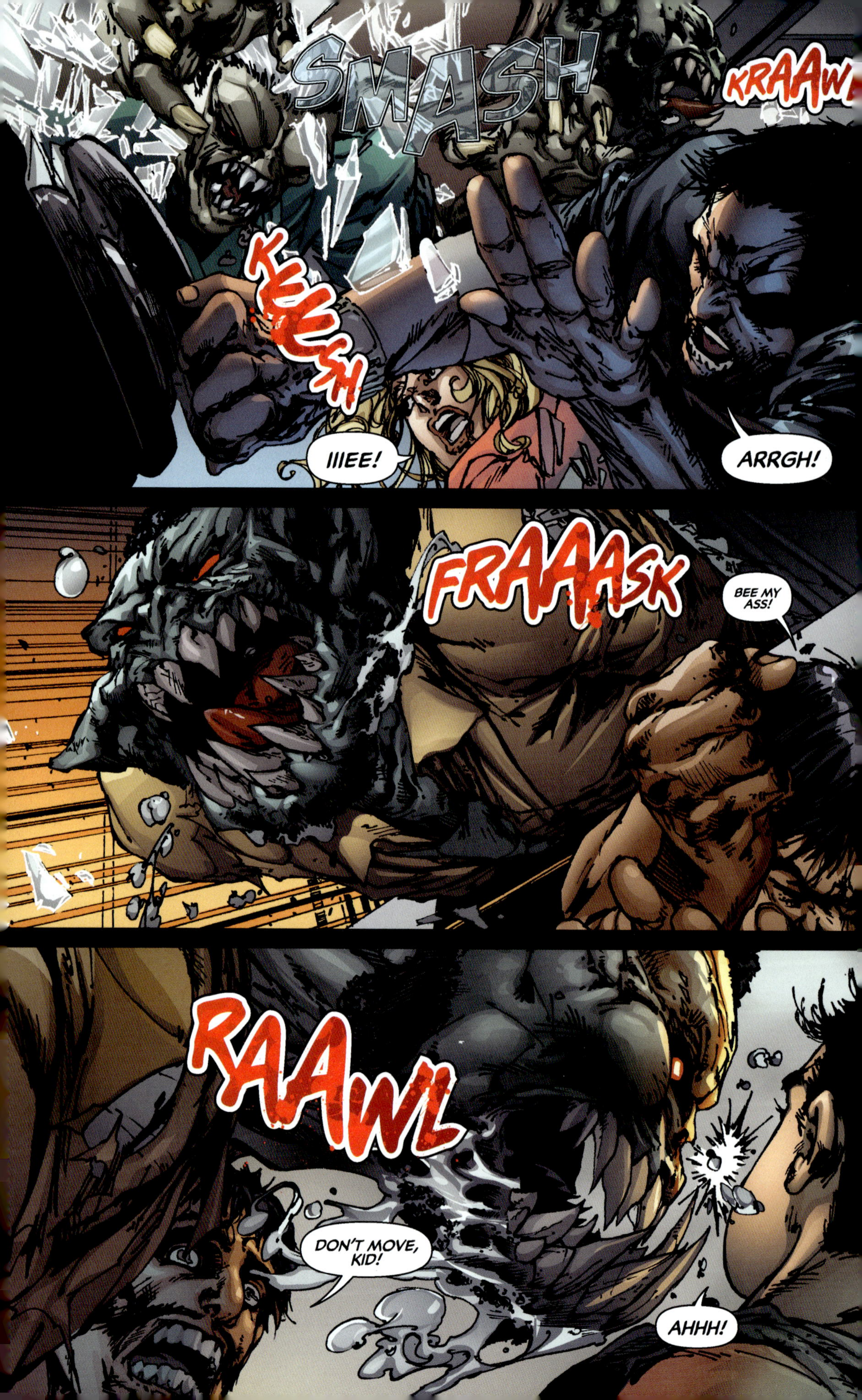
SMASH
KRAAW
IIIEE!
ARRGH!
FRAAASK
BEE MY ASS!
RAAWL
DON'T MOVE, KID!
AHHH!

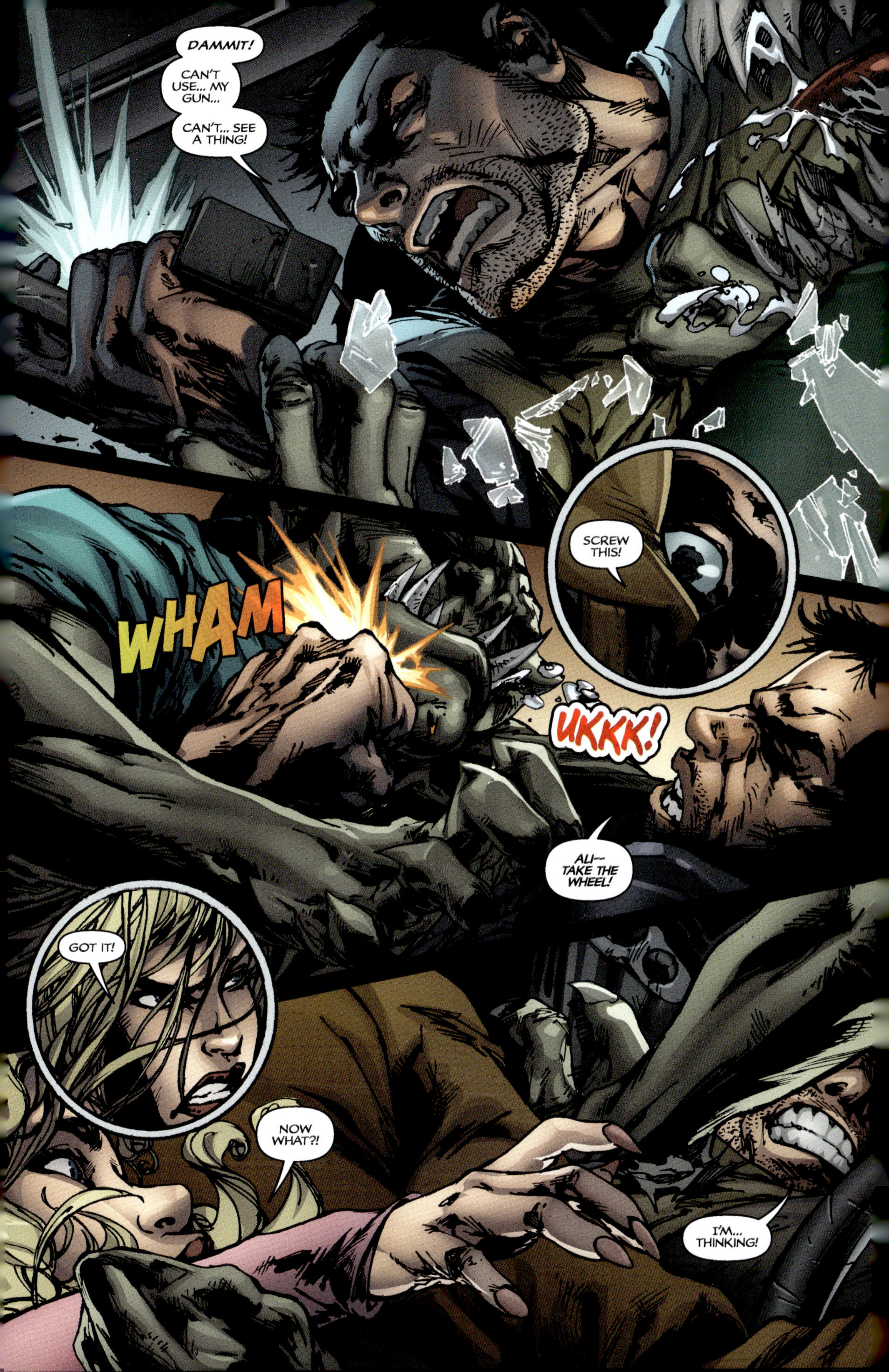
DAMMIT!
CAN'T USE... MY GUN...
CAN'T... SEE A THING!
SCREW THIS!
WHAM
UKKK!
ALI-- TAKE THE WHEEL!
GOT IT!
NOW WHAT?!
I'M... THINKING!

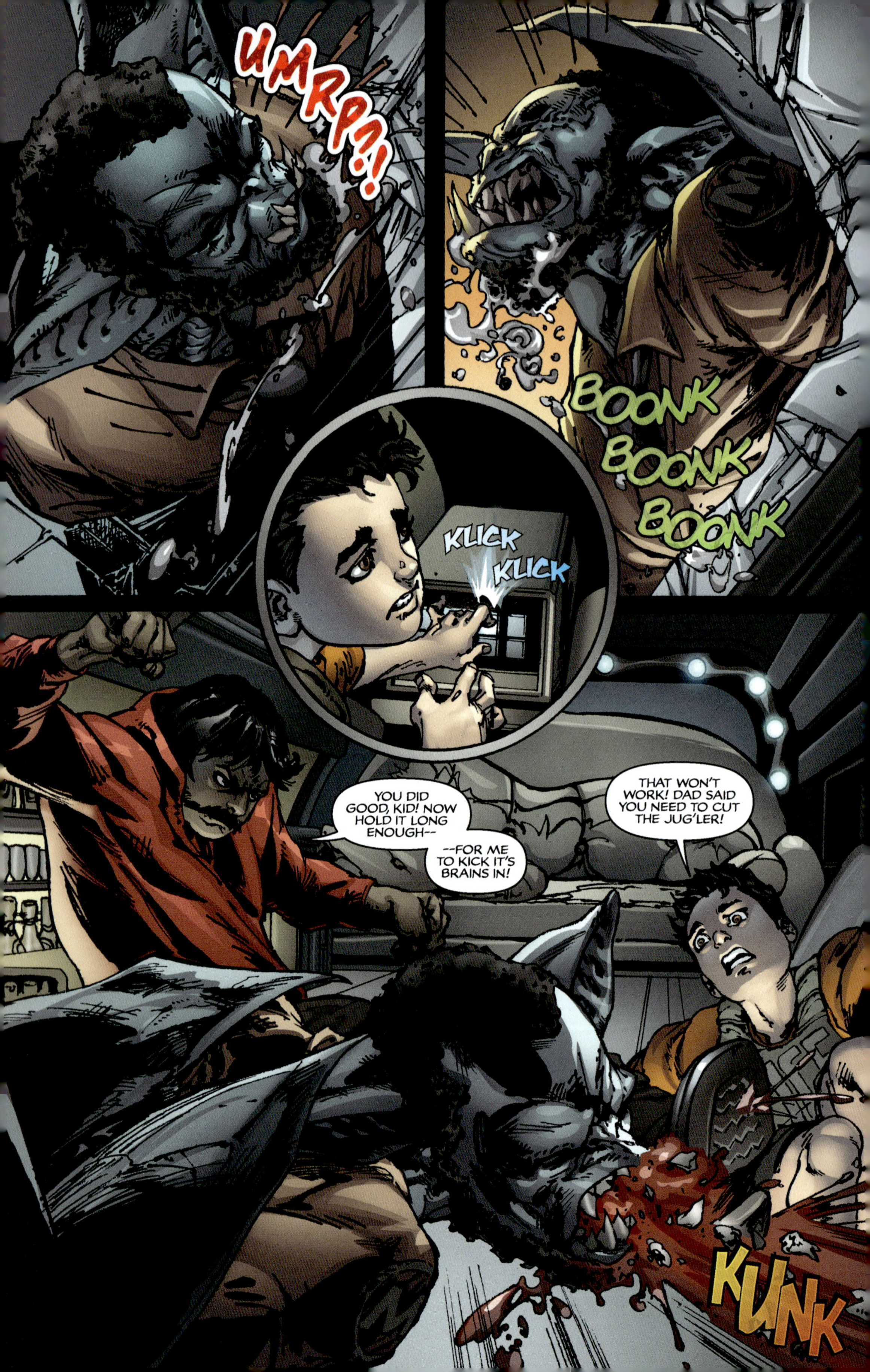
UMRP?!
BOONK
BOONK
BOONK
KLICK
KLICK
YOU DID GOOD, KID! NOW HOLD IT LONG ENOUGH--
--FOR ME TO KICK IT'S BRAINS IN!
THAT WON'T WORK! DAD SAID YOU NEED TO CUT THE JUG'LER!
KUNK

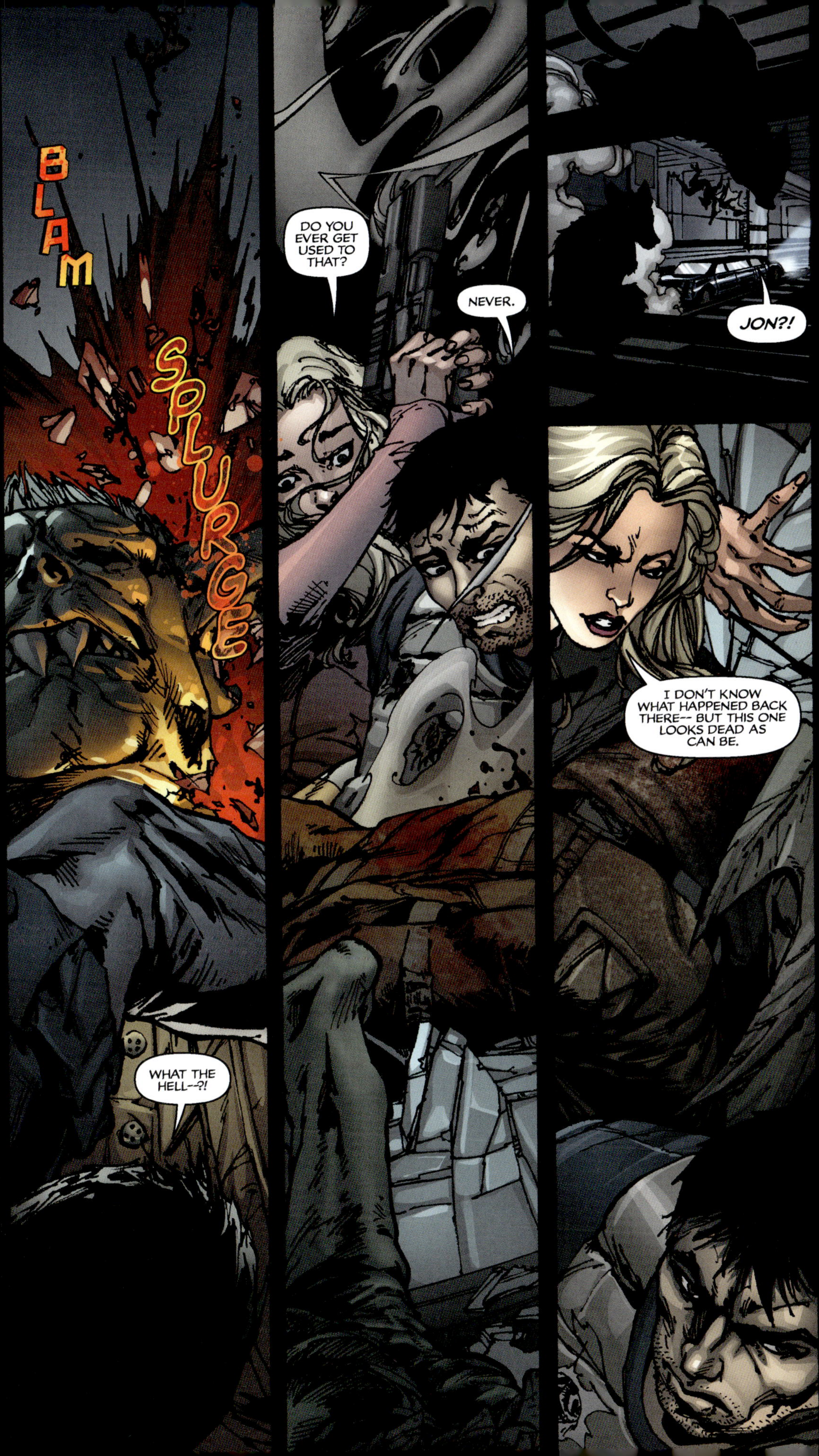
BLAM
SPLURGE
WHAT THE HELL--?!
DO YOU EVER GET USED TO THAT?
NEVER.
JON?!
I DON'T KNOW WHAT HAPPENED BACK THERE-- BUT THIS ONE LOOKS DEAD AS CAN BE.

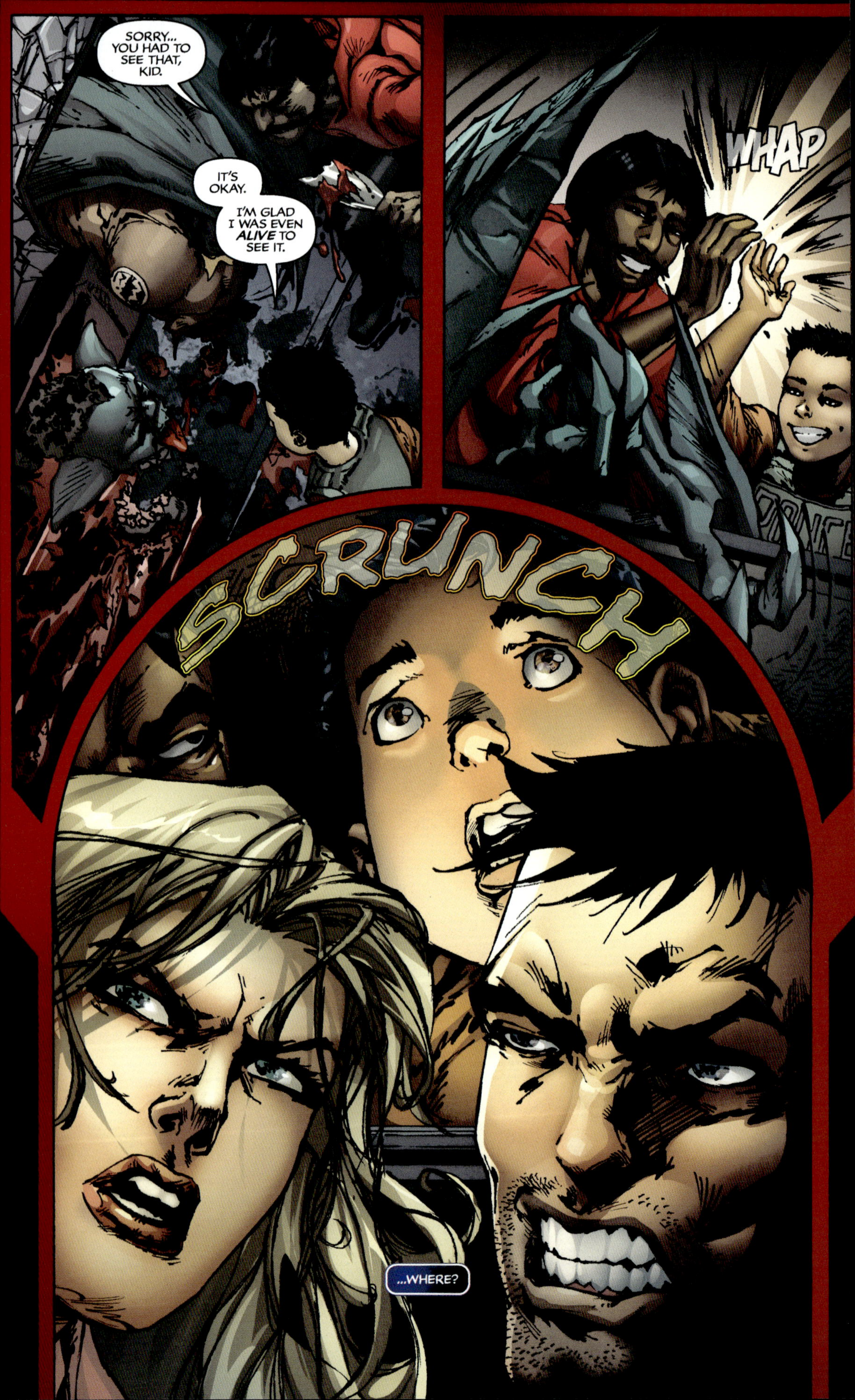
SORRY... YOU HAD TO SEE THAT, KID.
IT'S OKAY.
I'M GLAD I WAS EVEN *ALIVE* TO SEE IT.
WHAP
SCRUNCH
...WHERE?

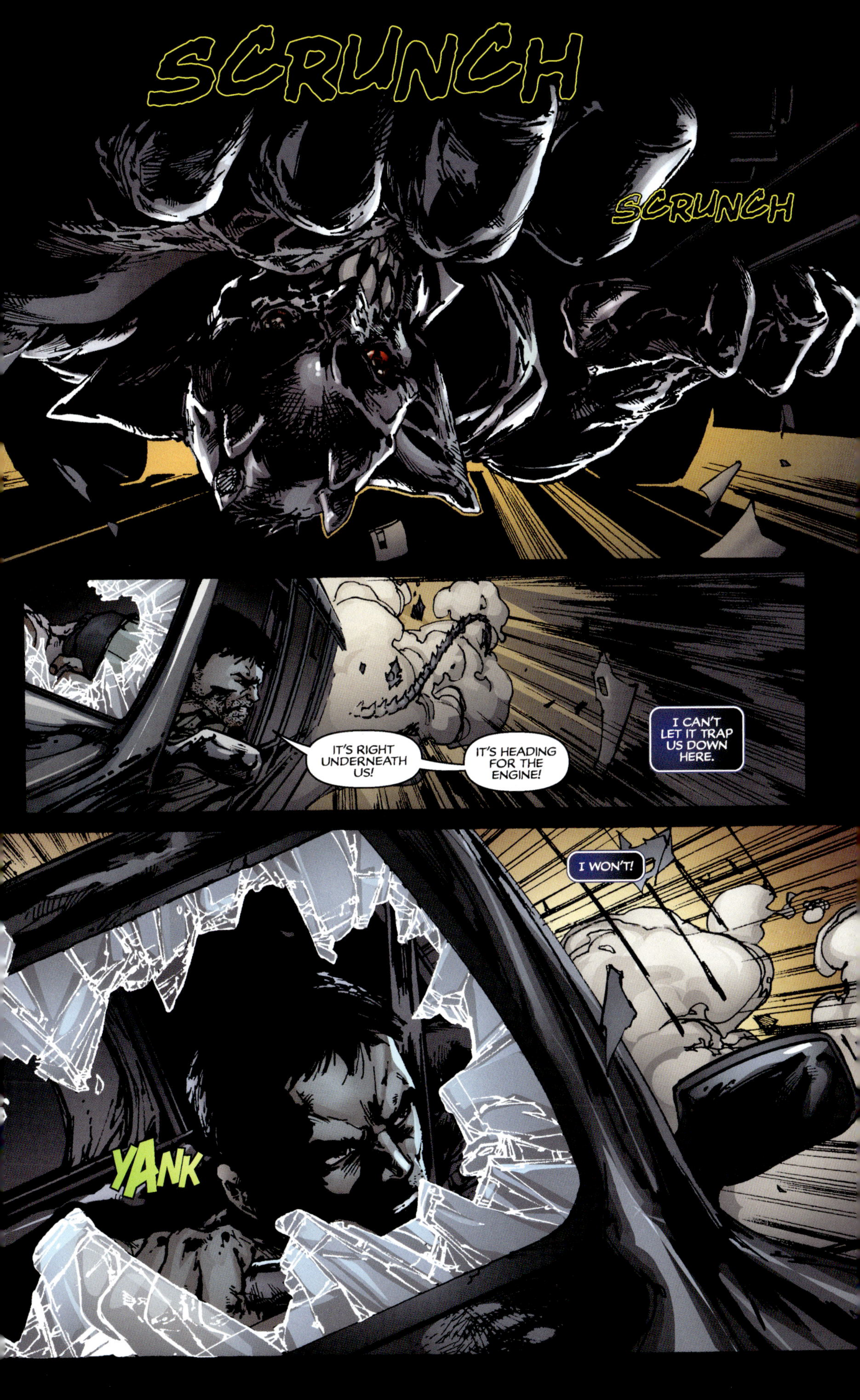
SCRUNCH
SCRUNCH
IT'S RIGHT UNDERNEATH US!
IT'S HEADING FOR THE ENGINE!
I CAN'T LET IT TRAP US DOWN HERE.
I WON'T!
YANK

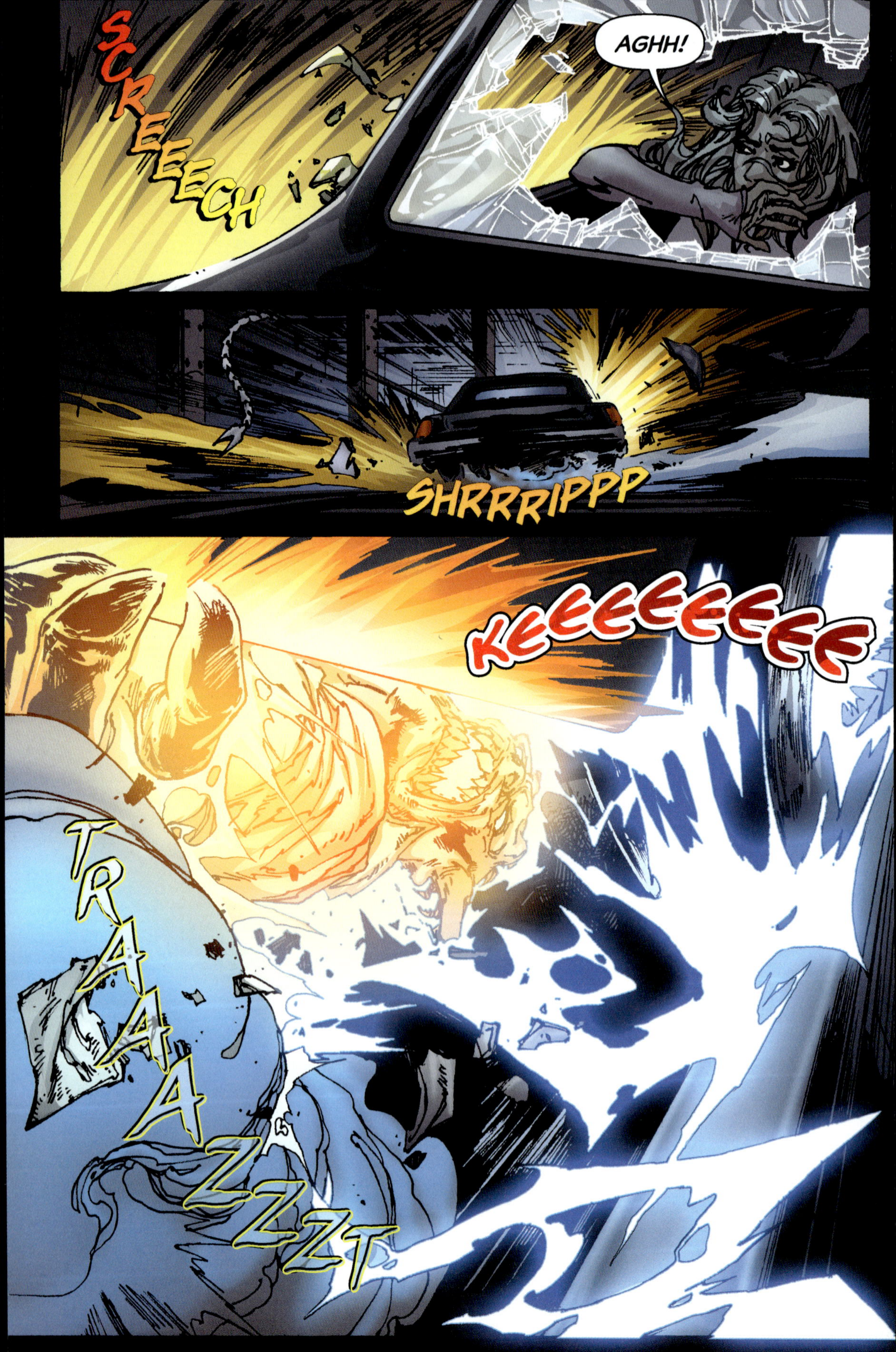
SCREEECH
AGHH!
SHRRRIPPP
KEEEEEEEEE
TRAAAZZZT

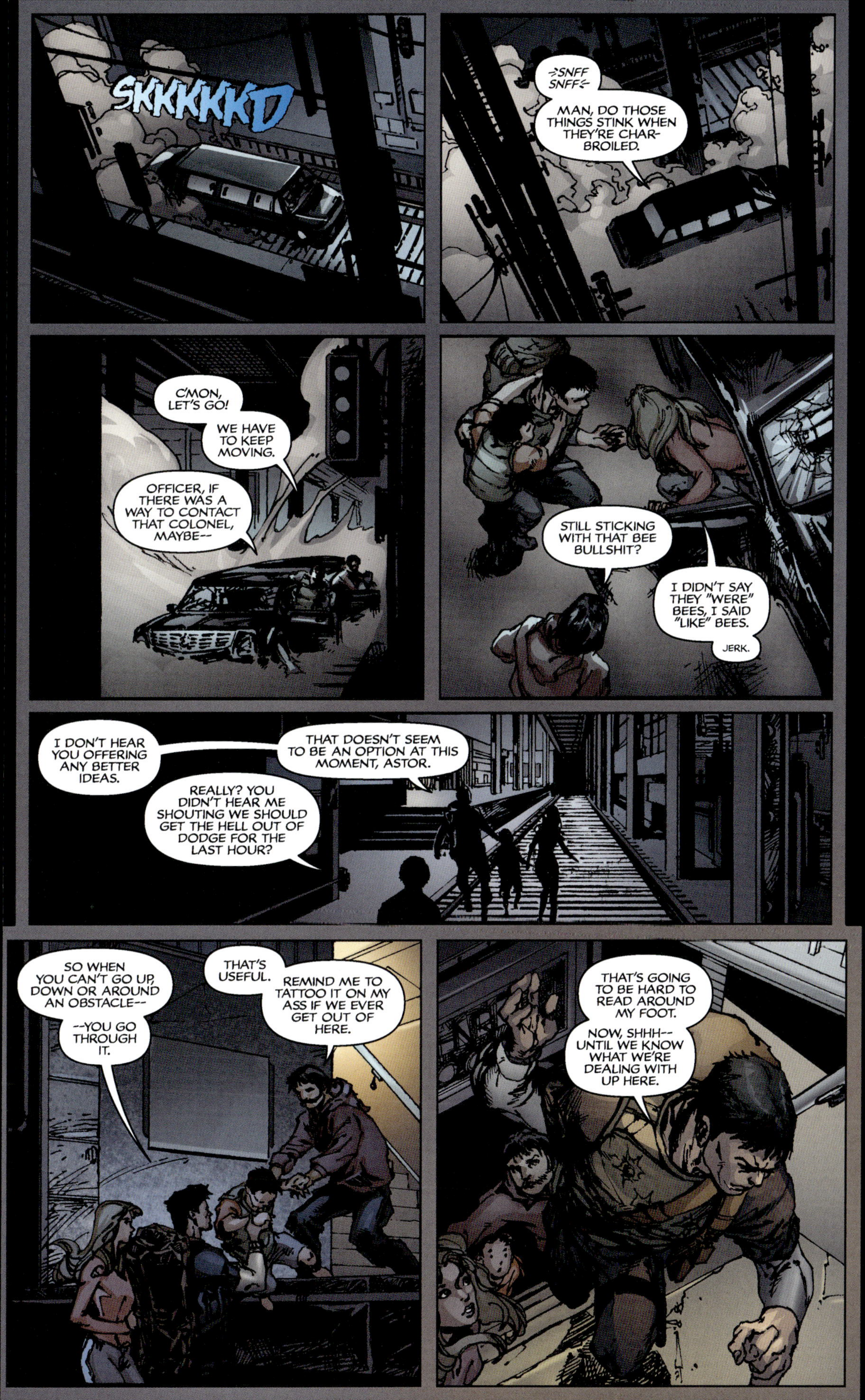
SKKKKKD
>SNFF SNFF<
MAN, DO THOSE THINGS STINK WHEN THEY'RE CHAR-BROILED.
C'MON, LET'S GO!
WE HAVE TO KEEP MOVING.
OFFICER, IF THERE WAS A WAY TO CONTACT THAT COLONEL, MAYBE--
STILL STICKING WITH THAT BEE BULLSHIT?
I DIDN'T SAY THEY "WERE" BEES, I SAID "LIKE" BEES.
JERK.
I DON'T HEAR YOU OFFERING ANY BETTER IDEAS.
THAT DOESN'T SEEM TO BE AN OPTION AT THIS MOMENT, ASTOR.
REALLY? YOU DIDN'T HEAR ME SHOUTING WE SHOULD GET THE HELL OUT OF DODGE FOR THE LAST HOUR?
SO WHEN YOU CAN'T GO UP, DOWN OR AROUND AN OBSTACLE--
--YOU GO THROUGH IT.
THAT'S USEFUL.
REMIND ME TO TATTOO IT ON MY ASS IF WE EVER GET OUT OF HERE.
THAT'S GOING TO BE HARD TO READ AROUND MY FOOT.
NOW, SHHH-- UNTIL WE KNOW WHAT WE'RE DEALING WITH UP HERE.

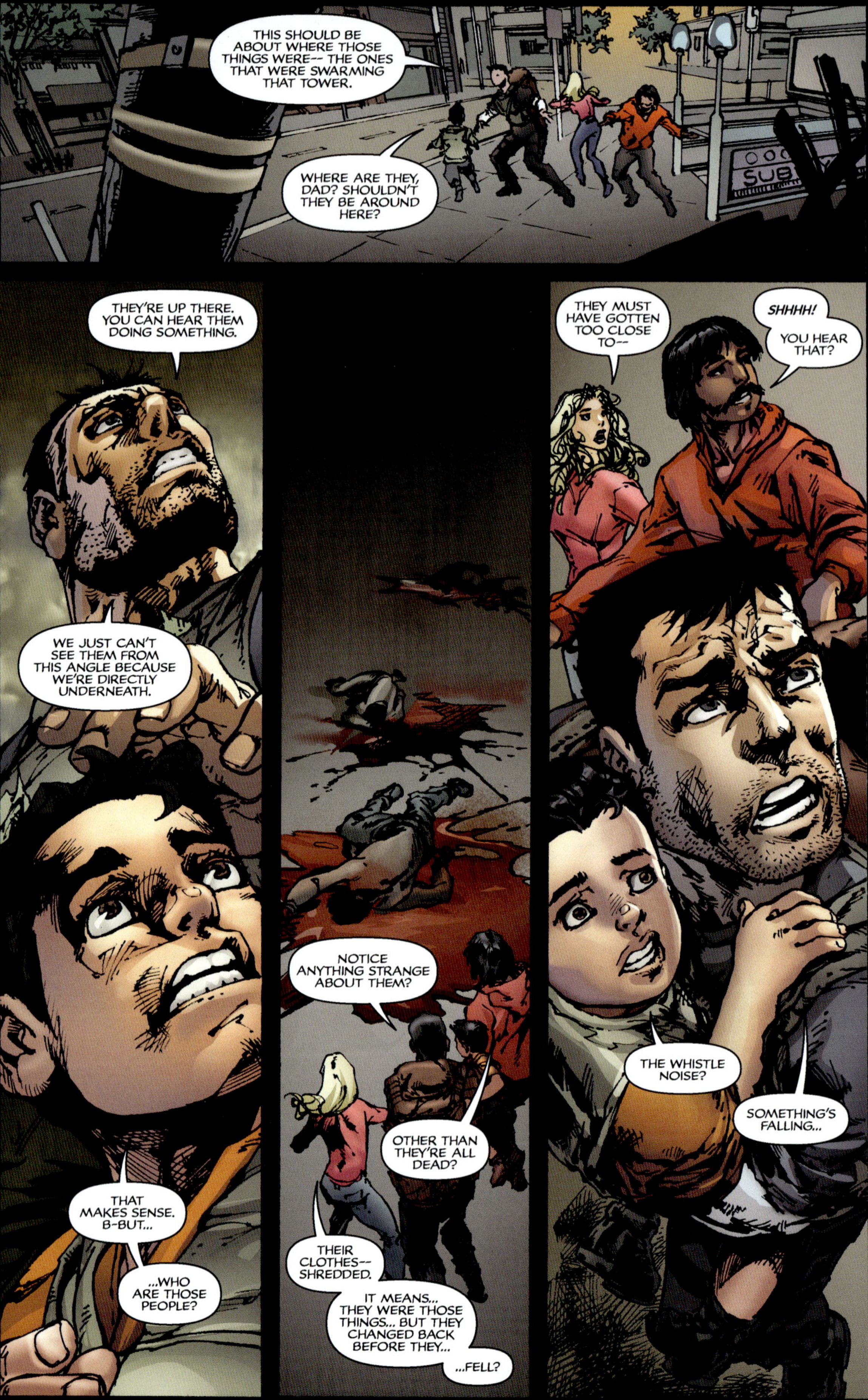
THIS SHOULD BE ABOUT WHERE THOSE THINGS WERE-- THE ONES THAT WERE SWARMING THAT TOWER.
WHERE ARE THEY, DAD? SHOULDN'T THEY BE AROUND HERE?
SUB
THEY'RE UP THERE. YOU CAN HEAR THEM DOING SOMETHING.
WE JUST CAN'T SEE THEM FROM THIS ANGLE BECAUSE WE'RE DIRECTLY UNDERNEATH.
THAT MAKES SENSE. B-BUT...
...WHO ARE THOSE PEOPLE?
NOTICE ANYTHING STRANGE ABOUT THEM?
OTHER THAN THEY'RE ALL DEAD?
THEIR CLOTHES-- SHREDDED.
IT MEANS... THEY WERE THOSE THINGS... BUT THEY CHANGED BACK BEFORE THEY...
...FELL?
THEY MUST HAVE GOTTEN TOO CLOSE TO--
SHHHH!
YOU HEAR THAT?
THE WHISTLE NOISE?
SOMETHING'S FALLING...

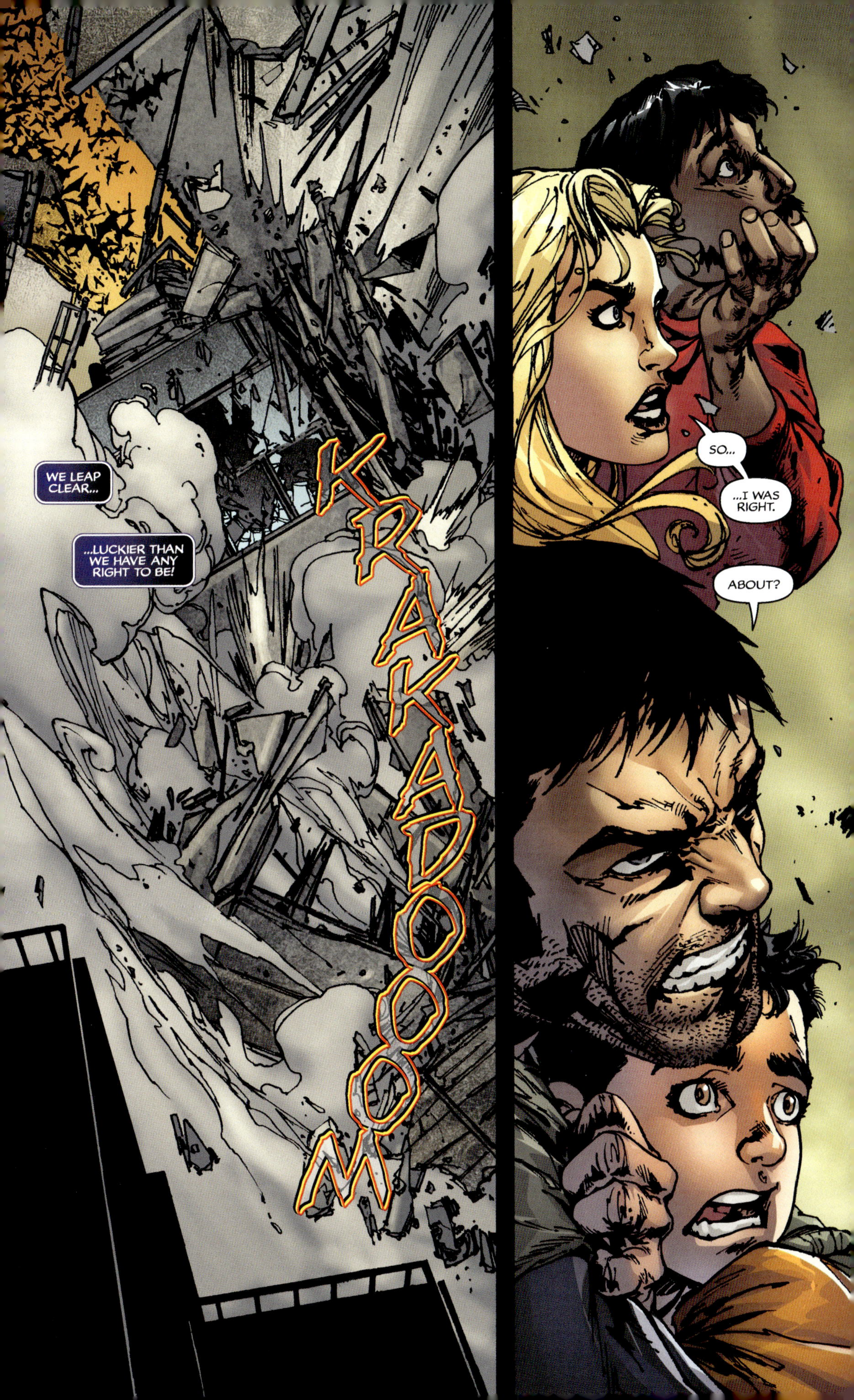
WE LEAP CLEAR...
...LUCKIER THAN WE HAVE ANY RIGHT TO BE!
KRAKADOOOOM
SO...
...I WAS RIGHT.
ABOUT?

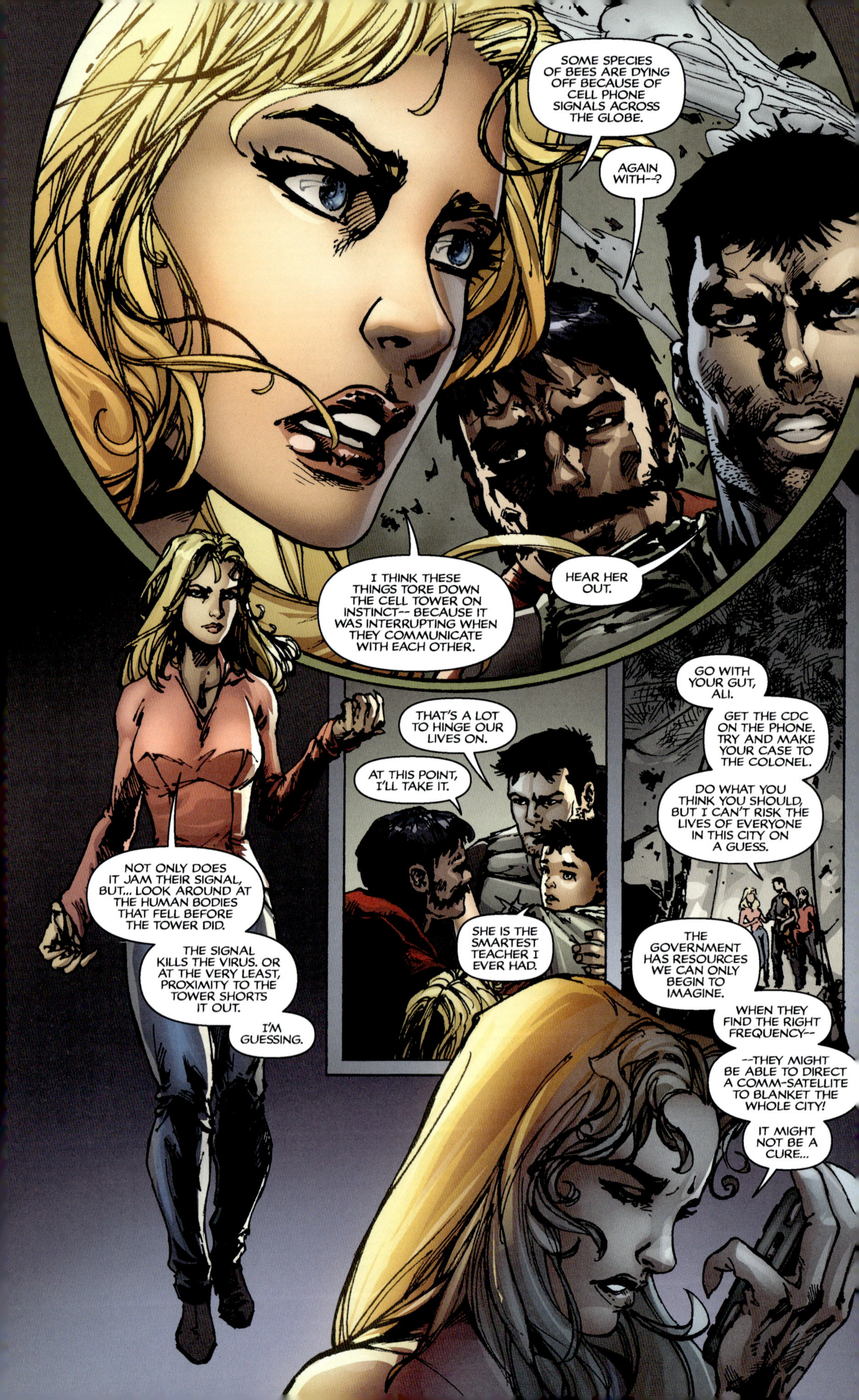
SOME SPECIES OF BEES ARE DYING OFF BECAUSE OF CELL PHONE SIGNALS ACROSS THE GLOBE.
AGAIN WITH--?
I THINK THESE THINGS TORE DOWN THE CELL TOWER ON INSTINCT-- BECAUSE IT WAS INTERRUPTING WHEN THEY COMMUNICATE WITH EACH OTHER.
HEAR HER OUT.
NOT ONLY DOES IT JAM THEIR SIGNAL, BUT... LOOK AROUND AT THE HUMAN BODIES THAT FELL BEFORE THE TOWER DID.
THE SIGNAL KILLS THE VIRUS. OR AT THE VERY LEAST, PROXIMITY TO THE TOWER SHORTS IT OUT.
I'M GUESSING.
THAT'S A LOT TO HINGE OUR LIVES ON.
AT THIS POINT, I'LL TAKE IT.
SHE IS THE SMARTEST TEACHER I EVER HAD.
GO WITH YOUR GUT, ALI.
GET THE CDC ON THE PHONE. TRY AND MAKE YOUR CASE TO THE COLONEL.
DO WHAT YOU THINK YOU SHOULD, BUT I CAN'T RISK THE LIVES OF EVERYONE IN THIS CITY ON A GUESS.
THE GOVERNMENT HAS RESOURCES WE CAN ONLY BEGIN TO IMAGINE.
WHEN THEY FIND THE RIGHT FREQUENCY--
--THEY MIGHT BE ABLE TO DIRECT A COMM-SATELLITE TO BLANKET THE WHOLE CITY!
IT MIGHT NOT BE A CURE...

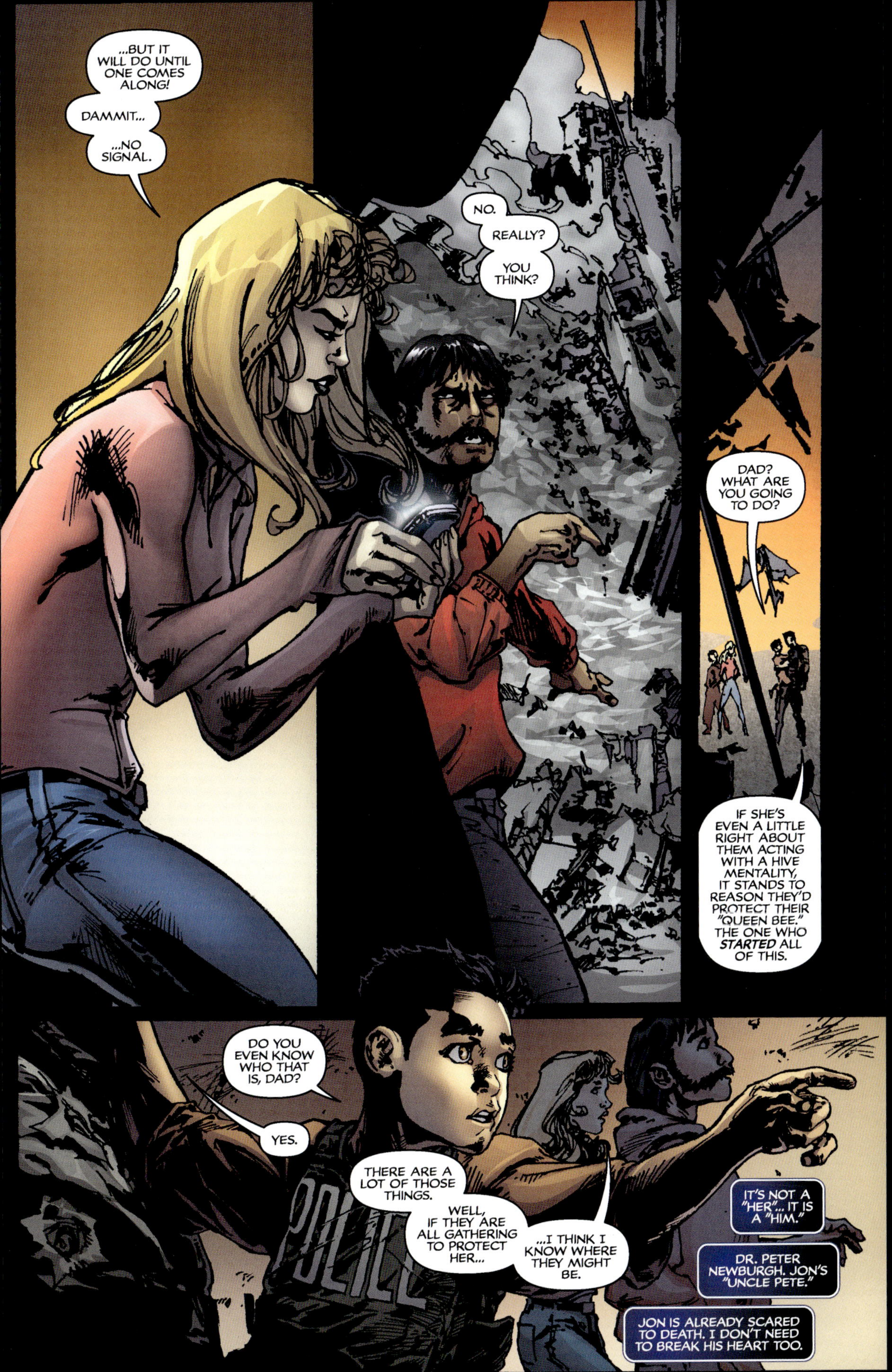
...BUT IT WILL DO UNTIL ONE COMES ALONG!
DAMMIT...
...NO SIGNAL.
NO.
REALLY?
YOU THINK?
DAD? WHAT ARE YOU GOING TO DO?
IF SHE'S EVEN A LITTLE RIGHT ABOUT THEM ACTING WITH A HIVE MENTALITY, IT STANDS TO REASON THEY'D PROTECT THEIR "QUEEN BEE." THE ONE WHO *STARTED* ALL OF THIS.
DO YOU EVEN KNOW WHO THAT IS, DAD?
YES.
THERE ARE A LOT OF THOSE THINGS.
WELL, IF THEY ARE ALL GATHERING TO PROTECT HER...
...I THINK I KNOW WHERE THEY MIGHT BE.
IT'S NOT A "HER"... IT IS A "HIM."
DR. PETER NEWBURGH. JON'S "UNCLE PETE."
JON IS ALREADY SCARED TO DEATH. I DON'T NEED TO BREAK HIS HEART TOO.
POLICE

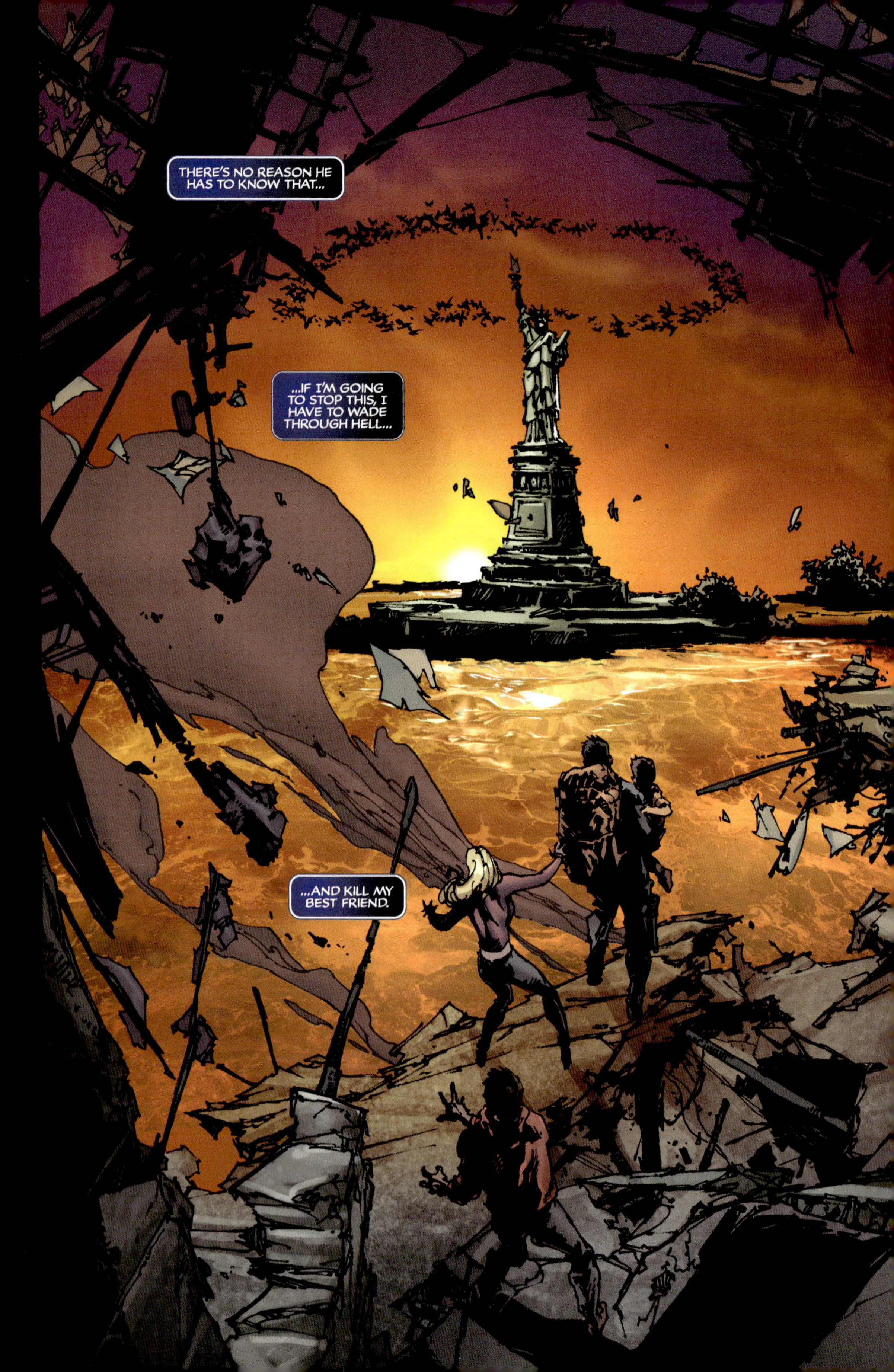
THERE'S NO REASON HE HAS TO KNOW THAT...
...IF I'M GOING TO STOP THIS, I HAVE TO WADE THROUGH HELL...
...AND KILL MY BEST FRIEND.

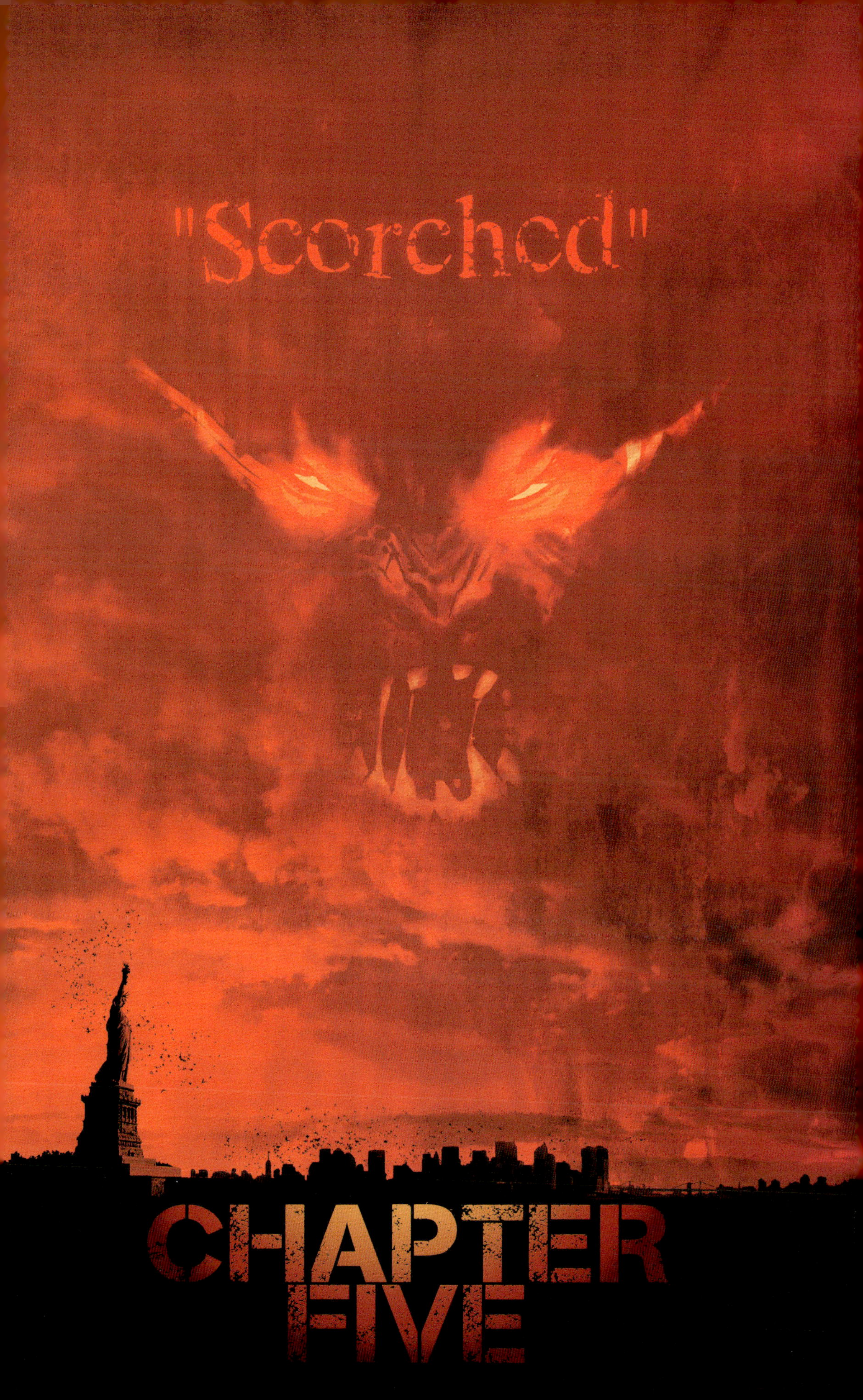
"Scorched"
CHAPTER
FIVE

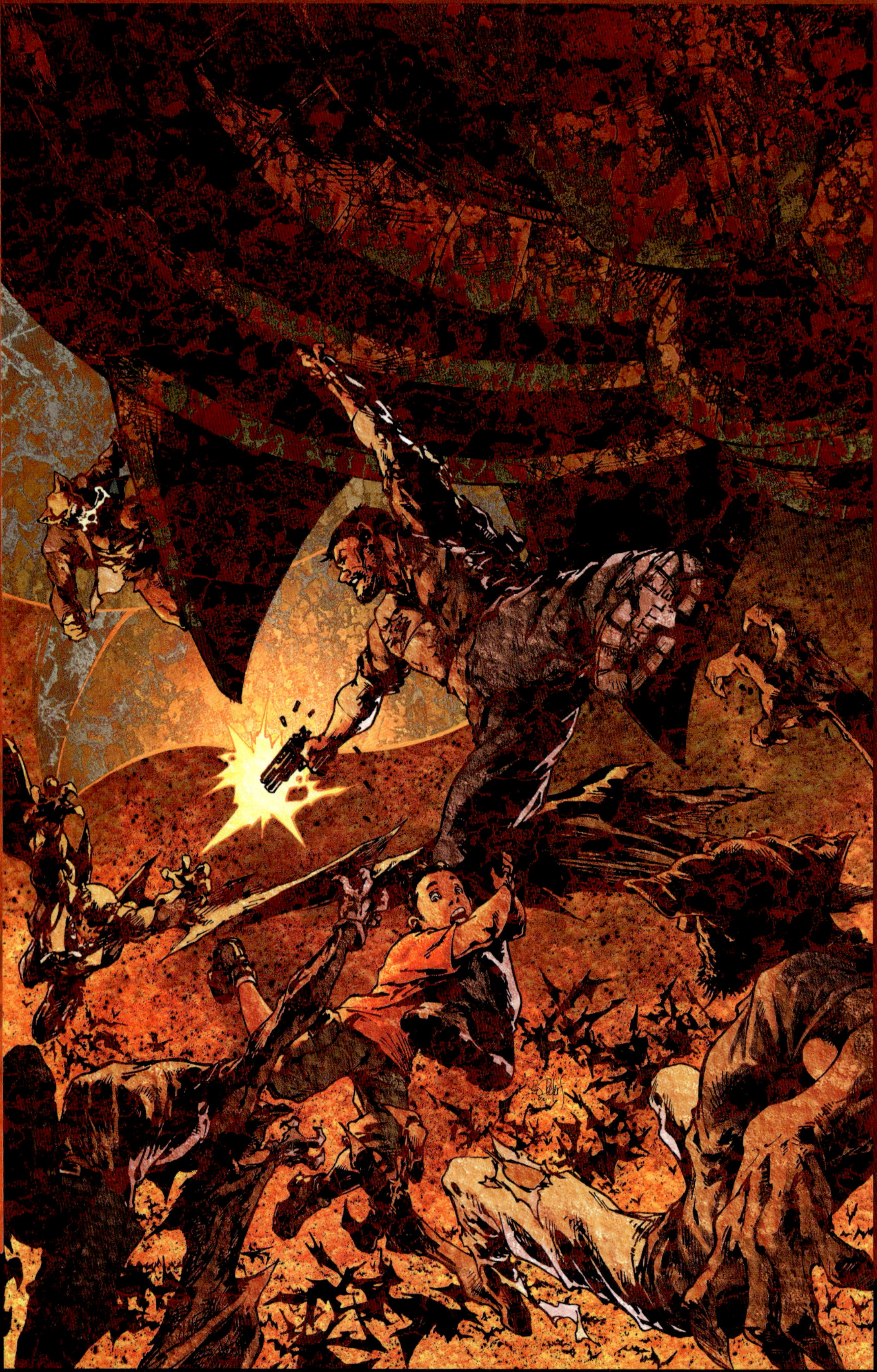

RETAILER "INFECTED" INCENTIVE EDITION COVER C TO
THE SCOURGE #5

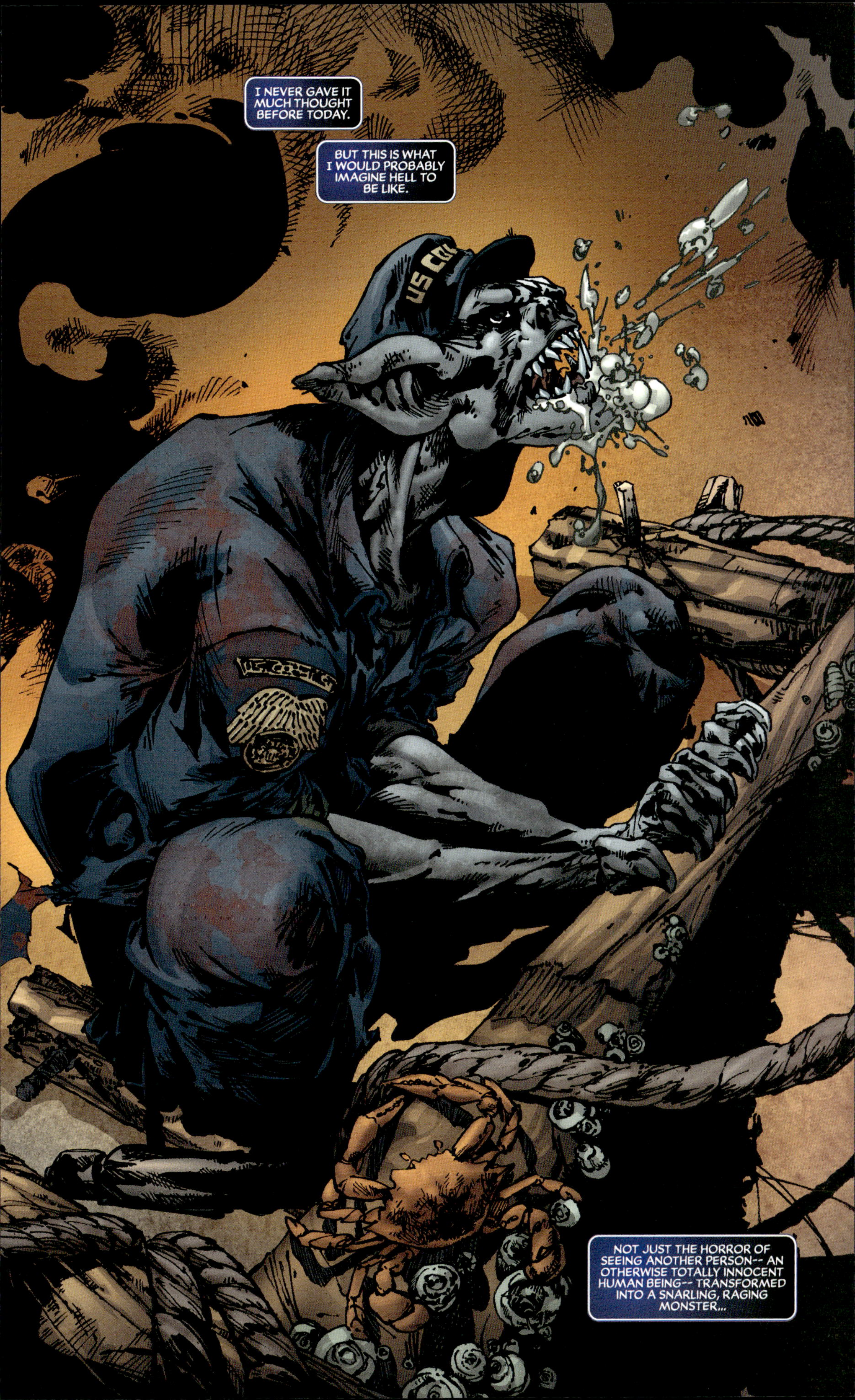
I NEVER GAVE IT MUCH THOUGHT BEFORE TODAY.
BUT THIS IS WHAT I WOULD PROBABLY IMAGINE HELL TO BE LIKE.
NOT JUST THE HORROR OF SEEING ANOTHER PERSON-- AN OTHERWISE TOTALLY INNOCENT HUMAN BEING-- TRANSFORMED INTO A SNARLING, RAGING MONSTER...

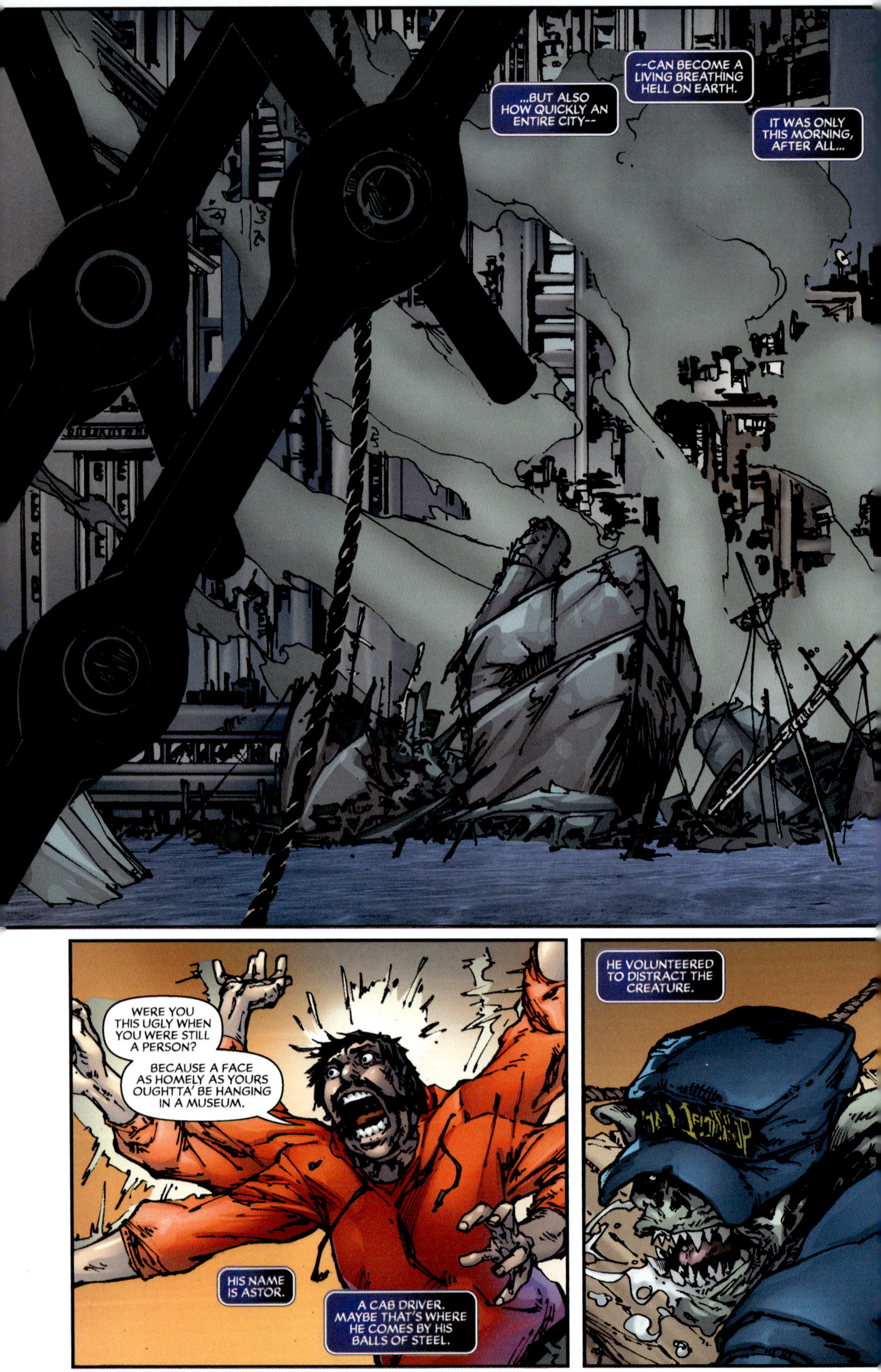
...BUT ALSO HOW QUICKLY AN ENTIRE CITY--
--CAN BECOME A LIVING BREATHING HELL ON EARTH.
IT WAS ONLY THIS MORNING, AFTER ALL...
WERE YOU THIS UGLY WHEN YOU WERE STILL A PERSON?
BECAUSE A FACE AS HOMELY AS YOURS OUGHTTA' BE HANGING IN A MUSEUM.
HIS NAME IS ASTOR.
A CAB DRIVER. MAYBE THAT'S WHERE HE COMES BY HIS BALLS OF STEEL.
HE VOLUNTEERED TO DISTRACT THE CREATURE.

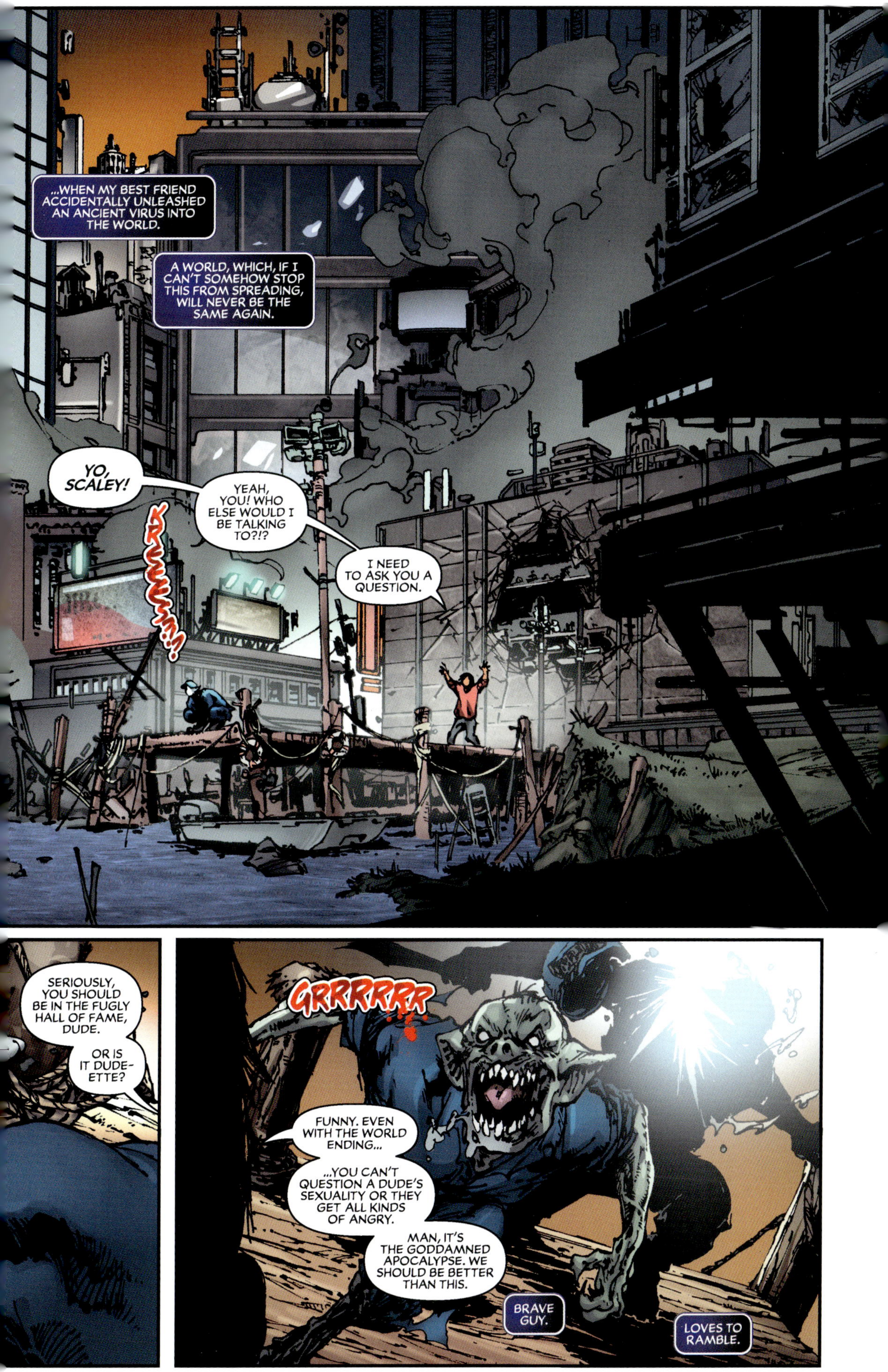
...WHEN MY BEST FRIEND ACCIDENTALLY UNLEASHED AN ANCIENT VIRUS INTO THE WORLD.
A WORLD, WHICH, IF I CAN'T SOMEHOW STOP THIS FROM SPREADING, WILL NEVER BE THE SAME AGAIN.
YO, SCALEY!
YEAH, YOU! WHO ELSE WOULD I BE TALKING TO?!?
I NEED TO ASK YOU A QUESTION.
SERIOUSLY, YOU SHOULD BE IN THE FUGLY HALL OF FAME, DUDE.
OR IS IT DUDE-ETTE?
GRRRRRR
FUNNY. EVEN WITH THE WORLD ENDING...
...YOU CAN'T QUESTION A DUDE'S SEXUALITY OR THEY GET ALL KINDS OF ANGRY.
MAN, IT'S THE GODDAMNED APOCALYPSE. WE SHOULD BE BETTER THAN THIS.
BRAVE GUY.
LOVES TO RAMBLE.

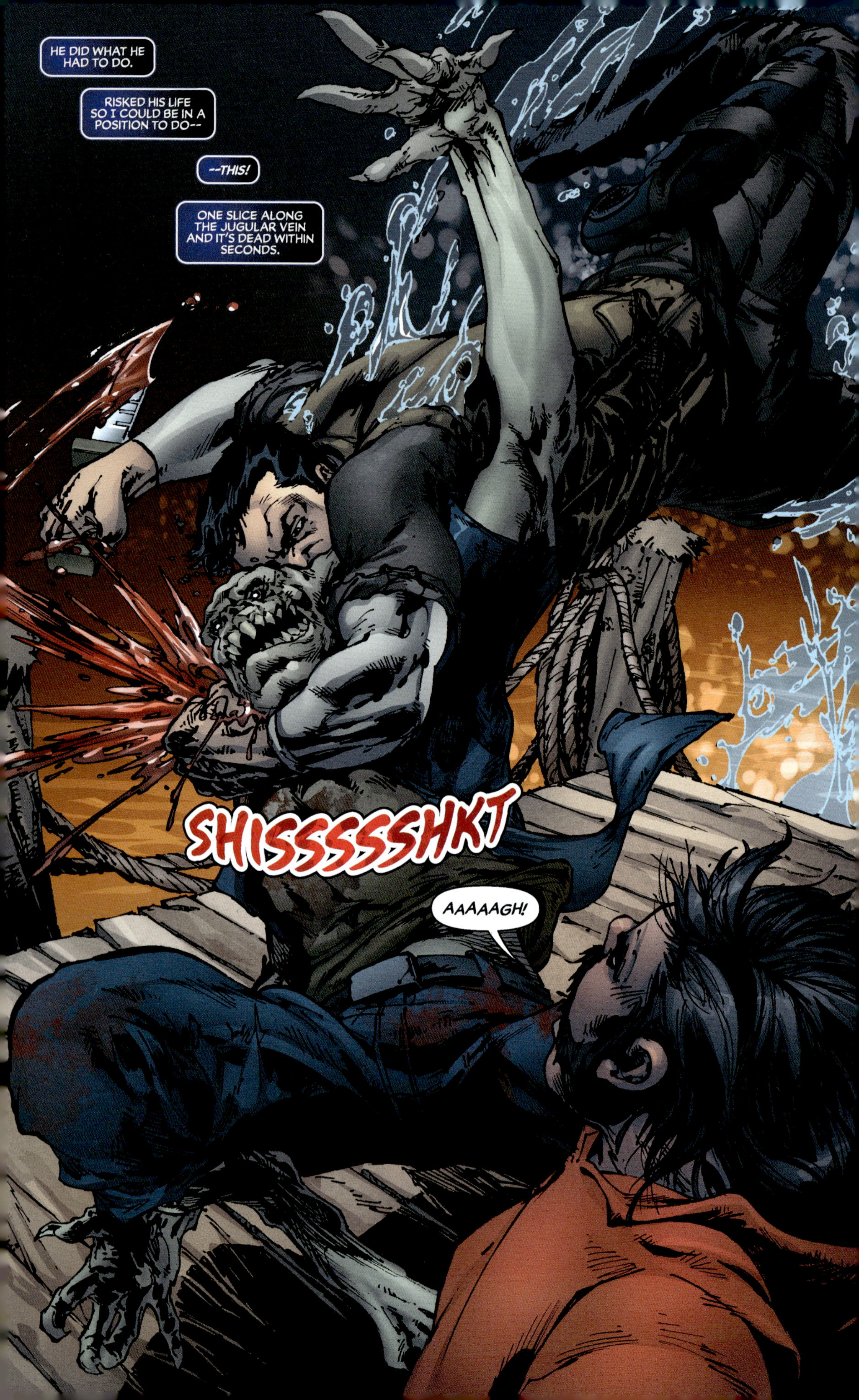
HE DID WHAT HE HAD TO DO.
RISKED HIS LIFE SO I COULD BE IN A POSITION TO DO--
--THIS!
ONE SLICE ALONG THE JUGULAR VEIN AND IT'S DEAD WITHIN SECONDS.
SHISSSSSHKT
AAAAAGH!

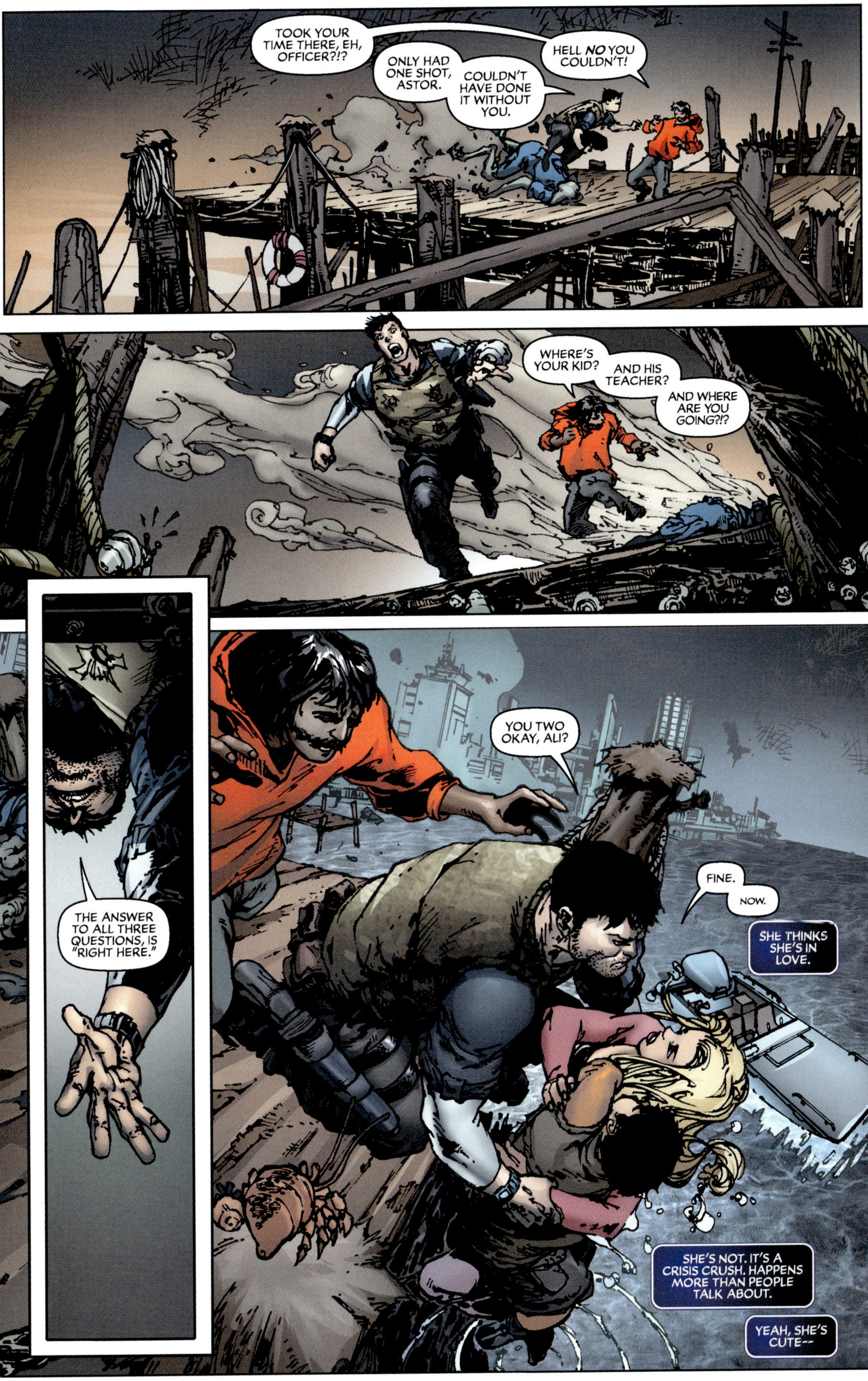
TOOK YOUR TIME THERE, EH, OFFICER?!?
ONLY HAD ONE SHOT, ASTOR.
COULDN'T HAVE DONE IT WITHOUT YOU.
HELL NO YOU COULDN'T!
WHERE'S YOUR KID?
AND HIS TEACHER?
AND WHERE ARE YOU GOING?!?
THE ANSWER TO ALL THREE QUESTIONS, IS "RIGHT HERE."
YOU TWO OKAY, ALI?
FINE.
NOW.
SHE THINKS SHE'S IN LOVE.
SHE'S NOT. IT'S A CRISIS CRUSH. HAPPENS MORE THAN PEOPLE TALK ABOUT.
YEAH, SHE'S CUTE--

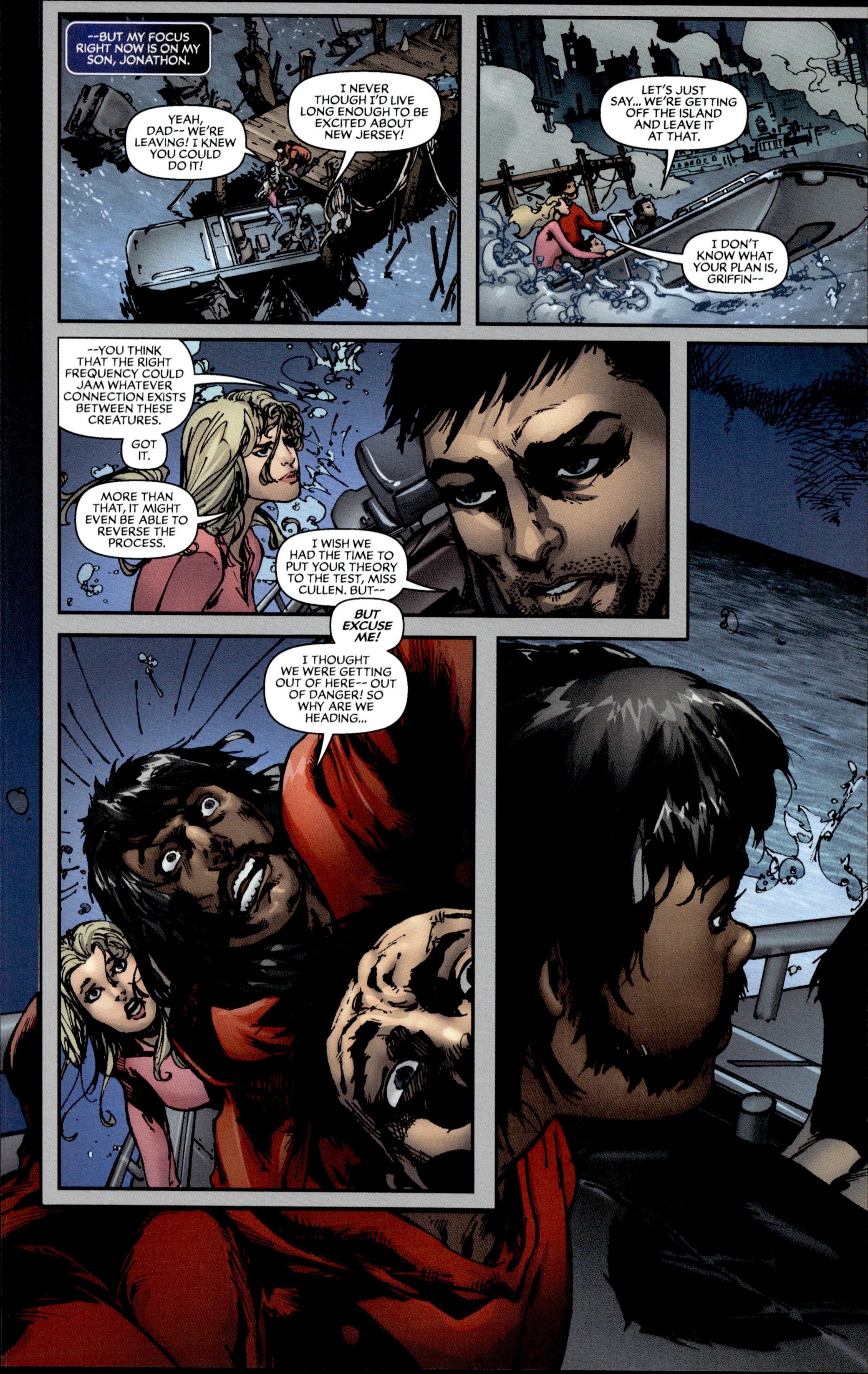
--BUT MY FOCUS RIGHT NOW IS ON MY SON, JONATHON.
YEAH, DAD-- WE'RE LEAVING! I KNEW YOU COULD DO IT!
I NEVER THOUGH I'D LIVE LONG ENOUGH TO BE EXCITED ABOUT NEW JERSEY!
LET'S JUST SAY... WE'RE GETTING OFF THE ISLAND AND LEAVE IT AT THAT.
I DON'T KNOW WHAT YOUR PLAN IS, GRIFFIN--
--YOU THINK THAT THE RIGHT FREQUENCY COULD JAM WHATEVER CONNECTION EXISTS BETWEEN THESE CREATURES.
GOT IT.
MORE THAN THAT, IT MIGHT EVEN BE ABLE TO REVERSE THE PROCESS.
I WISH WE HAD THE TIME TO PUT YOUR THEORY TO THE TEST, MISS CULLEN. BUT--
BUT EXCUSE ME!
I THOUGHT WE WERE GETTING OUT OF HERE-- OUT OF DANGER! SO WHY ARE WE HEADING...

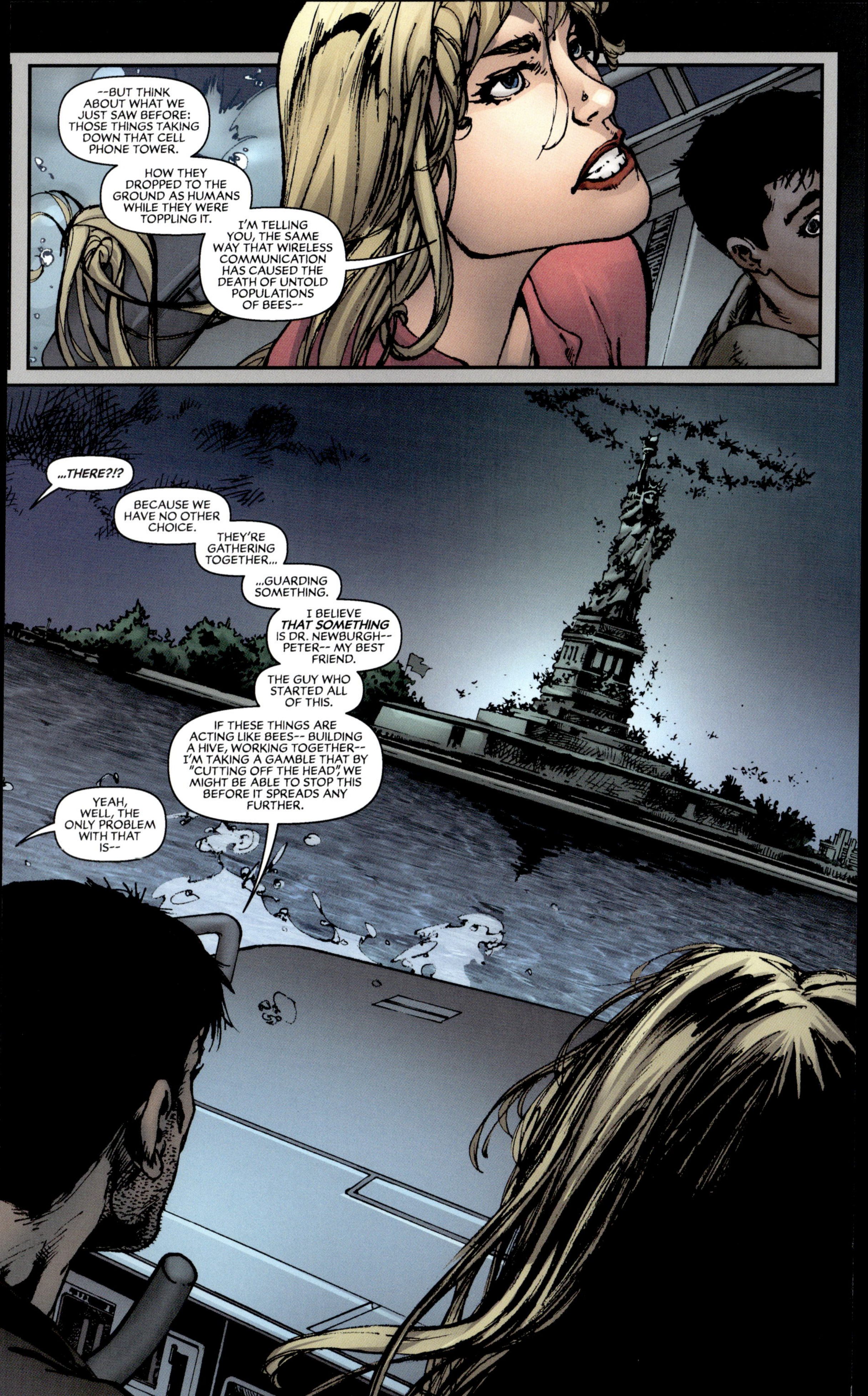
--BUT THINK ABOUT WHAT WE JUST SAW BEFORE: THOSE THINGS TAKING DOWN THAT CELL PHONE TOWER.
HOW THEY DROPPED TO THE GROUND AS HUMANS WHILE THEY WERE TOPPLING IT.
I'M TELLING YOU, THE SAME WAY THAT WIRELESS COMMUNICATION HAS CAUSED THE DEATH OF UNTOLD POPULATIONS OF BEES--
...THERE?!?
BECAUSE WE HAVE NO OTHER CHOICE.
THEY'RE GATHERING TOGETHER...
...GUARDING SOMETHING.
I BELIEVE *THAT SOMETHING* IS DR. NEWBURGH-- PETER-- MY BEST FRIEND.
THE GUY WHO STARTED ALL OF THIS.
IF THESE THINGS ARE ACTING LIKE BEES-- BUILDING A HIVE, WORKING TOGETHER-- I'M TAKING A GAMBLE THAT BY "CUTTING OFF THE HEAD," WE MIGHT BE ABLE TO STOP THIS BEFORE IT SPREADS ANY FURTHER.
YEAH, WELL, THE ONLY PROBLEM WITH THAT IS--

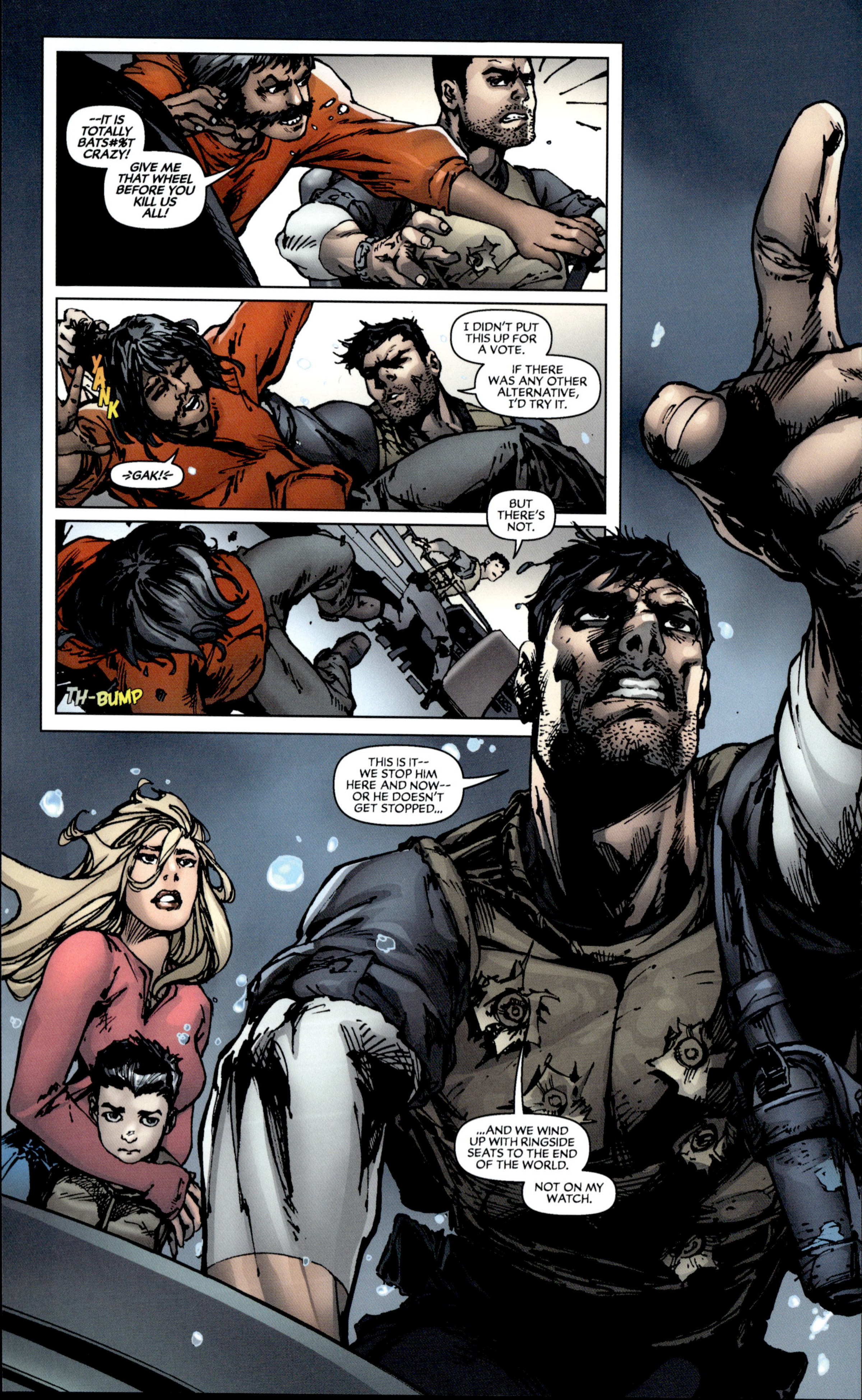
--IT IS TOTALLY BATS#%T CRAZY!
GIVE ME THAT WHEEL BEFORE YOU KILL US ALL!
YANK
I DIDN'T PUT THIS UP FOR A VOTE.
IF THERE WAS ANY OTHER ALTERNATIVE, I'D TRY IT.
GAK!
BUT THERE'S NOT.
TH-BUMP
THIS IS IT-- WE STOP HIM HERE AND NOW-- OR HE DOESN'T GET STOPPED...
...AND WE WIND UP WITH RINGSIDE SEATS TO THE END OF THE WORLD.
NOT ON MY WATCH.

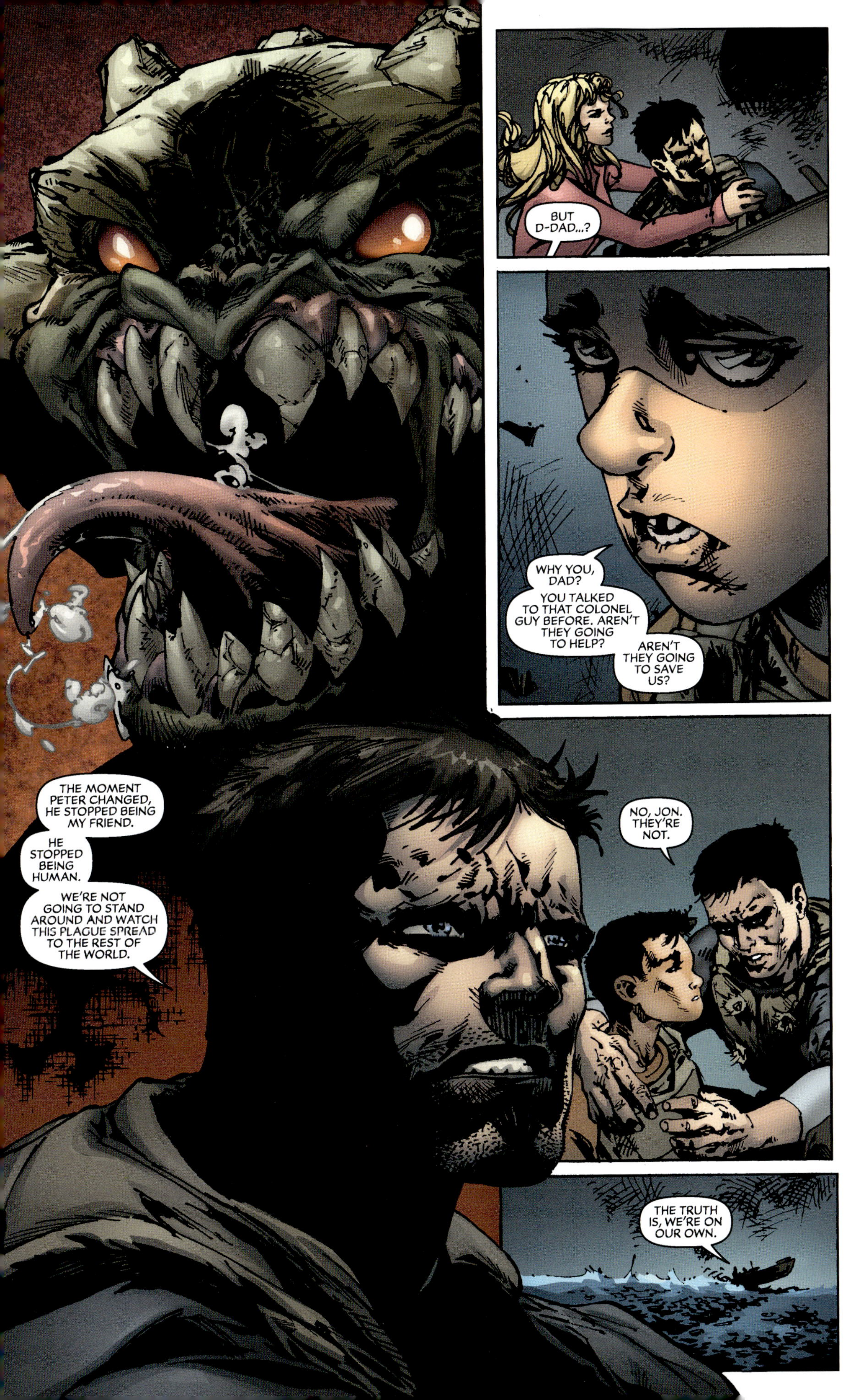
BUT D-DAD...?
WHY YOU, DAD?
YOU TALKED TO THAT COLONEL GUY BEFORE. AREN'T THEY GOING TO HELP?
AREN'T THEY GOING TO SAVE US?
THE MOMENT PETER CHANGED, HE STOPPED BEING MY FRIEND.
HE STOPPED BEING HUMAN.
WE'RE NOT GOING TO STAND AROUND AND WATCH THIS PLAGUE SPREAD TO THE REST OF THE WORLD.
NO, JON. THEY'RE NOT.
THE TRUTH IS, WE'RE ON OUR OWN.

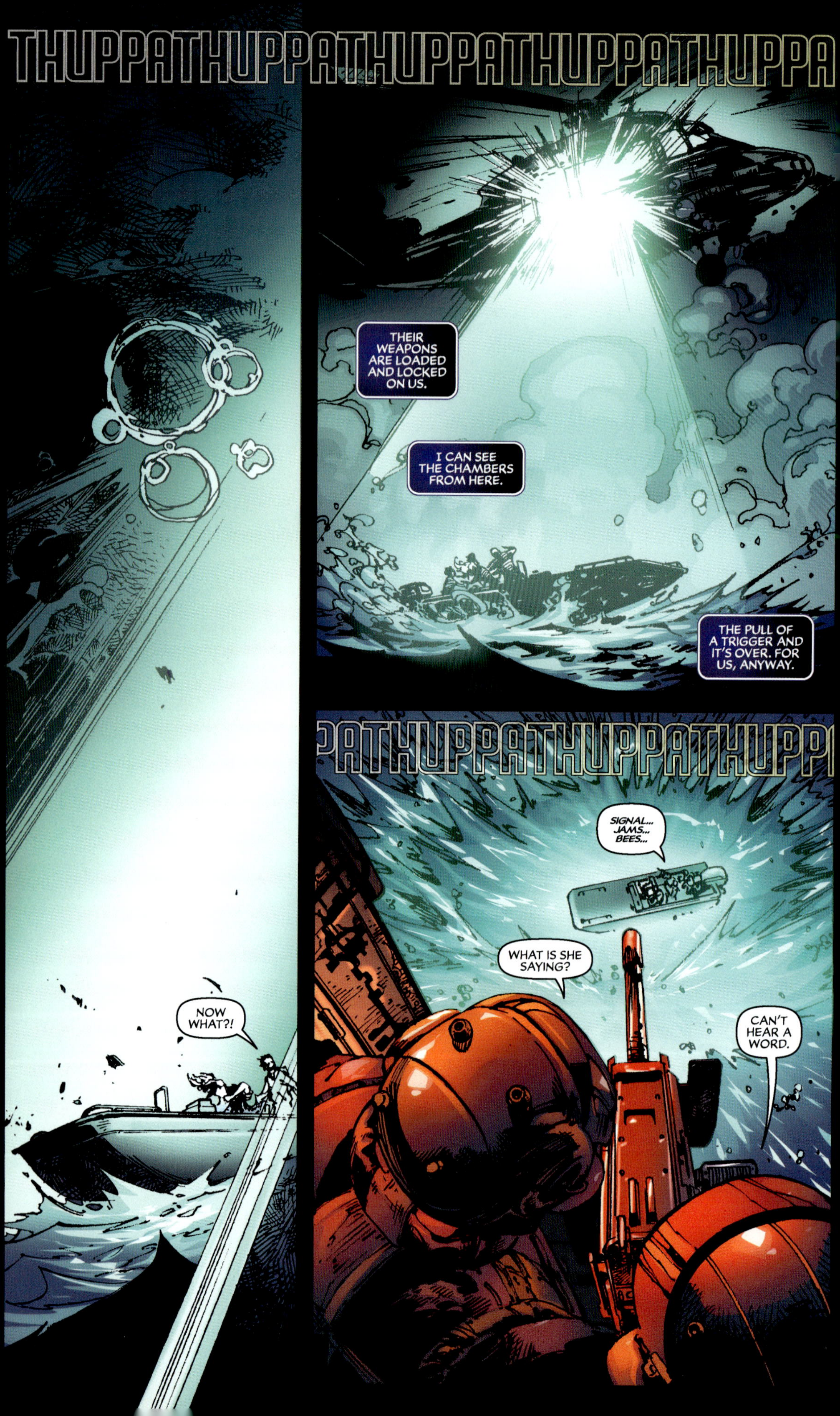
THUPPATHUPPATHUPPATHUPPATHUPPA
NOW WHAT?!
THEIR WEAPONS ARE LOADED AND LOCKED ON US.
I CAN SEE THE CHAMBERS FROM HERE.
THE PULL OF A TRIGGER AND IT'S OVER. FOR US, ANYWAY.
PATHUPPATHUPPATHUPP
SIGNAL... JAMS... BEES...
WHAT IS SHE SAYING?
CAN'T HEAR A WORD.

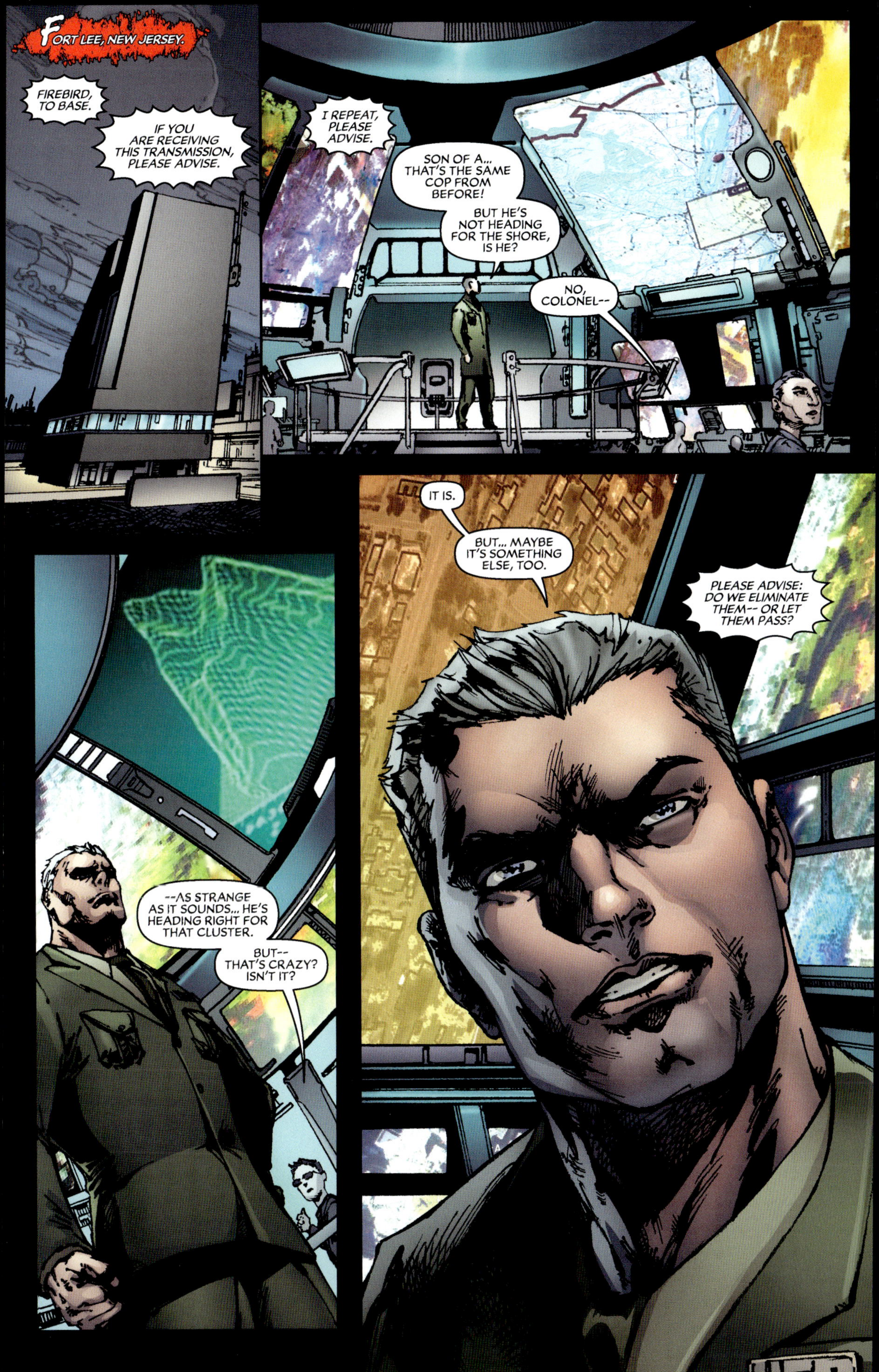
FORT LEE, NEW JERSEY.
FIREBIRD, TO BASE.
IF YOU ARE RECEIVING THIS TRANSMISSION, PLEASE ADVISE.
I REPEAT, PLEASE ADVISE.
SON OF A... THAT'S THE SAME COP FROM BEFORE!
BUT HE'S NOT HEADING FOR THE SHORE, IS HE?
NO, COLONEL--
--AS STRANGE AS IT SOUNDS... HE'S HEADING RIGHT FOR THAT CLUSTER.
BUT-- THAT'S CRAZY? ISN'T IT?
IT IS.
BUT... MAYBE IT'S SOMETHING ELSE, TOO.
PLEASE ADVISE: DO WE ELIMINATE THEM-- OR LET THEM PASS?

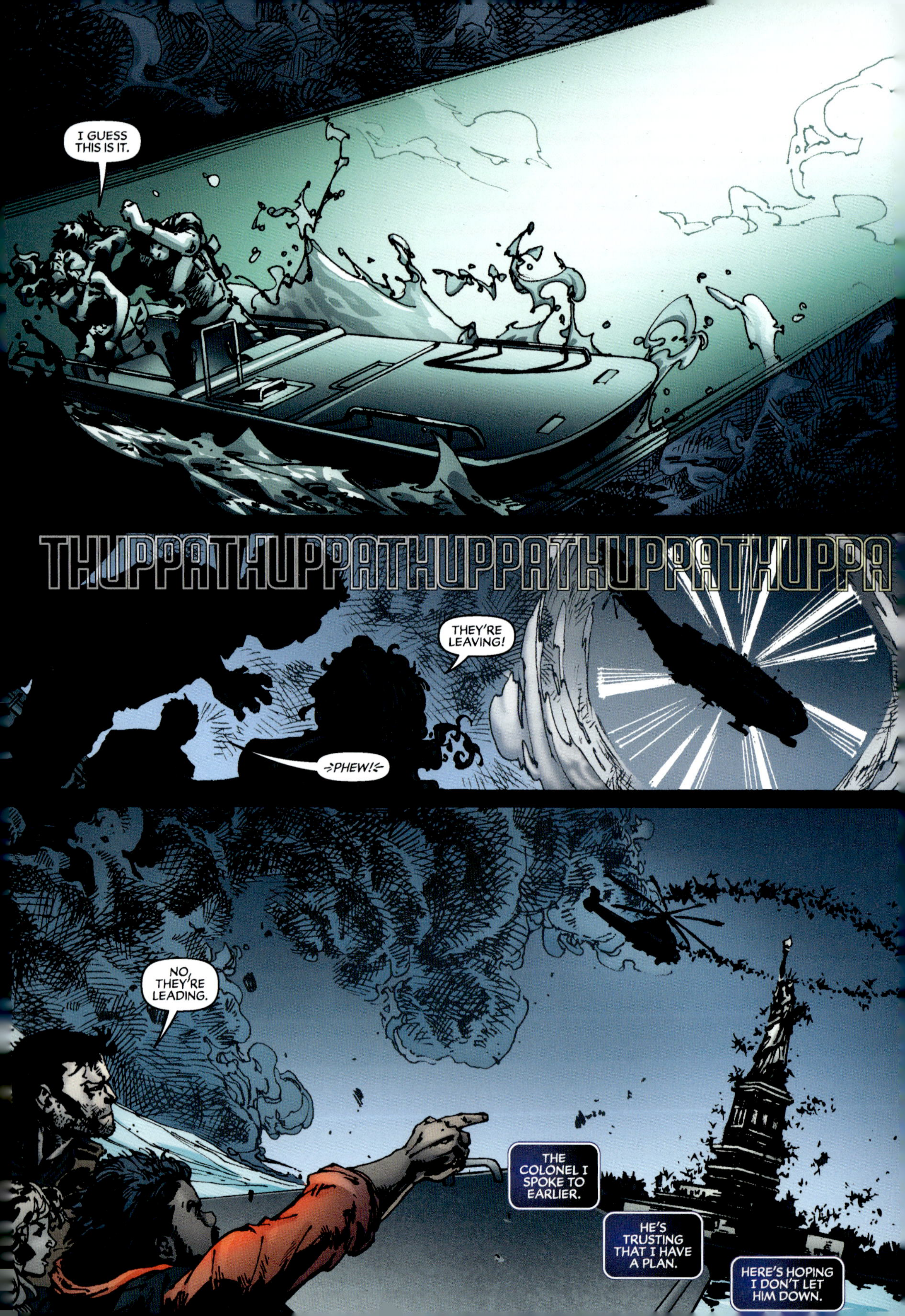
I GUESS THIS IS IT.
THUPPATHUPPATHUPPATHUPPATHUPPA
THEY'RE LEAVING!
PHEW!
NO, THEY'RE LEADING.
THE COLONEL I SPOKE TO EARLIER.
HE'S TRUSTING THAT I HAVE A PLAN.
HERE'S HOPING I DON'T LET HIM DOWN.

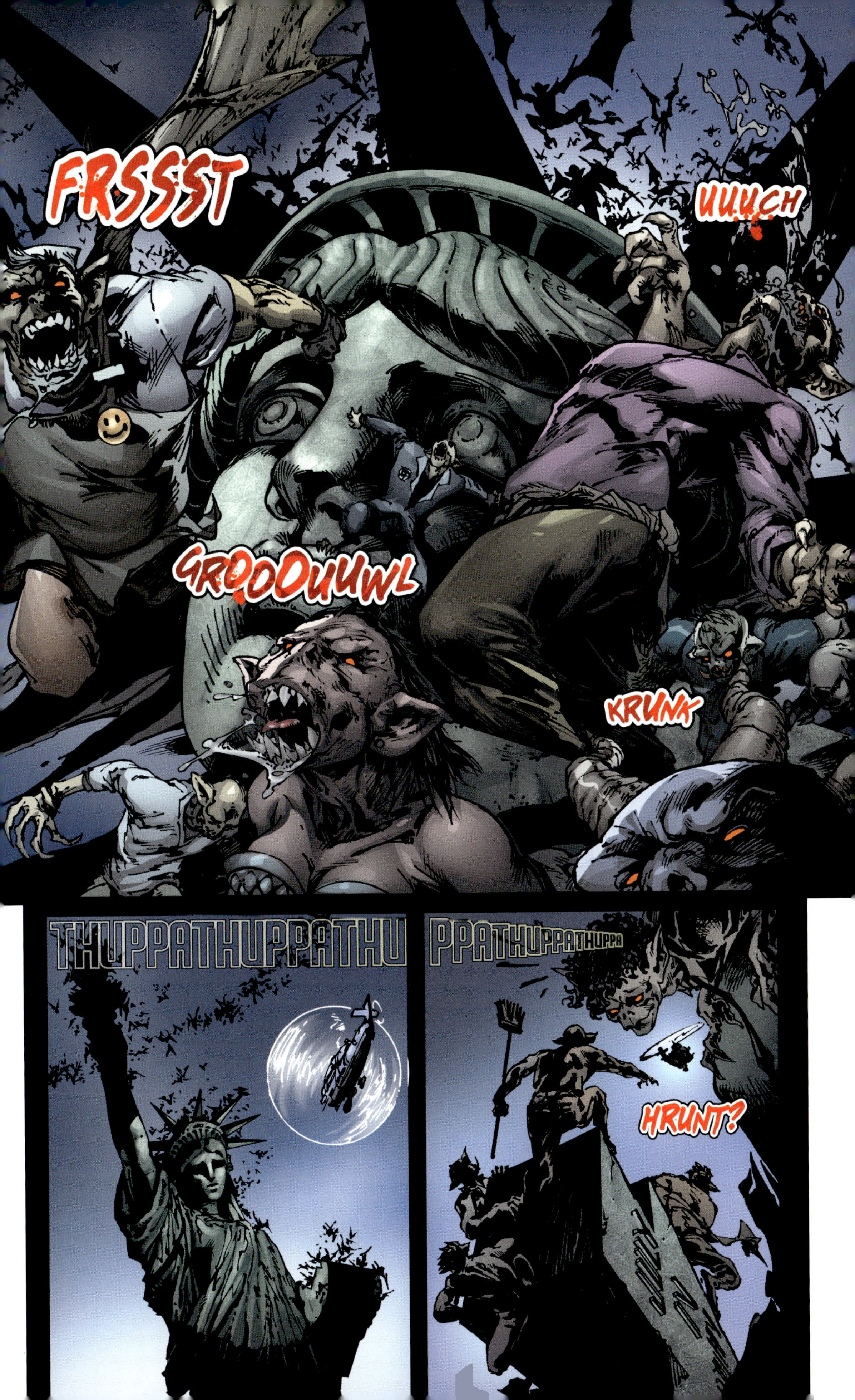
FRSSST
UUUCH
GROOOUUUWL
KRUNK
THUPPATHUPPATHU
PPATHUPPATHUPPA
HRUNT?

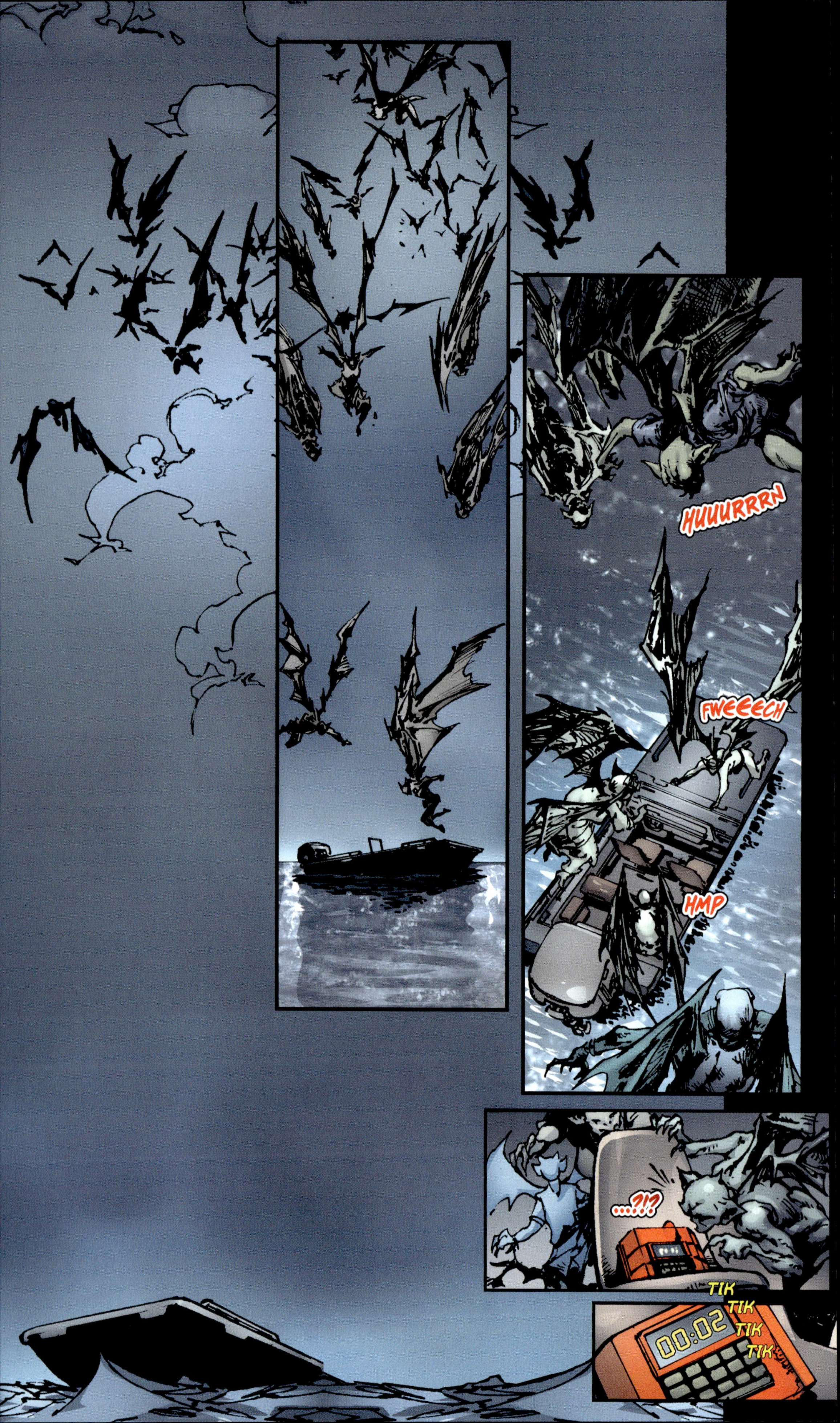
HUUURRRN
FWEEEECH
HMP
...?!?
00:02
TIK
TIK
TIK
TIK

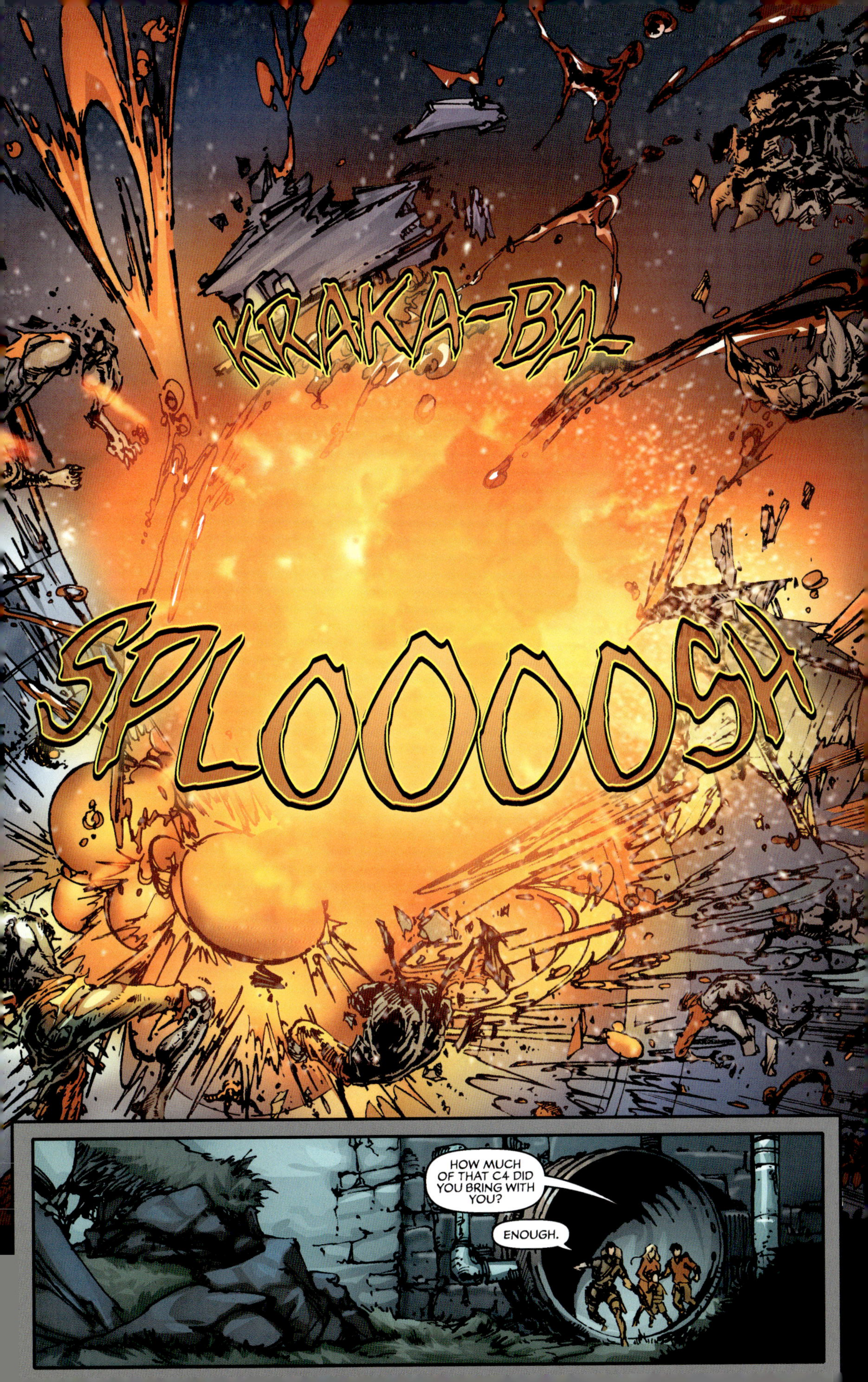
KRAKA-BA-
SPLOOOOSH
HOW MUCH OF THAT C4 DID YOU BRING WITH YOU?
ENOUGH.

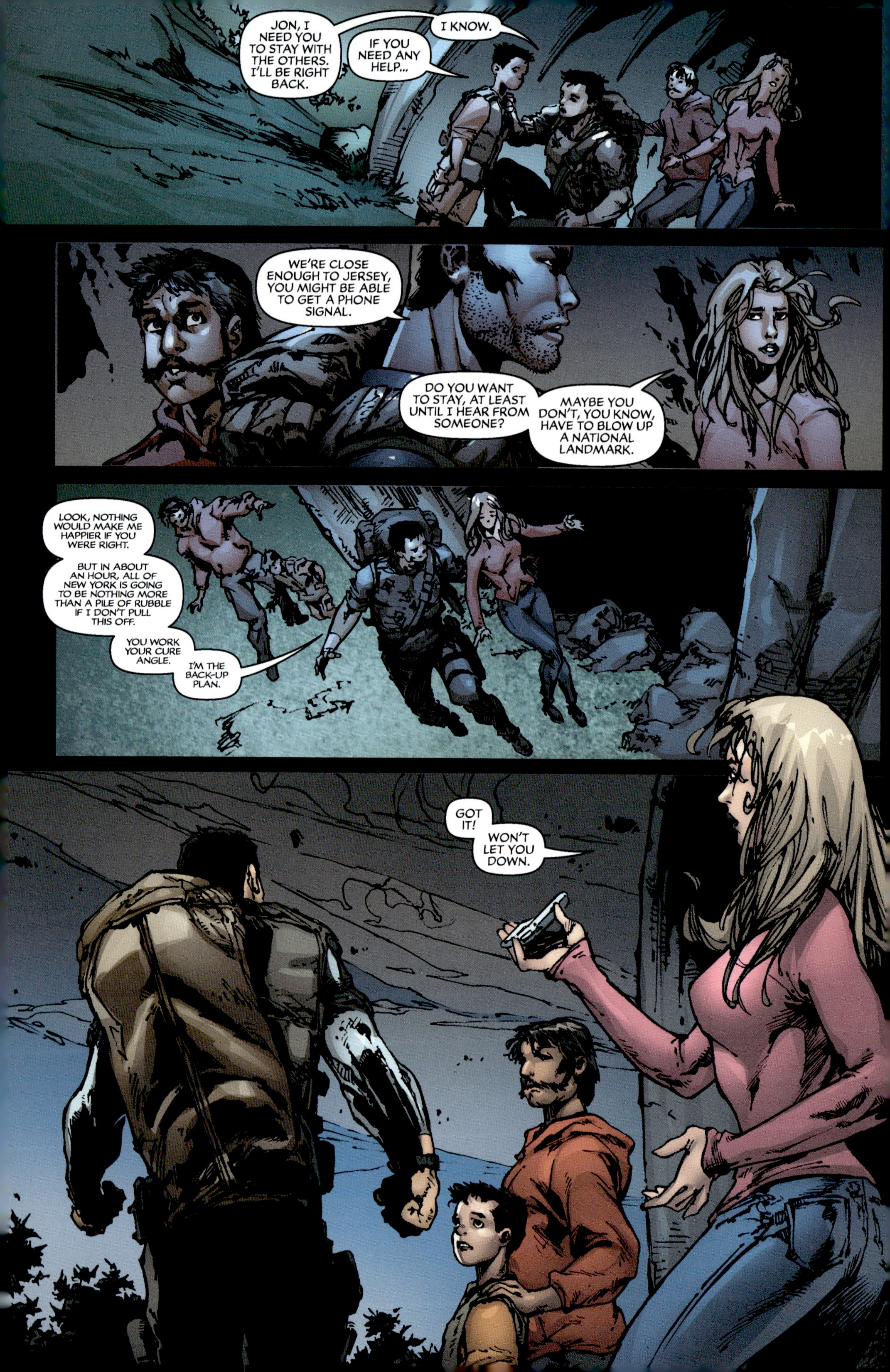
JON, I NEED YOU TO STAY WITH THE OTHERS. I'LL BE RIGHT BACK.
I KNOW.
IF YOU NEED ANY HELP...
WE'RE CLOSE ENOUGH TO JERSEY, YOU MIGHT BE ABLE TO GET A PHONE SIGNAL.
DO YOU WANT TO STAY, AT LEAST UNTIL I HEAR FROM SOMEONE?
MAYBE YOU DON'T, YOU KNOW, HAVE TO BLOW UP A NATIONAL LANDMARK.
LOOK, NOTHING WOULD MAKE ME HAPPIER IF YOU WERE RIGHT.
BUT IN ABOUT AN HOUR, ALL OF NEW YORK IS GOING TO BE NOTHING MORE THAN A PILE OF RUBBLE IF I DON'T PULL THIS OFF.
YOU WORK YOUR CURE ANGLE.
I'M THE BACK-UP PLAN.
GOT IT!
WON'T LET YOU DOWN.

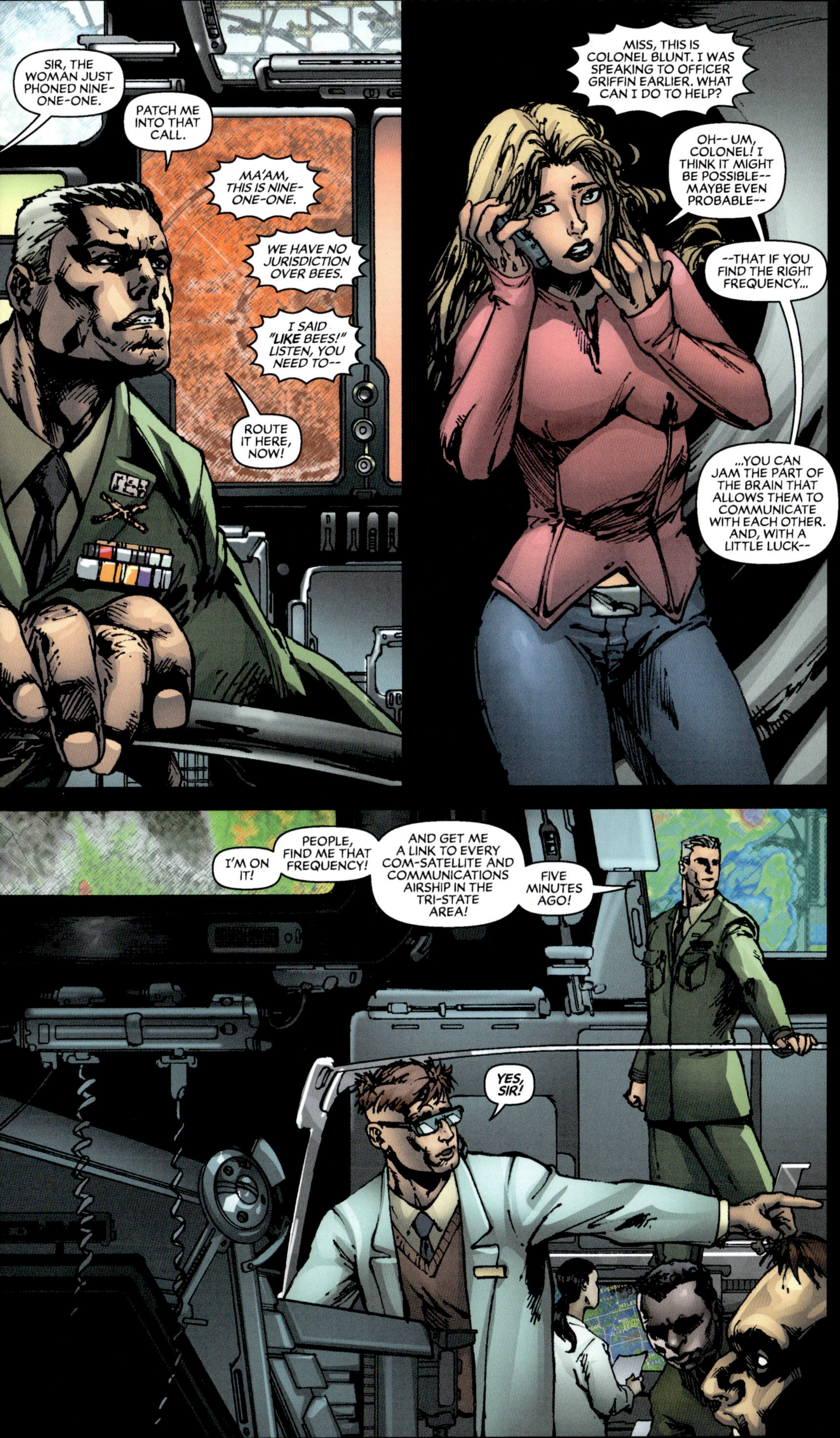
SIR, THE WOMAN JUST PHONED NINE-ONE-ONE.
PATCH ME INTO THAT CALL.
MA'AM, THIS IS NINE-ONE-ONE.
WE HAVE NO JURISDICTION OVER BEES.
I SAID "LIKE BEES!" LISTEN, YOU NEED TO--
ROUTE IT HERE, NOW!
MISS, THIS IS COLONEL BLUNT. I WAS SPEAKING TO OFFICER GRIFFIN EARLIER. WHAT CAN I DO TO HELP?
OH-- UM, COLONEL! I THINK IT MIGHT BE POSSIBLE-- MAYBE EVEN PROBABLE--
--THAT IF YOU FIND THE RIGHT FREQUENCY...
...YOU CAN JAM THE PART OF THE BRAIN THAT ALLOWS THEM TO COMMUNICATE WITH EACH OTHER. AND, WITH A LITTLE LUCK--
I'M ON IT!
PEOPLE, FIND ME THAT FREQUENCY!
AND GET ME A LINK TO EVERY COM-SATELLITE AND COMMUNICATIONS AIRSHIP IN THE TRI-STATE AREA!
FIVE MINUTES AGO!
YES, SIR!

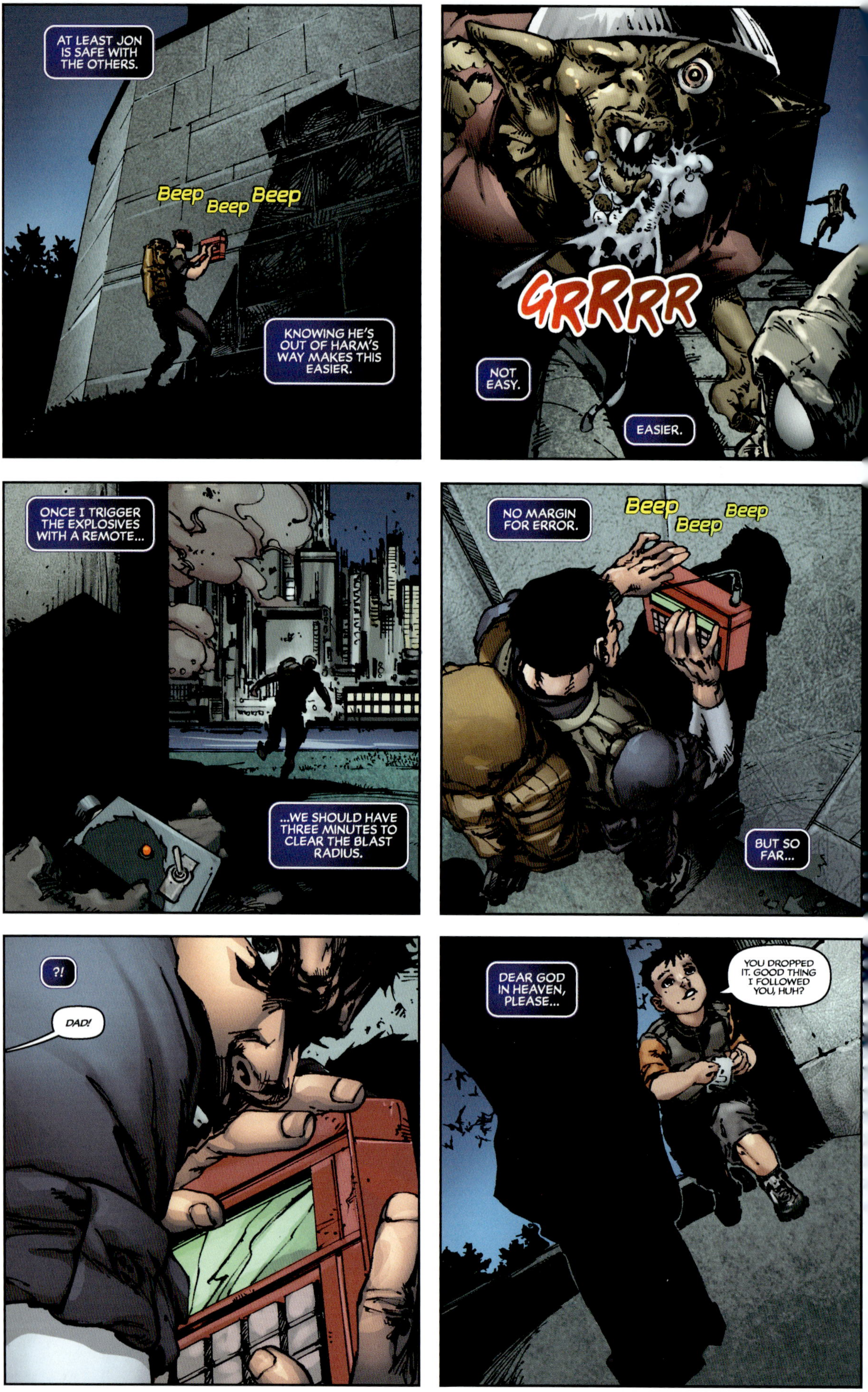
AT LEAST JON IS SAFE WITH THE OTHERS.
Beep Beep Beep
KNOWING HE'S OUT OF HARM'S WAY MAKES THIS EASIER.
GRRRR
NOT EASY.
EASIER.
ONCE I TRIGGER THE EXPLOSIVES WITH A REMOTE...
...WE SHOULD HAVE THREE MINUTES TO CLEAR THE BLAST RADIUS.
NO MARGIN FOR ERROR.
Beep Beep Beep
BUT SO FAR...
?!
DAD!
DEAR GOD IN HEAVEN, PLEASE...
YOU DROPPED IT. GOOD THING I FOLLOWED YOU, HUH?

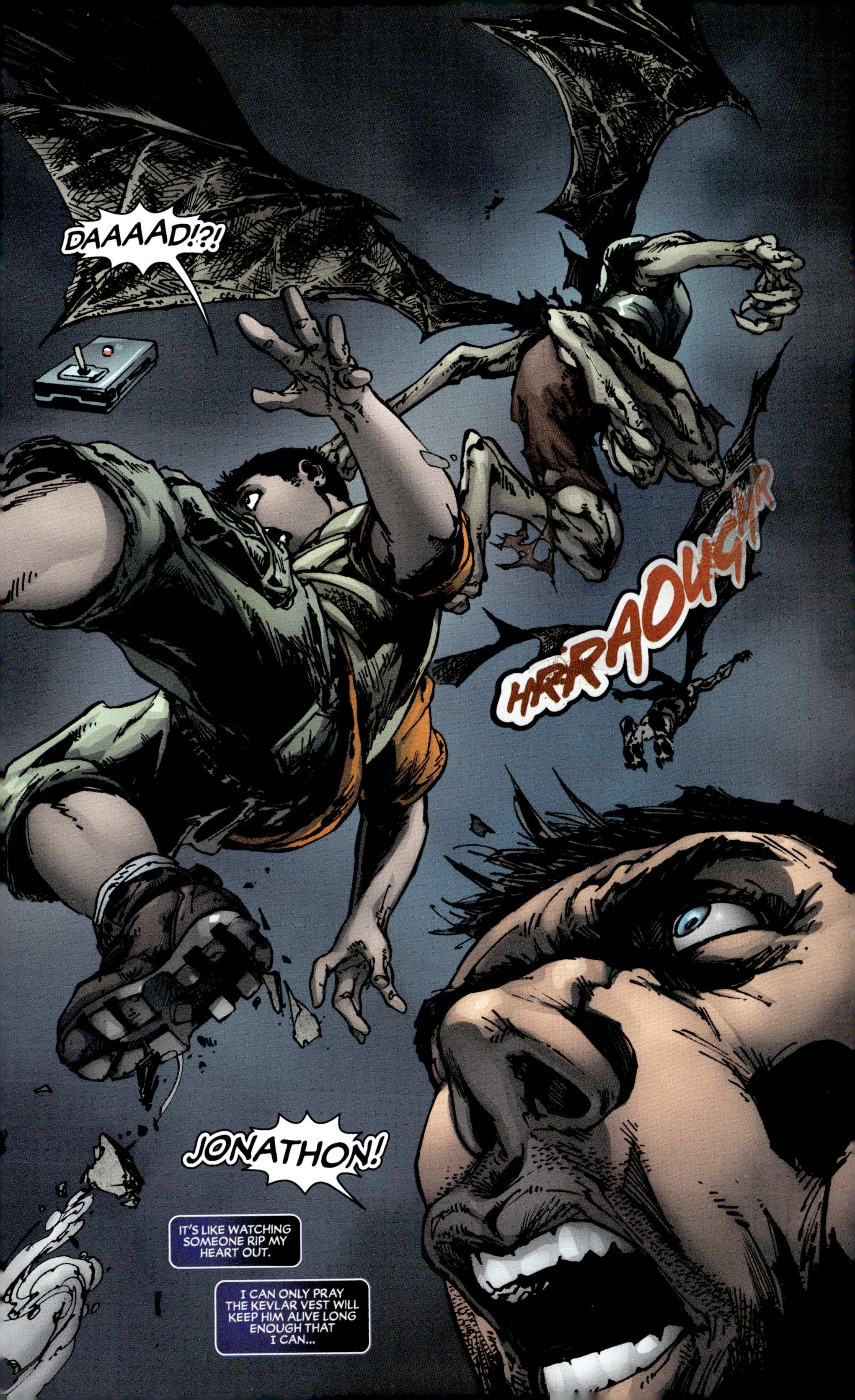
DAAAAD!?!
HRRRAOUGHR
JONATHON!
IT'S LIKE WATCHING SOMEONE RIP MY HEART OUT.
I CAN ONLY PRAY THE KEVLAR VEST WILL KEEP HIM ALIVE LONG ENOUGH THAT I CAN...

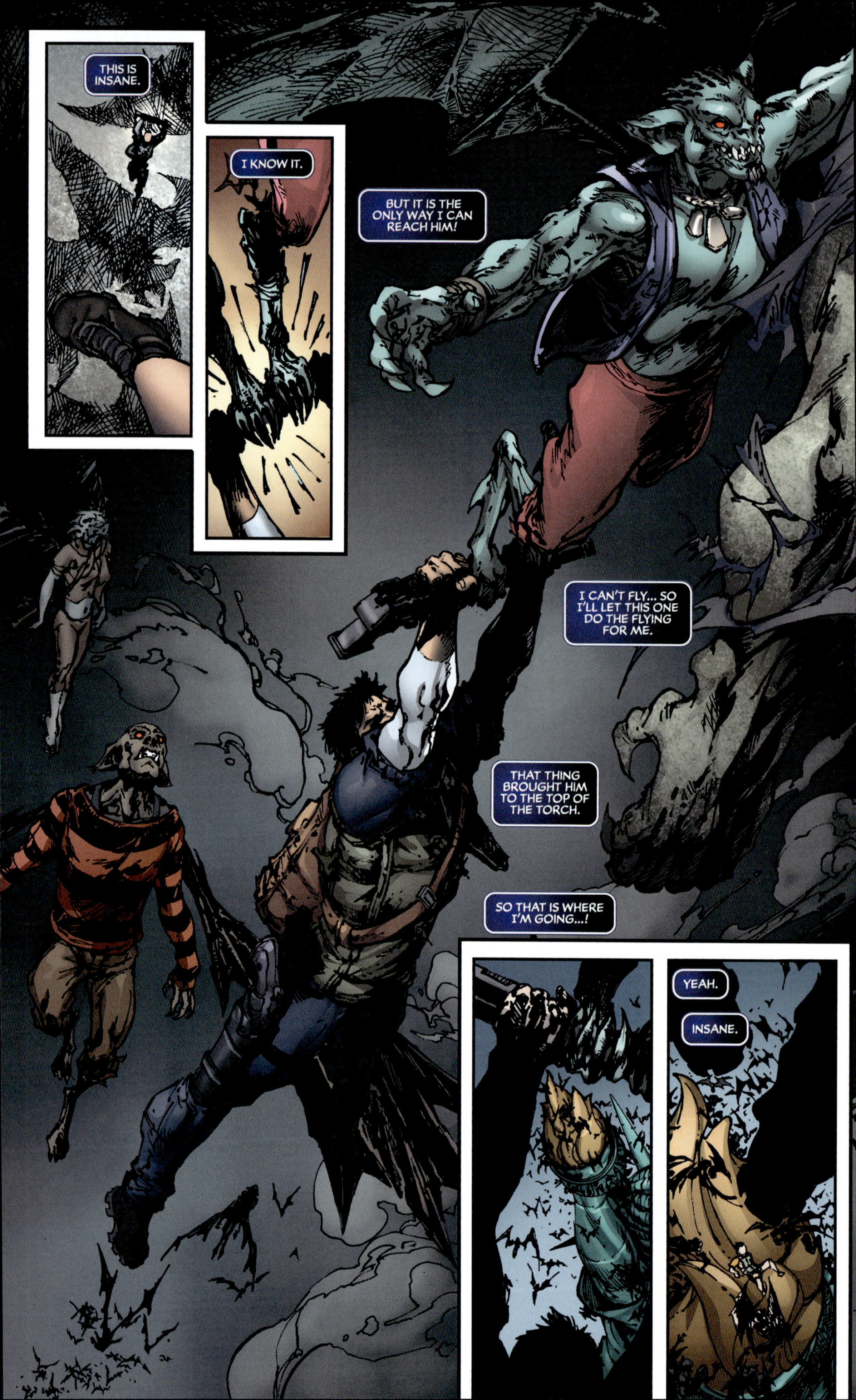
THIS IS INSANE.
I KNOW IT.
BUT IT IS THE ONLY WAY I CAN REACH HIM!
I CAN'T FLY... SO I'LL LET THIS ONE DO THE FLYING FOR ME.
THAT THING BROUGHT HIM TO THE TOP OF THE TORCH.
SO THAT IS WHERE I'M GOING...!
YEAH.
INSANE.

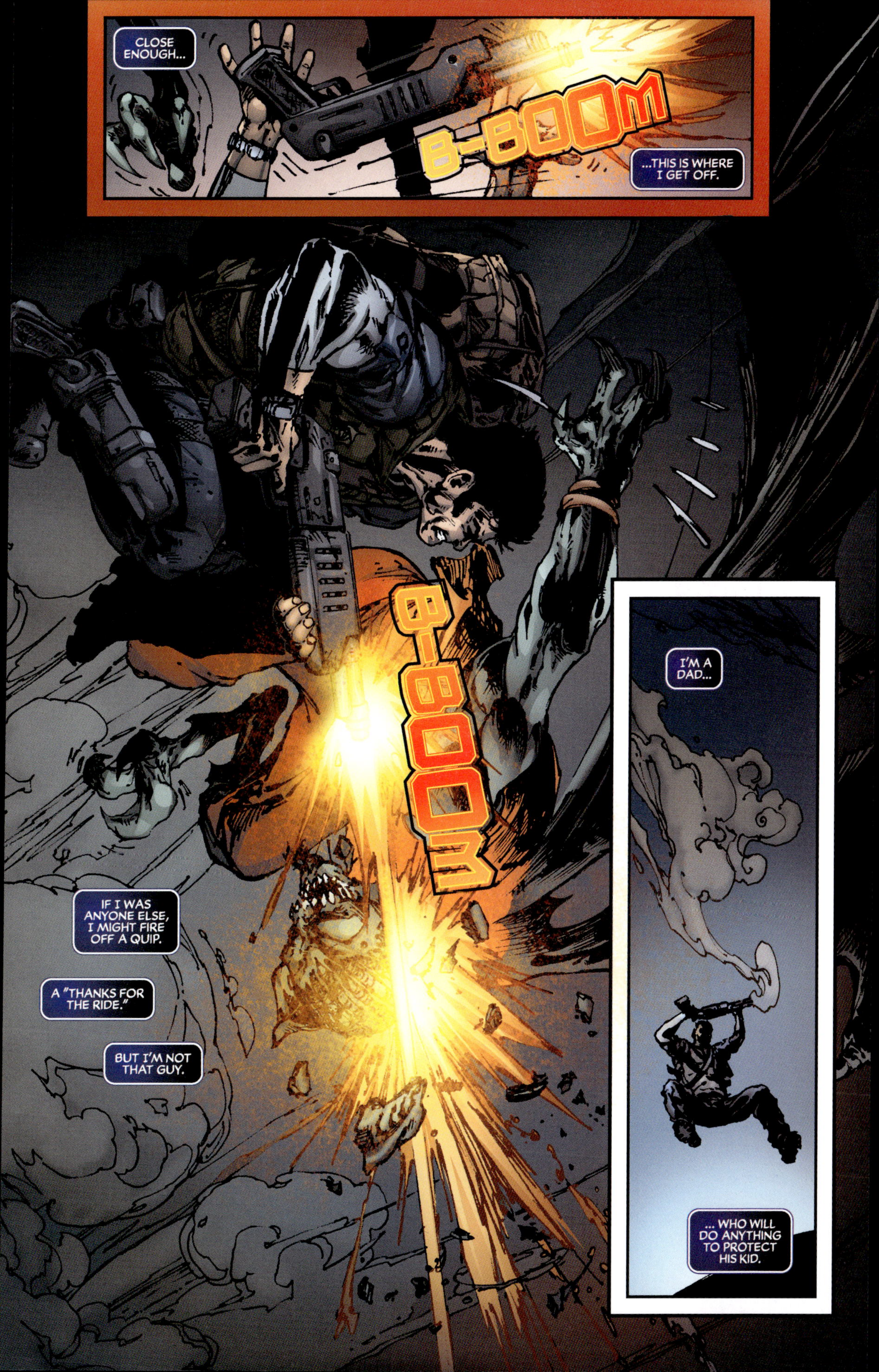

CLOSE ENOUGH...
B-BOOM
...THIS IS WHERE I GET OFF.
B-BOOM
IF I WAS ANYONE ELSE, I MIGHT FIRE OFF A QUIP.
A "THANKS FOR THE RIDE."
BUT I'M NOT THAT GUY.
I'M A DAD...
... WHO WILL DO ANYTHING TO PROTECT HIS KID.

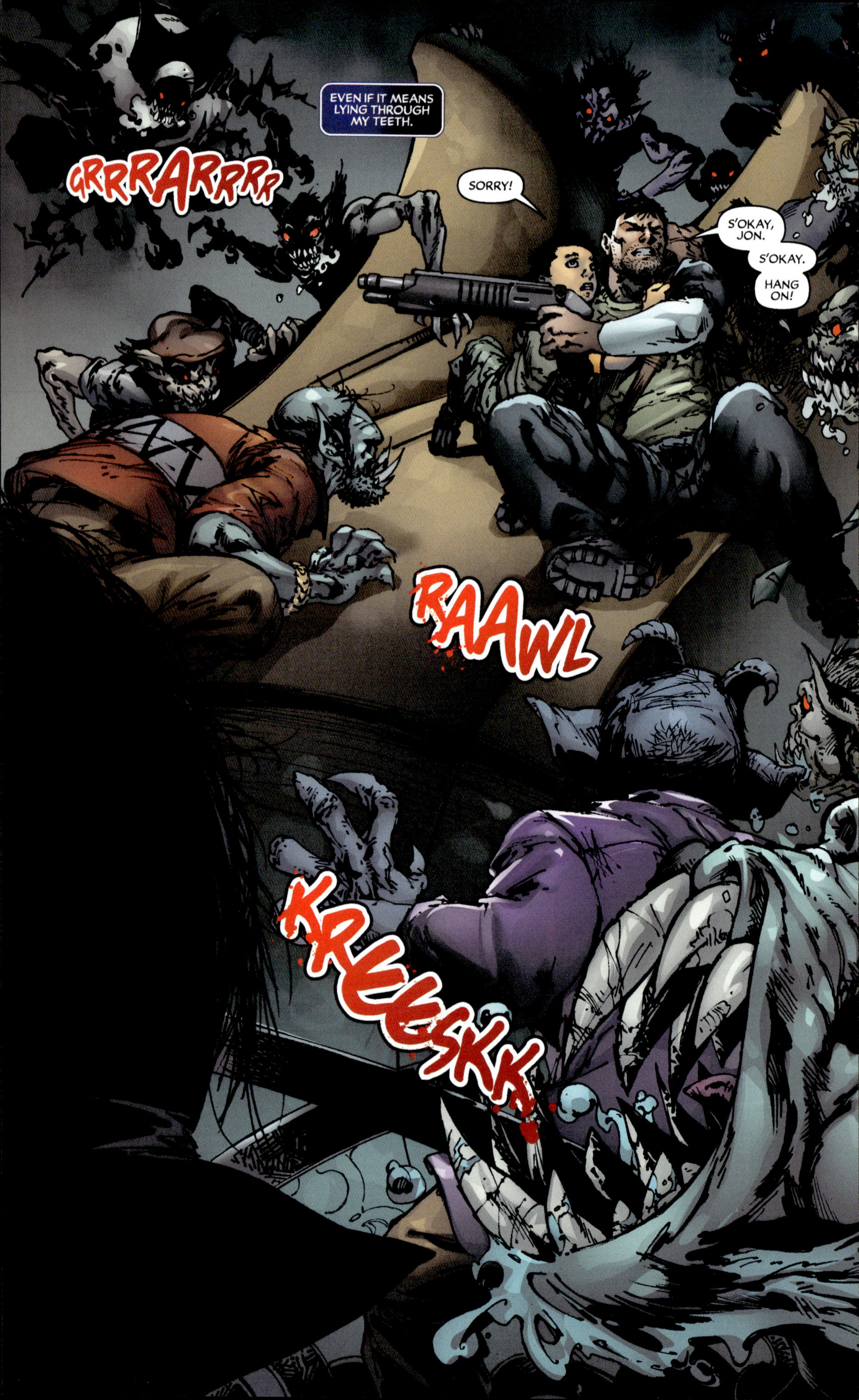
EVEN IF IT MEANS LYING THROUGH MY TEETH.
GRRRARRRRR
SORRY!
S'OKAY, JON.
S'OKAY.
HANG ON!
RAAWL
KREEESKK

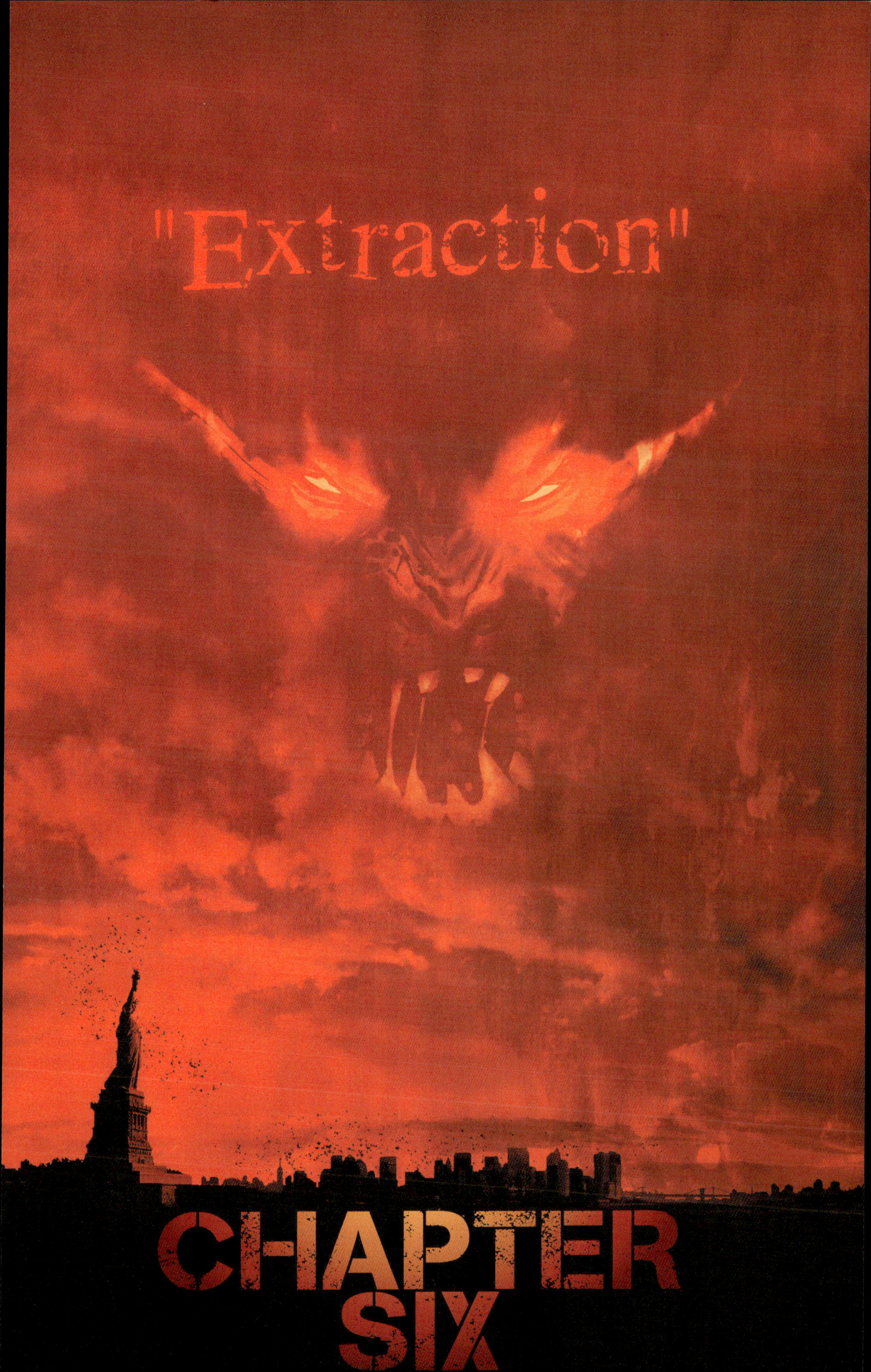
"Extraction"
CHAPTER
SIX

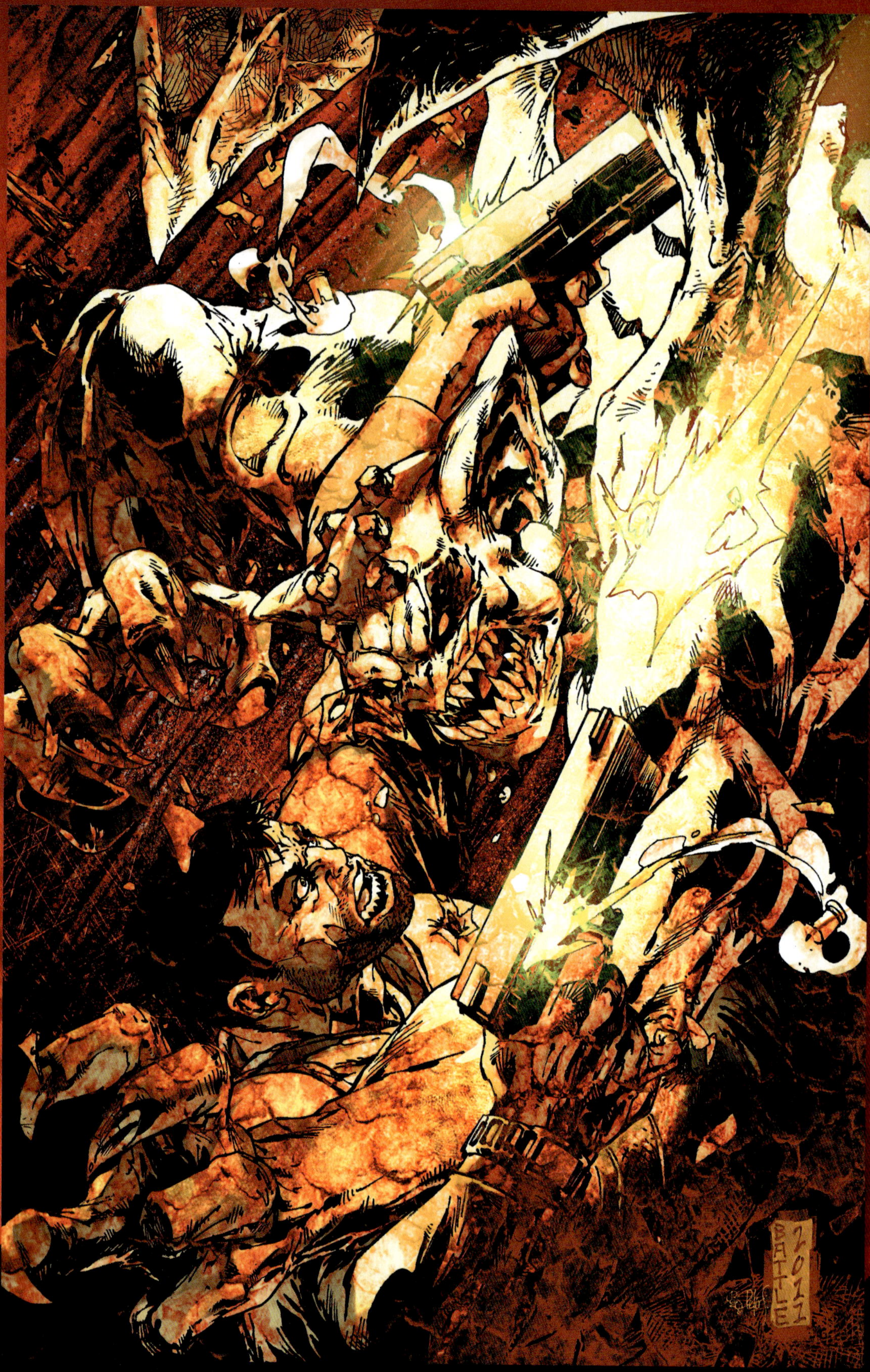
BATTLE 2011

Retailer "Infected" Incentive Edition Cover C to

THE SCOURGE #6

by

Eric **BATTLE** | Peter **STEIGERWALD**

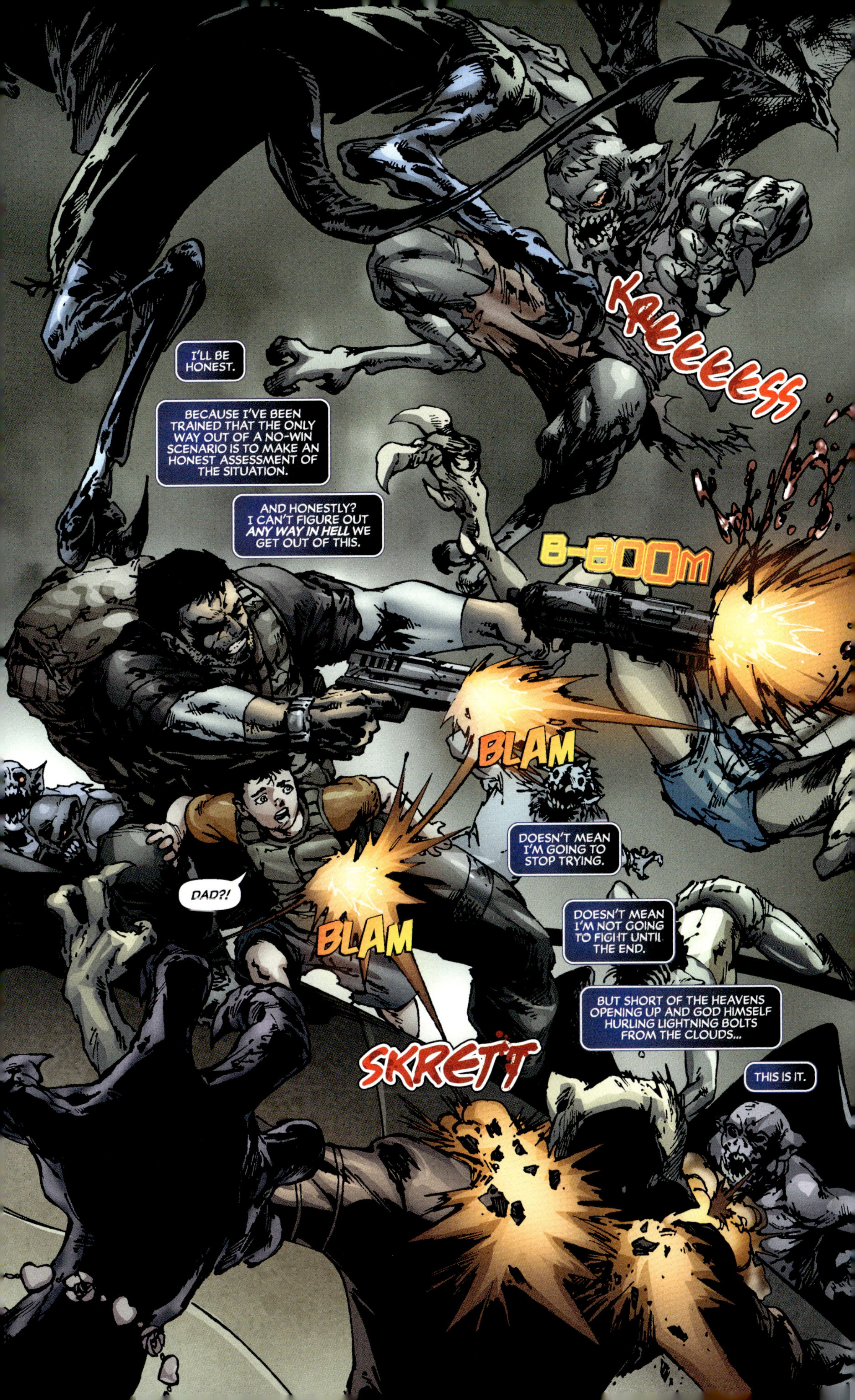
KREEEEESS
I'LL BE HONEST.
BECAUSE I'VE BEEN TRAINED THAT THE ONLY WAY OUT OF A NO-WIN SCENARIO IS TO MAKE AN HONEST ASSESSMENT OF THE SITUATION.
AND HONESTLY? I CAN'T FIGURE OUT *ANY WAY IN HELL* WE GET OUT OF THIS.
B-BOOM
BLAM
DOESN'T MEAN I'M GOING TO STOP TRYING.
DAD?!
BLAM
DOESN'T MEAN I'M NOT GOING TO FIGHT UNTIL THE END.
BUT SHORT OF THE HEAVENS OPENING UP AND GOD HIMSELF HURLING LIGHTNING BOLTS FROM THE CLOUDS...
SKRETT
THIS IS IT.

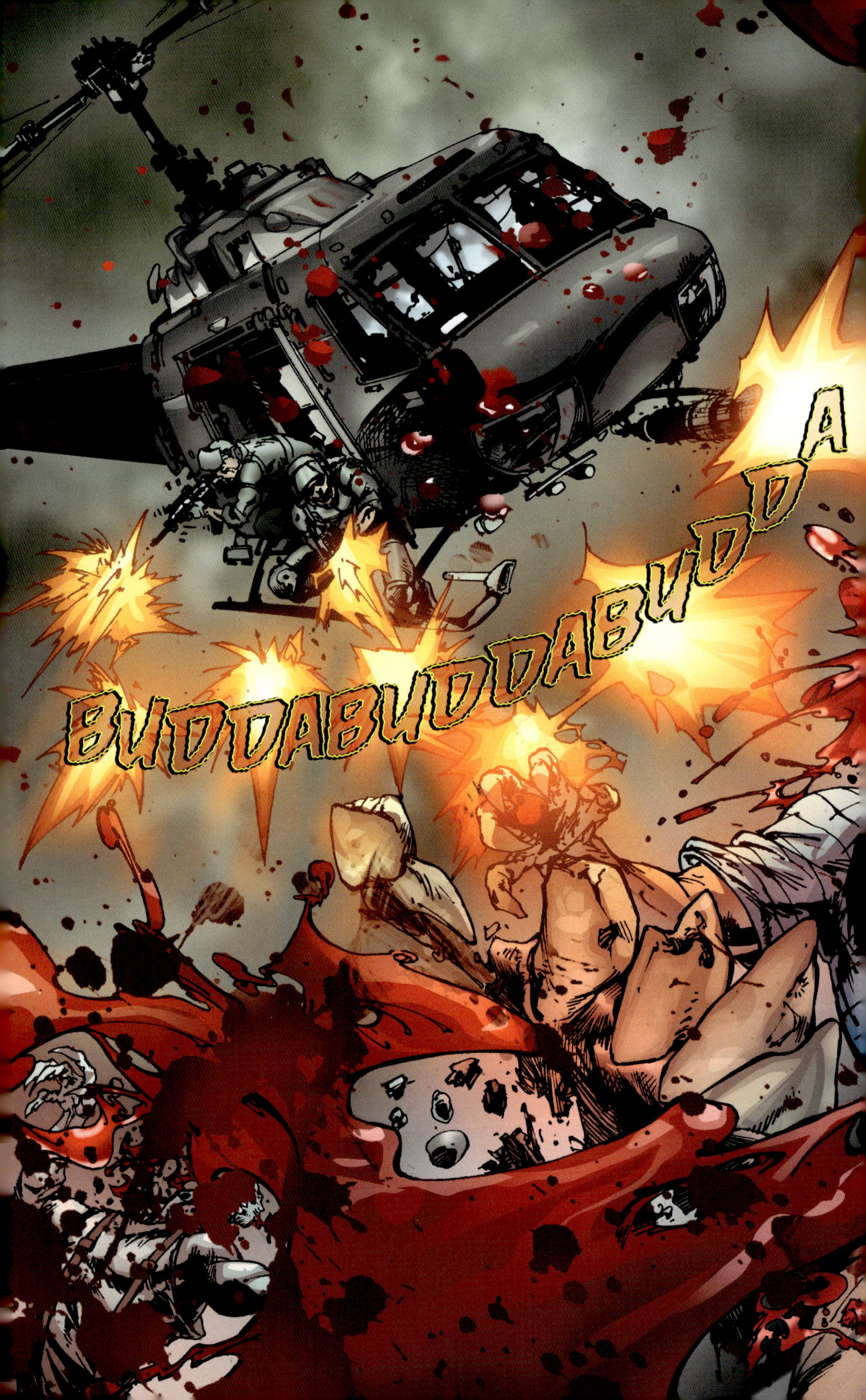
BUDDABUDDABUDDA

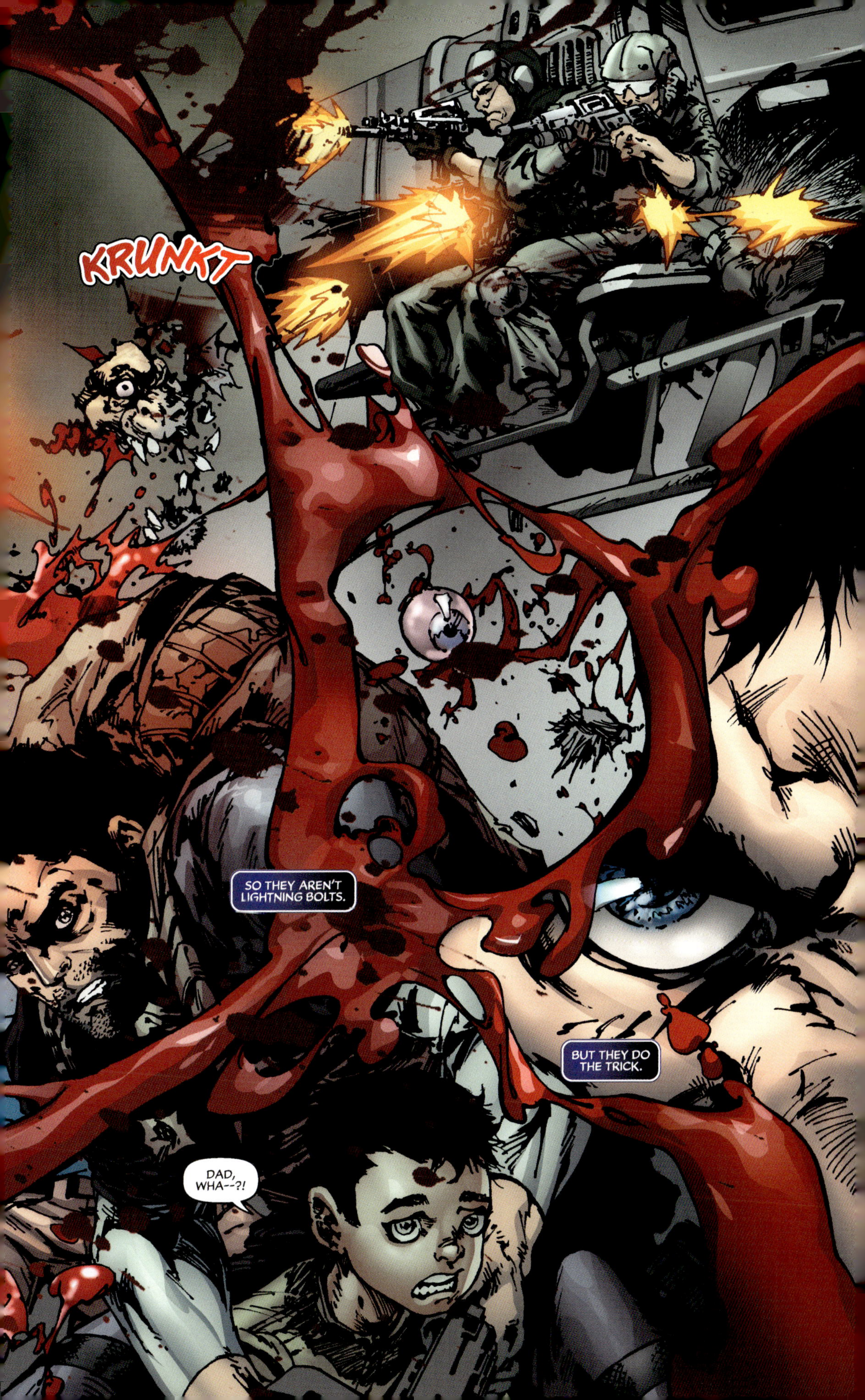
KRUNKT
SO THEY AREN'T LIGHTNING BOLTS.
BUT THEY DO THE TRICK.
DAD, WHA--?!

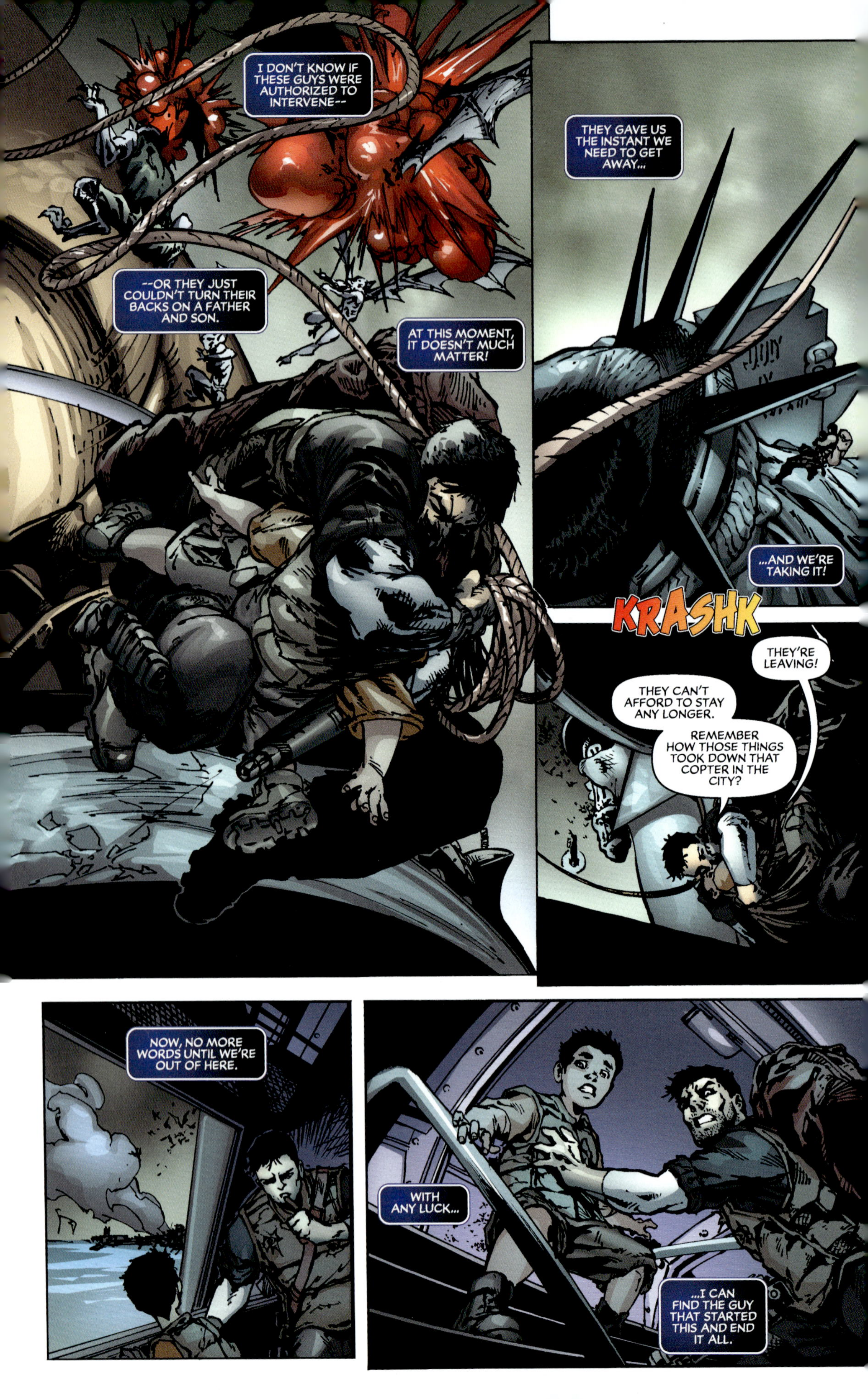
I DON'T KNOW IF THESE GUYS WERE AUTHORIZED TO INTERVENE--
--OR THEY JUST COULDN'T TURN THEIR BACKS ON A FATHER AND SON.
AT THIS MOMENT, IT DOESN'T MUCH MATTER!
THEY GAVE US THE INSTANT WE NEED TO GET AWAY...
...AND WE'RE TAKING IT!
KRASHK
THEY'RE LEAVING!
THEY CAN'T AFFORD TO STAY ANY LONGER.
REMEMBER HOW THOSE THINGS TOOK DOWN THAT COPTER IN THE CITY?
NOW, NO MORE WORDS UNTIL WE'RE OUT OF HERE.
WITH ANY LUCK...
...I CAN FIND THE GUY THAT STARTED THIS AND END IT ALL.

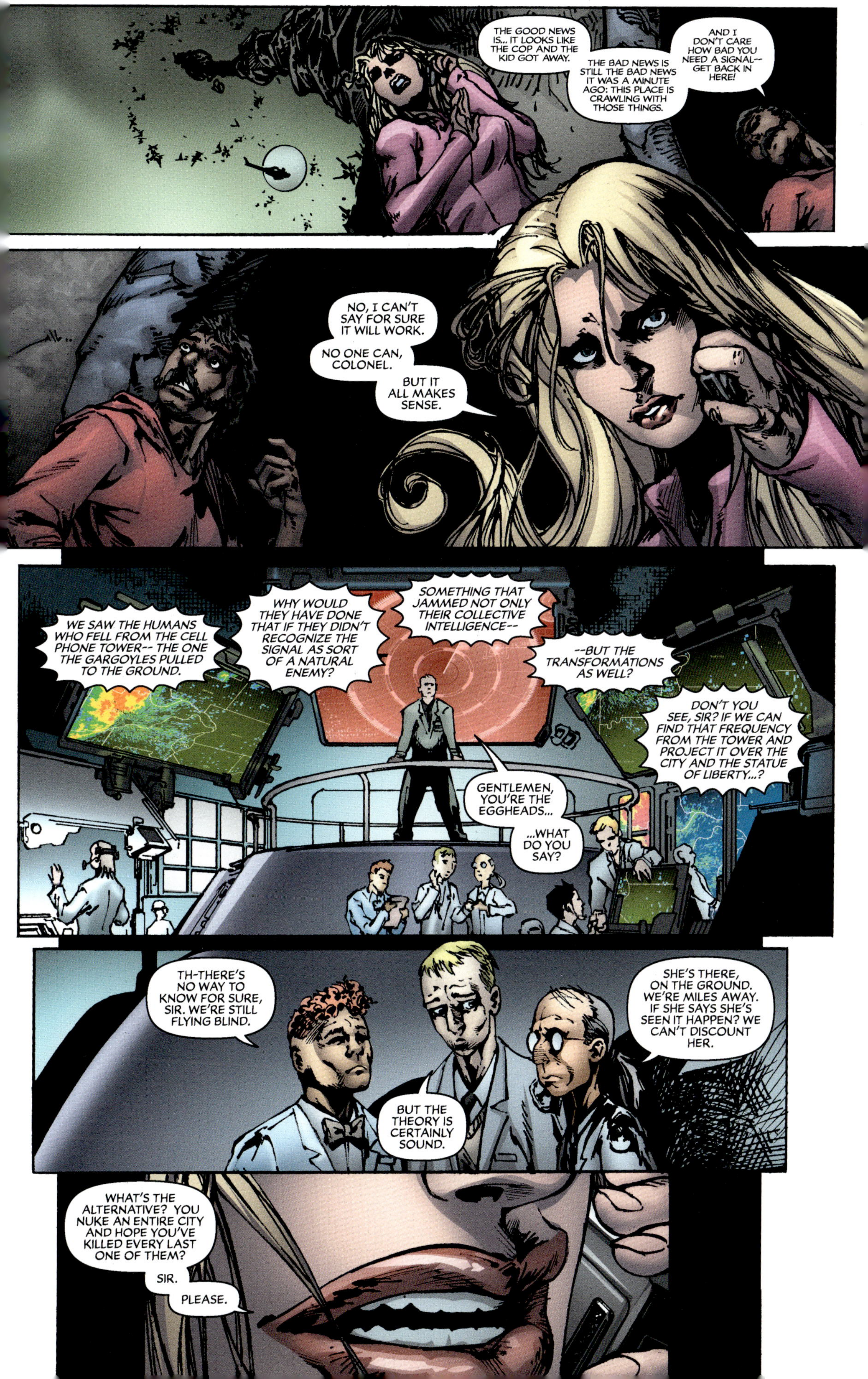
THE GOOD NEWS IS... IT LOOKS LIKE THE COP AND THE KID GOT AWAY.
THE BAD NEWS IS STILL THE BAD NEWS IT WAS A MINUTE AGO: THIS PLACE IS CRAWLING WITH THOSE THINGS.
AND I DON'T CARE HOW BAD YOU NEED A SIGNAL-- GET BACK IN HERE!
NO, I CAN'T SAY FOR SURE IT WILL WORK.
NO ONE CAN, COLONEL.
BUT IT ALL MAKES SENSE.
WE SAW THE HUMANS WHO FELL FROM THE CELL PHONE TOWER-- THE ONE THE GARGOYLES PULLED TO THE GROUND.
WHY WOULD THEY HAVE DONE THAT IF THEY DIDN'T RECOGNIZE THE SIGNAL AS SORT OF A NATURAL ENEMY?
SOMETHING THAT JAMMED NOT ONLY THEIR COLLECTIVE INTELLIGENCE--
--BUT THE TRANSFORMATIONS AS WELL?
DON'T YOU SEE, SIR? IF WE CAN FIND THAT FREQUENCY FROM THE TOWER AND PROJECT IT OVER THE CITY AND THE STATUE OF LIBERTY...?
GENTLEMEN, YOU'RE THE EGGHEADS...
...WHAT DO YOU SAY?
TH-THERE'S NO WAY TO KNOW FOR SURE, SIR. WE'RE STILL FLYING BLIND.
BUT THE THEORY IS CERTAINLY SOUND.
SHE'S THERE, ON THE GROUND. WE'RE MILES AWAY. IF SHE SAYS SHE'S SEEN IT HAPPEN? WE CAN'T DISCOUNT HER.
WHAT'S THE ALTERNATIVE? YOU NUKE AN ENTIRE CITY AND HOPE YOU'VE KILLED EVERY LAST ONE OF THEM?
SIR.
PLEASE.

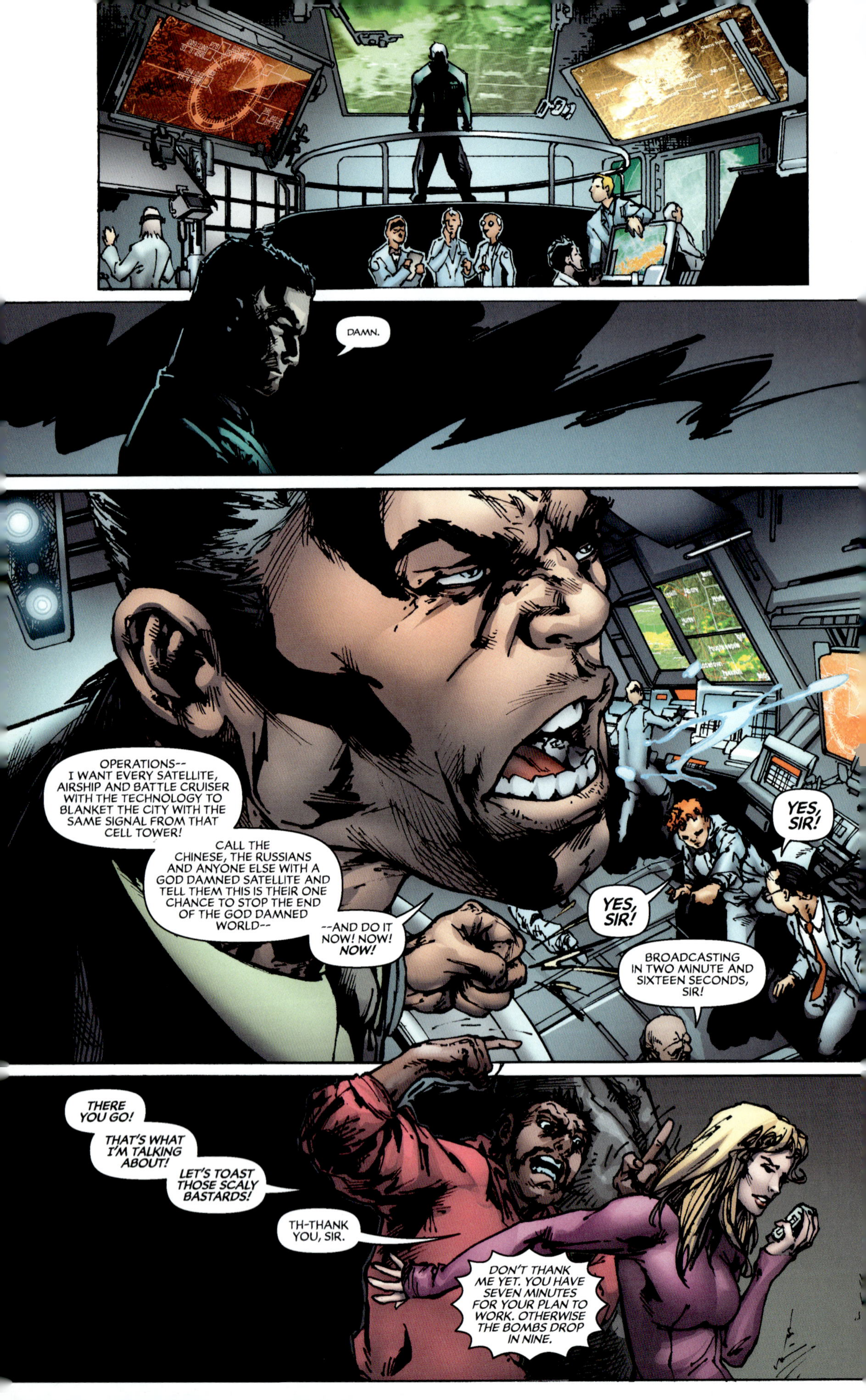
DAMN.
OPERATIONS-- I WANT EVERY SATELLITE, AIRSHIP AND BATTLE CRUISER WITH THE TECHNOLOGY TO BLANKET THE CITY WITH THE SAME SIGNAL FROM THAT CELL TOWER!
CALL THE CHINESE, THE RUSSIANS AND ANYONE ELSE WITH A GOD DAMNED SATELLITE AND TELL THEM THIS IS THEIR ONE CHANCE TO STOP THE END OF THE GOD DAMNED WORLD--
--AND DO IT NOW! NOW! NOW!
YES, SIR!
YES, SIR!
BROADCASTING IN TWO MINUTE AND SIXTEEN SECONDS, SIR!
THERE YOU GO!
THAT'S WHAT I'M TALKING ABOUT!
LET'S TOAST THOSE SCALY BASTARDS!
TH-THANK YOU, SIR.
DON'T THANK ME YET. YOU HAVE SEVEN MINUTES FOR YOUR PLAN TO WORK. OTHERWISE THE BOMBS DROP IN NINE.

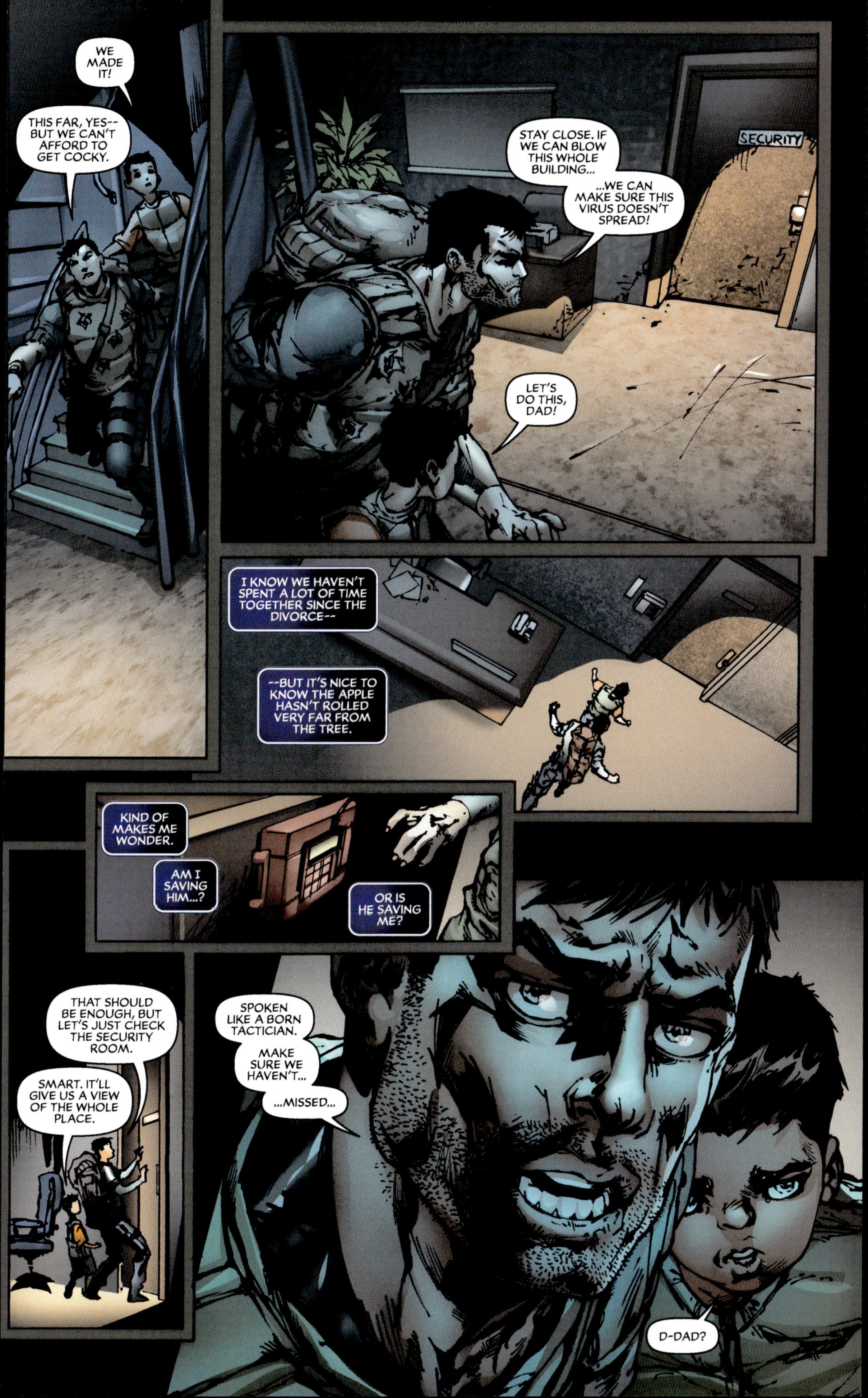

WE MADE IT!
THIS FAR, YES-- BUT WE CAN'T AFFORD TO GET COCKY.
STAY CLOSE. IF WE CAN BLOW THIS WHOLE BUILDING...
...WE CAN MAKE SURE THIS VIRUS DOESN'T SPREAD!
SECURITY
LET'S DO THIS, DAD!
I KNOW WE HAVEN'T SPENT A LOT OF TIME TOGETHER SINCE THE DIVORCE--
--BUT IT'S NICE TO KNOW THE APPLE HASN'T ROLLED VERY FAR FROM THE TREE.
KIND OF MAKES ME WONDER.
AM I SAVING HIM...?
OR IS HE SAVING ME?
THAT SHOULD BE ENOUGH, BUT LET'S JUST CHECK THE SECURITY ROOM.
SMART. IT'LL GIVE US A VIEW OF THE WHOLE PLACE.
SPOKEN LIKE A BORN TACTICIAN.
MAKE SURE WE HAVEN'T...
...MISSED...
D-DAD?

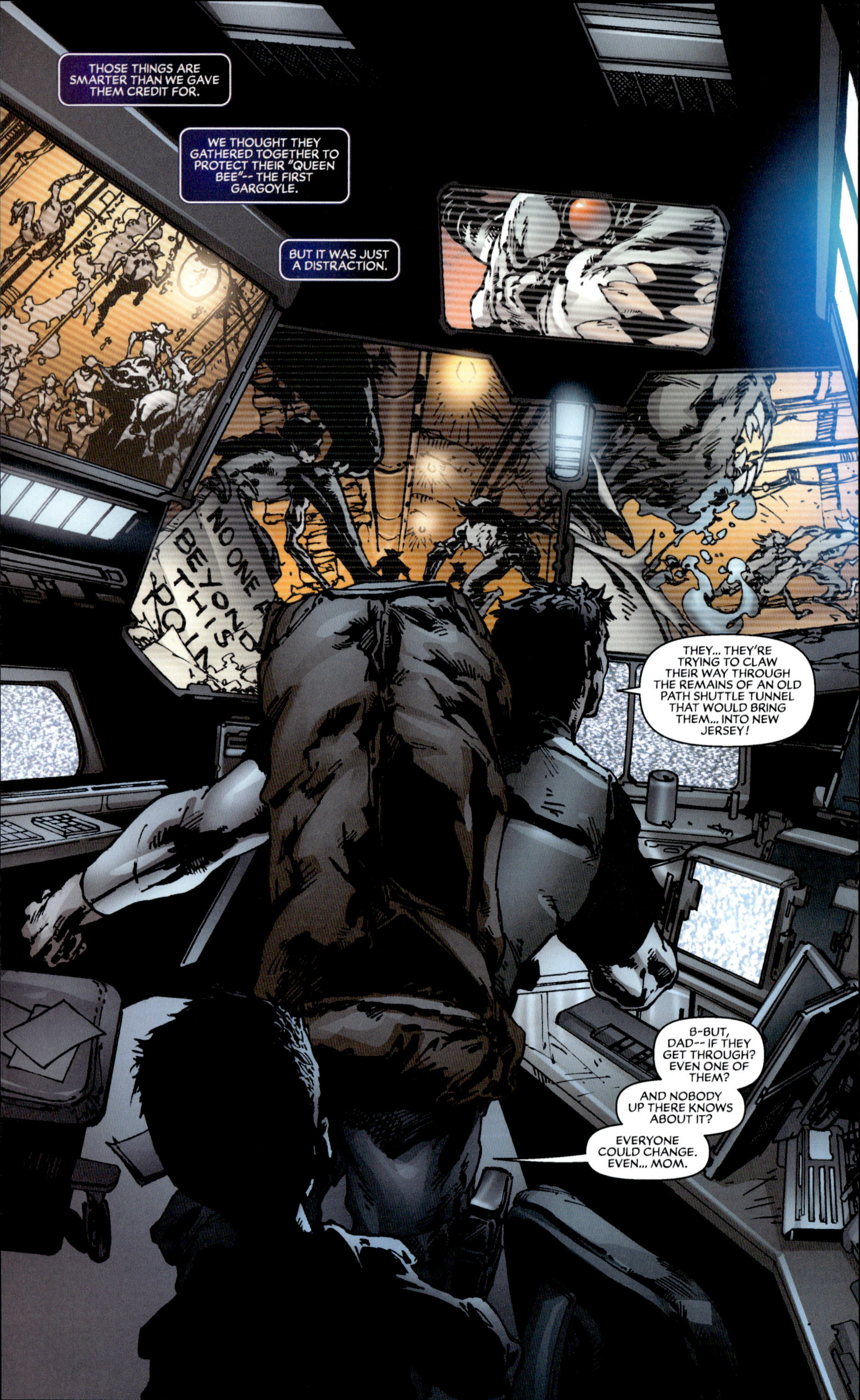
THOSE THINGS ARE SMARTER THAN WE GAVE THEM CREDIT FOR.
WE THOUGHT THEY GATHERED TOGETHER TO PROTECT THEIR "QUEEN BEE"-- THE FIRST GARGOYLE.
BUT IT WAS JUST A DISTRACTION.
NO ONE BEYOND THIS POIN
THEY... THEY'RE TRYING TO CLAW THEIR WAY THROUGH THE REMAINS OF AN OLD PATH SHUTTLE TUNNEL THAT WOULD BRING THEM... INTO NEW JERSEY!
B-BUT, DAD-- IF THEY GET THROUGH? EVEN ONE OF THEM?
AND NOBODY UP THERE KNOWS ABOUT IT?
EVERYONE COULD CHANGE. EVEN... MOM.

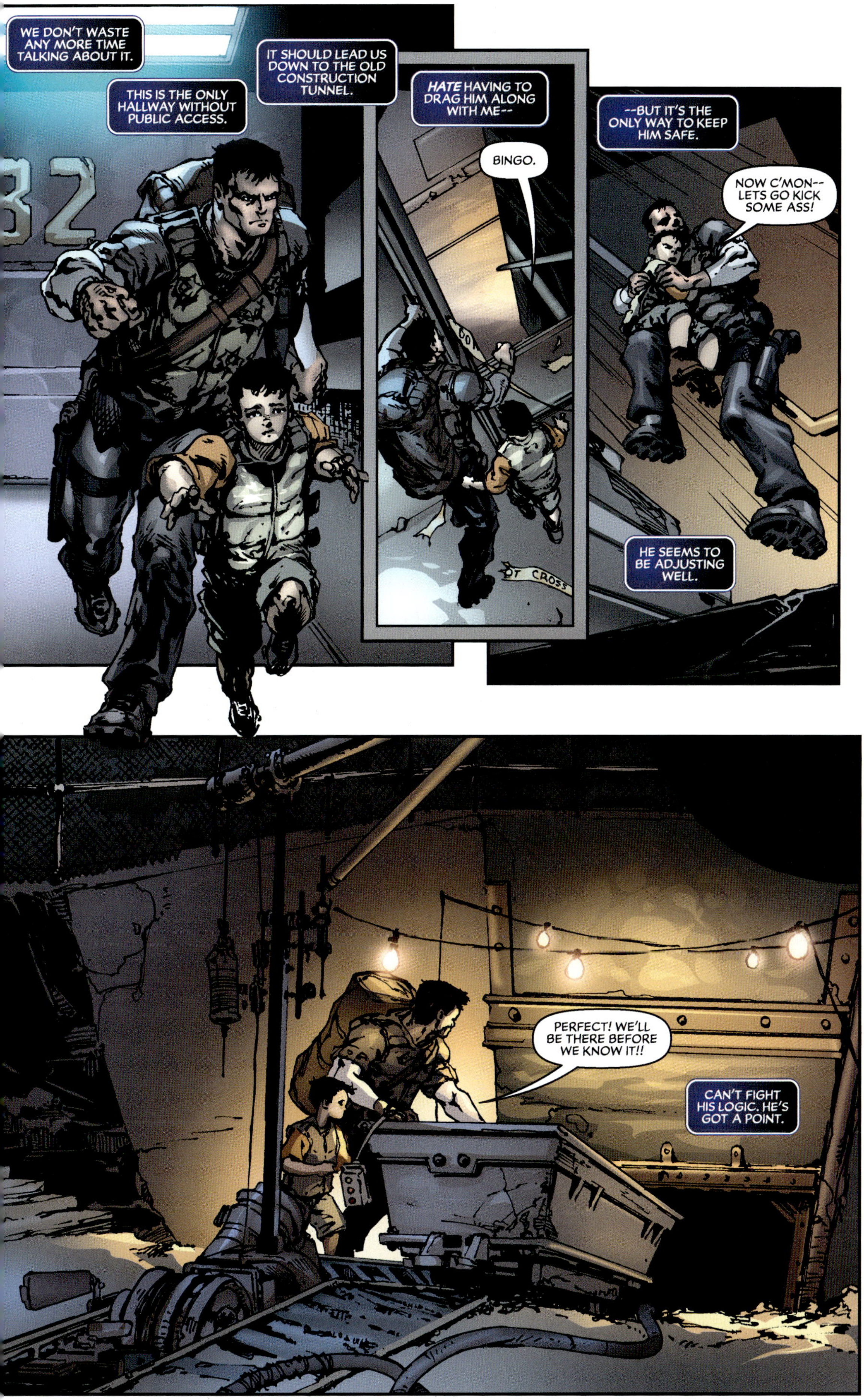
WE DON'T WASTE ANY MORE TIME TALKING ABOUT IT.
THIS IS THE ONLY HALLWAY WITHOUT PUBLIC ACCESS.
IT SHOULD LEAD US DOWN TO THE OLD CONSTRUCTION TUNNEL.
HATE HAVING TO DRAG HIM ALONG WITH ME--
BINGO.
--BUT IT'S THE ONLY WAY TO KEEP HIM SAFE.
NOW C'MON-- LETS GO KICK SOME ASS!
HE SEEMS TO BE ADJUSTING WELL.
PERFECT! WE'LL BE THERE BEFORE WE KNOW IT!!
CAN'T FIGHT HIS LOGIC. HE'S GOT A POINT.

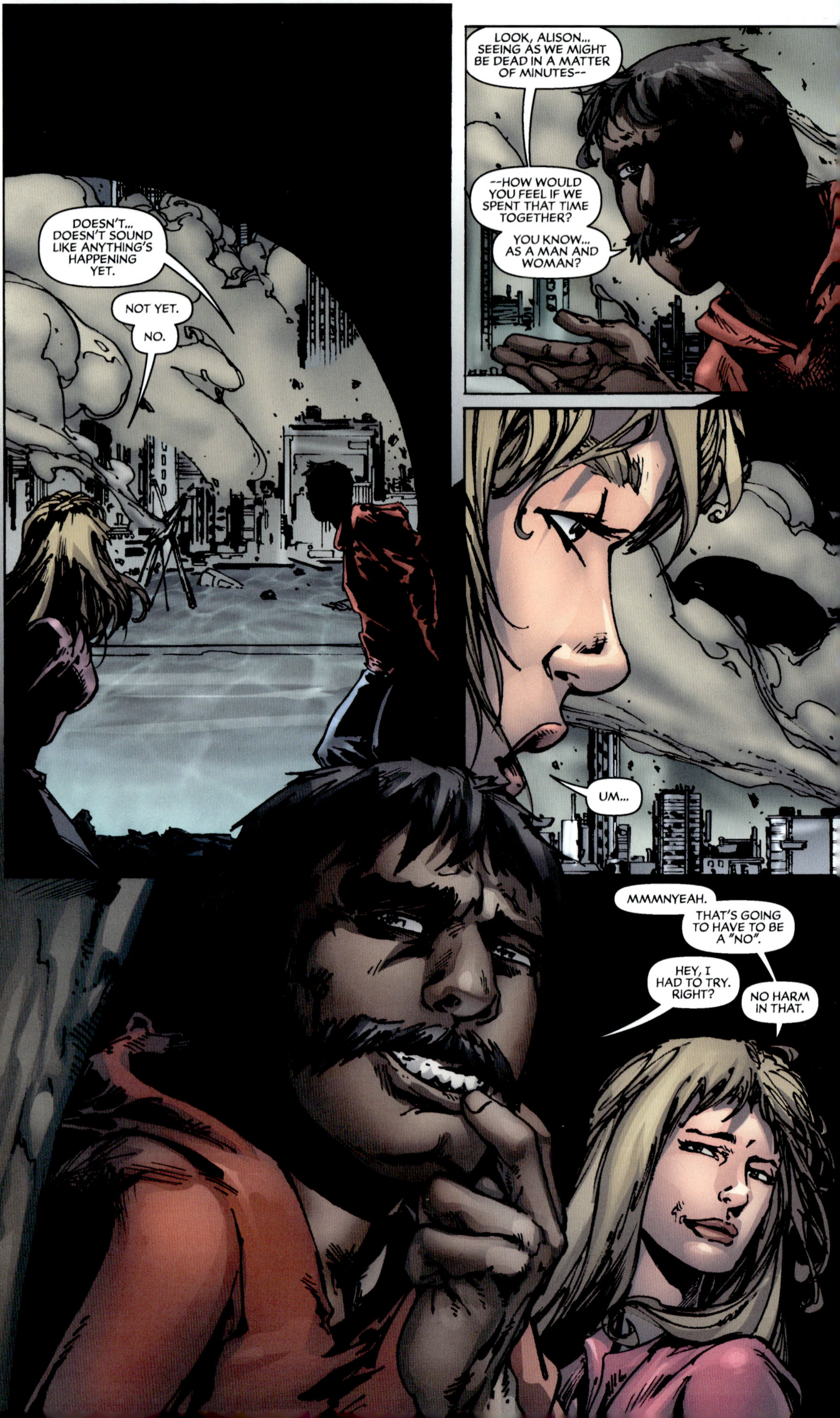
DOESN'T... DOESN'T SOUND LIKE ANYTHING'S HAPPENING YET.
NOT YET.
NO.
LOOK, ALISON... SEEING AS WE MIGHT BE DEAD IN A MATTER OF MINUTES--
--HOW WOULD YOU FEEL IF WE SPENT THAT TIME TOGETHER?
YOU KNOW... AS A MAN AND WOMAN?
UM...
MMMNYEAH.
THAT'S GOING TO HAVE TO BE A "NO".
HEY, I HAD TO TRY. RIGHT?
NO HARM IN THAT.

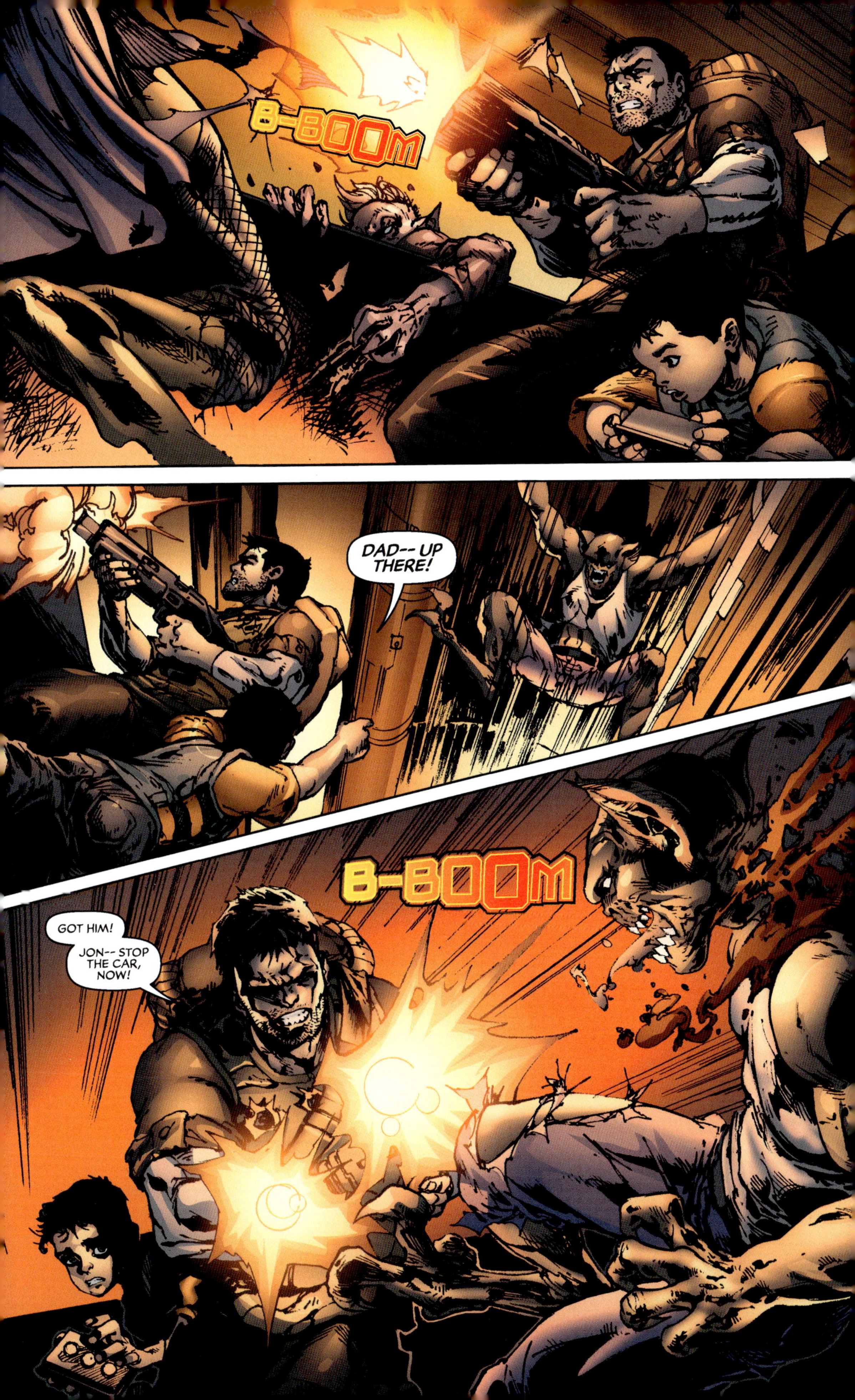
B-BOOM
DAD-- UP THERE!
B-BOOM
GOT HIM!
JON-- STOP THE CAR, NOW!

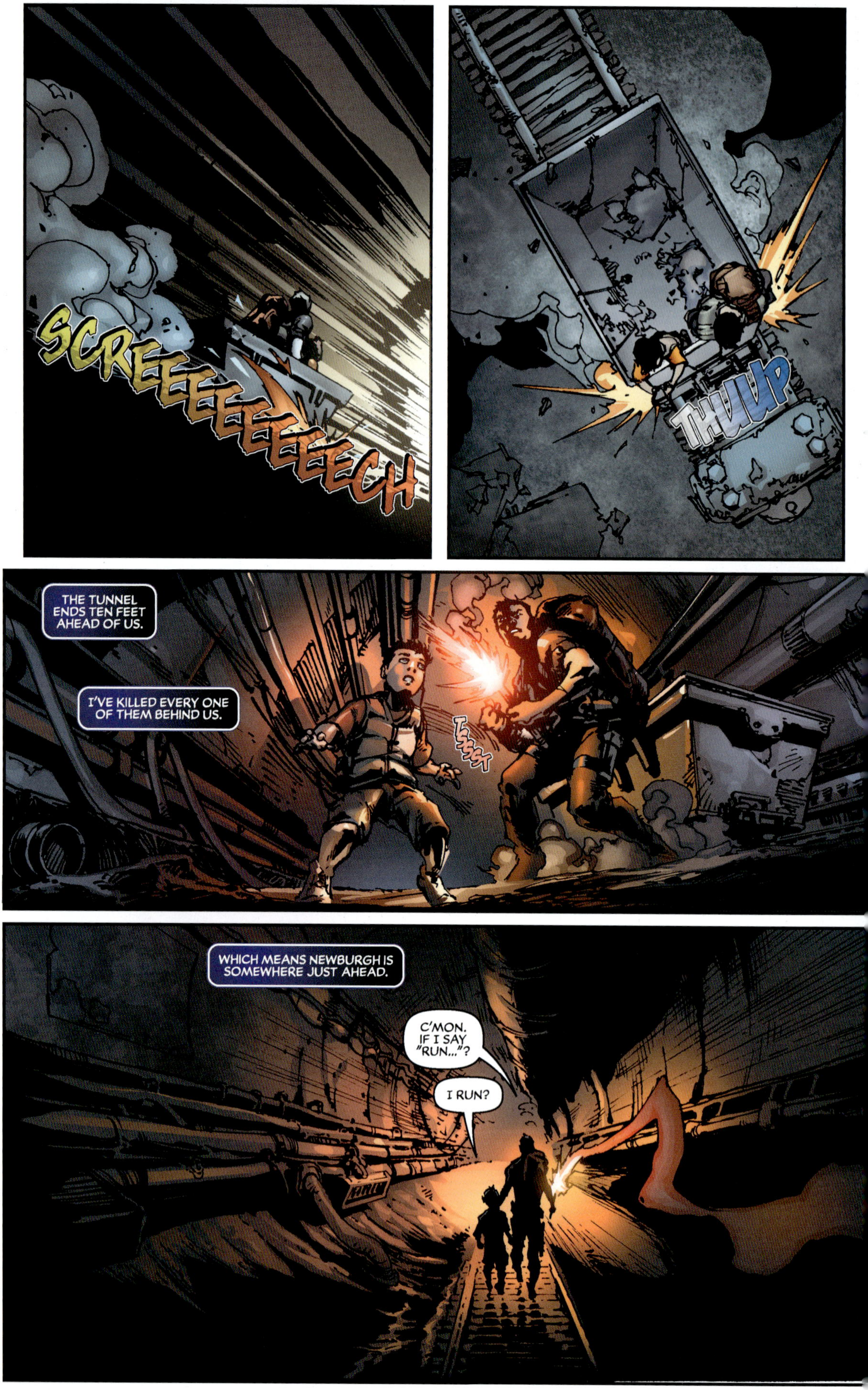
SCREEEEEEEEEEECH
THUUP
THE TUNNEL ENDS TEN FEET AHEAD OF US.
I'VE KILLED EVERY ONE OF THEM BEHIND US.
TSSSST
WHICH MEANS NEWBURGH IS SOMEWHERE JUST AHEAD.
C'MON. IF I SAY "RUN..."?
I RUN?

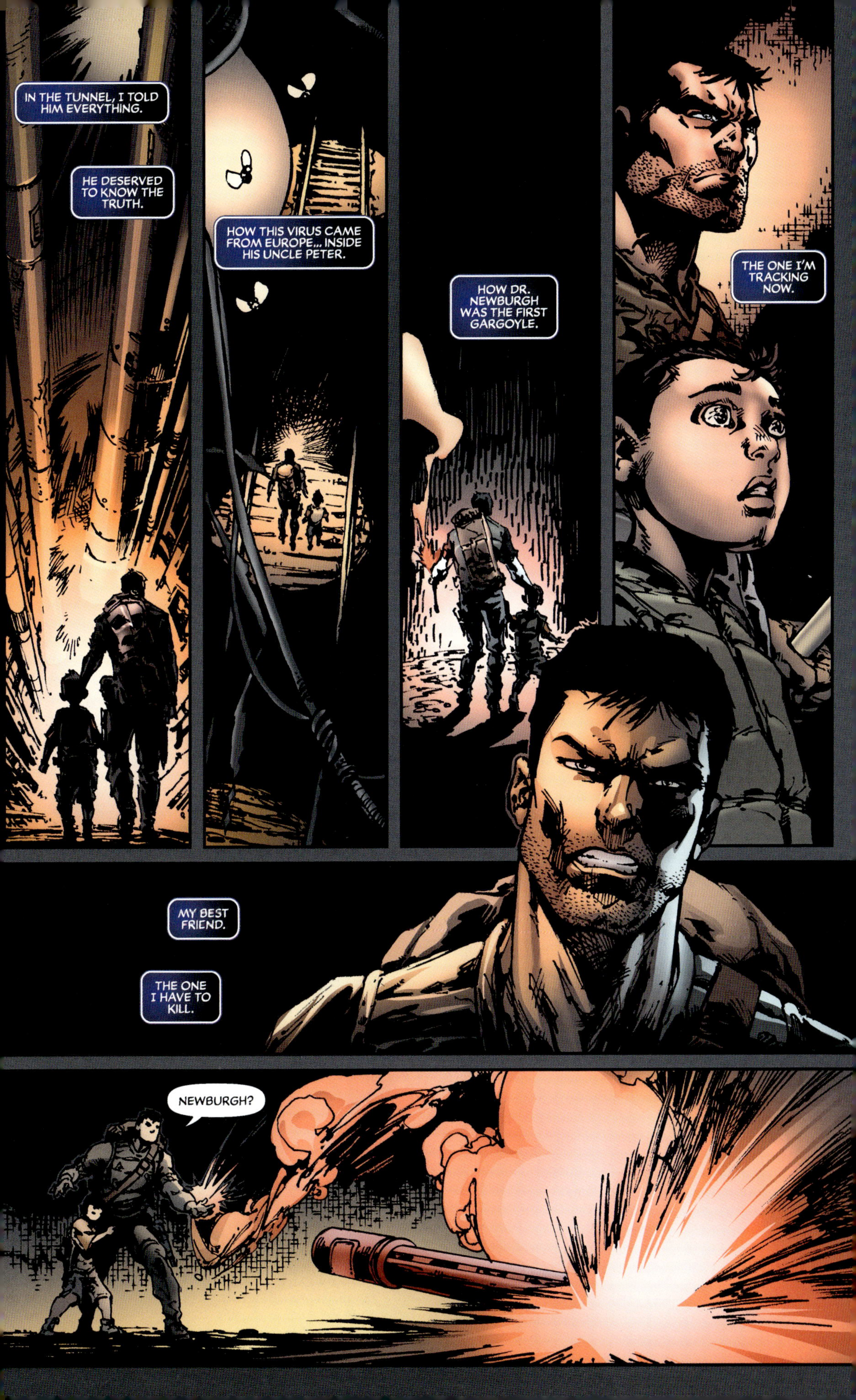
IN THE TUNNEL, I TOLD HIM EVERYTHING.
HE DESERVED TO KNOW THE TRUTH.
HOW THIS VIRUS CAME FROM EUROPE... INSIDE HIS UNCLE PETER.
HOW DR. NEWBURGH WAS THE FIRST GARGOYLE.
THE ONE I'M TRACKING NOW.
MY BEST FRIEND.
THE ONE I HAVE TO KILL.
NEWBURGH?

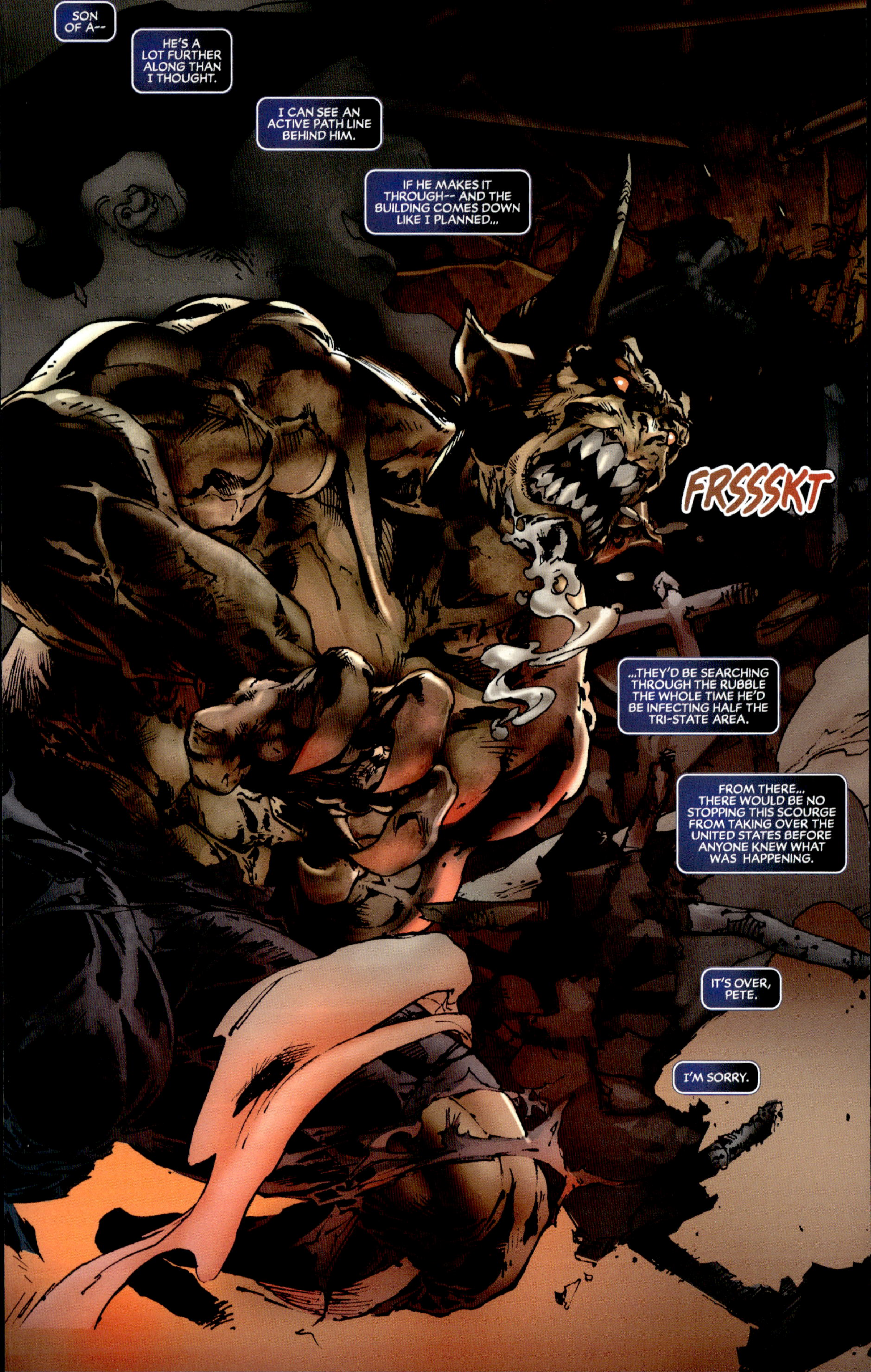
SON OF A--
HE'S A LOT FURTHER ALONG THAN I THOUGHT.
I CAN SEE AN ACTIVE PATH LINE BEHIND HIM.
IF HE MAKES IT THROUGH-- AND THE BUILDING COMES DOWN LIKE I PLANNED...
FRSSSKT
...THEY'D BE SEARCHING THROUGH THE RUBBLE THE WHOLE TIME HE'D BE INFECTING HALF THE TRI-STATE AREA.
FROM THERE... THERE WOULD BE NO STOPPING THIS SCOURGE FROM TAKING OVER THE UNITED STATES BEFORE ANYONE KNEW WHAT WAS HAPPENING.
IT'S OVER, PETE.
I'M SORRY.

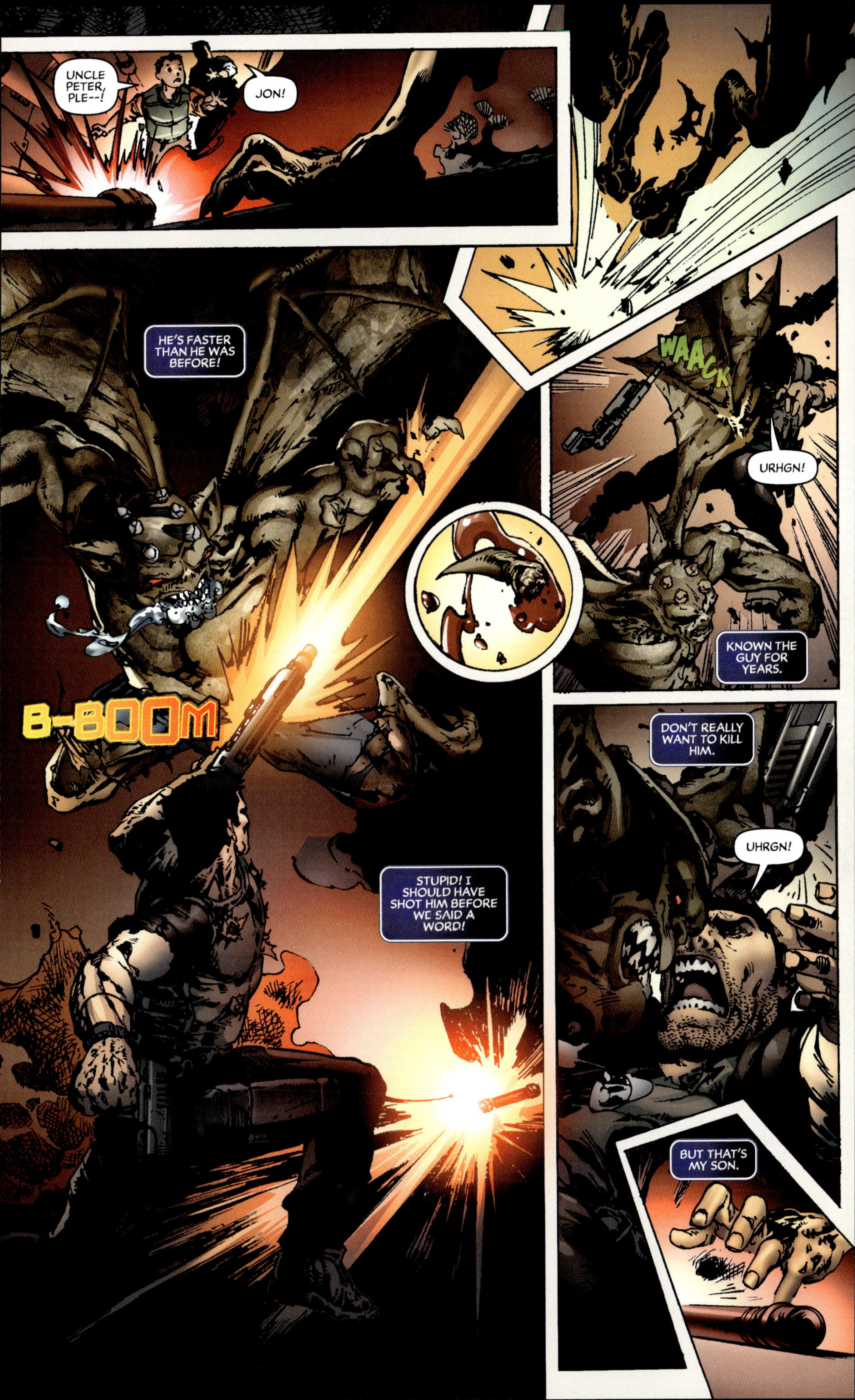
UNCLE PETER, PLE--!
JON!
HE'S FASTER THAN HE WAS BEFORE!
B-BOOM
WAACK
URHGN!
KNOWN THE GUY FOR YEARS.
DON'T REALLY WANT TO KILL HIM.
UHRGN!
STUPID! I SHOULD HAVE SHOT HIM BEFORE WE SAID A WORD!
BUT THAT'S MY SON.

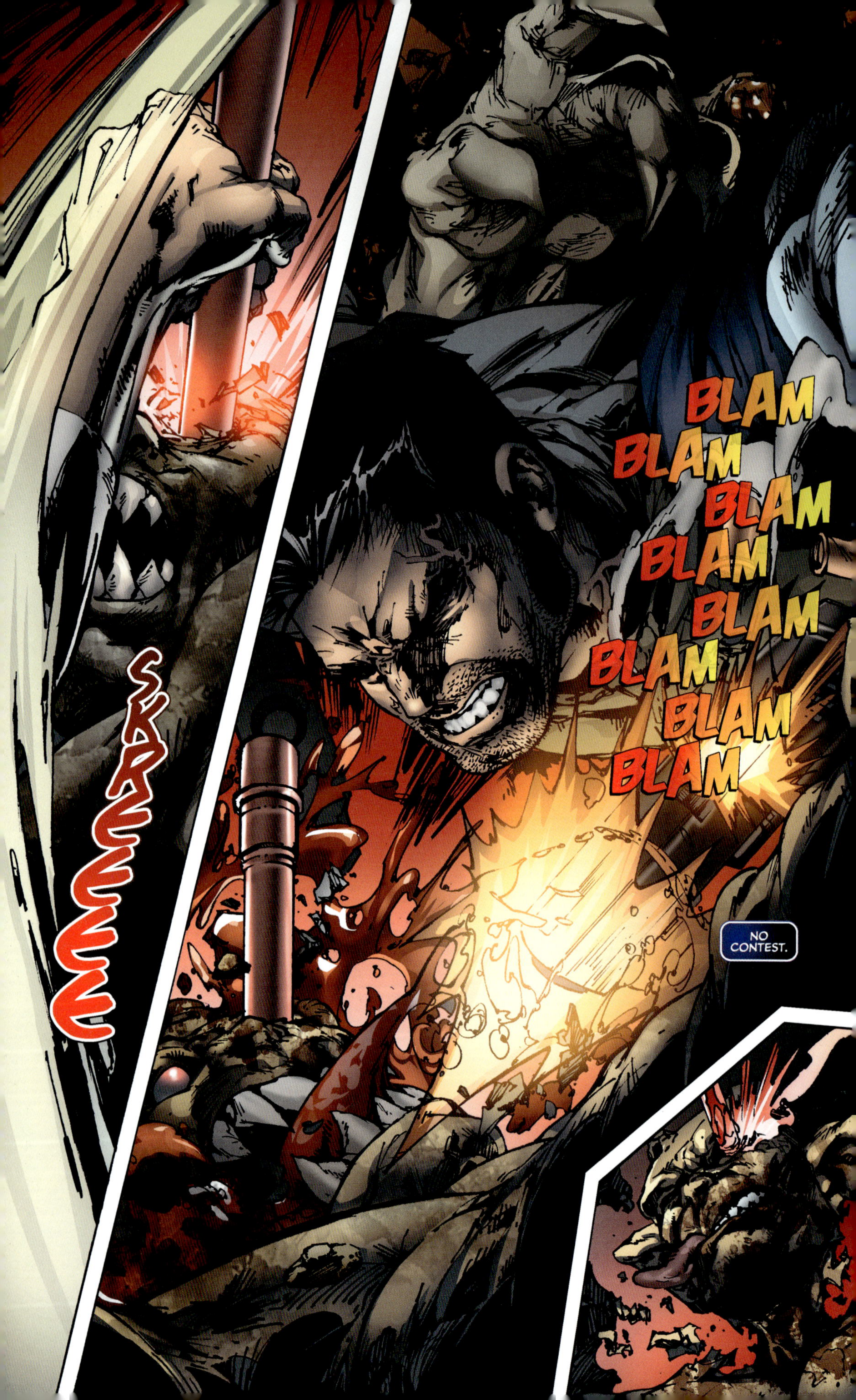
SKREEEEEE
BLAM
BLAM
BLAM
BLAM
BLAM
BLAM
BLAM
BLAM
NO CONTEST.

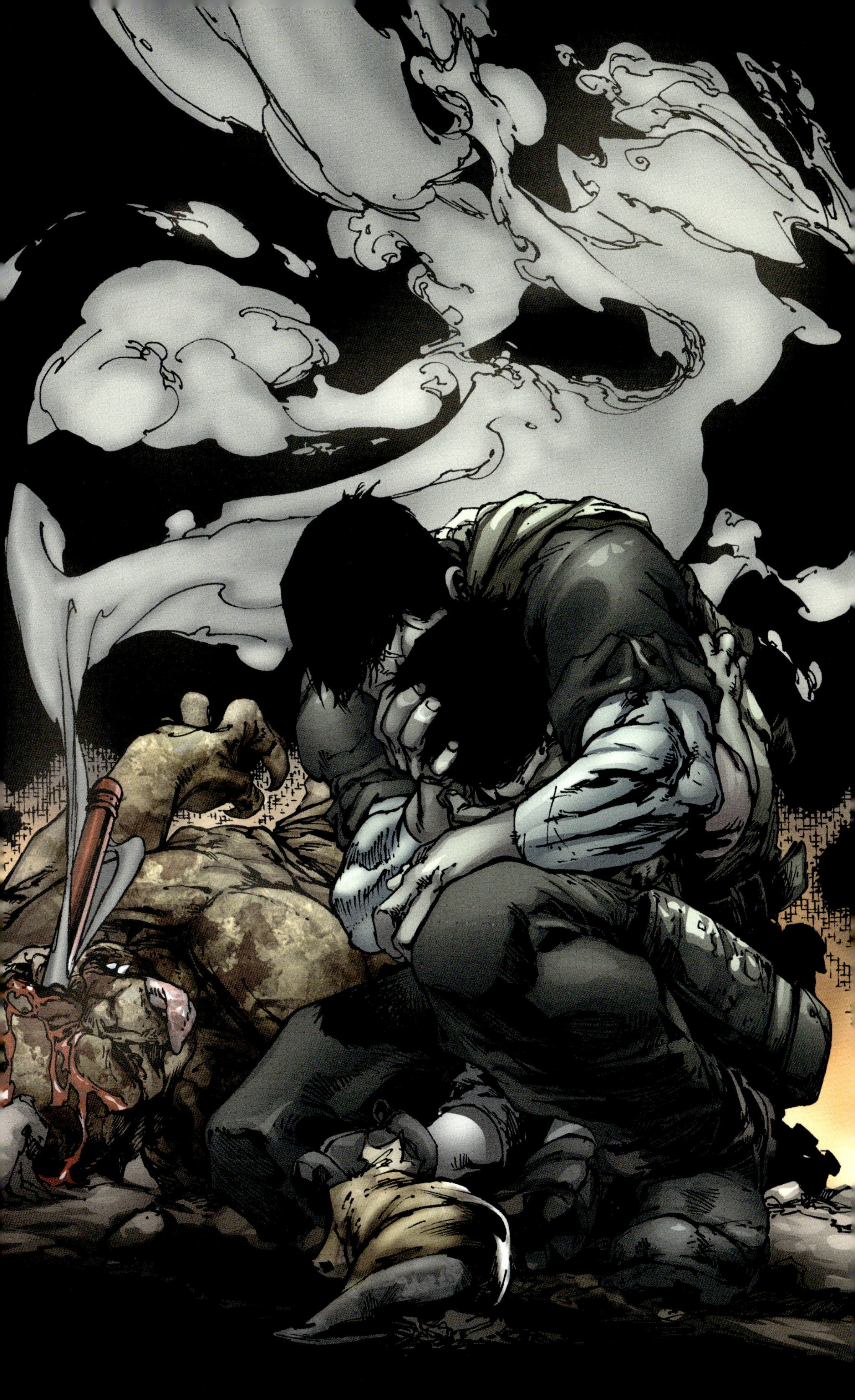

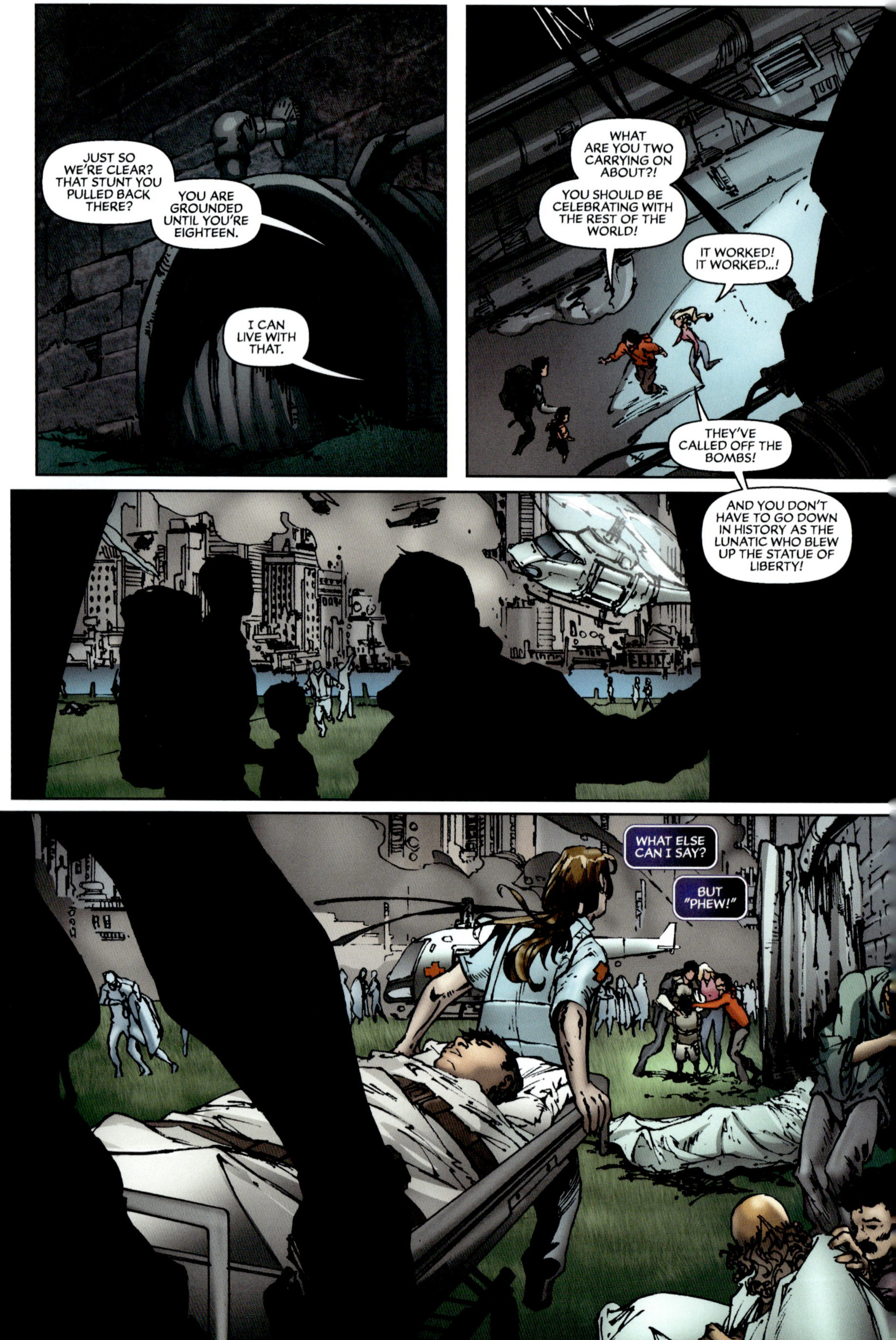
JUST SO WE'RE CLEAR? THAT STUNT YOU PULLED BACK THERE?
YOU ARE GROUNDED UNTIL YOU'RE EIGHTEEN.
I CAN LIVE WITH THAT.
WHAT ARE YOU TWO CARRYING ON ABOUT?!
YOU SHOULD BE CELEBRATING WITH THE REST OF THE WORLD!
IT WORKED! IT WORKED...!
THEY'VE CALLED OFF THE BOMBS!
AND YOU DON'T HAVE TO GO DOWN IN HISTORY AS THE LUNATIC WHO BLEW UP THE STATUE OF LIBERTY!
WHAT ELSE CAN I SAY?
BUT "PHEW!"

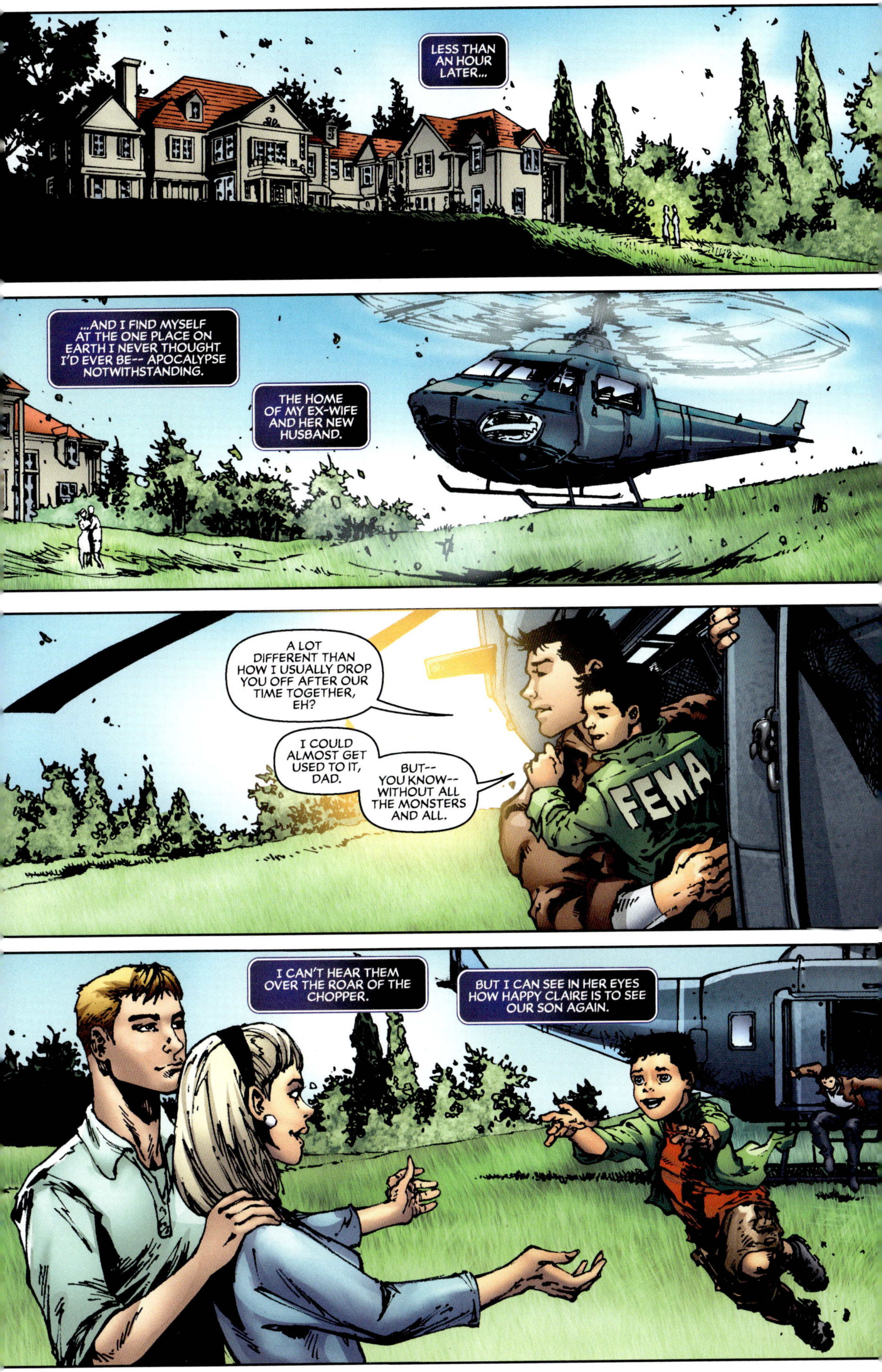
LESS THAN AN HOUR LATER...
...AND I FIND MYSELF AT THE ONE PLACE ON EARTH I NEVER THOUGHT I'D EVER BE-- APOCALYPSE NOTWITHSTANDING.
THE HOME OF MY EX-WIFE AND HER NEW HUSBAND.
A LOT DIFFERENT THAN HOW I USUALLY DROP YOU OFF AFTER OUR TIME TOGETHER, EH?
I COULD ALMOST GET USED TO IT, DAD.
BUT-- YOU KNOW-- WITHOUT ALL THE MONSTERS AND ALL.
FEMA
I CAN'T HEAR THEM OVER THE ROAR OF THE CHOPPER.
BUT I CAN SEE IN HER EYES HOW HAPPY CLAIRE IS TO SEE OUR SON AGAIN.

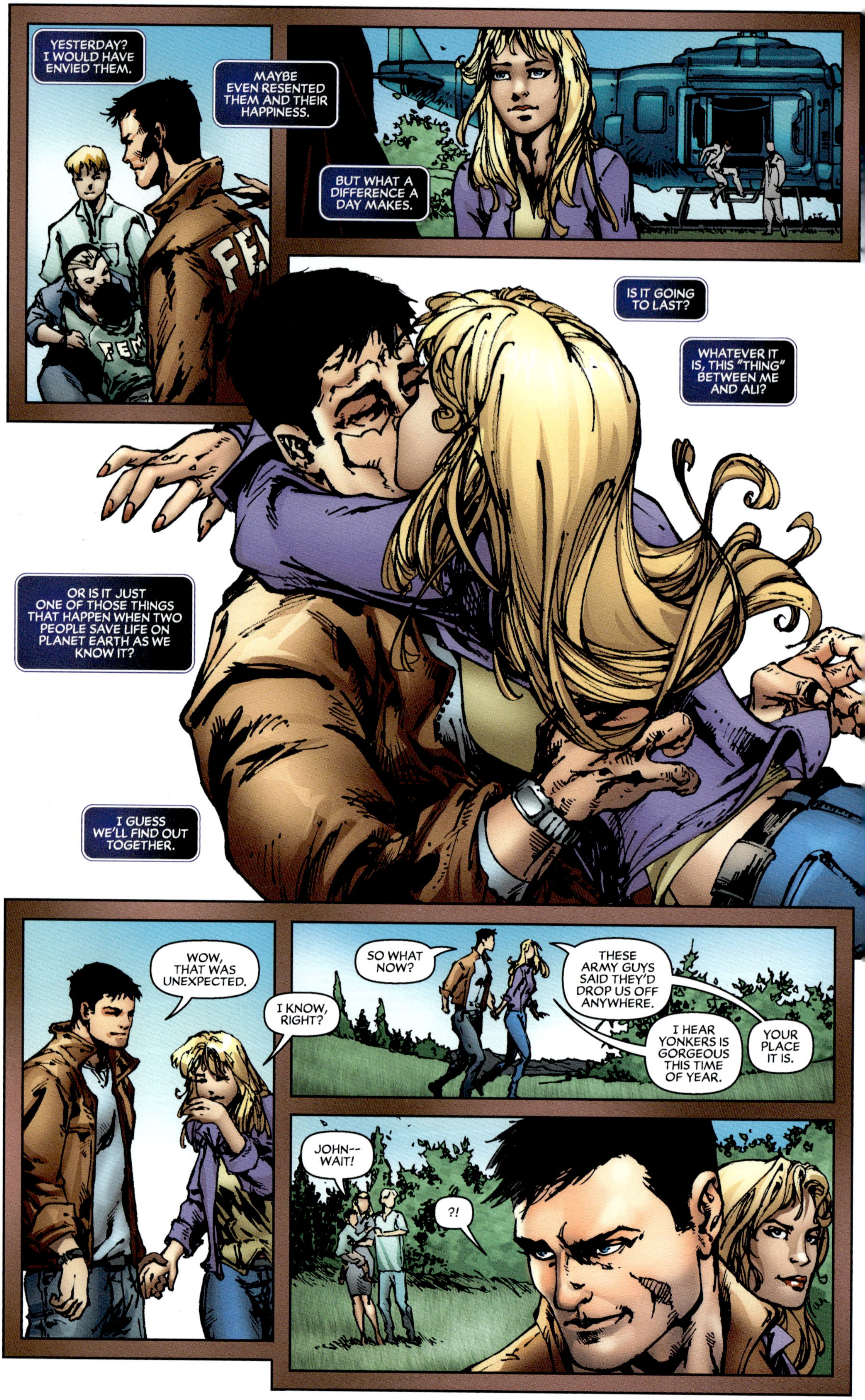
YESTERDAY? I WOULD HAVE ENVIED THEM.
MAYBE EVEN RESENTED THEM AND THEIR HAPPINESS.
BUT WHAT A DIFFERENCE A DAY MAKES.
IS IT GOING TO LAST?
WHATEVER IT IS, THIS "THING" BETWEEN ME AND ALI?
OR IS IT JUST ONE OF THOSE THINGS THAT HAPPEN WHEN TWO PEOPLE SAVE LIFE ON PLANET EARTH AS WE KNOW IT?
I GUESS WE'LL FIND OUT TOGETHER.
WOW, THAT WAS UNEXPECTED.
I KNOW, RIGHT?
SO WHAT NOW?
THESE ARMY GUYS SAID THEY'D DROP US OFF ANYWHERE.
I HEAR YONKERS IS GORGEOUS THIS TIME OF YEAR.
YOUR PLACE IT IS.
JOHN-- WAIT!
?!

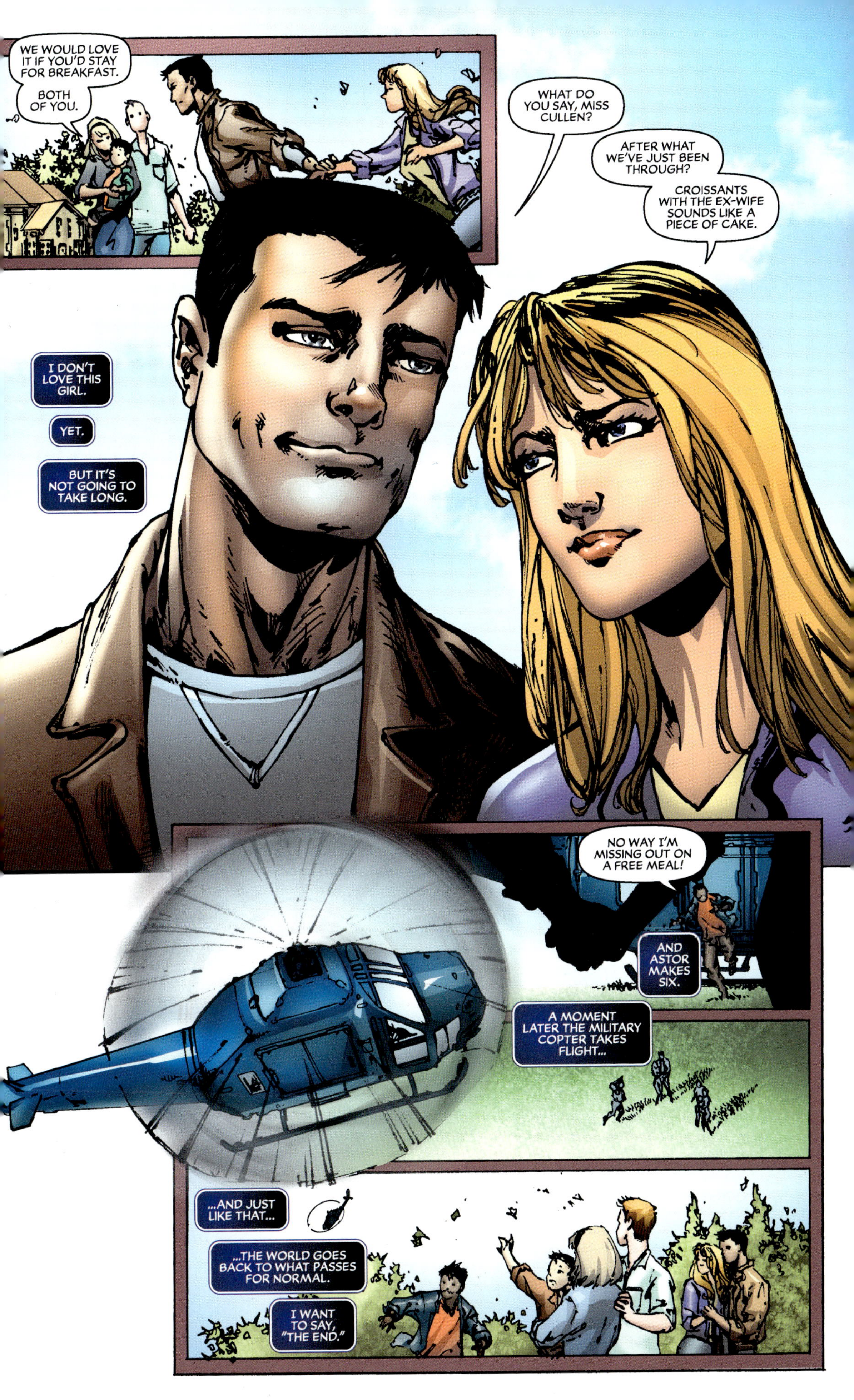
WE WOULD LOVE IT IF YOU'D STAY FOR BREAKFAST.
BOTH OF YOU.
WHAT DO YOU SAY, MISS CULLEN?
AFTER WHAT WE'VE JUST BEEN THROUGH?
CROISSANTS WITH THE EX-WIFE SOUNDS LIKE A PIECE OF CAKE.
I DON'T LOVE THIS GIRL.
YET.
BUT IT'S NOT GOING TO TAKE LONG.
NO WAY I'M MISSING OUT ON A FREE MEAL!
AND ASTOR MAKES SIX.
A MOMENT LATER THE MILITARY COPTER TAKES FLIGHT...
...AND JUST LIKE THAT...
...THE WORLD GOES BACK TO WHAT PASSES FOR NORMAL.
I WANT TO SAY, "THE END."

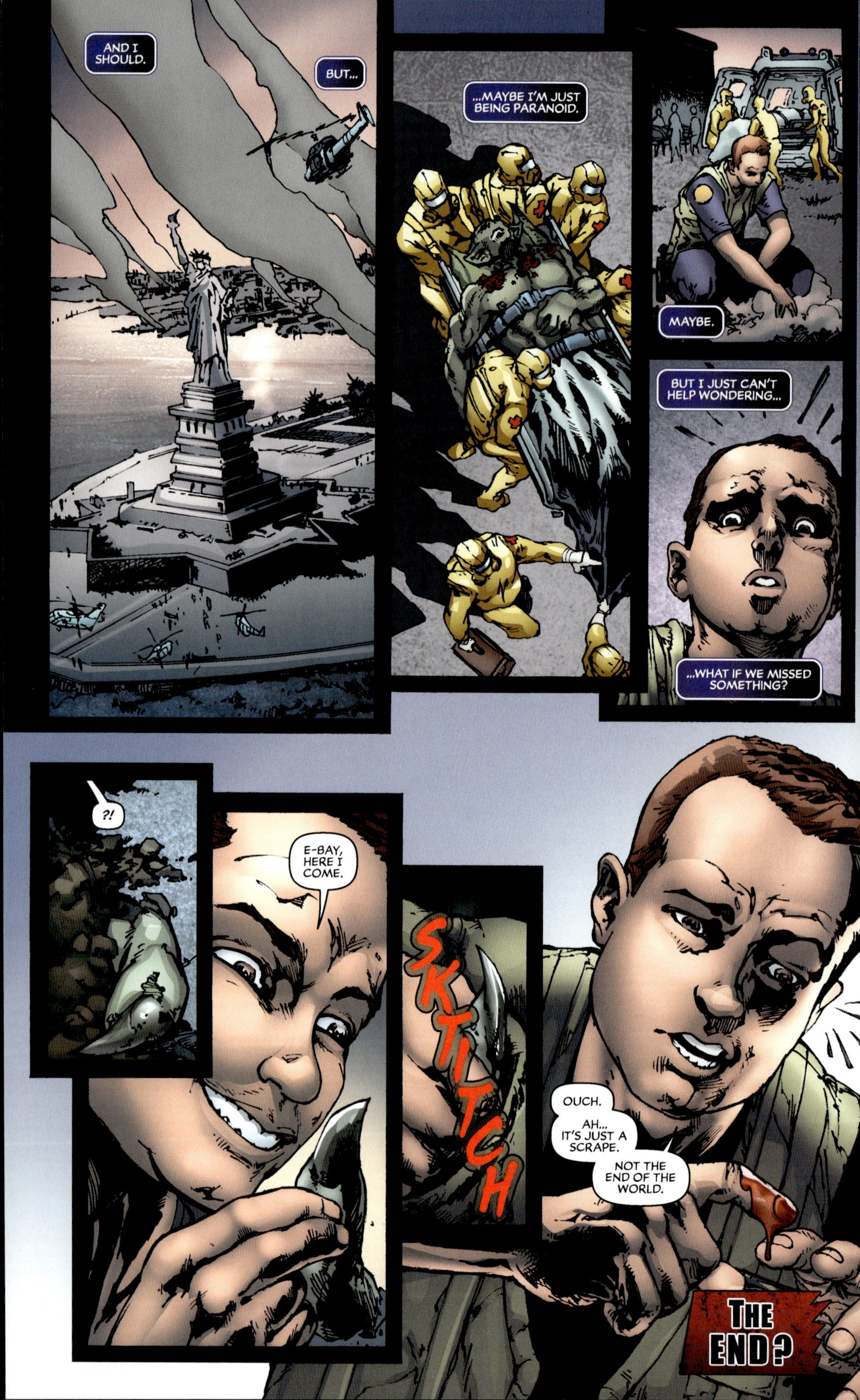
AND I SHOULD.
BUT...
...MAYBE I'M JUST BEING PARANOID.
MAYBE.
BUT I JUST CAN'T HELP WONDERING...
...WHAT IF WE MISSED SOMETHING?
?!
E-BAY, HERE I COME.
SKTITCH
OUCH.
AH... IT'S JUST A SCRAPE.
NOT THE END OF THE WORLD.
THE END?

COVER GALLERY

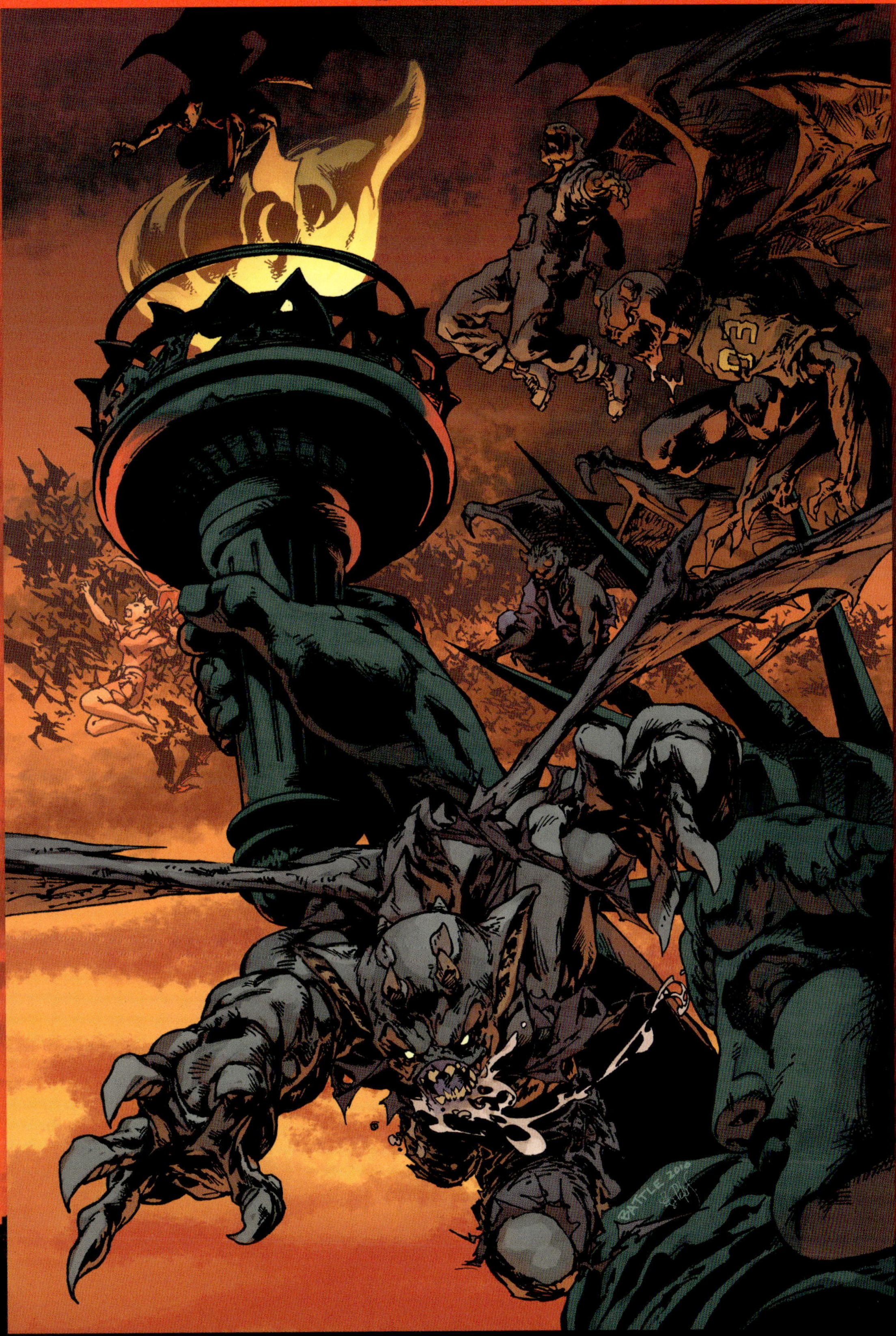

Direct Edition Cover A to
THE SCOURGE #0
by
Eric **BATTLE** | Mark **ROSLAN** | Peter **STEIGERWALD**

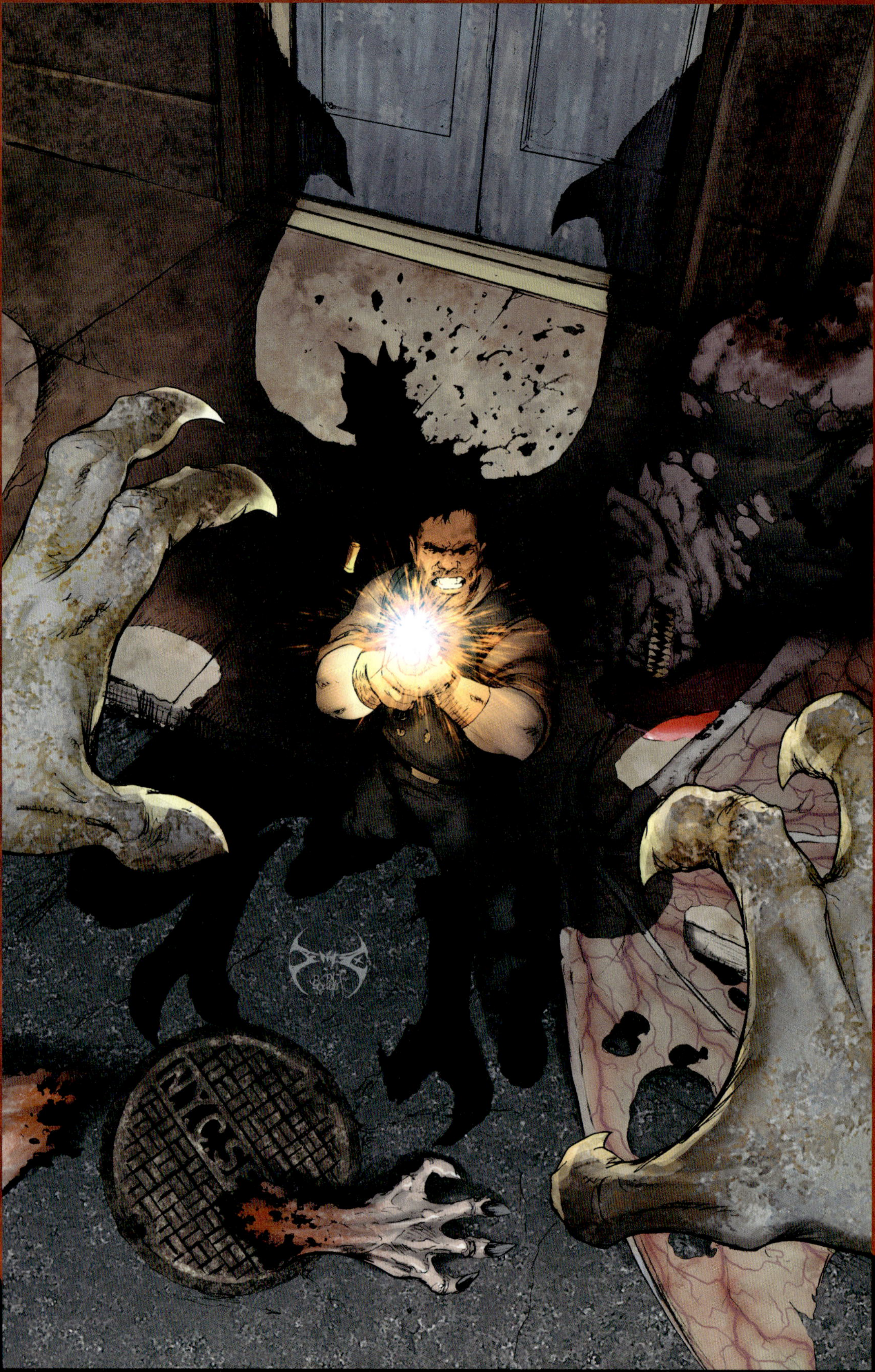

Direct Edition Cover B to

THE SCOURGE #0

by

Joe BENITEZ | Mark ROSLAN | Peter STEIGERWALD

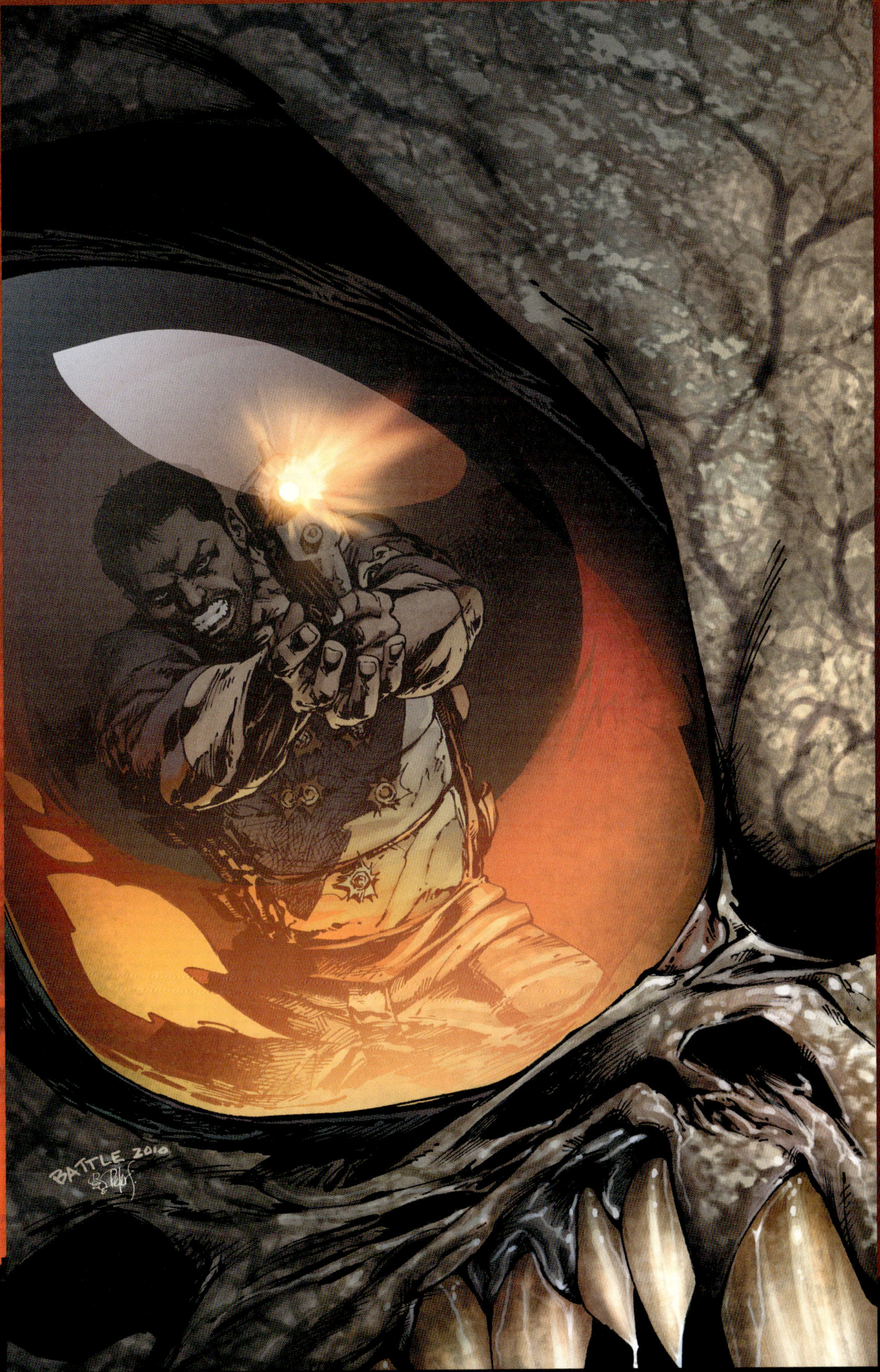
BATTLE 2010

COMIC-CON INTERNATIONAL: SAN DIEGO EXCLUSIVE EDITION COVER D TO

THE SCOURGE #0

BY

ERIC **BATTLE** | MARK **ROSLAN** | PETER **STEIGERWALD**

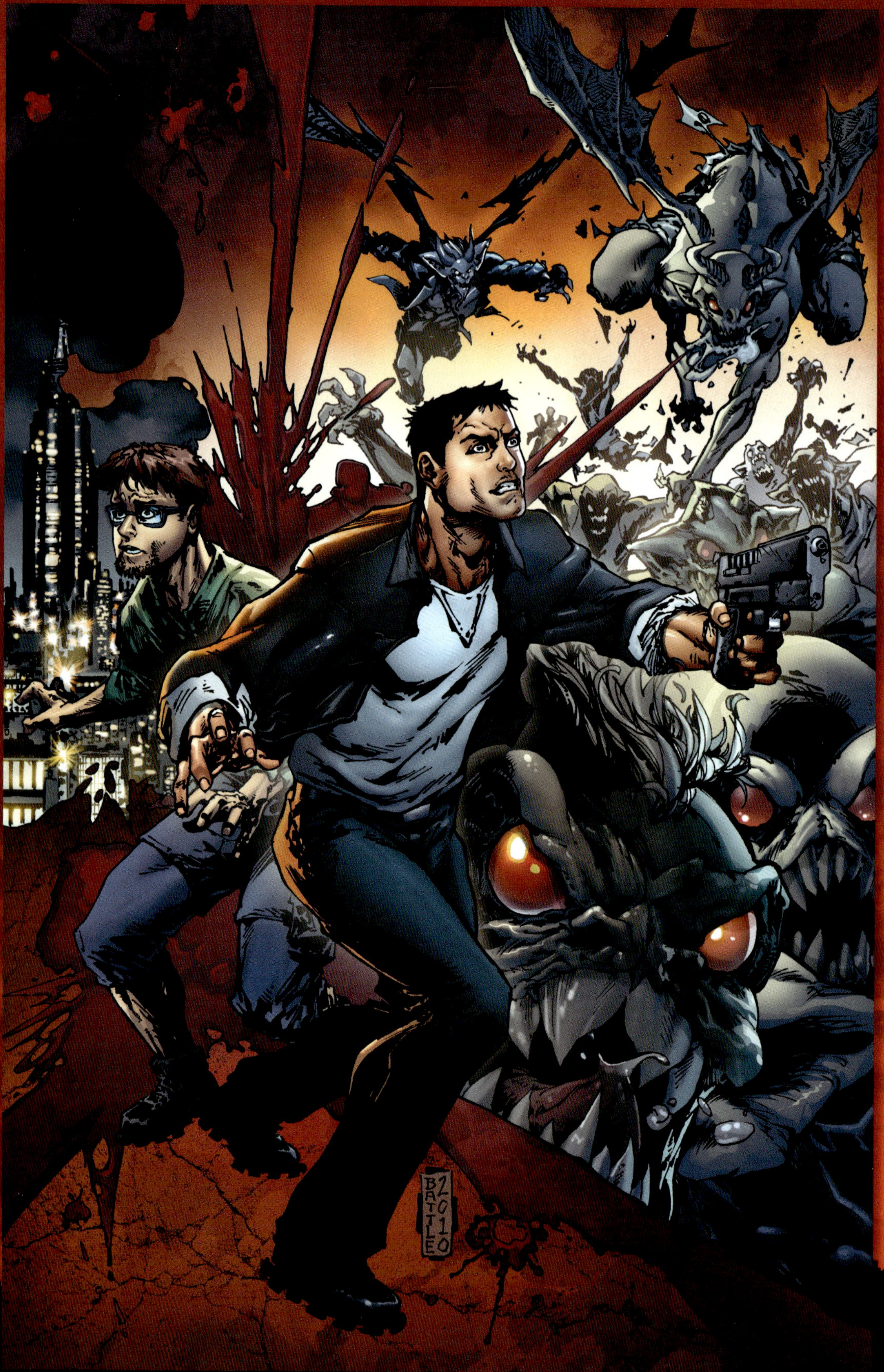
BATTLE 2010

Direct Edition Cover A to
THE SCOURGE #1
by
Eric BATTLE | Mark ROSLAN | David CURIEL

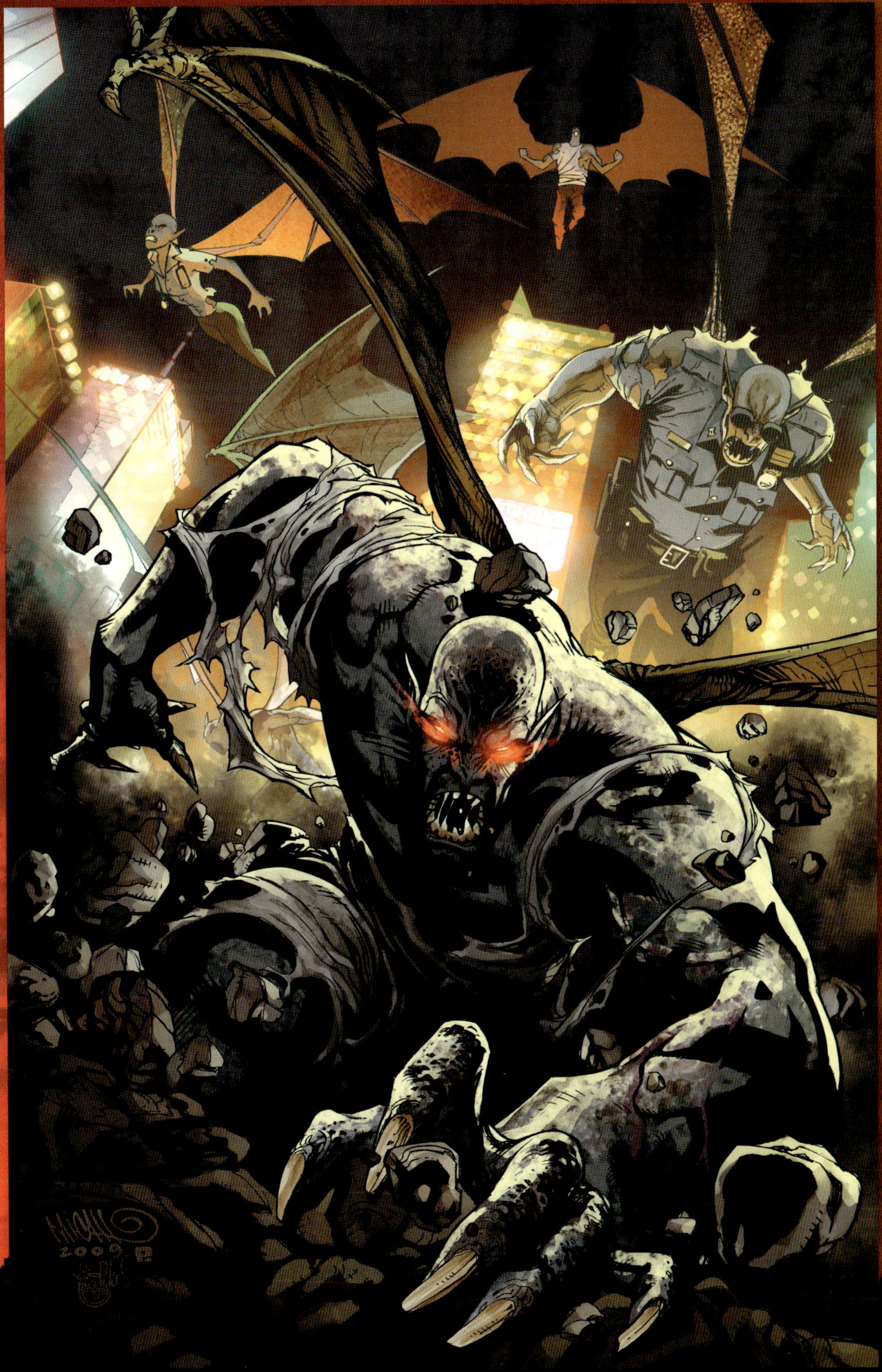

Direct Edition Cover B to
THE SCOURGE #1
BY
MICAH GUNNELL | MARK ROSLAN | PETER STEIGERWALD

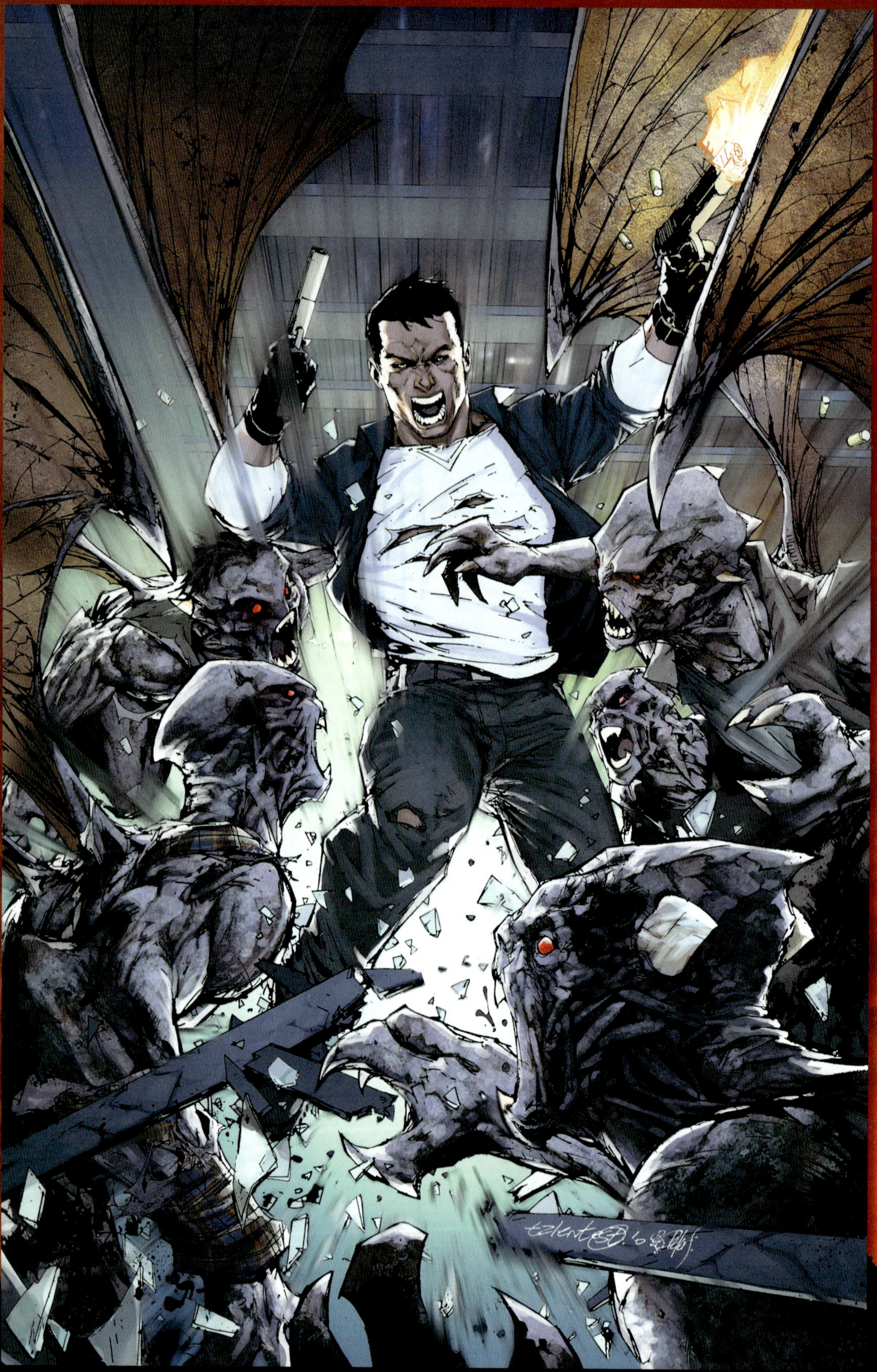

Direct Edition Cover C to
THE SCOURGE #1
BY
TALENT CALDWELL | MARK ROSLAN | PETER STEIGERWALD

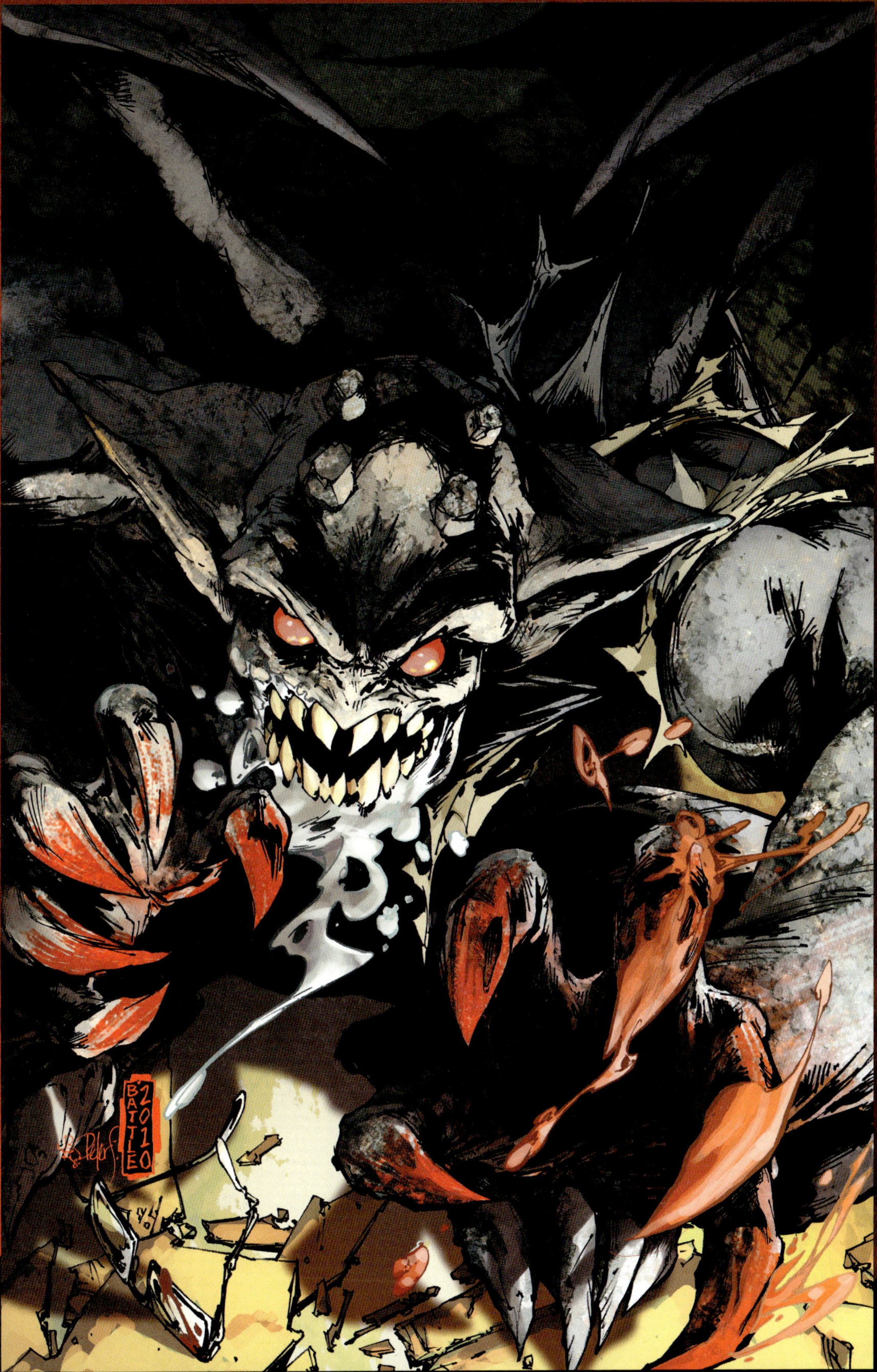

Canadian National Comic Expo Exclusive Edition Cover E to

THE SCOURGE #1

by

Eric **BATTLE** | Mark **ROSLAN** | Peter **STEIGERWALD**

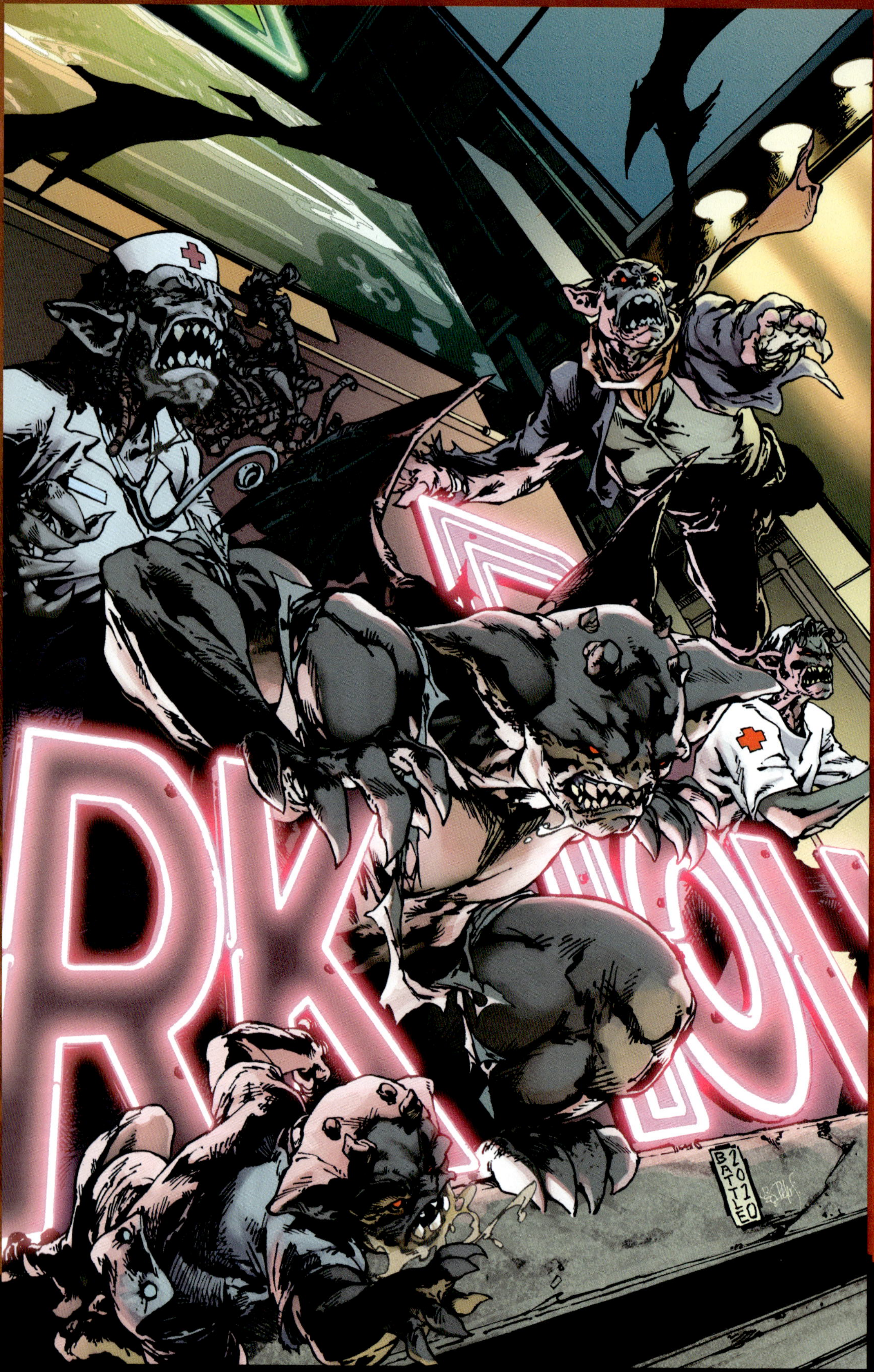

Direct Edition Cover A to

THE SCOURGE #2

by

Eric **BATTLE** | Mark **ROSLAN** | Peter **STEIGERWALD**

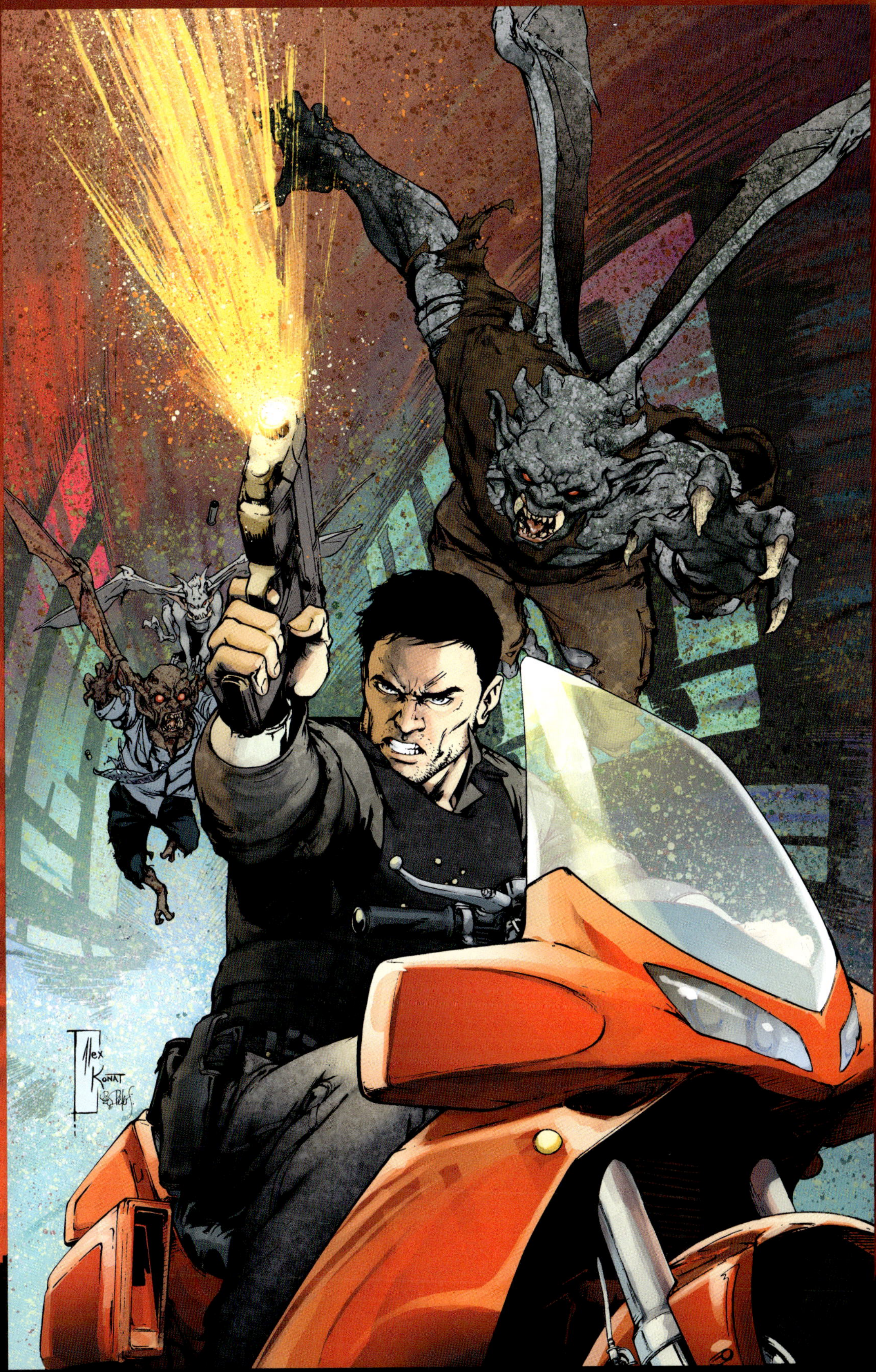

Direct Edition Cover B to
THE SCOURGE #2
BY
ALEX **KONAT** | MARK **ROSLAN** | PETER **STEIGERWALD**

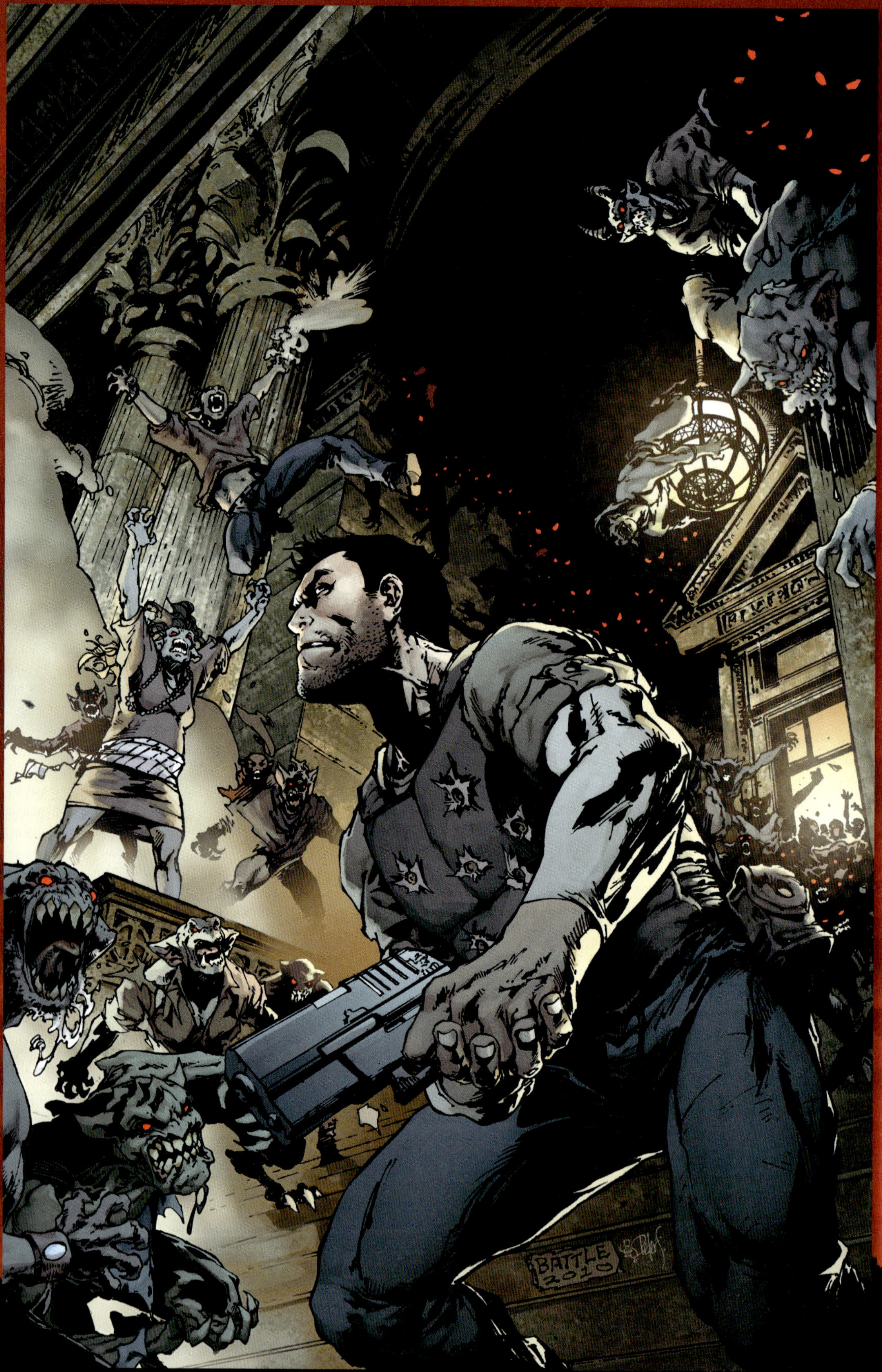
BATTLE
2010

Direct Edition Cover A to

THE SCOURGE #3

BY

ERIC BATTLE | MARK ROSLAN | PETER STEIGERWALD

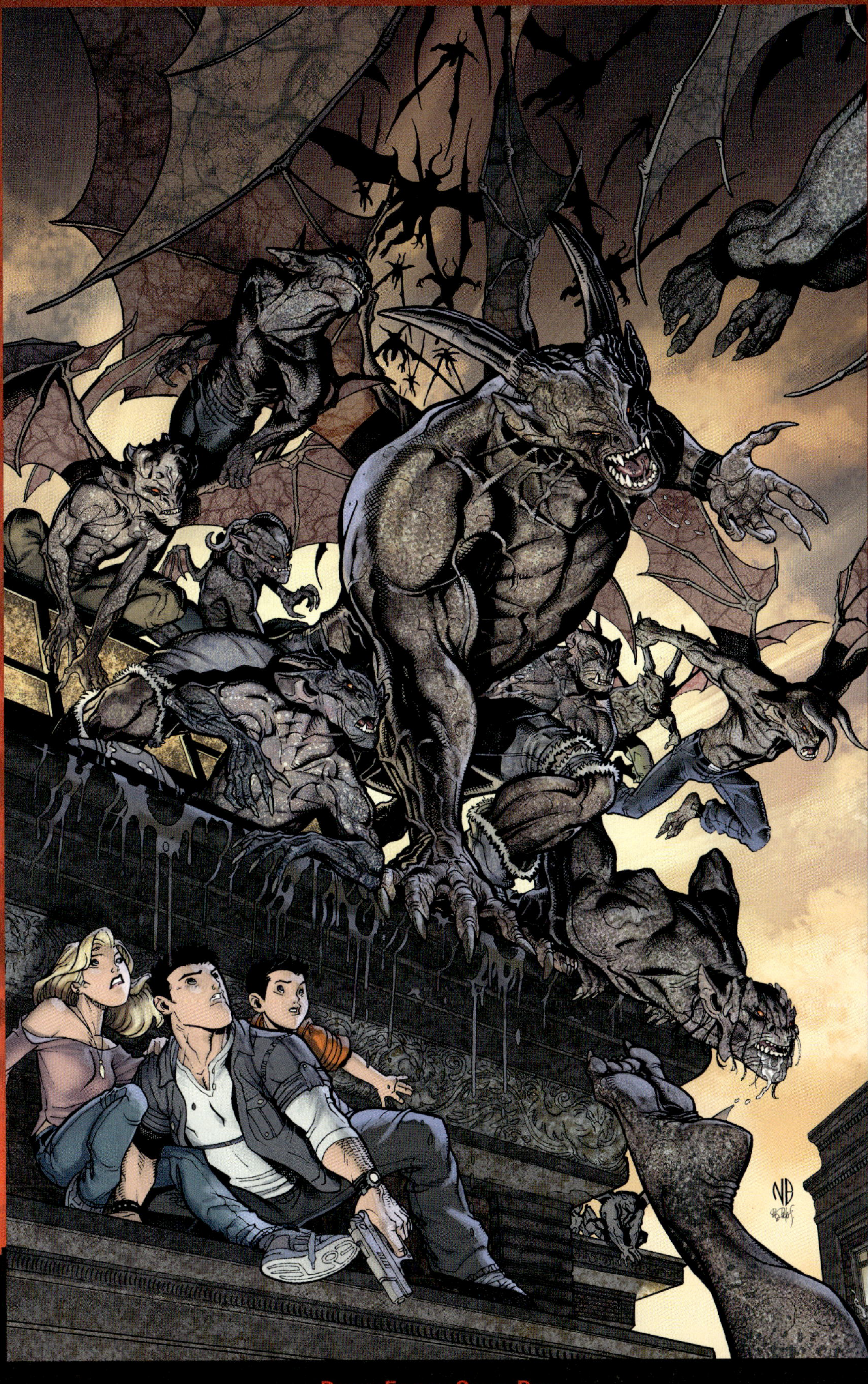

Direct Edition Cover B to
THE SCOURGE #3
BY
NICK BRADSHAW | PETER STEIGERWALD

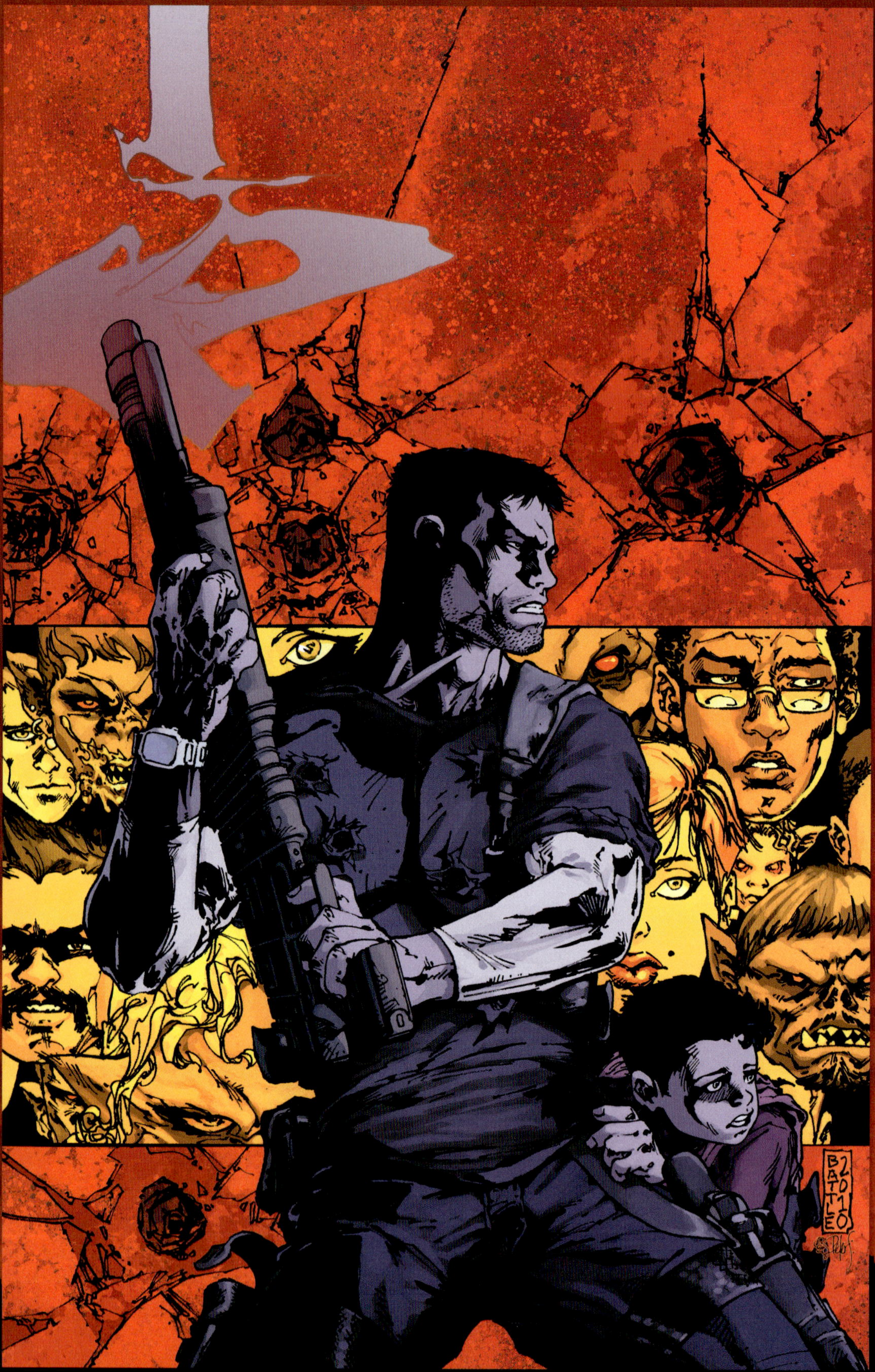

Direct Edition Cover A to

THE SCOURGE #4

BY

ERIC **BATTLE** | MARK **ROSLAN** | PETER **STEIGERWALD**

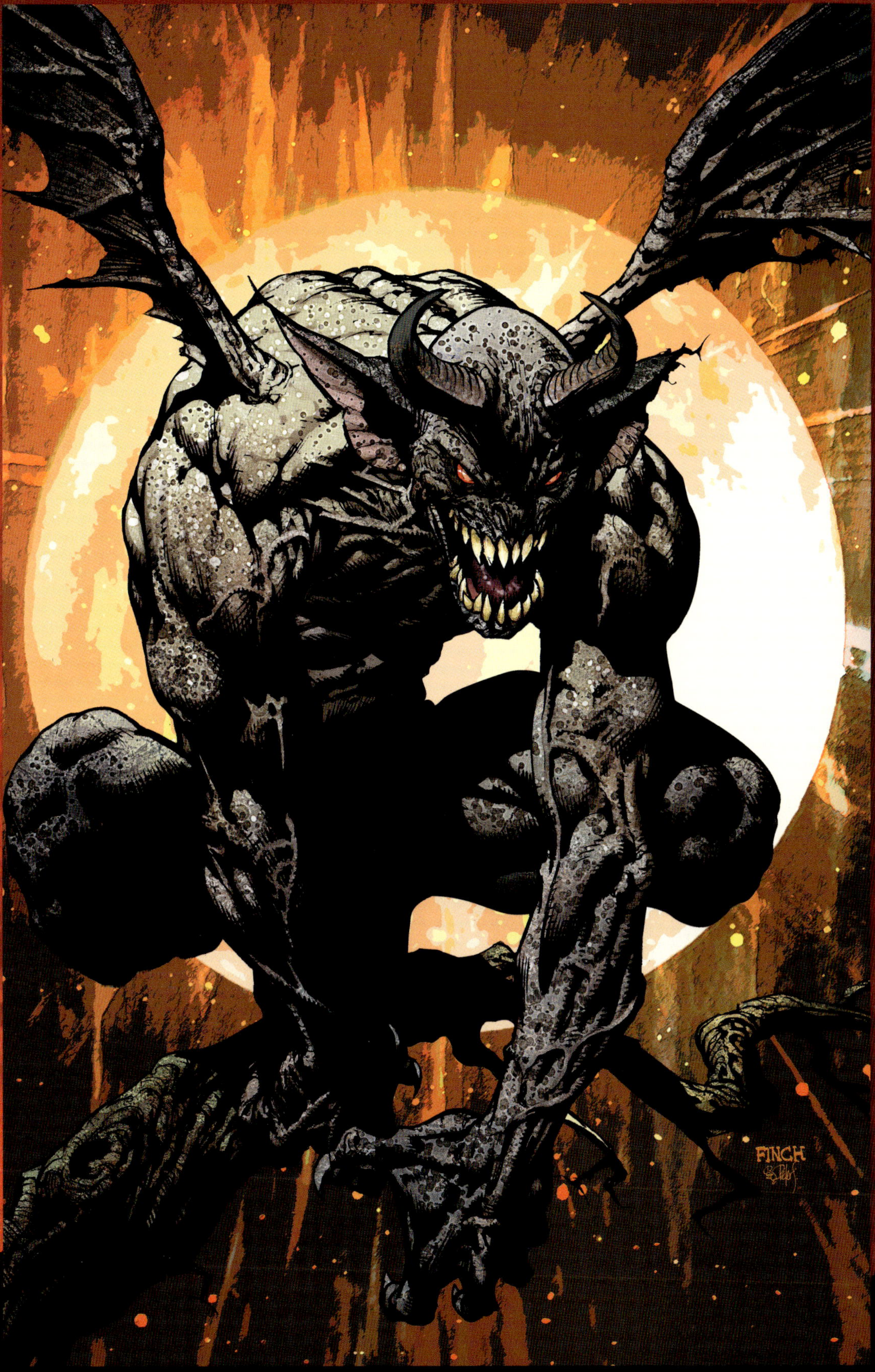
FINCH

DIRECT EDITION COVER B TO
THE SCOURGE #4
BY
DAVID FINCH | MARK ROSLAN | PETER STEIGERWALD

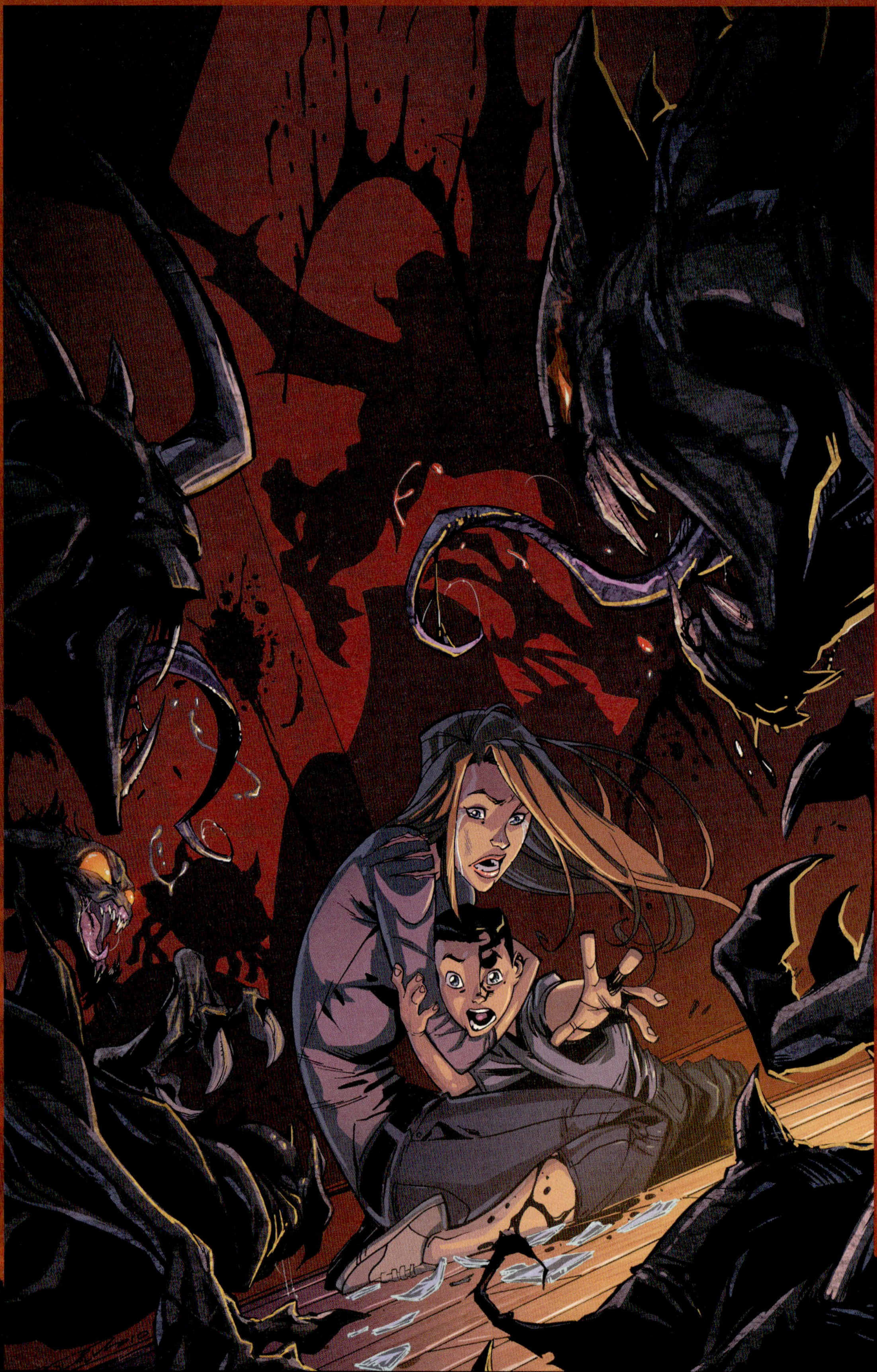

Direct Edition Cover C to
THE SCOURGE #4
by
Khary RANDOLPH Emilio LOPEZ

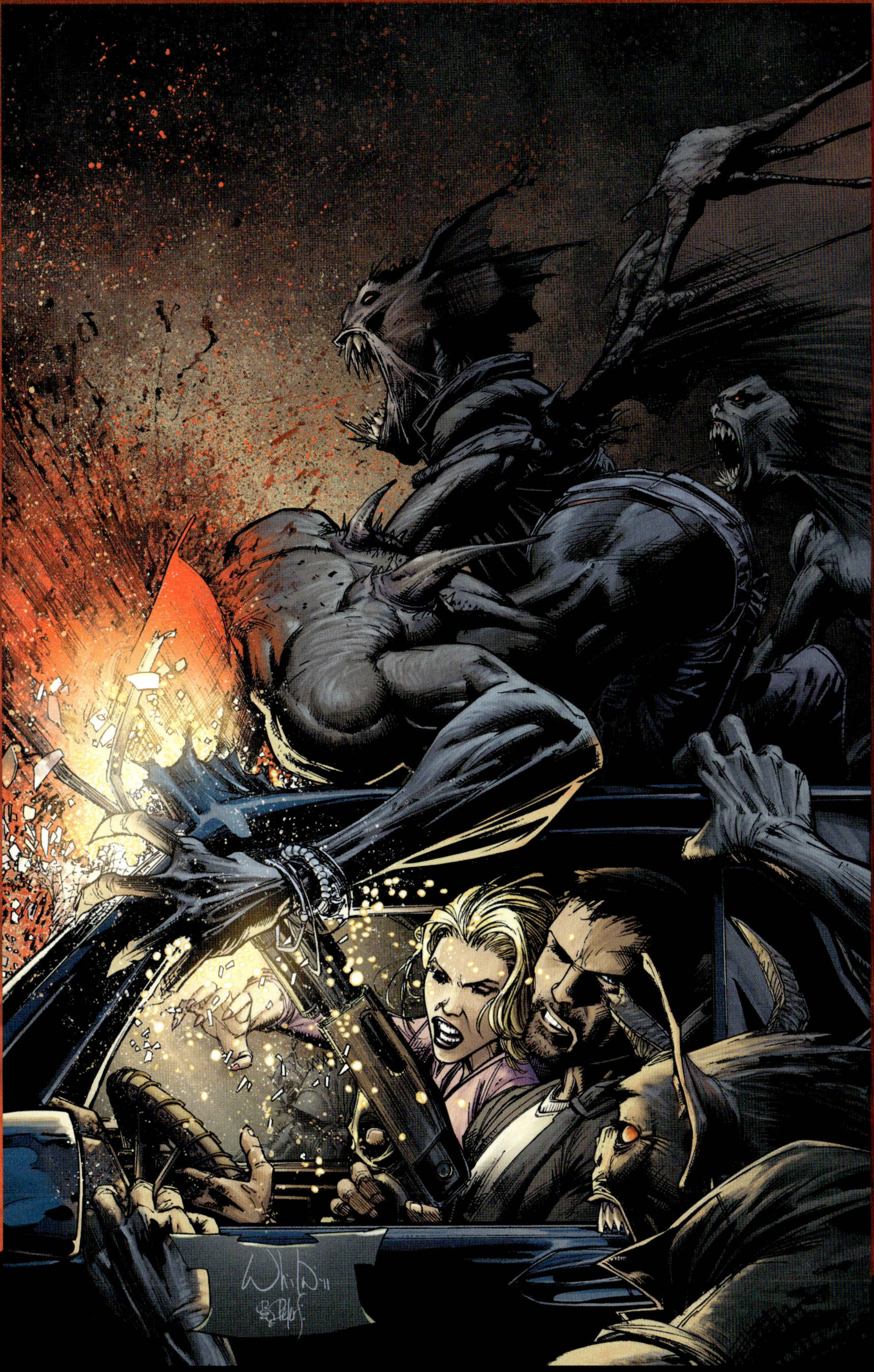

Direct Edition Cover D to
THE SCOURGE #4
BY
WHILCE PORTACIO | MARK ROSLAN | PETER STEIGERWALD

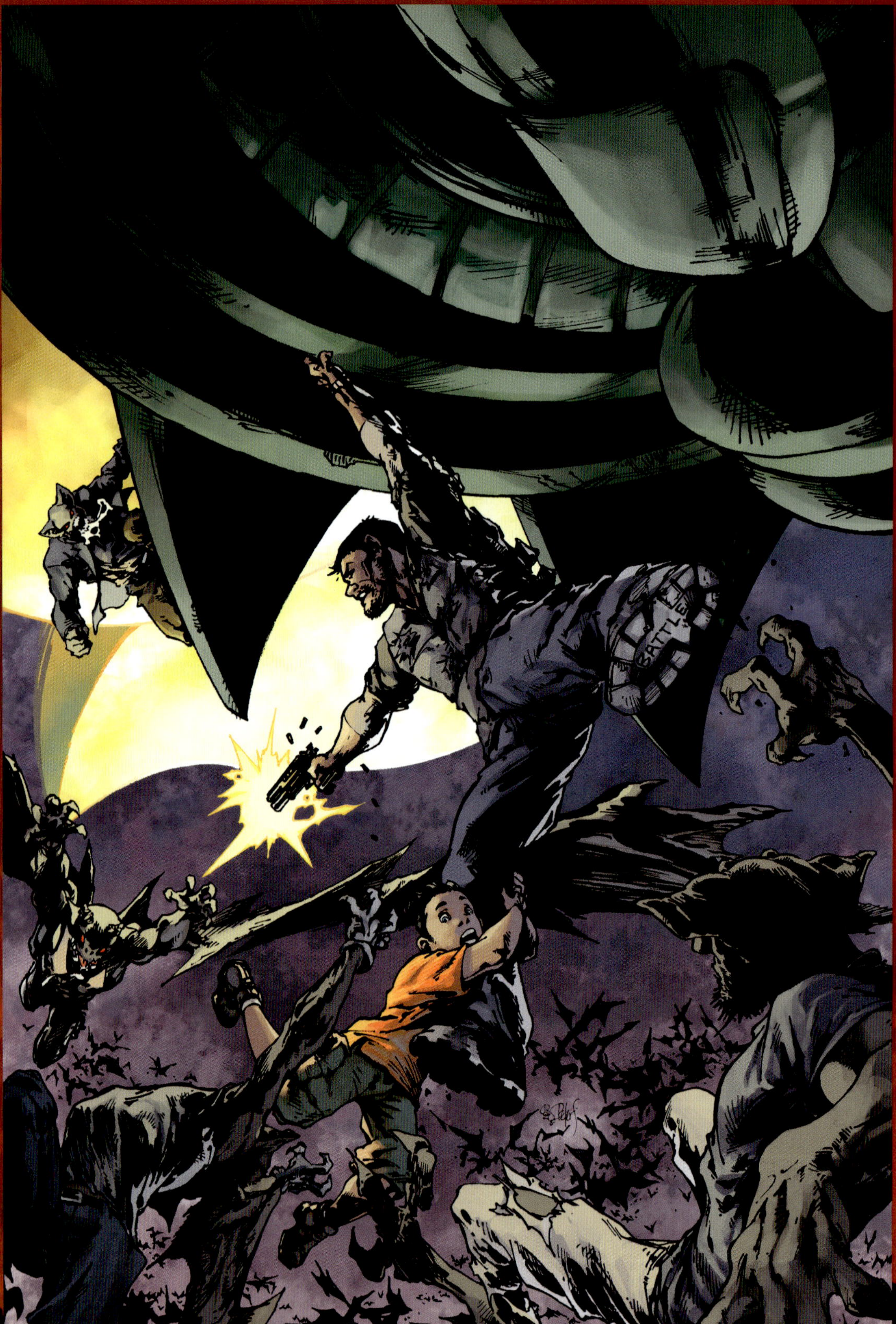

Direct Edition Cover A to
THE SCOURGE #5
by
Eric **BATTLE** | Mark **ROSLAN** | Peter **STEIGERWALD**

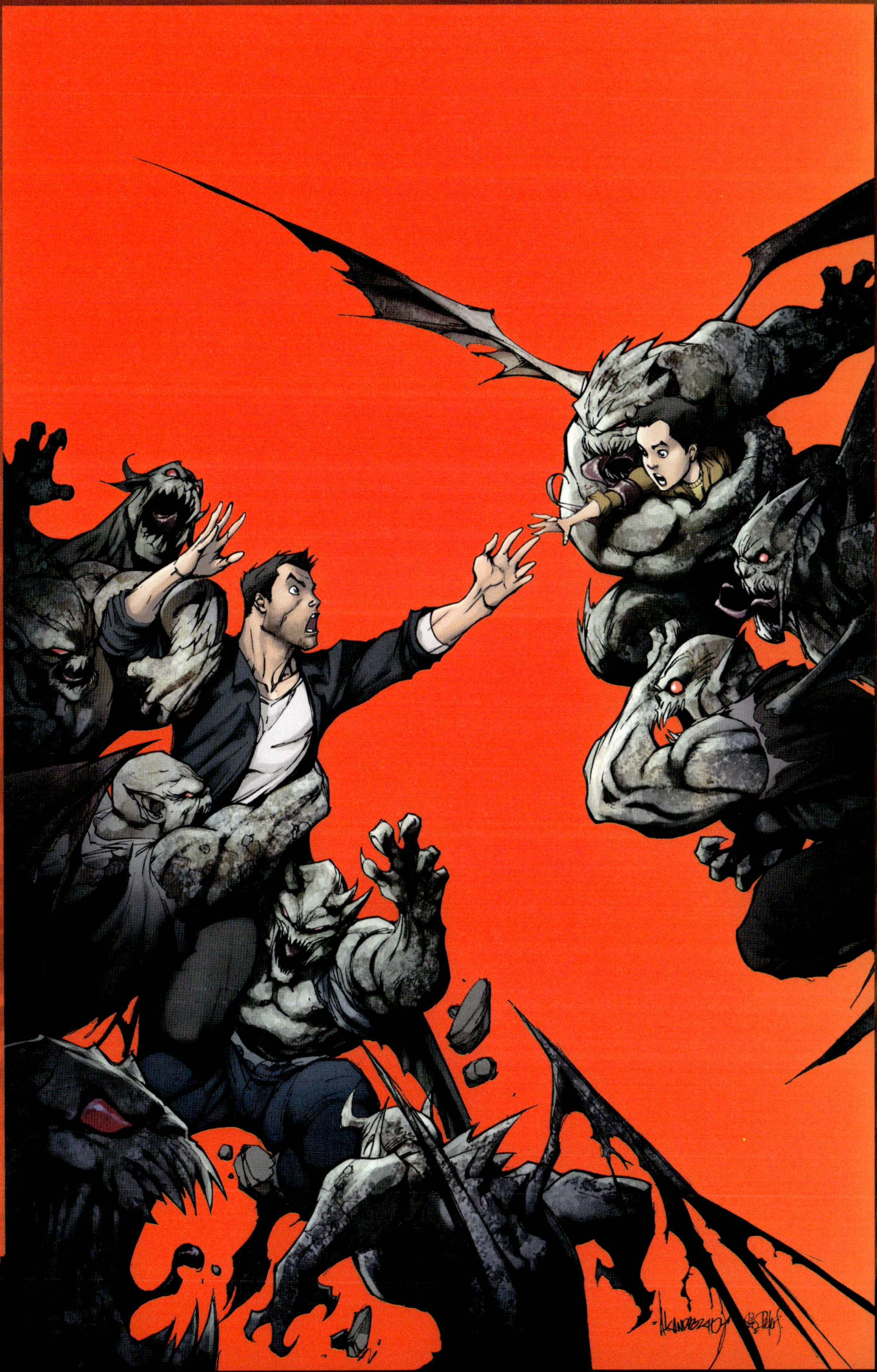

Direct Edition Cover B to
THE SCOURGE #5
BY
ALÉ GARZA | MARK ROSLAN | PETER STEIGERWALD

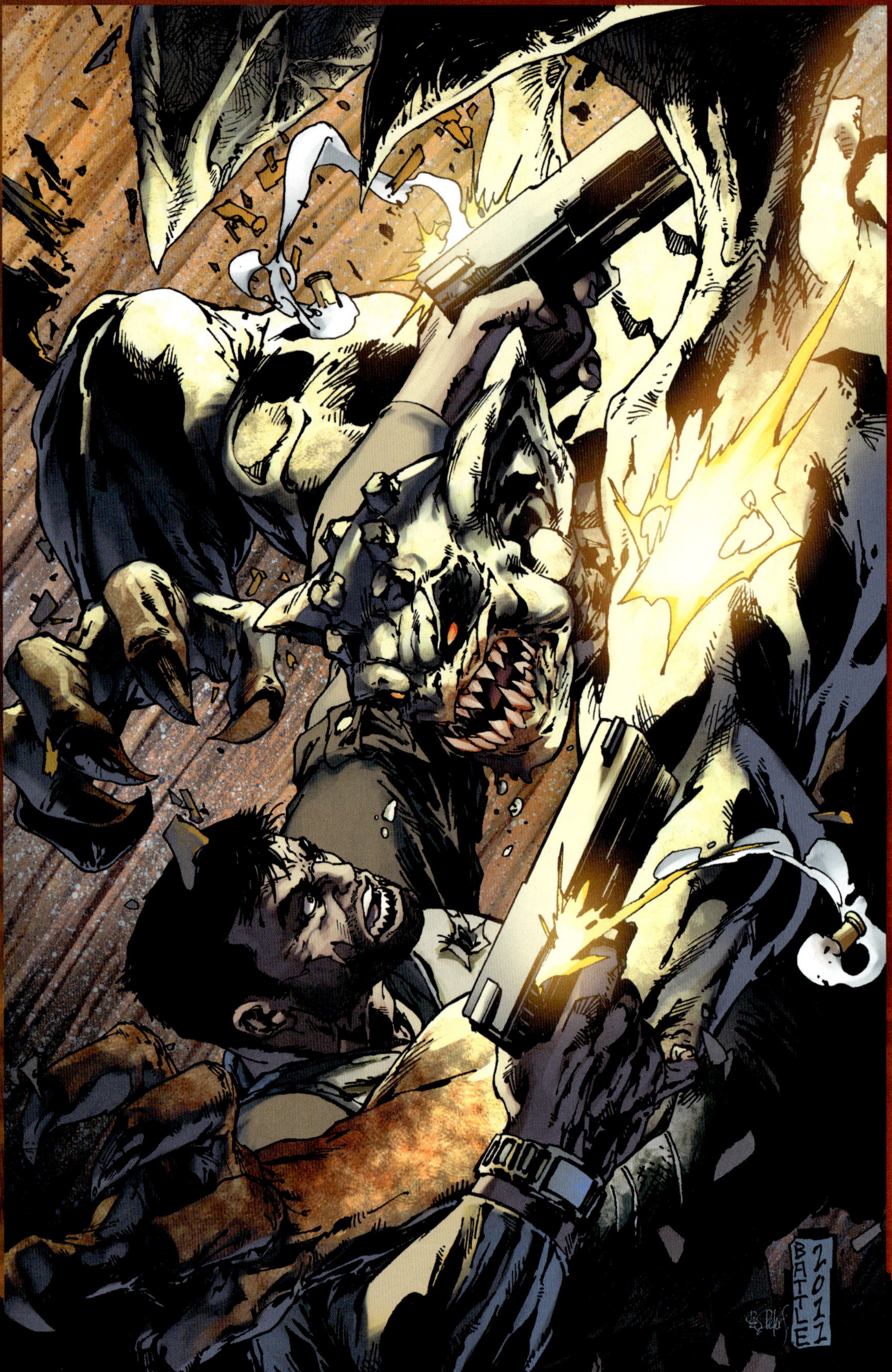
BATTLE 2011

Direct Edition Cover A to
THE SCOURGE #6
by
ERIC **BATTLE** | MARK **ROSLAN** | PETER **STEIGERWALD**

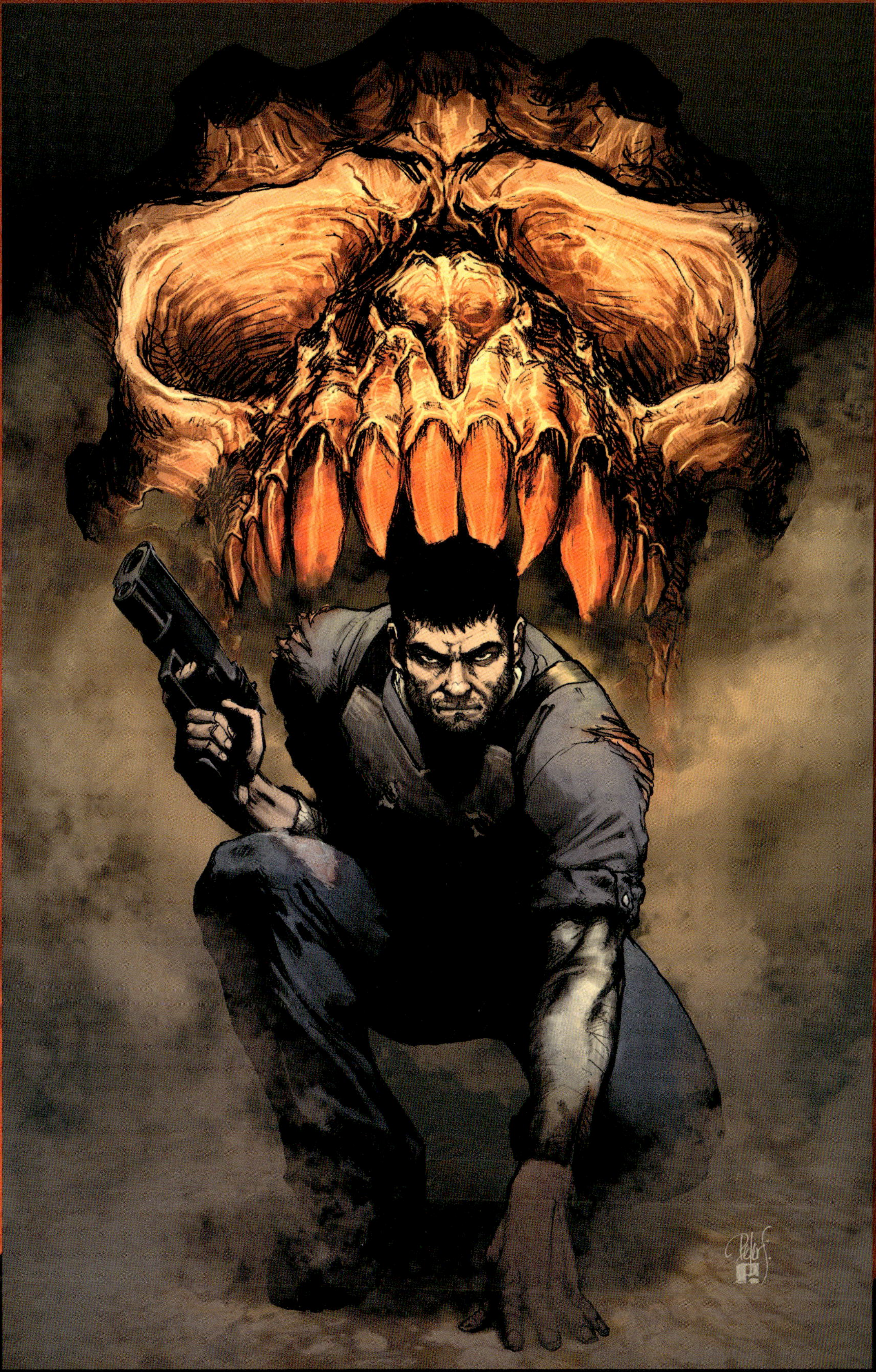

Direct Edition Cover B to
THE SCOURGE #6

STOCK YOUR ASPEN COMICS COLLECTION & EXPLORE MORE WORLDS OF ASPEN IN THESE COLLECTED GRAPHIC NOVELS!

Visit AspenComics.com & AspenStore.com for Previews, News and More.

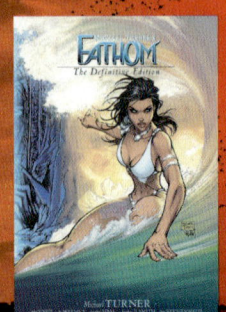

FATHOM VOL.1
THE DEFINITIVE EDITION
ISBN: 978-0-9774821-5-3
DIAMOND CODE: APR140878
PAGES: 496 | PRICE: $49.99

SOULFIRE VOL.1
THE DEFINITIVE EDITION
ISBN: 978-0-9823628-6-2
DIAMOND CODE: SEP100802
PAGES: 384 | PRICE: $39.99

FATHOM
VOL.2 - INTO THE DEEP
ISBN: 978-1-6317369-2-6
DIAMOND CODE: APR140879
PAGES: 320 | PRICE: $29.99

FATHOM
VOL.3 - WORLDS AT WAR
ISBN: 978-0-9774821-9-1
DIAMOND CODE: OCT090710
PAGES: 320 | PRICE: $29.99

FATHOM
VOL.4 - THE RIG
ISBN: 978-1-941511-07-7
DIAMOND CODE: DEC151020
PAGES: 260 | PRICE: $24.99

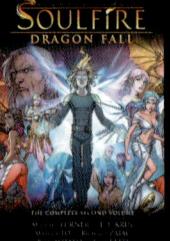

SOULFIRE
VOL.2 - DRAGON FALL
ISBN: 978-0-9854473-2-8
DIAMOND CODE: MAY141047
PAGES: 296 | PRICE: $29.99

SOULFIRE
VOL.3 - SEEDS OF CHAOS
ISBN: 978-1-941511-13-8
DIAMOND CODE: MAY161164
PAGES: 216 | PRICE: $19.99

SOULFIRE
VOL.4 - DARK GRACE
ISBN: 978-1-941511-22-0
DIAMOND CODE: AUG161263
PAGES: 216 | PRICE: $19.99

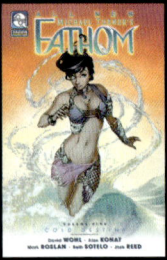

ALL NEW FATHOM
VOL.5 - COLD DESTINY
ISBN: 978-1-941511-14-5
DIAMOND CODE: MAY161165
PAGES: 216 | PRICE: $19.99

FATHOM BLUE
VOL.1
ISBN: 978-1-941511-27-5
DIAMOND CODE: NOV161180
PAGES: 176 | PRICE: $16.99

ASPEN UNIVERSE: REVELATIONS
VOL.1
ISBN: 978-1-941511-25-1
DIAMOND CODE: DEC161290
PAGES: 152 | PRICE: $14.99

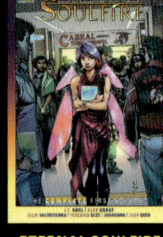

ETERNAL SOULFIRE
VOL.1
ISBN: 978-1-941511-26-8
DIAMOND CODE: NOV161181
PAGES: 176 | PRICE: $16.99

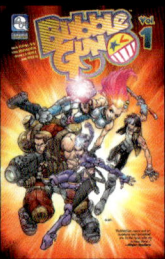

BUBBLEGUN
VOL.1 - HEIST JINKS
ISBN: 978-1-941511-15-2
DIAMOND CODE: JUN161159
PAGES: 136 | PRICE: $12.99

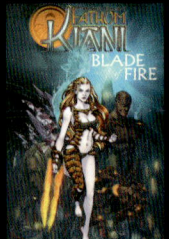

FATHOM: KIANI
VOL.1 - BLADE OF FIRE
ISBN: 978-0-9774821-8-4
DIAMOND CODE: FEB094065
PAGES: 152 | PRICE: $14.99

FATHOM: KIANI
VOL.2 - BLADE OF FURY
ISBN: 978-1-941511-06-0
DIAMOND CODE: NOV151077
PAGES: 128 | PRICE: $12.99

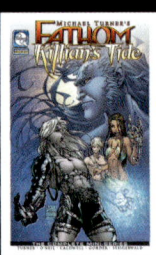

FATHOM: KILLIAN'S TIDE
VOL.1
ISBN: 978-1-941511-00-8
DIAMOND CODE: JUN140836
PAGES: 128 | PRICE: $12.99

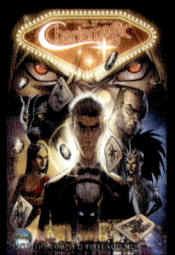

CHARISMAGIC
VOL.1 - HORSEMEN
ISBN: 978-0-9854473-7-3
DIAMOND CODE: MAR130847
PAGES: 184 | PRICE: $18.99

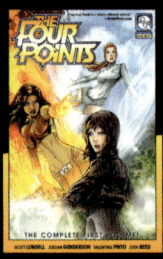

THE FOUR POINTS
VOL.1 - THE VANISHING
ISBN: 978-1-941511-10-7
DIAMOND CODE: MAR161113
PAGES: 136 | PRICE: $12.99

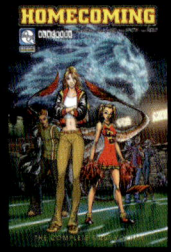

HOMECOMING
VOL.1
ISBN: 978-1-941511-18-3
DIAMOND CODE: JUN161160
PAGES: 120 | PRICE: $9.99

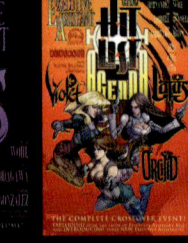

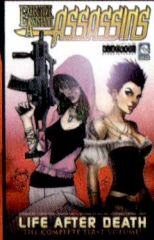

EXECUTIVE ASSISTANT: IRIS
VOL.1
ISBN: 978-0-9823628-5-3
DIAMOND CODE: AUG100788
PAGES: 200 | PRICE: $19.99

EXECUTIVE ASSISTANT: IRIS
VOL.2
ISBN: 978-098544730-4
DIAMOND CODE: MAY120880
PAGES: 160 | PRICE: $14.99

EXECUTIVE ASSISTANT: THE HITLIST AGENDA
ISBN: 978-098544731-1
DIAMOND CODE: MAY120881
PAGES: 224 | PRICE: $19.99

EXECUTIVE ASSISTANT: ASSASSINS VOL.1
ISBN: 978-1-941511-09-1
DIAMOND CODE: JAN161113
PAGES: 136 | PRICE: $12.99

JIRNI
VOL.1 - SHADOWS AND DUST
ISBN: 978-0-9854473-3-9
DIAMOND CODE: MAR140859
PAGES: 160 | PRICE: $14.99

LOLA XOXO
VOL.1
ISBN: 978-1-941511-03-9
DIAMOND CODE: OCT151122
PAGES: ... | PRICE: $24.99

SHRUGGED
VOL.1 - A LITTLE PERSPECTIVE
ISBN: 978-0-9774821-6-0
DIAMOND CODE: NOV083796
PAGES: 256 | PRICE: $24.99